ACCIDENT

Danielle Steel

Accident

Delacorte ▤ Press

LARGE PRINT EDITION

Published by
Delacorte Press
Bantam Doubleday Dell Publishing Group, Inc.
1540 Broadway
New York, New York 10036

Library of Congress Cataloging in Publication Data

Steel, Danielle.
    Accident / Danielle Steel.
        p.   cm.
    ISBN 0-385-30602-4
    ISBN 0-385-31116-8 (large-print ed.)
    ISBN 0-385-31215-6 (limited ed.)
    I. Title.
PS3569.T33828A23   1994
813'.54—dc20   93-31272
                                                        · CIP

Manufactured in the United States of America

Published simultaneously in Canada

March 1994

                10 9 8 7 6 5 4 3 2 1

NOV 01 1994   BVG

**This Large Print Book carries the
Seal of Approval of N.A.V.H.**

To Popeye,
who is always there
when it matters,
for the big things,
and little ones.
Every hour,
every moment
of every day,
I will always love you.
With all my heart
and love,
    d.s.

CHAPTER 1

It was one of those perfect, deliciously warm Saturday afternoons in April, when the air on your cheek feels like silk, and you want to stay outdoors forever. It had been a long, sunny day, and driving across the Golden Gate Bridge at five o'clock, into Marin, it took Page's breath away as she looked across the water.

She glanced over at her son, looking like a small blond replica of her, beside her, except that his hair was sticking up straight where his baseball cap had been, and there was dirt all over his face. Andrew Patterson Clarke had turned seven the previous Tuesday. And just sitting there, relaxing after the game, one could feel the strength of the bond between them. Page Clarke was a good mother, a good wife, the kind of friend anyone would be grateful for. She cared, she loved, she worked hard at whatever she did, she was there for the people who meant something to her, she was artistic in ways that always amazed her friends, she was unconsciously beautiful, and fun to be with.

"You were great this afternoon." She smiled over at him, one hand briefly leaving the wheel to ruffle the already tousled hair. Andy had the same thick, wheat-colored blond hair that she did, the same big blue eyes, and creamy skin, only his was well dusted with freckles. "I couldn't believe that ball you caught in the outfield. Looked like a home run to me." She always went to his games with him, and his school plays, and on field trips with his class and his friends. She did it because she loved it, and she loved him. It was obvious when he looked at her that he knew it.

"It looked like a homer to me too." He grinned, showing gums where both of his front teeth had been until recently. "I thought Benjie would get to home base for sure." He chortled mischievously as they reached the Marin County side of the bridge. ". . . but he didn't!"

Page laughed along with him. It had been a nice afternoon. She wished that Brad could have been there, but he played golf with his business associates every Saturday afternoon. It was a chance to relax and catch up with what they were all doing. It was rare for him to spend Saturday afternoons alone with her anymore. And when he did, there was always something else they had to do. Like Andy's games, or one of Allyson's swim meets, which always seemed to be held in the most godforsaken places. Either that, or their dog cut her paw, the roof leaked, the plumbing fell apart, or some other minor emergency had to be taken care of. There were no lazy Saturdays anymore, there hadn't been in years. She was used to it, and she and Brad stole whatever moments they could, at night when the kids were asleep, between his business trips, or on their rare weekends away together. Finding time for romance in busy lives was quite a feat, but somehow they managed to do it. She was still crazy about him, after sixteen years of marriage and two kids. She had everything she wanted, a husband she adored, and who

loved her, a secure life, and two wonderful
children. Their house in Ross wasn't elabo-
rate, but it was pretty and comfortable, it
was in a nice area, and with her constant
puttering and knack for improving things,
Page had made it really lovely. Her years as
an art student and an apprentice set designer in New York hadn't served her much,
but she had used her talents in recent years
to paint beautiful murals for herself and
friends. She had done a spectacular one at
Ross Grammar School. She had turned
their home into a place of real beauty. Her
paintings and murals and artistic touch had
turned an ordinary little ranch house into a
home that everyone admired and envied. It
was all Page's doing, and all who saw it
knew that.

She had painted a baseball game in full
swing on one wall of Andy's room as his
Christmas present the previous year, and he
really loved it. For Allyson, she had done a
Paris street scene the year she'd been in
love with all things French, and later a
string of ballerinas inspired by Degas, and
more recently she had turned Allyson's
room into a swimming pool with her magic
touch. She had even painted the furniture
in trompe l'oeil to match it. The reward was

that Allyson and her friends thought the room was "really cool," and Page was "wow . . . really rad . . . she's okay," which were high marks from the fifteen-year-old set.

Allyson was a sophomore in high school. Looking at them, Page was always sorry she hadn't had more children. She had always wanted more, but Brad had been adamant about "one or two," with the emphasis on one. He had been crazy about his little girl, and didn't see why they needed any more children. It had taken seven years to convince him to have another. That was when they moved out of the city, and into the house in Ross, when Andy was born, their little miracle baby, she called him. He was born two and a half months premature, after Page fell off a ladder doing a Winnie-the-Pooh mural in his bedroom. She had been rushed to the hospital with a broken leg, and she was already in labor. He had been in an incubator for two months, but in the end, he was absolutely perfect. She smiled, remembering it sometimes, how tiny he had been, how terrified they had been that they might lose him. She couldn't imagine surviving it, although she knew she would have . . . for Allyson, and Brad, but her life would never have been the same without him.

"Feel like an ice cream?" she asked as they took the Sir Francis Drake turn-off.

"Sure." Andy grinned again, and then laughed as she looked at him. It was impossible not to laugh at that big gummy grin.

"When are you going to get some teeth, Andrew Clarke? Maybe we ought to buy you some false ones."

"Naww . . ." He smiled, and then chuckled.

It was fun being alone with him, usually she had a carful of kids driving home from the game, but today one of the other mothers had done the honors, and she had gone to the game anyway, because she'd promised. Allyson was spending the afternoon with her friends, Brad was playing golf, and Page was caught up with all her projects. She was planning another mural for the school, and she had promised to take a look at a friend's living room and see what she'd recommend, but there had been nothing really pressing.

Andy had a double scoop of Rocky Road in a sugar cone, with chocolate jimmies, and she had a single scoop of coffee-flavored frozen yogurt, the nonfat kind that fooled you into thinking you were doing something really sinful. They sat outside together for a while, as Andy's ice cream got all over his face and dripped on his uniform, which Page said didn't matter. Everything had to be washed anyway, so what harm was there in a little ice cream. They watched people come and go, and enjoyed the warmth of the late afternoon sun. It was a gorgeous day, and Page talked about going on a picnic on Sunday.

"That would be neat." Andy looked pleased as the Rocky Road finally engulfed the tip of his nose, extending all the way to his chin, as Page felt overwhelmed with love for him as she watched him.

"You're cute . . . you know that? I know I'm not supposed to say stuff like that, but I think you're terrific, Andrew Clarke . . . and a great baseball player to boot . . . how did I ever get so lucky?"

He grinned again, even more broadly, and the ice cream was absolutely everywhere, even on her nose, as she kissed him.

"You're a great guy."

"You're okay, too . . ." He disappeared into his ice cream again, and then looked up at her with a question. "Mom . . . ?"

"Yeah?" Her yogurt was almost gone, but

his Rocky Road looked as though it was going to go on melting and dribbling and oozing forever. Ice cream had a way of growing in the hands of small children.

"Do you think we'll ever have another baby?"

Page looked surprised by the question. It wasn't the kind of thing boys usually asked. Allyson had asked her that several times. But now, at thirty-nine, she didn't think so. It wasn't that she felt too old, or was, given the ages people had babies these days, but she knew she'd never talk Brad into another child. He always insisted that all of that was behind him.

"I don't think so, sweetheart. Why?" Was he worried or just curious? She couldn't help but wonder.

"Tommy Silverberg's mom had twins last week. I saw them when I went to his house. They're pretty cute. They're identical," he explained, looking impressed. "They weighed seven pounds each, that's more than I weighed."

"It sure is." He had weighed barely three, thanks to his early appearance. "I'll bet they are cute. But I don't think we'll be having twins . . . or even one . . ." Oddly enough, she felt sad as she said it. She had always agreed with Brad, out of loyalty to him, that two children was a perfect family for them, but there were still times when, out of the blue, she found herself longing for another baby. "Maybe you should talk to Dad about it," she teased.

"About twins?" He looked intrigued.

"About another baby."

"It would be fun . . . kind of . . . they look like a lot of trouble though. Everything at Tommy's was a mess, they had all this stuff everywhere . . . you know, like beds and baskets . . . and swings, and there were two of everything . . . his grandmother was there helping, she cooked dinner, and she burned it. His dad did a lot of yelling."

"Doesn't sound like much fun to me." Page smiled, imagining the scene of total chaos surrounding the arrival of twins in a home where they were already poorly organized and had two other children. "But the beginning can be like that, till you get the hang of it."

"Was everything a mess like that when I was born?" He finally finished the ice cream and wiped his mouth on his sleeve and his hands on the pants of his baseball uniform as Page laughed while she watched him.

"No, but you sure are a mess now, kiddo. Maybe we'd better get you home and get all that stuff off you."

They climbed back into her station wagon, and headed home, chatting about other things, but his questions about the baby seemed to stay with her. For a moment, there was an old familiar pang of longing. Maybe it was just the warm, sunny day, or the fact that it was spring, but she suddenly wished that there would be other babies . . . romantic trips . . . more time with Brad . . . lazy afternoons in bed, with nowhere to go, and nothing to do except make love to him. As much as she loved her life, there were times when she wished she could turn the clock back. Nowadays, her life was so full of car pools, and helping with homework, and PTA, she and Brad only seemed to catch each other on the fly, or at the end of an exhausting day. And in spite of all that, there was still love and desire . . . but never enough time to indulge it. It was time that they never had enough of.

They pulled into their driveway a few minutes later, and Page noticed Brad's car as Andy gathered up his things. She looked over at him proudly. "I had a good time today," she said, still warm in the afternoon sun, and her heart full of all she felt for him. It had been one of those special days when you realize just how lucky you are, and are grateful for every precious moment.

"So did I . . . thanks for coming, Mom." He knew she didn't have to, and he was glad she came anyway. She was good to him, and he knew it. But he was a good boy, and he deserved it.

"Anytime, Mr. Clarke. Now go tell Dad about that famous catch. You made history out there today!" He laughed and ran into the house, as she picked up Allyson's bicycle sprawled across the walkway. Her roller blades were leaning up against the garage, and her tennis racket lay on a chair just outside the kitchen door with a can of balls she had "borrowed" from her father. She had obviously had a busy day, and as soon as Page walked into the house, she saw her on the kitchen phone, still wearing her tennis clothes, her long blond hair in a French braid, her back turned to her mother. She was concluding some plan, and then hung up and turned to face her. She was a beautiful girl, and it still startled Page sometimes

when she saw her. She was so striking looking, and she seemed so mature. She had a
woman's body, and a young girl's mind, and
she was always in motion, in action, in mid-
plan. She always had something to say, tell,
ask, do, somewhere she had to be, right
now, two hours ago, this minute . . . she
really *had* to! She had that look on her face
now, as Page rapidly shifted gears from the
easy roll of being with Andy. Allyson was
more intense, more like Brad, always on the
move, on the go, thinking ahead to what she
wanted to do next, where she had to be, and
what was important to her. She was more
intense than Page, more focused, not as
kind, or as gentle as Andy would be one
day. But she was a bright girl with a fine
mind and lots of good ideas and good intentions. Every now and then her common
sense went astray, and occasionally she and
Page would get into a roaring fight over
some typically teenage mistake she'd made,
but eventually Allyson usually made sense,
and calmed down enough to listen to her
parents.

At fifteen, none of her antics were very
surprising. She was trying her wings, testing
her limits, trying to figure out who she was
going to be, not Page, or Brad, but herself,

someone entirely different. In spite of her similarities to them, she wanted to be her own woman. Unlike Andy, who wanted to be just like his dad, and was actually so much like Page. In Allyson's eyes, he was just a baby. She had been eight when he was born, and she thought he was the cutest thing she'd ever seen. She had never seen anything as tiny. Like her parents, she was scared that he would die just after he was born, but there was no one prouder than Allyson when he finally came home. She carried him all around the house, from room to room, and whenever Page couldn't find him, she knew she'd find him in Allyson's bed, snuggled up to her, like a live doll. Allyson had been head over heels in love with him for years. And even now, she secretly indulged her little brother, buying him little treats and baseball cards, and occasionally she even went to his baseball games, although she hated baseball. But most of the time she was even willing to admit that she loved him.

"How'd you do today, runt?" She always teased him about how little he had been when he was born, but he was actually tall for his age now, and bigger than many of his classmates.

"Okay," he said modestly.

"He was the star of the game," Page explained. Andy blushed and walked away, to find his father, as Page called out a vague hello in the direction of their bedroom. She wanted to get dinner started before she went in to see her husband. "How was your day?" she asked her oldest child as she opened the refrigerator. They had no plans to go out that night, and it was so warm, she was thinking about making a picnic dinner or having Brad do a barbecue for them in the garden. "Who'd you play tennis with?"

"Chloe, and some other kids. There were some kids from Branson and Marin Academy at the club today. We played doubles for a while, and then I played Chloe. After that, we went swimming." She sounded unimpressed. She led a golden California life. To her it was no miracle, she always had, she'd been born there. For Brad from the Midwest, and Page from New York, the weather and the opportunities still seemed magical, but not to these children. To them it was a way of life, and sometimes Page envied them their easy beginnings. But she was also glad for them, this was exactly the life she wanted for her children. Easy, safe, healthy, comfortable, secure, protected from anything that could sadden or harm them. She had done everything she could to guarantee all of that for them, and she enjoyed watching them thrive and flourish.

"Sounds like a pretty good day. Do you have any plans for tonight?" If she didn't, or if Chloe came over to hang out with her, maybe she and Brad would go to a movie and Allyson could babysit. If not, it was no big thing if they had to stay home. She and Brad had made no special plans for that evening. It would have been nice to sit outdoors in the warm night air, talk and relax, and have an early evening. "What are you up to?"

Allyson turned to her nervously, with that look that said, you're about to ruin my whole life if you don't let me do what I've been planning to do all day. "Chloe's dad said he'd take us to dinner and a movie."

"Okay. It's no big deal. I was just asking." Allyson's face immediately relaxed, and Page smiled as she watched her. They were so predictable sometimes, and growing up still looked as though it was so painful. Even in a normal, happy home, every moment, every plan was fraught with anguish. It clearly wasn't easy.

"What movie?" Page put some meat in

the microwave to defrost it. She was going to make something simple.

"She didn't say. There are about three movies I want to see, and I still haven't seen *Woodstock,* they're playing it at the Festival. Her dad's taking us to dinner at Luigi's."

"Sounds like fun. It's nice of him to do that." Page pulled out some potato chips, and started to make the salad, as she glanced over her shoulder at her daughter. She was so beautiful, sitting perched on a stool at the kitchen counter. She looked like a model. She had huge brown eyes, like Brad's, her mother's golden hair, and a complexion that turned the color of honey the moment she saw the sun. She had long, shapely legs and a tiny waist. It was no wonder people stopped to stare at her, especially men lately. Page said to Brad sometimes that she wished she could put a sign on her that said she was only fifteen. Even thirty-year-old men turned to look at her in the street. She looked easily eighteen or twenty. "It's awfully nice of Mr. Thorensen to spend his Saturday night taking you girls out."

"He has nothing else to do," Allyson said, sounding fifteen, and Page laughed. Teenagers certainly brought one back to earth and reminded one of one's failures and misfortunes.

"How do you know?" His wife had left him the year before and right after the divorce, she had taken a job with a theatrical agent in England. She'd offered to take their three children with her, and put them in English boarding schools. She was American herself, but she thought the English school system was a lot better than anything here, but Trygve Thorensen had no intention of giving them up, and kept them with him. Sadly, after twenty years of suburban life, she was so sick and tired of being chauffeur, maid, and tutor to her children that she'd been willing to give it all up. Everything. Trygve, the kids, her whole life in Ross. She hated all of it. As far as Dana Thorensen was concerned, now it was her turn. She'd tried to tell him all along, but Trygve just didn't hear her. He wanted it to work so badly that he refused to see her anger and desperation.

They'd all been pretty badly shaken up when she left, and Page was shocked at her leaving her kids, but apparently it had all been too much for her for a long time. And everyone in Ross had always been impressed by how well Trygve managed his children, and how much he did with them. He was a free-lance political writer, and worked out of his home. It was a perfect setup for him, and unlike his wife, he never seemed to tire of his parental responsibilities and obligations. He had taken them on with the good humor and warmth he was so well known for. It wasn't easy, he admitted from time to time, but he was managing fine, and his kids seemed happier than they had in years. He seemed to find time for his work while the kids were in school, and late at night after they went to bed. And in the hours that they were around, he seemed to do everything with them. He was a familiar figure to all their friends, and well liked by most of them. It didn't surprise Page at all that he had offered to take a bunch of them to the movies and dinner at Luigi's.

His two boys were college age now, and Chloe and Allyson were the same age. Chloe had just turned fifteen at Christmas, and she was as pretty as Allyson, although very different. She was small, with her mother's dark hair, and her father's big blue Nordic eyes and fair skin. Both of Trygve's parents were Norwegian, and he had lived in Norway until he was twelve. But he was as American as apple pie now, although his friends teased him and called him the Viking.

He was an attractive man, and the divorcées of Ross had been greatly encouraged by his divorce, and somewhat disappointed since then. Between his work and his kids, he seemed to have no time at all in his life for women. Page suspected that it wasn't so much a lack of time as a lack of confidence or interest.

It was no secret that he had been deeply in love with his wife, and everyone also knew that in her desperation, she had been cheating on him for the last couple of years before she left him. She'd been something of a lost soul, and married life and monogamy were more than she could cope with. Trygve had done all he could, counseling, and even two trial separations. But he wanted so much more than she had to give. He wanted a real wife, half a dozen kids, a simple life, he wanted to spend their vacations going camping. She wanted New York, Paris, Hollywood, or London.

Dana Thorensen had been everything Trygve wasn't. They had met in Hollywood while they were scarcely more than kids. He had been trying his hand briefly at writing scripts, fresh out of school, and she had been a budding actress. She loved what she did, and hated it when he asked her to move to San Francisco. But she also loved him enough to try it. She tried to commute for a while, tried some repertory work with ACT in San Francisco. But none of it worked out for her, and she missed her friends, and the excitement of L.A. and Hollywood, and even working as an extra. She got pregnant unexpectedly, and Trygve surprised her by insisting on marrying her, and after that everything went downhill pretty quickly. She wound up playing a part she had never wanted. And when Bjorn, their second child, was born with Down syndrome, it was too much for her, and somehow she seemed to blame Trygve. She knew she didn't want more kids, she wasn't even sure she wanted to be married. And then Chloe came, and blew everything, as far as Dana was concerned. From then on, in her eyes, her life became a nightmare. Trygve tried to do all he could, and his political articles in *The New York Times,* and assorted magazines and foreign journals, were doing well by then. He managed to support all of them. But all Dana wanted was out. For more than half their marriage, she could barely be civil to him. All she really wanted was her freedom. And all Trygve wanted was to make it work. And he irritated Dana even more by being the perfect father. The impossible dream, married to the wrong woman.

He was patient, kind, always happy to include other children in their plans. He took groups of children camping and fishing with him, and was a major force in organizing the Special Olympics, at which Bjorn excelled, much to everyone's delight, except Dana's. She couldn't relate to any of them, even when she tried. And Bjorn was, in her eyes, the ultimate shame and disappointment. In the end, she was a woman whom no one liked, an angry soul, raging at a fate that others thought wasn't so bad. Her children were wonderful, even Bjorn with his special sweetness. And Trygve was a husband most women envied. But it came as no surprise when Dana began having frequent affairs. She seemed not to care who knew what she did, especially Trygve. In truth, she really wanted him to end it.

When she left him finally, everyone was relieved, except Trygve, who had allowed himself to drift slowly downstream for years, trying to pretend that it wasn't really as bad as it seemed. He told himself lies that only he believed, ". . . she'll get used to it . . . it was difficult for her to give up her career . . . leaving Hollywood had been so hard on her . . . marriage was harder for her than most, because she was so creative . . . and of course, Bjorn had been a terrible shock to her. . . ." He had made every possible excuse for her for twenty years, and couldn't believe it when she finally left him. Much to his surprise it was like the end of a constant pain. And even more surprising to him, he had absolutely no desire to try again and risk the same pain with someone else. He realized now just how bad it had been. He couldn't imagine marrying anyone again, or even a serious relationship. At first, he wouldn't even consider dating. All the women he knew in town seemed like vultures, waiting for fresh prey, and he had no intention of becoming their next victim. He was actually very happy alone, with his children, for the moment.

"He hasn't had a girlfriend, not a real one, since Chloe's mom left, and that was over a year ago. He just spends all his time with the kids, or writing about politics, but he does that at night. Chloe says he's writing a book now. But he likes going out with us, Mom. He says so."

"Lucky for all of you. But one of these days he might find someone a little more . . . ah . . . shall we say, mature, to spend his time with?" She smiled, as Allyson shrugged. She couldn't imagine him wanting to do anything else. For most of her life, Trygve Thorensen had made himself totally available to his children. It never occurred to her that he did it, not only because he liked them, and wanted to be with them, but also because he was avoiding the emptiness of a bad marriage.

"Besides, he likes to be with Bjorn. Mr. Thorensen is teaching him to drive."

"He's a decent guy." Page finished washing the lettuce and found a bowl to put it in, as Allyson helped herself to the potato chips. "How is Bjorn, by the way?" She hadn't seen him in a long time. He was less severely afflicted with the disorder than some, but still he had marked limitations.

"He's great. He plays baseball every Saturday, and now he's gone nuts over bowling." It was amazing to think about it. How did one even begin to cope with a situation like that? In a way, she could understand Dana Thorensen being overwhelmed by it, but not her subsequent behavior. Although they weren't close friends, she had known Trygve Thorensen for years, and she liked him. He didn't deserve all the troubles he'd had. No one did. And from what she could see, he was a terrific father.

"Are you spending the night at the Thorensens'?" Page asked, as she put the last of the lettuce leaves in a bowl, and wiped her hands. She hadn't seen Brad since she got home, and she wanted to go in and say hello, and check on Andy.

"No." Allyson shook her head as she stood up, left the potato chips on the counter, and grabbed an apple. Her body had long, lean lines, and she tossed her long blond braid over her shoulder. "They said they'd drop me off after the movies. Chloe has a track meet early tomorrow morning."

"On Sunday?" Page looked surprised as they left the kitchen.

"Yeah . . . I don't know . . . maybe it's practice . . . something."

"What time are you going out?"

"I said I'd meet her at seven." There was a long pause while the huge brown eyes locked on to her mother's. There was something there that Page couldn't quite figure out, and then it was gone again, just as quickly. Some secret, some thought, some private moment she didn't want to share with her mother. "Can I borrow your black sweater, Mom?"

"The cashmere one with the beads?" Brad had given it to her for Christmas. It was too hot, too dressy, and much too expensive for a fifteen-year-old girl. Page was not even amused at the suggestion, as Allyson nodded at the description.

"Hardly. That's not exactly appropriate for Luigi's, and the Festival, wouldn't you say?"

"Yeah . . . okay . . . how about the pink one?"

"Better."

"Can I?"

"Okay . . . okay . . ." She sighed and shook her head with a rueful grin, as they went their separate ways. Allyson to her room, and Page to find her husband. Sometimes she felt as though there were obstacles and hurdles standing between them. It was as though she and Brad had to finish a marathon every day before they could finally share a private moment . . . take me . . . drop me . . . pick me . . . give me . . . can I . . . would you . . . where is my . . . where . . . how . . . when . . .

and then, as she turned the corner to their bedroom, she saw him. She still found him breathtaking at times. Brad Clarke was the definition of tall, dark, and handsome. He stood six feet four inches tall, had short dark hair, big brown eyes, and powerful shoulders. He had narrow hips, long legs, and a smile that still made her legs turn to water. He had been leaning over a suitcase on the bed, and he stood up with a long slow smile, just for her, as she came through the doorway.

"How was the game?" He smiled ruefully. He never got to Andy's games anymore, he was always too busy. Sometimes, with their busy schedules, and his, he felt as though he never saw them.

"It was great. Your son was a hero." She grinned as she stood on tiptoe to kiss him.

"So he says." His hand went easily to the small of her back, as he pulled her closer. "I missed you."

"Me too . . ." She nestled close to him for a minute before walking across the room to collapse in a comfortable chair, while he went back to his packing. Usually he packed on Sunday afternoons, and left on business trips on Sunday nights, when he had to, which was often. But sometimes, when he had enough time, he packed on Saturdays, so they'd have more time together on Sundays. "You feel like doing a barbecue tonight? It's so pretty out, and I just defrosted some steaks. It's just the two of us, and Andy. Allyson's going out with Chloe."

"I'd love to," he looked chagrined as he walked toward her, "but I couldn't get a seat on the flight to Cleveland tomorrow night. I have to catch a nine o'clock tonight. I should probably leave around seven." She looked crestfallen as he told her his plans. She'd been looking forward to seeing him all afternoon, and spending a quiet evening, maybe sitting in the moonlight in the garden. "Baby, I'm really sorry."

"Yeah . . . me too . . ." She looked genuinely depressed at the news. "I've been thinking about you all day." She smiled at him as he sat on the arm of her chair. She was trying to be a good sport, and she should have been used to his trips by then, but in some ways she wasn't. She always missed him.

"I guess Cleveland on a Sunday won't exactly be a treat for you." She felt sorry for him. The ad agency where he worked expected so much from him. But he was their star attraction, the man who roped them in like dazed steer. There were legends about him in the business, about being able to bring in new clients like little lambs, and even more remarkable, keep them.

"As long as I'm stuck there, I thought I'd play golf with the president of the company I'm seeing. I called him this afternoon, and we're meeting at his club tomorrow morning. At least it won't be a total waste of time." He kissed her on the lips then, and she felt the old familiar thrill race through her. "I'd rather be here with you and the kids," he whispered as her arms went around his neck.

"Forget the kids . . ." she said hoarsely, and he laughed.

"I like that idea . . . save it till Tuesday night . . . I'll be back by bedtime."

"I'll remind you of that on Tuesday," Page whispered as they kissed again, and Andy exploded into their bedroom.

"Allie left the potato chips out and Lizzie's eating them! She's gonna be sick all over the kitchen!" Lizzie was their golden Lab, and she had a notoriously indiscriminating appetite and equally famous delicate stomach. "Come on, Mom! She's gonna get sick if you let her eat them!"

"Okay . . . I'm coming . . ." Page smiled ruefully at Brad, and he gently patted her behind as she followed Andy back to the kitchen. As advertised, there was a carpet of potato chip crumbs all over the kitchen, and Lizzie was happily devouring the last of them when they got there. "You're a pig, Lizzie," Page said tiredly, as she cleaned up the last of the mess, and wished Brad weren't going to Cleveland. She had really wanted to spend some time with him. Their life seemed to belong to everyone but them, and just today she had really longed for some quiet time with her husband. She turned to look at Andrew then, as Lizzie tried to lick the last of the potato chips she was holding. "Want a hot date with your old Mom? Dad has to go to Cleveland tonight. We could go out for pizza." They could also eat pizza at home, or the steaks she had defrosted for all of them, but suddenly she didn't feel like being at home without Brad. And it might be more fun to just go out with Andy. "What do you say?"

"I'd love to!" He looked delighted as he and Lizzie left the kitchen again, and Page put the salad and the steaks back in the fridge. Then she went back to the bedroom to see her husband. It was six-thirty by then, he had finished packing, and he was almost dressed to leave for the airport. He was traveling in a dark blue double-breasted blazer and beige slacks, the collar of his blue shirt was open, and he looked young and handsome. It made her feel suddenly tired and old to look at him. He was out in the world, making things happen, meeting clients, doing business, spending time with grown-ups, and she was at home, ironing his shirts and chasing children. She tried to put it into words as she washed her face and combed her hair, and he laughed at what she was saying.

"Yeah . . . sure . . . you don't do a thing . . . you just run a house better than anyone in the world . . . take great care of our kids and everyone else's . . . and in your 'spare' time you do murals for the school and all your friends, advise my clients on how to redecorate their offices, and our friends on how to redo their homes, and then here and there you do a little painting. Damn shame you never do anything, Page." He was teasing her, but all that he said was true and she knew it. It just seemed so insignificant sometimes, as though she didn't *really* do anything. Maybe it was because she just did whatever she did for friends, or as favors. She hadn't been paid for her artwork in years, not since her days right after art school when she worked as an apprentice on Broadway. She had loved that. It seemed light years ago now, painting scenery, designing sets, and on one production off-off-Broadway, they had even consulted her about the costumes. And now all she did was dress her children for Halloween, or at least that was what it felt like.

"Believe me," Brad went on, as he put his suitcase in the hall, and turned to hold her again, "I'd rather do what you do than be spending my Saturday night on a plane to Cleveland."

"I'm sorry." Her life was a lot easier than his, and she knew it. Thanks to him. He worked hard to support them, and he did well. Her parents had a little bit of money, but his had had nothing till the day they died. And everything Brad had done, he had done himself, the hard way. He had crawled his way up, worked hard, and become successful. And one day, he would probably run the ad agency where he worked. If not, he'd run another one. He was much in demand, greatly admired, and the agency was anxious to keep him happy.

Like tonight, he'd be flying first class, and staying at the Tower City Plaza in Cleveland. They didn't want to take any chances on his getting fed up, or burnt out, or a better offer.

"I'll be back Tuesday night . . . I'll call you later." He walked toward the children's rooms, kissed Allyson, who was looking particularly grown up in her mother's pink cashmere sweater and a little bit of makeup. The sweater had a round neck and short sleeves, and she was wearing it with a short white skirt, and her long blond hair loose around her shoulders. Her hair almost reached her waist and cascaded seductively around her face and seemed to float around her like a halo. "Wow! Who's the lucky guy?" It was impossible not to notice her, or the way she looked. She was a real beauty.

"Chloe's father." She grinned.

"I hope he's not into young girls, or I may not let you go out with her anymore. You look hot, Princess!"

"Oh Daddy!" She rolled her eyes in embarrassment, but she liked it when he thought she looked pretty, and he was always lavish with his compliments. For her,

her mother, and even Andy. "He's really old!"

"Oh, great! Thanks a lot! I think Trygve Thorensen is two years younger than I am." Brad was forty-four, although he didn't look it.

"You know what I mean."

"Yeah . . . unfortunately, I do . . . anyway, kiddo, be a good girl for your Mom this week. I'll see you Tuesday night."

"Bye, Dad. Have fun."

"Oh yeah. Big time. In Cleveland. Besides, what would I do to have a good time without all of you?"

"You leaving now, Dad?" Andy appeared under his arm, and stood very close to him. He loved being near his father.

"Yup. I'm leaving you in command. Take care of your mother, please. You can report to me on Tuesday night, and tell me if the ladies followed your orders." Andy grinned toothlessly in response. He loved it when his father put him in charge, it made him feel so important.

"I'm taking Mom out to dinner tonight," he announced seriously, "for pizza."

"Make sure she doesn't eat too much . . . it might make her sick . . ." Brad said conspiratorially to his young aide, "you know, like Lizzie!"

"Yuk!" Andy made a face, and they all laughed. Andy followed his parents to the front door. Brad took his car out of the garage, and then got out to toss his suitcase in the trunk, and then hug Page and Andy.

"I'm going to miss you guys, take care," he said as he got into the car again.

"We will." Page smiled. She should have been used to his leaving by then, but she wasn't. It was easier when he left on Sunday night. She expected that, but this way she felt cheated. She had wanted more time with him, and now he'd be gone. Besides, as much as he traveled, it was impossible not to think of the dangers. What if something happened to him one day? What if . . . she knew she'd never live through it. "Take care . . ." she whispered as she leaned into the window of the front seat and kissed him, thinking that she should have taken him to the airport. But he liked having his car there when he got home. And on Tuesday night it would have been complicated for her to pick him up, so this was simpler. "I love you."

"I love you too," he said softly, and then leaned around her to wave at Andy again.

She stepped back, and they waved, and he drove off. It was exactly five minutes to seven.

They went back into the house, hand in hand, and she felt lonely again, but tried not to. It was stupid. She was a grown woman, she didn't have to be that dependent on him. And he would be back in three days. You'd think he'd be gone for a month from the way she was feeling.

Allyson was ready by then, and she looked really lovely. She had on the tiniest bit of mascara, and a pale pink gloss on her lips that barely shimmered. She looked clean and healthy and young. Youth at its most exquisite moment. She was the same age as the models they put on the cover of *Vogue,* and in some ways, Page thought, she looked better than they did.

"Have a good time, sweetheart. And I'd like you home by eleven." It was an ordinary curfew, and Page was always firm about it.

"Mom!"

"Never mind that. Eleven is perfectly reasonable, and you know it." She had just turned fifteen, and Page didn't see why she had to stay out any later.

"What if the movie gets out later than that?"

"Eleven-thirty then. Any later than eleven-thirty, forget the movie."

"Thanks a lot!"

"You're welcome. Do you want a ride to Chloe's?"

"No, thanks, I'll walk. See you later." She slipped out of the house, while Page went to get her sweater and her handbag out of their bedroom. The phone rang as she picked up her bag. It was her mother in New York. She explained that she and Andy were on their way out to dinner, and she'd call her back the next day. And by the time Page and Andy got back in the car, with their things, Allyson was long gone, and had probably already reached Chloe's.

"Well, young man, what'll it be? Domino's or Shakey's?"

"Domino's. We went to Shakey's last time."

"Sounds fair to me." Page flipped on the radio in the car, and let Andy pick the music. He picked the rock-and-roll station that he knew Allyson liked. He had very odd musical tastes for a seven-year-old boy, and he got them mostly from his older sister.

They got to the restaurant in five minutes, and Page felt better by then. Her moment of melancholy was gone, and she and Andy had a good time. They always did when they were together. He told her about all his friends, and what they did in school, and he explained to her how when he grew up he had decided to be a teacher. When she asked him why, he said it was because he liked taking care of little kids, and he liked the long summer vacations.

"Or maybe I'll be a baseball star, for the Giants or the Mets."

"That would be nice too." She smiled, he was always fun and easy to be with.

"Mom?"

"Yes?"

"Are you an artist?"

"More or less. I used to be, but I don't do it very seriously anymore. I haven't in a long time." He nodded, thinking about it.

"I like the mural you did at school."

"I'm glad. I like it too. It was fun to do. I think I'm going to do another one." He seemed pleased, and when they finished their pizza, he paid for them, and left the amount for the tip that she told him to. Then he put an arm around her waist and they walked back to the station wagon parked outside.

Ten minutes later, they were home, and after his bath, he joined her in her bed to watch TV. Eventually, she let him fall asleep in her bed, and smiled as she tucked him in and kissed him. At seven he was already a big boy, but he was still her baby, and always would be. In her own way, Allyson was still her baby too. Maybe children always are, at any age. She smiled, thinking of her, in the borrowed pink cashmere, and how pretty she looked when she left to have dinner with the Thorensens.

Page thought of Brad then too. And when she checked for messages on the machine, she discovered that he had called her from the airport. He had probably known they would be out, but he had just called to tell her he loved her.

She watched a movie on TV then. She was tired and would have gone to sleep, but she wanted to wait up for Allyson. Page had not yet reached the point of being able to assume that she would come in. She wanted to know for sure, so she sat up and waited.

At eleven o'clock she watched the news. Nothing too remarkable had happened, and Page saw with relief that there had been no disasters in the air, or at the airport. Whenever Brad was traveling, she was always nervous that something terrible might happen to him. But nothing had. There had been the usual shootings in Oakland, the gang wars, the politicians insulting each other, and a minor crisis at a water treatment plant. And other than that, there had been an accident on the Golden Gate Bridge, and a few minutes before they had closed the bridge, but at least Page knew that she didn't have to worry about that. Brad was in the air, and Allyson had stayed in Marin, with the Thorensens. Andy was in bed next to her. All her chickens were accounted for, thank God. It was something to be grateful for, as she glanced at the clock and waited for Allyson to come home by eleven-thirty. It was eleven-twenty by then, and knowing her well, Page knew she would come racing through the door at eleven twenty-nine, eyes bright, hair flying . . . and probably with a huge spot of spaghetti sauce on the borrowed pink cashmere sweater. Page smiled to herself, thinking of it, as she settled deeper into her bed, to watch the weather.

CHAPTER 2

———◆———

As Allyson hurried down the walk when she left her house, she was already five minutes late for her appointment with Chloe. Her house was three blocks from Allyson's, but she didn't even have to go that far this time. Allyson and Chloe had agreed to meet at the corner of Shady Lane and Lagunitas, halfway between their two homes, and just around the corner from Chloe's.

Chloe was already there when Allyson arrived, breathless and flushed in the slightly too warm pink cashmere sweater.

"Wow! That's neat!" Chloe admired. "Is it your mom's?" She no longer had the vast

pool of her mother's wardrobe to draw
from, and she had borrowed the black
sweater she was wearing from the older sister of a girl in school. Or actually, Chloe's
friend had stolen it from her older sister,
and assured Chloe that they'd all be dead if
it wasn't returned, without fail, by Sunday
morning. It was a black turtleneck sweater,
and she was wearing it with a black leather
miniskirt she'd borrowed from another
friend, and a pair of black tights her mother
had forgotten in a drawer when she left for
England.

"You look cool," Allyson nodded, impressed with the sophisticated outfit. She
started to worry then that she looked like
Little Bo Peep next to Chloe. But in any
case, their looks were very different. The
black sweater and skirt set off Chloe's shining dark hair, in sharp contrast to her
creamy white skin. She was a very pretty
girl, and she stood next to Allyson, looking
like a nervous ballerina. She had done
eleven years of ballet, and it showed in her
every movement. She was hoping to trans-
fer to the San Francisco Ballet School in the
fall, and had just been accepted after a series of gruelling auditions. Allyson was
looking at her uncomfortably, as Chloe

looked at her watch repeatedly and glanced down the street with obvious expectation. "Stop it! You're making me a wreck! Maybe we shouldn't have done it," Allyson said, looking ready to cry, and suddenly remorseful.

"How can you say a thing like that?" Chloe looked terrified. "They're the two best-looking guys in the whole school. And Phillip Chapman is a senior!" Phillip was Allyson's date, and Jamie Applegate was the boy Chloe had been dreaming of since she was a freshman. He was a junior now, and both boys were on the swimming team.

It was Jamie who had set up the date, and Chloe who had arranged it. She had consulted with Allyson immediately, who said that her mother would never let her go out with a senior. She had only had a few very tentative dates by then, usually to go to movies with boys she had known all her life, or in a large group of friends, and so far always dropped off and picked up by their parents. None of their sophomore friends had driver's licenses yet, so transportation was all-important. There were parties, of course, and she had gone steady for a few weeks before Christmas, but they were sick of each other by the New Year. There had never been a real date with a real boy who picked her up in a real car and took her out for a real dinner. Until tonight. This was very real, a little too much so.

After considerable consultation with Allyson and her other friends, Chloe had decided that her father wouldn't want her going out with Jamie Applegate, at least not in a car, driven by him. She knew instinctively that her father would complain that she scarcely knew him. Maybe if Jamie spent some time with them, came to dinner once or twice, hung around with them, maybe her father would feel different. But certainly not in time for this once-in-a-lifetime opportunity that she had to seize now, or surely it would never come again. *Carpe diem.* Seize the day. And she had. She had convinced Allyson that the only way was to lie to their parents. Just this once. This one time wouldn't hurt anything, and if they liked the boys after that, and wanted to go out with them again, then they could lay all the groundwork with their parents. This was like a tryout.

Allyson wasn't sure about it at first, but Phillip Chapman was so beautiful, so overwhelming in his coolness and seniority, there was no way she could resist a chance to go out with him. Chloe was right. After endless phone calls, and whispered conversations at school, they accepted, and made arrangements to meet the boys around the corner from Chloe's house.

"Not allowed to go out with boys?" Jamie teased when she gave him the address, and told him where they'd be waiting for them.

"Of course I am. I just don't want my older brothers bruising you if they don't like you," she said, trying to dream up an excuse, but Jamie looked unconcerned as he wrote down the address and promised to tell Phillip Chapman. Phillip had a car, and he'd be driving them to dinner at Luigi's.

"Dutch treat?" Chloe had asked nervously. That would pose a problem too. She had already spent all of her allowance on a pair of shoes she wasn't supposed to buy. Sometimes life got incredibly complicated at fifteen. And she had loaned Penny Morris another five when she couldn't even afford to, but Jamie only laughed at her question. He had bright red hair, a great smile, and Chloe liked everything about him.

"Don't be stupid. We invited you." It was the real thing. A genuine date with two honest-to-goodness upperclassmen. It was so exciting they giggled about it all week. They could hardly wait for the big evening. And now, suddenly it was here. But the boys were late, and Allyson wondered if it was all a big joke, and they'd been made fools of.

"Maybe they won't come," she said anxiously, half terrified and half relieved. "Maybe they were just kidding. Why would Phillip Chapman want to go out with me? He's seventeen, practically eighteen, he's graduating in two months, and he's the captain of the swim team."

"So what?" Chloe frantically reassured, but she was every bit as worried as Allyson that the boys were only playing with them, and might not show up for the evening. "You're beautiful, Allie. He's lucky to be going out with you," she said gently.

"Maybe he doesn't think so." But as she said the words, an old gray Mercedes came around the corner, and stopped neatly in front of them. Phillip was driving, and Jamie was next to him. The boys were wearing blazers and slacks, both were wearing ties, and both looked incredibly handsome to Allyson and Chloe.

Phillip quietly took it all in, and then smiled at Allyson. "Hi . . . sorry we were late. I had to stop and get gas, and I couldn't find a station that sold diesel." Jamie was helping Chloe into the backseat by then, he looked dazzled by the shining black hair, the big blue eyes, and the little black leather skirt. He told Chloe how pretty she looked, as Allyson got in, and Phillip said hi to Chloe. They were a cute group, and they all looked about eighteen as they took off in the direction of Luigi's. "Seat belts, please," Phillip said sternly as they drove off, sounding very grown up, and making them all feel very important. And then he looked at Allyson, and spoke softly as their two friends chattered in the backseat as though they'd been going out for Saturday night dinner for years, and had never been nervous for a single moment.

"You look really nice," Phillip said, looking at her. "I'm glad you could make it."

"So am I." Allyson blushed and smiled, wishing she weren't so nervous.

"Are your folks uptight about us or the car?" he asked honestly, and for an instant Allyson was tempted to pretend that neither was a problem. And then she shrugged with a shy smile and decided to be honest. Maybe it was okay to be straight with him.

He seemed like a nice guy, and she liked him.

"Probably both. I didn't ask. They don't really want me driving with kids. It's sort of a dumb rule, but they get really nuts about it."

"They're probably right. But I'm a really careful driver. My father taught me to drive when I was nine." He glanced over at her again with a slow smile. "Maybe I could come over and meet them sometime. That might help a little bit." Or not, depending on how her parents felt about her going out with a boy nearly three years older than she was. Or maybe they'd like him. It was hard to tell. He certainly was polite, and nice, and respectable. Phillip Chapman was no juvenile delinquent.

"I'd like that," she said softly, in awe of his willingness to make her comfortable, and put things right with her parents.

"So would I."

They chatted on the way to Luigi's, and Chloe giggled a lot from the backseat. Jamie was telling her outrageous stories about the swim team, most of them lies, according to Phillip, who was far more serious, but nice to be with. By the time they'd ordered dinner, Allyson had decided that she really liked him.

He surprised her when he ordered wine for Jamie and himself, and offered to share it with them. They had fake ID's, but the waiter didn't even ask, he just brought them two glasses of the house red, and then turned his back when the girls took sips from their glasses. Phillip didn't even finish it but at dessert, Allyson noticed that he drank two cups of very strong black coffee.

"Do you always drink wine?" She couldn't help asking. Her parents only let her sip champagne at Christmas. She'd had beer a couple of times, but she hated it. And tonight the wine had been exciting but it hadn't tasted much better.

"Sometimes," he answered. "I like a glass of wine when I'm having a good time. I drink it at home, with my parents. And they don't mind my having some when I'm out with them." But they would have minded a lot his ordering it with a fake ID, for another minor, and with the intention of driving after he drank it. And Phillip knew that. But out with two pretty girls, he was feeling very daring.

"Doesn't it bother you when you drive?" she asked, concerned.

"No," he said firmly. "It doesn't really get to me. I wouldn't want to drink more than a glass though. And I had two cups of coffee."

"I saw that." Allyson smiled. "I'm glad you did." She was honest with him. He was handsome, and very grown up, but she found that she could be fairly outspoken with him, and he seemed to like that.

"Were you worried?"

"A little."

"Don't be." He smiled, and put a hand over her own, resting on the table. They looked into each other's eyes, and then away. For Allyson, it was all a little overwhelming. They looked over at Jamie and Chloe then, chattering away about Chloe's move to the San Francisco Ballet School. Jamie was telling her how good he'd thought she was in a performance he'd been dragged to by his sister.

"Thank you," she beamed. She was crazy about him, and his praise meant a lot to her. "Did you like it?"

"No." He grinned. "I hated it, but I thought you were great, and so did my sister."

"She used to do ballet with me, before she quit."

"I know. She was lousy, but she says you're good."

"Maybe . . . I don't know . . . sometimes I think it's too much work, and sometimes I really love it."

"Sounds like swimming." Phillip smiled, and then suggested they all go into the city for cappuccino. "How about Union Street? We can walk around for a while, and maybe go somewhere for coffee. How does that sound?"

"Nice," Jamie volunteered.

"Really nice," Chloe agreed. For an instant, Allyson had a wave of nervousness about going into the city. No one knew they were going there. But then again, what harm could it do? Union Street was pretty tame, and coffee was not exactly racy.

"As long as I'm home by eleven-thirty, it's cool with me," she volunteered, trying not to worry.

"Let's go then."

Phillip left a handsome tip, and they got back in his car outside Luigi's. It was actually his mother's car, he explained. They usually let him drive an old station wagon, but it was so disreputable-looking, he had borrowed her fifteen-year-old Mercedes instead, since his parents were in Pebble Beach for the weekend.

They drove across the Golden Gate Bridge, paid the toll, and drove east on Lombard Street, and then south on Fillmore, to Union. After an endless search, they found a parking place, and began strolling past the shops and restaurants. It was a busy Saturday, a warm night, and it was fun just being there. Allyson felt terribly grown up, as she walked along with Phillip's arm around her shoulders.

He was tall and handsome, and he told her about his college plans. He had just been accepted at UCLA, and he was excited about going in September. He had thought a lot about Yale, but his parents hadn't really wanted him to go East. They were older, he was an only child, and they liked the idea of his being a little closer. He said he had liked UCLA better anyway, and that maybe Allyson could come down and visit him in September. The very idea of it dazzled her. She couldn't even begin to imagine explaining that to her parents. She laughed just thinking of it, and he understood it.

"Maybe that's a little too much of a leap for the first night, hmm? How about some coffee?" He seemed to understand a lot of things, and as they sat drinking cappuccino until almost eleven o'clock, she liked him better and better. He leaned across the table once, and almost brushed her lips with his own, as he bent to tell her something. It was almost as though Chloe and Jamie weren't there by then, they were so engrossed in their own conversation.

There was no wine drunk at the coffeehouse, and they stood up to leave at five to eleven. They ambled slowly back to the car, but they knew that at that hour of night, they would have no trouble getting back to Ross in time for Allyson's curfew.

"I had a great time," she said softly to Phillip, as she put on her seat belt.

"So did I." He smiled, and yet he seemed so much older that she really wondered if he would want to take her out again, or if he was just being kind to her this evening. It was hard to say, but she would have liked to get to know him better.

He drove quietly and smoothly up Lombard Street, toward the bridge, and then onto the Golden Gate Bridge. It was a perfect evening. Every star in the sky seemed to be out and sparkling. The water shimmered in the moonlight, the lights around the bay seemed brilliant. The air was gentle and warm in just the way it almost never is in San Francisco, the fog having disappeared entirely for the night. It was the most romantic night Allyson had ever seen, or could remember.

"It's so beautiful," she whispered almost to herself as they crossed the bridge, and from the backseat there was a burst of giggles.

"Do you two have your seat belts on?" Phillip asked, sounding serious again, and Jamie laughed.

"Mind your own business, Chapman."

"I'm going to pull over after the bridge, if you don't. Put them on, please." But there was no sound of buckling-up from the backseat. In fact, there was a noticeable silence, and Allyson didn't want to turn around to look at them. So with an embarrassed smile, she glanced at Phillip.

"What are you doing tomorrow night, Allyson?" he asked her.

"I . . . I don't know . . . I'm not allowed to go out on Sunday nights." It was time to be honest with him. She was no senior. She was fifteen years old, and she had to live by rules, whether or not she liked him. She had enjoyed tonight, but it was too nervous-making sneaking out and doing something she shouldn't. She liked the idea of his meeting her family, but she didn't want to sneak out to meet him again, no matter what Chloe decided to do about Jamie.

But Phillip didn't seem upset by what she'd said. He knew how old she was, but she was mature for her age, and she was a knockout. He had enjoyed her company, and he was willing to play by the rules in order to further their friendship. "I've got practice tomorrow afternoon, I thought maybe I could come by afterwards, if that's okay, and just hang out for a while . . . meet your parents . . . how does that sound?"

"Terrific." She beamed. "You really wouldn't mind doing that?" He shook his head, and glanced over at her with a look that made her heart melt. "I thought maybe . . . I don't know . . . I thought you'd think it was a pain in the neck to deal with all that."

"I knew what to expect when I asked you out tonight. I was surprised I didn't have to meet your parents. And then I figured you probably hadn't told them the truth. We can't go on doing that forever."

"No." She shook her head, relieved by his attitude. "We can't . . . or I guess I couldn't . . . and if my parents found out, they'd kill me. . . ."

"So will my mother when she finds out I took her car, if she does find out. . . ." He grinned, looking like a kid himself. They both laughed. They'd been outrageous tonight, and they knew it, but they were all good kids. They didn't mean any harm, it was all in good fun, and high spirits.

They were more than halfway across the bridge by then, and Jamie and Chloe were whispering softly in the backseat, their murmurings dotted by an occasional silence. Phillip had pulled Allyson closer to him, as close as he could within the confines of her seat belt. She had loosened it, and started to take it off, but he wouldn't let her. He took his eyes from the road then, for just a single instant, looked at her long and hard, and then as he glanced back at the road, he saw it. But too late. It was only a flash of light, a bolt of lightning hurtling toward them, almost in their faces by then. Allyson was looking at him when it hit, and in the backseat they never saw it. It was an arc of light, a crash of thunder, a mountain of steel, an explosion of glass everywhere as it hit them. It was the end of the world in a single moment, as the two cars met and crashed and twirled furiously around each other like two enraged bulls, as everywhere around them cars swerved not to hit them, horns, shrieks, the sound of an explosion, and then suddenly silence.

There was glass everywhere, iron wrapped around steel, there was a long scream in the night, horns honking in the distance, and at last the long slow wail of a siren. And then, slowly at first, and suddenly faster, people ran from their cars, and rushed toward the two cars, locked together, seemingly in death, frozen together in a rictus of horror, one tangled ball of steel . . . one mass . . . as people ran to help them, and the sirens wailed closer. It was impossible to believe that anyone had survived it.

CHAPTER 3

Two men were the first to approach what was left of the old gray Mercedes. It was apparent by then that a black Lincoln had hit them head-on. The engine was crushed, and the two cars seemed to have merged into one. Except for the color, it was almost impossible to distinguish between them. A woman was wandering nearby, murmuring to herself and whimpering, but she appeared unharmed, and two other motorists went to her, as the two men peered into the gray Mercedes. One man had brought a flashlight with him and was wearing rough clothes, the other one was a young man in jeans, and had already said he was a doctor.

"Do you see anything?" the man with the flashlight asked, feeling his whole body shake as he looked inside the Mercedes. He had seen a lot of things, but never anything like this. He had almost hit another car as he swerved to avoid them. There was traffic stopped everywhere, in all lanes, and no one was moving across the bridge now.

It was dark in the car at first, in spite of the lights overhead, everything was so crushed and so condensed that it was hard to see who was in it. And then, they saw him. His face was covered with blood, his whole body compressed into an impossible space, the back of his head crushed against the door, his neck at an awful angle. It was obvious instantly that he was dead, although the doctor searched for a pulse, and couldn't find one.

"The driver's dead," the doctor said quietly to the other man, who shone his flashlight into the backseat, and found himself staring into a young man's eyes. He was conscious and seemed alert, but he said not a word as he stared at the man with the flashlight.

"Are you all right?" he asked as Jamie

Applegate nodded. There was a cut over one eye, and he had hit his forehead on something, possibly Phillip. He looked dazed, but he seemed otherwise unhurt, which was nothing less than amazing.

The man with the flashlight tried to open the door for him, but everything was so jammed that he couldn't.

"The highway patrol will be here in a minute, son." He spoke calmly, and Jamie nodded again. He seemed unable to speak, and it was obvious that he was in shock. He just went on staring at the two men, and the man with the flashlight felt sure that at the very least the boy had a concussion.

The doctor moved back to look at Jamie through the open window, and offer what encouragement he could, when they heard a deep groan from the backseat, next to him, and then a sharp cry that became a scream. It was Chloe. Jamie turned to stare at her as though unable to understand how she had gotten there beside him.

The doctor ran around the car as quickly as he could, and the man with the flashlight tried to shine the light on her from where he stood on Jamie's side, and then all at once they saw her. She had been crushed between the front and back seats, the entire

front seat had been shoved back by the
force and mass of the Lincoln, and she
seemed to have the seat jammed into her
lap. They couldn't see her legs, and she began sobbing hysterically, telling them she
couldn't move, and screaming that it hurt,
as they tried to calm her. Jamie continued
to stare at her, looking confused, and then
he said something vague to Phillip.

"Hang in there," the man with the flashlight said to both of them. "Help's on the
way." They could all hear the wail of the
sirens approaching, but her screams seemed
even more piercing.

"I can't move . . . I can't . . . I can't
breathe . . ." She was panting and out of
breath, hyperventilating in her panic, as the
young doctor quietly took charge of her,
and talked to her very calmly.

"You're all right . . . you're fine . . .
we're going to get you out of here in a minute . . . now, try to breathe slowly . . .
here . . . hold my hand . . ." He reached
in and took her hand in his own, and he saw
that there was blood on her hands where
she had touched her legs, but in spite of the
flashlight he couldn't see what had happened. The best news was that she was conscious and talking to him. No matter how

damaged her legs were, she was alive, and there was every reason to hope she would make it.

The man with the flashlight left them for an instant then. He had just seen that there was an unconscious girl in the front seat. At first she had been almost invisible, she was lying so far down on the seat, and there was so much metal pressed against her. But they had suddenly noticed her face and her hair, as they tried to examine Chloe. The doctor kept busy talking to Chloe as she sobbed, while the man with the flashlight tried to pull open the front passenger door to free the girl lying under the dashboard. But to no avail. The door was bent beyond hope of opening it, and the young girl on the front seat never moved as he reached in through the broken glass of the window and tried to touch her. He said something in an undervoice to the doctor who, glancing at her, said he suspected that she was dead like the driver. But a moment later, he checked, leaving the other man to continue talking to Chloe. He was surprised to find a pulse when he touched her neck, it was thin and thready, and he could detect almost no breath at all. Her entire head and face were covered with blood, her hair matted with it, the sweater she had worn was a deep red, she had cuts everywhere and had clearly sustained a major head injury in the collision. She was barely alive, hanging on by the merest thread, and he thought it unlikely she would live long enough for them to save her. There was nothing he could do for her, and even if her breathing stopped or her pulse, he couldn't have administered CPR. She was positioned too awkwardly, and was obviously much too badly damaged. All he could do was stand there and keep an eye on her, feeling helpless. From what he could see, both of the young people in the front seat were a loss. Only the two in the back had been extremely lucky.

"Christ, they're taking forever, aren't they?" The man with the flashlight said under his breath, looking at the carnage in the car. With the flashlight, they could see more clearly how much blood had been lost. Both of the girls seemed to be bleeding profusely.

"It just feels that way," the doctor said softly. He had ridden an ambulance as part of his residency in New York ten years before, and he had seen a lot of ugly things, on the highways, in the streets, and in the ghettos. He had delivered his share of babies in back hallways too, but he had seen more scenes like this one, and frequently with no survivors. "They'll be here in a minute."

The other man was sweating profusely and Chloe's screams were getting to him. And he was afraid to look at Allyson's face, she was in such bad shape. He wasn't even sure she had a face left.

And then, finally, they came. Two fire engines, an ambulance, and three police cars. Several people had called from their car phones and reported how bad the accident was, others had approached the two cars cautiously, and learned that there were four passengers in the smaller car, two of them badly injured. The driver of the other car had been miraculously untouched except for a few scratches and bruises, and she was sobbing hysterically by the side of the road, in the arms of a stranger.

Three of the firemen and two cops approached the car simultaneously, along with both paramedics. The other policemen tried to take charge of the traffic, directing it slowly around the two cars, and getting it moving in one direction. Their own vehicles had added to the confusion and the roadblock, and the single file of cars heading north barely crawled past the two cars and the emergency vehicles, as people stared at the carnage.

"What have we got?" The highway patrolman glanced in first, and shook his head when he looked at Phillip.

"He's gone," the doctor was quick to explain, and the first of the paramedics confirmed it. Over. One life. Finished in a single moment. No matter how young he had been, or how bright, or how kind, or how much his parents loved him. He was dead, with no reason, no plan, no purpose. Phillip Chapman was dead at seventeen, on a balmy Saturday night in April.

"We can't get any of the doors open," the doctor explained, "the girl in the backseat is trapped, I think she's got some pretty severe injuries to her lower extremities. He's okay." He motioned to Jamie still staring at them in confusion. "He's in shock, and we need to get him to the hospital right away to check him out. But I think he's probably going to be all right. Maybe a concussion."

The paramedics had reached in to touch Allyson by then, as the firemen ran to call for the Jaws of Life and a five-man team to free them. "What about the girl in the front seat, Doc?"

"She doesn't look like she's going to make it." He had continued to check her pulse, she was still alive, but she was losing ground rapidly, and until the heavy equipment came, there was nothing they could do to free her. The paramedics were moving quickly to start an IV on her anyway, and one of them gently strapped a small sandbag under her head to keep her from damaging it further. "She's got an obvious head injury," the doctor exclaimed, "and God knows what else in there." She was totally engulfed by the mass of steel, most of her body was inaccessible to them, and all of it looked as though it might be broken. More than ever, it seemed unlikely that she would make it.

Chloe began screaming more alarmingly just then, and it was difficult to know if she had listened to what they said about her friends, or was simply in more pain. It was impossible to reason with her. Most of the time, she seemed completely oblivious to where she was, she just kept screaming about her legs, and she said her back hurt. As awful as it was, the medical team thought it was encouraging that she still had feeling. Too many of the accidents they saw involved people who seemed to experience almost no pain, mostly because their spinal cords had been severed.

"Okay, sweetheart, we're gonna get you out of here in a minute. You just hang on. We're gonna get you home in just a little minute." The fireman almost crooned to her, as the highway patrol managed to pry Phillip's door open with a crowbar, while carefully opening the broken window with a blanket. They pulled his body gently from the car, and one of the firemen assisted in putting his body on a gurney. They covered him immediately with a drape, and rolled his body slowly toward the ambulance. Shocked motorists looked on, and some people cried as they realized he had been killed in the car crash. Shocked tears of grief for a total stranger.

The open door allowed the doctor to slip in next to Allyson, and get a better fix on her condition, but it wasn't good. She was breathing even more irregularly by then, and the paramedics quickly put an airway through her mouth, and then attached a bag to it with an oxygen tube extending from it. The doctor knew they were "bagging," as it was called, to help her breathe, and he knew, as they did, that the IV and the oxygen could only help her. Her arms were too lacerated to even allow them to get a blood pressure cuff on her, but the doctor didn't need it. He could see what was happening to her. She was dying in their hands, and if they didn't free her soon, she would be gone just like Phillip. She might not make it anyway, but even covered with blood, it was easy to see how young she was, and he wanted her to make it.

"Come on, little girl . . . come on . . . don't you quit on me now . . ." It almost sounded like praying, as he turned and snapped at the paramedic. "Come on, more oxygen." They all watched tensely as the paramedics gave it to her and a moment later they added something to her IV. But they were clutching at straws, and they all knew it. If they didn't get her to the hospital soon, she just wasn't going to make it.

And then, finally, the Jaws of Life rumbled up, and the five-man crew leapt out and came running. They assessed the situation within milliseconds, had a brief consultation with the people on the scene, and then moved swiftly into action.

Chloe was starting to lose consciousness by then, and one of the firemen was giving her oxygen through the open window. It was Allyson who had to be freed first, Allyson who was almost dead, who had no hope at all unless they could pry her from the car in minutes, maybe seconds. No matter how great Chloe's distress, she had to wait. She was not in as great danger. And they couldn't move her anyway until the front seat was removed, and Allyson with it.

While one man stabilized the vehicle with wedges and chocks so that nothing more would move, a second man on the team deflated the tires, and two others moved with lightning speed to remove the remaining glass from all the windows. The fifth conferred with the patrolmen and paramedics on the scene, and then rapidly joined his partner, to help remove the rear window. The young people within had all gently been covered by tarps, so that no random piece of falling glass would hurt them. The windshield took two of them to remove, with one man using a flathead ax around the edges. Eventually, the windshield came away, and they actually folded it almost like a blanket. They slid it swiftly under the car with practiced hands, moving like a highly practiced ballet team. Two others removed the rear window. Only slightly more than a minute had passed since they'd arrived on the scene, and the doctor watched them, thinking that if Allyson survived at all it would be thanks to them and their speedy, almost surgical reactions.

With a tarp still covering Allyson, one of the rescuers moved inside, removed the keys and cut the seat belts. And then, as one group, they began flapping the roof, using a hydraulic cutter, and hand hacksaws. The noise was terrifying, and Jamie whimpered piteously, as Chloe began to scream again. But Allyson never stirred, and the paramedics continued pumping oxygen into her through the air tube.

Within moments, they pulled the roof off the car, drilled a hole in the door, and inserted the Jaws of Life in the door to force it open. The machine itself weighed close to a hundred pounds and took two men to hold, and made a sound as loud as a jackhammer. Jamie was crying openly by now, and the noise of the spreader was so intense that it even drowned out Chloe's screaming. Only Allyson was oblivious to all they were going through, and one of the paramedics was lying next to her on the driver's side, keeping track of the IV and her air tube, and making sure she was still breathing. She was, but barely.

They removed the door entirely, and

then moved swiftly to work pulling away the dashboard and the steering. They used nine-foot chains and a giant hook to pull it away, and before it was even fully freed, the paramedics had slipped a backboard under Allyson to immobilize her further. But as they did, the entire car was open to the night air, the front end gone, the roof open, the doors off, and Allyson could finally be moved now. And they could see, as the paramedics bent over her, how acute her wounds were. She looked as though she'd received blows at the front of her head, and the side as well. Her head must have bounced around like a marble when the car hit her. And her seat belt had been so loose, it was almost as though she hadn't worn one.

But all their manpower was concentrated now on moving her, ever so gently, to the gurney. Speed was of the essence, and yet every movement had to be infinitely delicate and carefully planned, or they might do her further cervical or spinal damage. She was barely clinging to life as the head of the paramedic team shouted "Go!" and they ran as smoothly as they could to the waiting ambulance with the gurney. Two more ambulances had arrived on the scene

by then, and the newly arrived paramedics
turned their attention to Chloe and Jamie.
It was exactly midnight as the ambulance
sped off the bridge with Phillip's body, Allyson, and the young doctor. One of the
highway patrolmen had said he'd bring his
car to Marin General to him. The doctor
didn't feel comfortable letting her go to the
hospital with only the paramedics, although
he felt that what he could do for her was
minimal. She needed a neurosurgeon immediately, but he wanted to be there in the
meantime. He still didn't think she'd live.
But she might. And if there was any chance
at all, he wanted to help her.

More patrol cars had arrived by then, a
fourth ambulance and two more fire trucks.
The traffic was still moving single file into
Marin, and the bridge was still closed from
Marin County into San Francisco, and the
traffic looked as though it was backed up to
forever.

"How is she?" one of the firemen asked,
referring to Chloe, as the paramedics
waited for the rescue team to free her. She
was bleeding profusely from both legs and
hysterical. They had an IV going on her by
then and she had fainted several times
when they tried to move her.

"She's in and out of consciousness," one of the paramedics explained. "We'll have her out in a minute." They had to rip away the seat in order to get her, and it was blocked in from every angle. The machines they used literally tore it to shreds, and disposed of it on the pavement, and ten minutes later, Chloe's legs were exposed, crushed, broken, she had compound fractures of both legs, with the bones protruding. And as they lifted her from the car as carefully as they could, on a backboard, she finally lost consciousness completely.

The second ambulance sped off with its sirens screaming in the night, just as the firemen helped Jamie from the car. He was free now, and as they pulled him out of it, he sobbed and clung to the firemen like a small child in total panic.

"It's all right, son . . . it's all right . . ." He had seen a lot, and he was still confused and dazed. He still couldn't understand what had happened. They put him gently in the last ambulance, and he was taken to Marin General like the others, just as the news truck arrived. They were late getting to the scene this time, but the bridge had been blocked solid.

"Christ, I hate nights like this," one fireman said to another. "Makes you never want to let your kids out of the house again, doesn't it?" They both shook their heads, as the extraction team continued to attempt to untangle the mass of steel sufficiently so that both cars could be towed off the bridge, as the TV cameraman filmed it.

They were all amazed that the Mercedes had been so completely destroyed. But it was old and it must have collided with the Lincoln at an odd angle. If it hadn't been a Mercedes, of whatever age, they would probably all have been dead, and not just Phillip.

The other driver was still sitting dazed by the roadside by then, leaning on a stranger. She was wearing a black dress and white coat. And she looked disheveled, but there were no bloodstains on her. Even the white coat was still clean, which seemed incredible, given the condition of the young people in the Mercedes.

"Isn't she going to the hospital?" one of the firemen asked a highway patrolman.

"She says she's okay. There are no apparent injuries. She was damn lucky. But she's pretty shook up. She feels terrible about the boy. We're going to run her home in a minute."

The fireman nodded, glancing at her. She was an attractive, expensively dressed woman in her early forties. Two women were still standing next to her, and someone had brought her some bottled water. She was crying softly into a handkerchief and shaking her head, unable to believe what had happened.

"Any idea what did happen?" a reporter asked a fireman, but he only shrugged in answer. He had no fondness for the media, or their ghoulish interest in other people's disasters. It was clear enough what had happened here. A life had been lost, maybe two by then, if Allyson hadn't made it. What did they want to know? Why? How? What did it really matter? The results were unalterable, no matter whose fault the accident had been.

"We're still not sure," the fireman said noncommittally, and then a few minutes later to one of his colleagues, "It looks like they both may have drifted over the center line just enough to create a disaster." One of the highway patrolmen had just explained it to him. "You look away for a minute . . . She was further over the line than they were in the end, but she says she wasn't. And there's no reason to disbelieve her. She's Laura Hutchinson," he said, sounding impressed, as the second fireman raised his eyebrows.

"As in Senator John Hutchinson?"

"You got it."

"Shit. Imagine if she'd been killed." But it was no better that one or two kids were. "You think the kids were drunk or on drugs?"

"Who knows? They'll check it out at the hospital. Could be. Or it could just be one of those flukes where you never figure out who did what to who. It's not real clear-cut from the position of the cars, and there isn't a hell of a lot left." What there was, was being hacked into pieces so it could be removed. And they were starting to hose down the oil and debris, and the blood that had spattered on the pavement.

It would be another hour or two before bridge traffic could resume, and even then there would be only one lane open in each direction until the early morning, when the last of the wreckage was towed away to be examined.

The camera crews were getting ready to leave by then. There was nothing left to see, and the Senator's wife had refused to comment on the other driver's death. The highway patrol had protected her from them very discreetly.

It was twelve-thirty when they finally took her home to her house on Clay Street in San Francisco. Her husband was in Washington, D.C., and she had gone to a party in Belvedere. Her children were asleep in bed, and the housekeeper opened the door to them and began to cry when she saw Mrs. Hutchinson's disheveled state and heard the story.

Laura Hutchinson thanked them profusely, insisted that she didn't need to go to the hospital, and would see her own doctor the next morning, if there was any need for it. And she made them promise that they would call her to tell her of the other young people's condition.

She already knew that the young driver was dead, but they hadn't yet told her that Allyson would probably not survive until morning. The highway patrolmen felt sorry for her, she was so distraught, so frightened, so desperately upset by what had happened. She had cried terribly when she saw Phillip's body covered with the drape and removed. She had three children of her own, and the thought of these young people dying in an accident was almost more than she could bear to think of.

The patrolman who brought her home suggested that she take a tranquilizer that night, to calm her nerves, if she had any in the house, or at least have a strong drink. She looked as though she needed it, and he was sure that the Senator wouldn't mind his suggestion.

"I haven't had a drink all night," she said nervously. "I never drink when I go out without my husband," she explained.

"I think it would do you good, ma'am. Would you like me to get you one now?"

She hesitated, but he could sense that she would, and he went to the bar and poured her a drink himself. A good strong drink of brandy. She made a terrible face as she drank it down, but she smiled at him once she did, and thanked him. They had been wonderful to her all night, and she assured them that the Senator would be very grateful to know how kind they had been to her.

"Not at all." He thanked her and left, and went to rejoin his partner outside, who inquired if he had thought to take her in to the hospital for an alcohol check, so they could rule that out in their investigation.

"For chrissake, Tom. The woman is a senator's wife, she's a nervous wreck over the accident, she saw a kid die, and she told me herself she hadn't had a drink all night. That's good enough for me." The other highway patrolman shrugged, his partner was probably right. She was a senator's wife, she wasn't going to hit the highway at eleven o'clock at night half crocked and hit a bunch of kids. No one could be that dumb, and she looked like a nice woman.

"I just poured her a brandy anyway, so it's too late now, if you wanted me to go back in and ask for it. The poor thing needed a stiff drink. I think it did her good."

"Might do me good too." The patrolman grinned. "Did you bring me one?"

"Shut up. Christ . . . run an alcohol check . . ." He laughed. "What else did you want me to do? Fingerprint her?"

"Sure. Why not. The Senator would have probably set us up for a commendation." The two men laughed and drove off into the night. It had already been a long night for them, and it was only one-thirty in the morning.

CHAPTER 4

At eleven-fifty, Page was watching an old movie on TV, and she sat up in bed a little straighter. Allyson was twenty minutes late, and her mother was not amused. At midnight, she was even less so.

Andy was sleeping peacefully at her side, and Lizzie was asleep on the floor near the bed. Everything was quiet and tranquil in the house, except Page, who was getting madder by the minute. Allyson had promised to be home no later than eleven-thirty, which was half an hour later than Page wanted her home in the first place. And there was absolutely no excuse for her violating her curfew.

Page thought of calling the Thorensen home, but she knew there was no point. If they were still at the movies, or out having ice cream somewhere, there would be no answer anyway. She figured they had probably gone out to eat somewhere after the movie, and Allyson obviously hadn't told Chloe's father that she had to be home by eleven-thirty.

By twelve-thirty, Page was enraged, and by one o'clock she was very worried. She was just deciding to abandon her reticence and call the Thorensen home, when the phone rang at five after one. She assumed that it was Allyson asking if she could spend the night at Chloe's. Page was beyond livid by then, and would have liked to shake her daughter.

"No, you may *not*!" was the way she answered.

"Hello?" The voice at the other end sounded confused, and Page sounded even more so. It wasn't Allyson at all, but a stranger. She couldn't even imagine who would call her at this hour, unless it was a mistake, or an obscene phone call.

"Is this the Clarke residence?"

"Yes? Who is this?" A sudden electric tingle of fear ran down her spine, and she ignored it.

"This is the highway patrol, Mrs. Clarke. This is Mrs. Clarke?"

"Yes." The word was a whisper, as sudden fear clutched her throat and held it.

"I'm sorry to tell you that your daughter has been in an accident."

"Oh my God." Her whole body came alive, and her mind was filled with terror. "Is she alive?"

"Yes, but she was unconscious on the way to Marin General. She was very seriously hurt." Oh God . . . oh God . . . what does "very seriously" mean? How bad is that? Is she okay? Will she live? How hurt is she?

"What happened?" It was a pathetic croak from deep in Page's throat.

"A head-on collision on the Golden Gate Bridge. They were hit by an oncoming southbound vehicle on their way into Marin County."

"Into Marin? From where? That can't be." She was willing to quibble about where Allyson had been, maybe if she won the argument, it would mean that she had never been there and nothing had happened to her after all.

"I'm afraid it was. She's in Marin General now, Mrs. Clarke. You need to get there pretty quickly."

"Oh God . . . thank you . . ." She hung up without saying more, and frantically dialed information. They gave her the number for Marin General, and she asked for the emergency room. Yes, Allyson Clarke was there, yes, she was still alive, and no, they were unable to give her any further information. The doctors were all busy with her, and couldn't talk to Page. Allyson Clarke was listed in critical condition.

Tears sprang to her eyes, and her hands shook violently as she dialed her neighbor. She had to leave Andy with someone . . . she had to call . . . had to get dressed . . . had to get there . . . The phone answered after four rings, as Page sobbed silently, praying that Allyson would be alive when she got there.

"Hello?" A sleepy voice finally answered.

"Jane? Can you come?" Page sounded breathless and felt as though she couldn't get enough air. What if she fainted? What if . . . what if Allyson died . . . oh God, no . . . please, no . . .

"What's wrong?" Jane Gilson knew her well, and she had never known Page to panic. "What is it? Are you sick? Is someone there?" Had there been an intruder?

"No," it was a terrible mouse squeak of terror, "it's Allie. She's had an accident . . . head-on . . . she's in Marin General, in critical condition . . . Brad's gone . . . I have to leave Andy . . ."

"Oh my God . . . I'll be there in two minutes." Jane Gilson hung up, and Page ran to her closet and tore on jeans and the first sweater she could find. It was the old blue one she wore to garden in, covered with holes and spots and permanently faded. But she didn't even see it as she put it on, and slipped her feet into loafers. She never thought of combing her hair, and then she ran to the pad in the den where Brad always left the name and number of his hotel when he traveled. She knew she'd find it there. She'd wait to see Allyson first, before she called, in case the news was better than she feared. But at least she could call him from the hospital, after she saw her. But this time, there was no hotel and no number. Nothing. There was a blank page. For the first time in sixteen years, he had forgotten to leave the information. It was like fate playing a bad joke on them, but she didn't have time to worry about it now. She could call someone from Brad's office and figure something out later. Right now she had to get to the hospital and see her baby.

She grabbed her bag as the front door rang, and she ran to let in Jane Gilson. Jane's arms went around her old friend. She had known the Clarkes since they'd moved in, before Andy was born, and Allyson since she was seven.

"She'll be all right . . . you know she will. Page, calm down. It probably all sounds worse than it is. Just take it easy." She would have liked to drive her there herself, but her own husband was gone. He had gone camping with her kids, both home from college for their spring vacation. And there was no one else to leave with Andy. He was still sound asleep in his mother's bed, completely unaware of what had happened. "What do you want me to tell him when he wakes up, in case you're not back yet?"

"Just tell him Allyson got sick, and I had to go to the hospital with her. I'll call you from there and let you know what's happening. And if Brad calls, for God's sake, Jane, get his number."

"Right . . . now go . . . and drive safely."

Page ran out into the warm night, her hair flying, her purse under her arm, jumped into the car, and a moment later she shot out of the driveway. She tried to talk to herself all the way, telling herself to stay calm, to breathe, alternately reassuring herself that Allyson would be okay, and begging God that she would be. She still couldn't believe it had happened.

The hospital was eight minutes away, and she parked in the first space she found. She forgot her keys in the car, and ran into the building. The emergency unit was alive with lights, and people running around, dashing into rooms, and half a dozen people sat in a corridor, waiting for treatment. A woman in labor walked by looking uncomfortable, leaning heavily against her husband. But all Page wanted to see was her little girl . . . her baby. She noticed the reporters then, two of them taking notes from a highway patrolman.

She went to the desk and asked a nurse where she might find her, and the woman's face sobered instantly as she glanced up at

Page. She had a pretty face and kind eyes, and as she looked at Page, she felt a wave of sympathy for her. Page was dead white and shaking.

"You're her mother?"

Page nodded, feeling her body shake more. "Is she . . . is she . . ."

"She's alive." Page's legs went weak, as the woman came around the desk and held her firmly. "She's very, very badly hurt, Mrs. Clarke. She has a severe head injury. Our neurosurgical team is with her now, and we're waiting for our head of services. When he gets here, we'll be able to tell you more. But she's hanging in." She led Page to a chair, and helped her to sit down. It was as though the whole world had turned upside down in a single moment. "Would you like a cup of coffee?" She looked sympathetically down at her, and Page tried not to cry as she shook her head, but it was hopeless. The tears instantly overflowed as she tried to absorb what the woman had said . . . neurosurgeons . . . neurosurgical team . . . she's very, very badly hurt . . . but why? How? How had it happened? "Are you okay?" the nurse asked rhetorically. It was obvious that she wasn't, as she blew her nose and shook her head,

and wished she could turn the clock back.
And she had been so angry at her for missing her curfew. It was unbearable to think
of it. While she was being angry, Allyson
was being hit head-on . . . it didn't even
bear thinking.

"Was anyone else hurt?" Page finally
managed to croak, and the nurse looked at
her sadly as she nodded.

"The driver was killed. And another
young girl was severely injured."

"Oh my God . . ." *Killed?* . . . Trygve
Thorensen dead? How in God's name had
this happened? And as she thought of it,
she saw a man emerge from one of the
emergency rooms who looked astonishingly
like him. He walked out of the treatment
room in a daze and seemed to stare at Page,
without actually seeing who she was. It was
Page who suddenly realized that it was
Trygve. But how was this possible? The
nurse had said he was dead. Was it all a lie?
A bad joke? A bad dream? Was she crazy,
or dreaming? But the nightmare was all too
true, as she looked at him, and she knew it.
The nurse discreetly moved away, and
Trygve stood looking down at Page, with
tears flowing unchecked down his own
cheeks.

"Page, I'm so sorry . . ." He reached out and took her hand in his own, and held it for a moment. "I should have known . . . I guess I should have seen it coming, but I wasn't paying attention . . . I don't know how I could have been so stupid." She stared at him in horror. He hadn't been paying attention, and their children had been critically injured . . . how could he even say this to her? And why had the nurse told her he was dead, when he wasn't?

"I don't understand," Page said, staring up at him in anguish, as he sat down slowly next to her, shaking his head, still unable to believe what had happened.

"I'm beginning to. I should have known when I saw her go out in that outfit. She was wearing a black leather skirt she'd borrowed from somewhere, and black stockings that must have been Dana's . . . I'm a damn fool. I was working on something with Bjorn, and I just let it slide by. She said she was going out with you, so I figured she was okay . . . I wish to hell now that I'd stopped her."

"Out with *me*? You mean . . . you weren't driving?" A rush of fresh fear overcame her as she understood him. They hadn't been out with him at all. But then who had they been with, and who was the driver?

"No, I wasn't."

"Allyson said you were taking them to dinner at Luigi's, and a movie. It never occurred to me that you weren't . . ." And then, suddenly, as she thought about it, the pieces of the puzzle fit together for her too. The borrowed cashmere sweater, the white skirt, the fact that she scampered off to Chloe's, and didn't let Page drive her there. "How could I have been so stupid?"

"I guess we both were." He stared at her through his tears, and she began to cry again. "You should have seen Chloe when she came in . . . she's got multiple compound fractures of both legs, a shattered hip, broken pelvis, internal injuries. They're removing her spleen now, and she may have damaged her liver. They have to replace the hip, put the pelvis together with pins . . . she may never walk again, Page . . ." His tears went unchecked. "And all she wanted was to get into that ballet school. Oh Christ . . . how did this happen?"

Page nodded, numbed by what she'd just heard. Chloe unable to walk again . . . and Allyson with a severe head injury. She looked at Trygve then, no longer able to blame him. "Did you see Allyson?" She was almost afraid to herself, and yet she wanted to desperately, but they had told her she had to wait until the neurosurgeons had finished their evaluation. But what if she died first, and Page wasn't there . . . what if . . . what if.

"No, I didn't," Trygve said soberly, drying his tears for a moment. "I asked to, but they wouldn't let me. They just took Chloe to surgery. They think it'll take six to eight hours, maybe longer. It's going to be a long night." Or not. That would be even worse, for Page. For Allyson, it could all be over very quickly.

"They told me Allyson had a severe head injury, but that was all they'd say," he said softly.

"That's all they said to me too. I'm not even sure what that means. Is she brain damaged? Will she die? Could she be all right again?" Tears filled Page's eyes as she talked in circles and he listened. "She's with the neurosurgeons now."

"You just have to believe that she'll be all right. Right now that's all we have."

"But what if she isn't?" Page was grateful to have someone to talk to, and at least he knew all the terrors that she was feeling, except that Chloe was alive, and no matter how badly battered, she seemed not to be in mortal danger.

"Try not to ask yourself too many questions," he said. "I keep doing that about Chloe . . . what if she can't walk . . . what if she's paralyzed . . . will she ever be able to walk or dance or run . . . or have children? A few minutes ago, I found myself planning where to put ramps for her wheelchair. You have to force yourself to stop doing that. We just don't know yet. Live it minute by minute." Page nodded, knowing what he meant. One minute, she found herself trying to figure out what she would tell Brad if Allyson died, the next she refused to believe it.

"Do you know who was driving?" Page asked somberly, remembering what the nurse had said, that he was dead. And she had assumed it was Trygve.

"Only his name. A boy called Phillip Chapman, he was seventeen. That's all I know. And Chloe was in no condition to answer questions."

"I've heard of him. I think I've met his parents. How do you suppose they knew him?"

"God knows . . . school . . . one of

their sports teams . . . the tennis club
. . . they're growing up, you know. I never
went through anything like this with the
boys though. Not with Nick at any rate."
And, of course, Bjorn would have been different. "I guess girls are a little more enter-
prising, or at least ours are." He tried to
make her smile, but Page was beyond it.
What if she never grew up? Never had a
real date? Or a boyfriend? Or a husband?
Or a baby? What if this was it? Fifteen brief
years, and then over. Just the thought of it
brought tears to her eyes again, and Trygve
took her hand in his, and held it, when he
saw her crying.

"Don't, Page . . . try not to panic."

"How can I not? How can you say that?"
She took her hand away and began to sob.
"She may not even live. She may end up
like the boy who was driving." He nodded
miserably, and she blew her nose in terror
and despair, and then looked up at him
again. "Were they drinking?" It was the first
thing that came to mind when she thought
of a seventeen-year-old driver and an accident like this one.

"I don't know," he told her honestly.
"The nurse told me that they're taking
blood tests from all of them, to check the

alcohol levels in their blood. I suppose they could have been," he said dismally, as a reporter approached them. He had been watching them talk for a while, and Trygve had seen him ask the nurse at the desk some questions after he finished with the highway patrolman.

Page was still crying when the man in jeans and a plaid shirt walked up to them. He had on a plastic tag from the newsroom, running shoes, and he was carrying both a small cassette recorder and a notebook.

"Mrs. Clarke?" he asked very directly, and stood very close to her, watching her reactions.

"Yes?" She was so dazed she didn't realize who he was, and for an instant, she thought he might be a doctor. She looked up at him with a terrified air, as Trygve watched him with suspicion.

"How's Allyson doing?" he asked, sounding as though he knew her. He had gotten her name from the nurse.

"I don't know . . . I thought you would know . . ." But Trygve was shaking his head, and then she noticed the man's badge with his photograph, name, and network. "What do you want from me?" She looked confused and frightened by the intrusion.

"I just wanted to know how you are . . . how Allie is . . . did she know Phillip Chapman very well? What kind of kid was he? Was he a wild guy? Or do you think . . ." He pressed as hard as he could until Trygve cut him off abruptly.

"I don't think this is the time . . ." Trygve took a step closer to him, and the young reporter looked unaffected.

"Did you know that Senator Hutchinson's wife was the other driver? Not a scratch on her," he said provocatively. "How does that make you feel, Mrs. Clarke? You must be pretty angry." Page's eyes grew wide as she listened to him, unable to believe what she was hearing. What was this man trying to do to her? Make her crazy? What difference did it make who the other driver was? Was he nuts as well as insensitive? She looked up at Trygve helplessly, and saw that he was furious at the reporter's questions. "Do you think the young people in the car might have been drinking, Mrs. Clarke? Was Phillip Chapman her steady boyfriend?"

"What are you doing here?" She stood up, and stared him in the eye with a look of outrage. "My daughter may be dying, and it's none of your business how well she knew that boy, or who the other driver was, or how I feel about it." She was sobbing so hard, she could hardly get the words out. "Leave us alone!" She sat down and dropped her face into her hands, as Trygve moved between her and the reporter.

"I want you to leave us alone now." He was as immovable as a wall between Page and the young man from the newsroom. "Get out of here. You have no right to do this." He growled at him, wanting to sound ominous, but like Page, his voice was shaking.

"I have every right. The public has a right to know about this kind of thing. What if they weren't drinking? What if the Senator's wife was?"

"What's the point of this?" Trygve said angrily. What were these people doing there? This had nothing to do with the public, or anyone caring about the truth, or their rights. It had to do with prying, and bad taste, and hurting people who were already deeply wounded.

"Did you ask for an alcohol check on the Senator's wife?" His eyes fought his way back to Page, and she stared dumbly up at both men. It was all too much for her at this point. All she could think about was Allie.

"I'm sure the police did everything they were supposed to, why are you doing this? Why are you making trouble here? Can't you understand what you're doing?" Page asked him miserably. He seemed to be refusing to leave them.

"I am seeking the truth. That's all. I hope your daughter will be okay," he said without emotion, and then sauntered off to talk to someone else. He and his cameraman were in the waiting room for another hour, but they didn't bother Page again. But Trygve was still outraged by the man's attitude and his daring to pursue Page at a moment like this one. And he resented the inflammatory, sleazy style and implications that were designed to enrage them. It was utterly disgusting.

They were both shaken after the reporter walked away, and at first they didn't even notice a redheaded boy approach them half an hour later. Page had never seen him before, but he looked vaguely familiar to Trygve.

"Mr. Thorensen?" he asked nervously. He was very pale, and looked a little dazed, but he looked directly at Chloe's father as he stood before him.

"Yes?" Trygve looked at him without any

warmth or recognition. It was the wrong night for people to come up and chat with him. All he wanted to do was wait for Chloe to come out of her surgery, and pray that her life wouldn't be ruined forever. "What is it?"

"I'm Jamie Applegate, sir. I was with Chloe in . . . in the accident . . ." His lip trembled as he said the words, and Trygve looked up at him in horror.

"Who are you?" He stood to meet him then, and the boy looked sick as he faced him. He had a mild concussion and had had a few stitches over the eyebrow, but other than that he was untouched by the horror that had changed the other three lives forever.

"I'm a friend of Chloe's, sir. I . . . we . . . took her out to dinner."

"Were you drunk?" Trygve fired at him without mercy or hesitation, but Jamie shook his head. They had just done a blood test on him to prove that. And he had passed it very respectably, as had Phillip.

"No, sir. We weren't. We went to dinner, at Luigi's in Marin. I had one glass of wine, but I wasn't driving, and Phillip had less than that, maybe half a glass, if that, and then we went to have cappuccino on Union Street, and came home."

"You're all under age, son." Trygve said quietly, but he made his point. "None of you should have been drinking. Not even half a glass of wine." Jamie knew he was right, as he went on to explain what had happened. "I know. You're right, sir. But no one was drunk. I just don't know what happened. I never saw it. We were in the backseat, talking . . . and the next thing I knew, I was here. I don't remember what happened, except that the highway patrol said someone hit us, or we hit them. I just don't know. But Phillip was a good driver . . . he made us all wear our seat belts and he was totally sober." He started to cry as he said it. His friend was dead and he had lived through it.

"Do you think it was the other driver's fault?" Trygve asked him calmly. He was touched by what the boy had said, and Jamie was obviously very badly shaken.

"I don't know . . . I don't know anything, except that . . . Chloe and Allyson . . . and Phillip . . ." He began to sob, thinking of his friends, and without hesitation Trygve put his arms around him. "I'm so sorry . . . I'm so sorry . . ."

"So are we . . . it's all right, son . . .
it's all right . . . you were a lucky boy tonight . . . that's fate . . ." It chooses one,
it crushes a life, then darts away. It strikes
like lightning.

"But it's not fair . . . why did I walk
away from it, and they . . ."

"Sometimes it just happens like that. You
have to be very grateful." But all Jamie Applegate felt was guilt. He didn't want Phillip
to be dead . . . or Chloe and Allyson to be
so badly hurt . . . why did he only have a
little bump on his head? Why couldn't it
have been him behind the wheel instead of
Phillip?

"Is someone taking you home?" Trygve
asked him gently, unable to be angry at
him, in the face of what had happened.

"My father'll be here in a minute. But I
saw you sitting here, and I just wanted to
say . . . to tell you . . ." He glanced from
Trygve to Page, and started crying again.

"We know." Page reached up and
squeezed his hand, and he bent to hug her,
and she found herself sobbing as she em-
braced him. His father finally came for him,
and there was anger, and tears, and re-
proaches. Jamie's father, Bill Applegate,
was understandably upset by what had hap-

pened, but also relieved that Jamie had survived it. He had cried when they told him Phillip Chapman had died, but he was also deeply grateful that his own child hadn't. He was a respected man in the community, and Trygve had met him a few times at school events and sports games.

He talked to Page and Trygve for a while, piecing together what had happened, and he apologized on behalf of Jamie for the deception. But they all knew it was too late for apologies, it was too late for anything, except surgery, and miracles, and prayers. They all knew that. And Bill Applegate said he'd be in close touch with them, to check on Allyson and Chloe. And before they left, he also asked Jamie if they'd been drunk, and Jamie continued to insist that they weren't, and for some reason, they all believed him.

Trygve looked at Page after the Applegates left, and shook his head. "I feel sorry for him . . . except a part of me is still so angry." He was angry at everyone, Phillip for getting them into the accident, Chloe for lying to him, and the other driver, if it was her fault. But who knew what had really gone on? Who would ever know? The head highway patrolman had explained to him a short while before that the force of the collision had been so monumental that it was going to be next to impossible to determine who was at fault, and from the position of the cars, they couldn't tell for sure who had slipped over the line or why. The blood tests showed alcohol in Phillip's blood, but not enough to consider him drunk. And the Senator's wife had appeared to be sober, so they hadn't even bothered. They could only assume that Phillip had gotten distracted, maybe by Allyson, and perhaps the accident had been his fault after all. But nothing would ever be certain.

All Page could think of was the condition that Allyson was in, and how badly she wanted to see her. It was another hour before the nurse approached her again. The neurosurgeons were ready to see her.

"Can I see Allyson?"

"In a minute, Mrs. Clarke. The doctors would like to see you first, so they can explain her condition to you." At least there was still something to explain, and as she stood up, Trygve looked at her with a worried expression. He was a good friend, they had met at a thousand school events, sports teams, and an occasional picnic, and although they had never been close friends, she had always liked him, and their daughters had always been bosom buddies, ever since the Clarkes had moved to Marin County.

"Do you want me to come in with you?" he asked, and she hesitated, and then nodded. She was terrified by what they were going to say, and even more so of seeing her daughter. She wanted to see her more than anything, but she was desperately afraid of what she would have to face when she saw her.

"Do you mind?" Page whispered apologetically as they hurried down the hall to where the neurosurgical team was waiting for them.

"Don't be silly," Trygve said as they began to run. They looked like brother and sister as they hurried down the hall, both of them so blond and Scandinavian-looking. He was a pleasant man, with healthy good looks, and a gentle manner. It was easy to be with him. She had never felt as comfortable with anyone. They were partners in disaster.

The door to the conference room looked ominous as they pushed their way through, and there were three men in surgical gowns and caps waiting around an oval table.

Their masks were down around their necks, and Page noticed with a shudder that one of them still had blood on his gown, and she prayed that it wasn't her daughter's.

"How is she?" She couldn't restrain the words, it was all she wanted to know. But the answer was not as simple as the question.

"She's alive, Mrs. Clarke. She's a strong girl. She sustained a tremendous blow, and an ugly injury. A lot of people wouldn't have made it this far. But she has, and we hope that's a good sign. But there's a long way to go right now.

"What she has sustained are essentially two kinds of injuries, each with its own particular complications. Her first injury occurred at the moment of impact. Her brain was decelerated against the skull, and to put it simply, pretty badly shaken around. It may well have been rotated, and in the process, nerve fibers probably got stretched, and arteries and veins would have gotten torn. This can cause a tremendous amount of damage.

"Her second injury actually appears to be more frightening than the first, but may not be. She has an open wound where the skull was cut through, and the bone of the skull had been broken. Her brain is actually exposed right now, in that area, probably where she was struck by some sharp piece of steel in the car just after the impact." Page made a horrifying little sound as she listened, and clutched Trygve's hand without thinking. She felt ill thinking of what they had just said, but she was willing herself not to faint or throw up. She knew she had to absorb what they were saying.

"There's a good possibility . . ." the chief surgeon went on relentlessly. He knew how unpleasant this was for them, but he also knew that he had to explain it. They had a right to know what had happened to their daughter. He was assuming that Trygve was Allyson's father. "There's a good chance that the area away from the open wound is actually undamaged. We often see very minor long-term disability from these open head wounds. It's the first injury that has us worried. And of course, the obvious complications from both situations. She's lost a fair amount of blood, and her blood pressure would have dropped severely anyway from the trauma. She's badly weakened by the blood loss. In addition, there's a loss of oxygen to the brain. How much we don't know, but the damage could be fairly catastrophic . . . or very slight. We just don't know yet. Right now, we need to get in there and help her. We need to lift the bone that was depressed in the fracture, to relieve some of the pressure. We need to address the wound. And there's some additional repair work we're going to have to do around the eye sockets. She sustained a tremendous blow, which could ultimately blind her.

"We have other concerns too. Infection, of course, and she's having quite a bit of trouble with her breathing. That's to be expected, in this type of injury, but again it could cause some catastrophic complications. We're keeping the breathing tube through her trachea that the paramedics put in and we've had her on a respirator since she got here. We've already done a CT scan on her which gave us some very important information." He looked at Page, who sat staring at him, and for a moment he wondered if she had understood him. She looked totally dazed, and the girl's father seemed no better. He decided to try talking to him, since the girl's mother seemed so unable to absorb it.

"Have I made all of this clear, Mr. Clarke?" he asked hopefully, sounding frighteningly calm, and almost without emotion.

"I'm not Mr. Clarke," Trygve croaked, as overwhelmed as Page by what he had told them. "I'm just a friend."

"Oh." The chief surgeon looked disappointed. "I see. Mrs. Clarke? Do you understand me?"

"I'm not sure. You're telling me that she has two major injuries, basically a shaking of the brain, and an open wound which results from a fracture of her skull. And as a result of the damage, she may die, or she may have permanent brain injury . . . and she may be blind . . . is that about it?" she asked with tears welling up in her eyes. "Did I understand it?"

"More or less. Our next concern after the surgery will be a possibility of what we call 'third' injury. There could have been second injuries as well, but she avoided them by wearing her seat belt. In third injuries, we look for acute swelling of the brain, blood clots, and severe bruising. This could be a very serious problem. It's not likely to occur until at least twenty-four hours after the injury, so it's a little difficult to predict at this moment."

Page asked the one thing she'd wanted to

ask ever since she'd heard, but she was also afraid to hear the answer. "Is there any chance she'll ever be okay again . . . I mean normal? Is that possible, given all that's happened?"

"Possible, as long as we all understand that there are degrees of normal. Her motor skills could be affected, for a time, or even indefinitely. They could be affected in minor ways, or very major ones. Her reasoning processes can be affected, her personality could change. But on the whole, yes, if she is very, very lucky, and blessed with a small miracle, she could be normal." But he didn't look to Page as though he thought it likely.

"Do you consider that likely?" She was pushing and she knew it, but she wanted to know.

"No, I don't. I think it's unlikely to sustain this extensive an injury and not see any long-term ill effects, but I do think that if all goes well, they could be relatively minor . . . *if we're lucky.* I'm not making you any promises, Mrs. Clarke. Right now, she's in a lot of trouble, and we can't ignore that. You're asking me for best case, and I'm telling you what's possible, but not necessarily what will happen."

"And worst case?"

"She won't make it at all . . . or if she does she'll be severely impaired."

"Meaning what?"

"She could remain in a coma permanently, or be extensively brain damaged if she regains consciousness at all, loss of motor skills, powers of reason. She could in essence be severely brain damaged, if she has sustained too great a shock, too many injuries, and we are unable to repair them. How much swelling occurs in the brain will have a lot to do with it as well, and how successful we are in controlling the swelling. We'll need all our skill, Mrs. Clarke, and a lot of luck . . . and so will your daughter. We'd like to operate immediately, if you'll sign the papers."

"I haven't been able to reach her father." Page felt a lump in her throat the size of her fist. "I may not be able to get hold of him until tomorrow . . . I mean today . . ." She felt and sounded panicked as Trygve watched her, aching for what she was going through, and unable to help her.

"Allyson can't wait, Mrs. Clarke . . . we're talking minutes here. We've already done a CT scan on her, as I said, and skull X rays. We have to get in as soon as possible, if we're going to save her, or any normal brain function whatsoever."

"And if we wait?" She had to ask Brad, she was his child too. It wasn't fair to him to proceed without him.

He looked at her honestly for a long moment. "I don't think she'll live another two hours, Mrs. Clarke. And if she does, I don't think there will be any viable brain function left, she'll probably be blind too." But what if he was wrong? Whatever happened to the theories about second opinions? The trouble was, they didn't have time. They barely had time for one, if he was saying Allyson wouldn't live another two hours without brain surgery. What choice was there?

"You don't leave me many options, Doctor," Page said miserably, as Trygve squeezed her hand, and she held his tightly.

"There aren't any, Mrs. Clarke. I'm sure your husband will understand that, when you reach him. We'd like to do everything we can." She nodded as she looked at him, not sure if she trusted him or not. But she had to, she had no choice. Allyson's life depended on their skill and their good judgment. And what if she lived, but was totally brain damaged as they had warned, or was in a coma for the rest of her life? What kind of victory would that be? "Will you sign the consent forms now?" he asked quietly, and after a long moment's hesitation, she nodded.

"When are you going to operate?" she asked hoarsely.

"In about half an hour," he said calmly.

"May I be with her until you do?" Page asked, feeling panicked. What if they never let her see her again? What if this was the last time she ever saw her? Why hadn't she held her for longer that night before she went out? Why hadn't she said all the things to her she had meant to say in her brief lifetime? Without even knowing it, she found herself crying again, as the doctor leaned over and touched her shoulder.

"We're going to do everything we can for her, Mrs. Clarke. You have my word." He looked around at his two associates, who had said very little in the past half hour. "And you have one of the best neurosurgical teams in the country. Trust us." She nodded, unable to say more to him, and he stood up and offered to take her to her daughter.

"She's deeply unconscious, Mrs. Clarke, and she's sustained a number of minor injuries as well. In some ways, it looks worse than it is. A lot of what you'll see will heal. Her brain is another story."

But nothing he said to her prepared her for what she saw when they let her into the room where Allyson lay, watched by a resident and two specially trained ICU nurses. There was a breathing tube in her throat, another tube in her nose, a transfusion in one arm, an IV in her leg, and machines and monitors everywhere. And in the midst of it all, beautiful little Allyson, her face so battered, her own mother could scarcely recognize it, and her head covered by a sterile drape that concealed the hair they were going to cut off in only moments.

It was almost impossible to recognize her, except that Page would have known her anywhere, would have found her, and recognized her as her child. She would have known her with her heart, if not her eyes, and she went to her now, and stood quietly beside her.

"Hello, sweetheart." She bent low, and spoke softly into her ear, praying that with some distant part of her, her daughter would hear her. "I love you, baby . . . everything's going to be fine . . . I love you, Allie . . . we all love you . . . we love you . . ." All she could say were the same words over and over, as she cried, and stroked Allie's arm and her hand, and the one cheek that hadn't been damaged. She looked so battered and so pale, and if it weren't for the monitors, Page would have thought more than once she was dead. Her heart ached as she looked at her, unable to believe what had happened. "Baby, we all love you . . . you have to get better. For all of us . . . me . . . and Daddy . . . and Andy . . ."

Page stood next to her for a long time, and then finally, they asked her to leave so they could prepare Allyson for surgery. She asked if she could stay, but they said she really couldn't. She wanted to know what they were going to do to her, and they explained that they wanted to start her on some drugs, and they had to shave her head, and put a catheter in place. There was a lot for them to do, and Allyson would be aware of none of it. But it would have been much too upsetting for Page to watch it.

"May I . . . could I . . ." She found she couldn't say the words and then she forced herself to. "May I have a piece of her hair?" It sounded horrible, even to her, except that she wanted to have it.

"Of course," one of the ICU nurses said gently. "We'll take good care of her, Mrs. Clarke, I promise." Page nodded and turned to Allyson again, she bent close to her ear, and kissed her gently.

"I'll always love you, sweetheart . . . always and always." It was something she had said to her when she was a little girl, and maybe in some remote part of her, she might remember.

Page was blinded by tears as she left the room, and she literally had to tear herself away from Allyson's bedside. It was unbelievably painful knowing that she might never see her alive again, and yet, she reminded herself again and again, there was no choice. They had to operate on Allyson now, if there was any hope at all that they'd save her.

She found Trygve waiting for her again in the hall, and he ached when he saw her. Everything she had just been through was written on her face. She looked ghastly. He had only gotten a glimpse of the child as Page went in, and it had torn at his heart to see her. Chloe had been bad enough, but this was much worse. And having heard what the doctor said, he secretly thought there was a good chance they might lose her.

"I'm sorry, Page," he whispered, and then pulled her into his arms, as she stood there and cried for a long time. There was nothing else she could do. It was the longest night of both their lives, a never-ending nightmare. He knew that Chloe was still in surgery, a nurse had come to say that it was going well, but that it would go on for several more hours.

The nurse from the desk brought the papers for Page to sign, and after she did, Trygve insisted that they go to the cafeteria for a cup of coffee.

"I don't think I could drink it."

"Water then. You need a change of scene. It's going to be a long day." It was already four in the morning, and the chief neurosurgeon had told Page that the operation would take twelve to fourteen hours. "Maybe you should go home for a couple of hours, and get some rest," he said with a look of concern. They had grown closer in the past few hours than they had in eight years, and she was grateful to have him with her. She would have gone crazy alone, and she knew it.

"I'm not going anywhere," Page said

stubbornly. And he understood. He didn't want to leave Chloe either. But in his case, his oldest son, Nick, was at home to take care of Bjorn, and he had explained as much as he knew when he left, and he'd called home since then. But in Page's case, she had Andy to worry about, and he'd probably be panicked without his mother and sister.

"Who did you leave Andy with?" Trygve asked as they sipped bad coffee in the cafeteria. Both of their daughters were in surgery by then, and Page had finally, reluctantly, agreed to go with him.

"I left him with our neighbor, Jane Gilson. Andy likes her, he'll be all right when he wakes up. And I can't help it. I can't leave now. I'm going to have to do something about finding Brad in a few hours though. It's the first time in sixteen years he forgot to leave a number."

"That's always the way." Trygve looked rueful. "Dana went skiing with friends once and forgot to leave me the number too, and of course that was the weekend that Bjorn got lost, Nick broke his arm, and Chloe came down with pneumonia. I had a great time."

Page smiled thinking of it. He was such a

good guy, and he'd been so decent to her tonight. It was still difficult to assimilate what had happened. "I don't know what I'm going to say to Brad. He and Allie are so close . . . it'll kill him."

"It's a nightmare for everyone . . . and the poor kid who was driving . . . imagine what his parents must be feeling."

They had an opportunity to see it firsthand, when the Chapmans arrived at Marin General at six o'clock in the morning. They were a nice-looking couple in their late fifties. She had well-groomed white hair, and Mr. Chapman looked like a banker. Page saw them arrive at the front desk, looking exhausted and worn. They had driven all the way from Carmel the moment they had been called, unable to believe what had happened. Phillip was their only child, they had had him late, and had never been able to have any others. He was the light of their life, which was why they hadn't wanted him to go East to college. They couldn't bear the idea of his being so far away, and now he couldn't be farther. He was gone from their life forever.

Mrs. Chapman stood with her head bowed, crying softly as they listened to the doctor, her husband had an arm around her and cried openly as he told them that Phillip had been killed instantly from a head injury and a broken neck that had severed both his spinal cord and his brain stem. There had been no hope of his surviving from the moment of impact.

The doctor told them too that there had been a small amount of alcohol in his blood, not enough to make him legally drunk, but maybe enough for a boy his age to be slightly affected. He did not say that the accident was due to him, it still remained unclear who had hit whom, or why. But the implication was there, and the Chapmans looked horrified when they heard it. The doctor in the examining room told them that the other driver had been Senator Hutchinson's wife, and that she was devastated over it, not that that changed anything for the Chapmans. Phillip was dead, no matter who the other driver had been. Mrs. Chapman's grief turned suddenly to anger as she listened to him and the implication that Phillip might have been drinking. She asked if the other driver had been checked too, and was told that she hadn't. The patrolmen at the scene had been certain she was sober. There had been no suspicion about her at all. And as he listened, Tom Chapman grew visibly angry. He looked outraged by what they'd just told them. He was a well-known attorney, and the idea that Phillip had been tested, and even subtly slurred, while the Senator's wife was assumed without reproach seemed like an appalling injustice, and one that he wasn't going to stand for.

"What are you telling me? That because my son was seventeen, half a glass of wine, or roughly its equivalent, makes him presumed guilty of this accident? But a grown woman who may well have drunk a great deal more than he, and possibly been severely affected by it, is above the law because she's married to a politician?" Tom Chapman was shaking with grief and rage as he spoke to the young doctor who had just told him that Laura Hutchinson had not been checked for alcohol, only because the patrolmen on the scene "assumed" she was sober.

"Don't you dare imply that my son was drunk!" Tom Chapman roared at him, as his wife began to cry again beside him. Their anger was a buffer against the inconsolable grief they were feeling. "That's slander. The blood test showed that he was nowhere near legally drunk, not even close to it. I know my boy. He doesn't drink, or if he does, rarely, and very little, and certainly not if he's driving." But he wouldn't be doing anything anymore, and suddenly Tom Chapman's anger began to fade as he began to realize what had happened. He wanted to blame someone, to hurt someone as much as he was hurting. He wanted it to be the other driver's fault, not his son's . . . but much more than that, he wanted it never to have happened. Why had they gone to Carmel? Why had they left him alone, and trusted him? He was only a boy after all . . . a child . . . and now look what had happened. His eyes welled up with tears again, and he turned to his wife with a look of desperation. For a moment, the brief burst of rage had helped assuage the pain, but now it hit him again full force, and when he took his wife in his arms in the emergency room, they were both crying, and the issue of blame no longer seemed important.

A photographer took their picture as they sat in a corner of the emergency room. They looked confused at the flash of light. So much had already happened to them, it was just one more incomprehensible moment. And when they realized that the press had photographed them, they were understandably outraged by the intrusion. In the midst of their grief, they were being subjected to indignity as well, and Tom Chapman looked as though he were going to physically assault the man who had taken their picture, but of course he didn't. He was in great distress, but he was a reasonable person. But it was then that they understood that their agony was going to become a news event because of who the other driver had been. It was news, something hot, something to tantalize people with. Was it the Senator's wife's fault, or was she a very lucky innocent victim? Was it the Chapman boy's fault? Was he drunk? Irresponsible? Merely young? Or was there some malfeasance on the part of Laura Hutchinson? Were any or all of them into drugs? The fact that a seventeen-year-old boy had died, his parents' lives had been shattered, another child had been crippled, and a third nearly killed was merely more fodder for the press, or better yet for the tabloids.

The Chapmans looked devastated as they left the hospital, but the most devastating of all had been seeing Phillip. Mary Chapman knew she would never forget the horror of that moment, of seeing him broken and pale, so deathly still as they stared at him and cried, and bent to kiss him. Tom sobbed openly, and Mary bent over him and gently touched his face with her hands, and then kissed him. All she could think of was the first moment she had seen him, seventeen years before, when she had held him in her arms, and been overwhelmed by the sheer joy of being his mother. She knew she would always be, time could never take that from her, but death had taken Phillip from her. She would never see him laugh again, or run across the lawn, slam the front door, or tell her a joke. He would never surprise her again, with one of his harmless pranks, or his sweet surprises. He would never bring her flowers. She would never see him grow old. She would see him forever as he was now, heartbreakingly still, his soul gone on to another place. For all their love for him, and his for them, in one swift unexpected moment, Phillip had left them.

It made the next photographer's attack on them as they left even more repulsive. But seeing what was happening, Tom Chapman vowed to see that Phillip wasn't blamed for this disaster. If need be, he would clear his son's name. He didn't want

Phillip's memory sullied by innuendo, or used to protect the Senator's wife, or the Senator's seat in the next election. Tom Chapman felt certain that his son was not to blame, and he was not going to allow anyone to say anything different. He said as much to his wife, as they drove away, but she seemed not to hear him. All she could think of was Phillip's face when she had kissed him.

The night seemed interminable to all of them, as Page sat with Trygve. Both girls were still in surgery then, and Trygve and Page were beginning to feel as though they had been there forever.

"I keep thinking about the options," Page said quietly as the sun came up over Marin, and she tried to view it as a hopeful sign. It was another gorgeous spring day, but she no longer felt excited by the warm weather. In her heart, winter had come, with ice and snow, and all its desolation.

"I keep thinking about what Dr. Hammerman said . . . she might end up brain damaged, or severely affected in some way, physically or mentally. How would we ever begin to deal with that? How do you live with something like that?" she said absentmindedly, talking almost as much to herself

as to him, and suddenly she remembered
Bjorn, and felt awful. "I'm sorry, Trygve
. . . I wasn't thinking."

"It's all right. I understand what you
must be going through. Or at least I can
guess at it . . . I feel a little bit that way
about Chloe's legs, and I remember what it
was like when they told us Bjorn had Down
syndrome." He was being honest with her,
they were both trying to understand what
adjustments might lie ahead.

She looked over at him. His hair was as
rumpled as hers, and he had worn jeans and
an old plaid shirt, bare feet and an ancient
pair of sneakers. She looked down at her
gardening sweater then, and remembered
that she hadn't bothered to comb her hair.
She didn't really care, and it made her smile
to realize what they looked like. "We're a
sight, the two of us." She grinned. "Actually, you look better than I do. I ran out of
the house so fast, I'm surprised I remembered to get dressed at all."

Trygve grinned at her for the first time all
night, looking very boyish and very Nordic
with his big blue eyes and blond lashes.
"These are Nick's jeans, and Bjorn's shirt.
God only knows whose shoes. I don't think

they're mine. I found them in the garage. I was about to drive here barefoot."

She nodded, knowing only too well what he had felt when he heard the news. She couldn't bear to think of it, and she still had to tell Brad, yet another nightmare to survive. If only she could tell him that Allyson was still alive, and there was some hope. But it was unlikely they would know by the time she reached him.

"I was just thinking about Bjorn," Trygve said softly, as he leaned back in his chair with a thoughtful look. "It was awful when they first told us. Dana hated everyone and everything, mostly me, because she didn't know who else to hate. And Bjorn, too, at first. She just couldn't accept that we hadn't had a perfect baby. She talked about him being a vegetable, and painted a grisly picture of what the future would be like. She wanted to put him in an institution."

"Why didn't you?" She was intrigued, and felt she could ask him anything. She knew Brad would have balked at accepting a child who wasn't normal.

"I don't believe in that. Maybe it's the Norwegian upbringing, or just me. I don't think you walk away from things because they're difficult. I never have anyway," he smiled ruefully again, thinking of his twenty years in a bad marriage, "though I probably should have in some cases. But that's part of life to me, old people, kids, people with infirmities, people with limitations. This is not a perfect world, and it's not fair to expect that. I don't know, I just thought we ought to make the best of it. Dana said she wanted no part of it, so it became my mission to help Bjorn. And actually, we were very lucky. He isn't as severe as some. He's limited, but he has a lot of capabilities too. He's very gifted with carpentry, he's artistic in a childlike way, he loves people, he's incredibly affectionate, he's very loyal, he's a great cook, he's got a good sense of humor, he's responsible, to a point, and he's even learning to drive a car now. But he'll never be like Nick, or you, or me. He'll never go to college, or run a bank, or be a doctor. He's Bjorn, and he's good at what he can do . . . he loves sports, and kids, and people. And maybe he'll have a good life in spite of his limitations. I certainly hope so."

"You've given him a lot," Page said softly. "He's a lucky man." He wanted to tell her he thought Brad was too. From what he'd seen that night, he thought she was a remarkable woman. She had taken a blow that would have shattered most people on the spot, and she was weathering it, and helping him, and still managing to think about everyone else, her husband, her son, even the Chapmans.

"He deserves it, Page. Bjorn is a great guy. I can't even bear to think of what his life might have been like in an institution. Maybe he'd never have grown to this point, or maybe he would have. I don't know. He buys our groceries, you know, and he's very proud of it. Sometimes, I can rely on him more than I can on Chloe." They both smiled at that, teenage girls definitely had their own sets of limitations.

"Doesn't it make you angry sometimes, wishing he would have been more?"

"He never could have, Page. This was the very best he could be. Maybe it's easier that way. All I am is proud." They both knew it would be different if Allyson were seriously brain damaged, after all she had been.

"I just keep asking myself how you adjust to it. Maybe you have to throw away all the old measuring sticks, and start all over again, grateful for every step, every word, every tiny bit of growth and accomplishment . . . but how do you forget? How do you forget what she was, and learn to accept so little?"

"I don't know," he said sadly, unable to even fathom it. "Maybe you just have to be grateful she's alive, and take it from there," he said, as she nodded her head, realizing how lucky she'd be if Allyson lived through it.

"I guess I'm not even there yet."

It was almost eight in the morning by then, and Page decided to call one of Brad's associates, to see if she could locate him in Cleveland.

With apologies, she woke Dan Ballantine and his wife, and explained briefly to Dan what had happened. She said that Brad was planning to play golf with the president of the company in Cleveland that day and if Dan had no clues as to what hotel he'd used, maybe he could call the president and leave a message with him for Brad to call her. It was a roundabout way to get hold of Brad, but it was the best she could think of. And Dan promised to get on it right away, and leave the number at Marin General for Brad without saying too much to frighten him. Dan told her too how sorry he was about the accident, and hoped Allie'd be okay.

"Me too," Page said, thanking him again for his help. And it was less than an hour later when Dan called her in the emergency room. He had called the president of the company they were dealing with in Cleveland, and he did have an appointment with Brad the next day. But according to him, they had never made plans to play golf, or meet on Sunday morning.

"That's odd. Brad said . . . never mind, I probably misunderstood. I'll just have to wait till he calls," she said tiredly. She was too exhausted to worry about why he had said he was playing golf with the man when he wasn't. She figured it had probably gotten canceled, and Dan had misunderstood. At least they had tried, so he'd hear eventually. And maybe by then the news would be a little better.

"They couldn't locate him," she said to Trygve as she came back and sat down next to him in an uncomfortable chair. His beard had grown overnight, though it was pale, and he looked as tired and worn-out as she did. "He'll call eventually, and Jane will tell him to call here. Poor guy. It makes me sick to think of telling him."

"I know. I called Dana in London while you were on the phone. She just got back from a weekend in Venice. She was horrified, and blamed me, as usual. It was all my fault, why did I let her out of the house, why didn't I know who she was going with, what was wrong with me not to suspect she was up to no good. Maybe she's right. I was awfully dumb, but once in a while you have to trust them, or they drive you nuts. You can't play cop constantly, and to tell you the truth, most of the time she's pretty good. Just now and then, she does something foolish."

"Allie's like that too. It's pretty rare for her to go off the deep end. I guess they were just trying their wings. Normal stuff, I guess . . . except for some very rotten luck in this instance."

"Yeah, really . . . anyway, Dana says it's all my fault."

"Do you believe that?" Page asked quietly.

"Not really. But a part of you always wonders. She could be right, you know. Though I don't like to think so."

"She's not right, and you know it. This isn't your fault. It's a miserable twist of fate, but it's no one's fault, except maybe the other driver's." They both wanted to feel it was Laura Hutchinson's fault, and not Phil-

lip Chapman's. At least if the accident had
been a terrible stroke of fate, and not Phillip's fault, it might be easier to bear. Or
maybe it wouldn't make any difference.

And before they could discuss it anymore, the orthopedic surgeon came to tell
him that Chloe's operation had gone well.
She had lost a lot of blood, and she would
be uncomfortable for quite a while, but they
felt optimistic that she would regain the use
of her legs. The pelvis was in place, the hip
had been replaced, and she had steel rods
and pins in both legs which would be removed in a year or two. There would be no
more ballet, but with any luck at all, there
would be walking and even dancing . . .
and maybe even one day, children. A lot
would depend on how the next few weeks
went, but the surgeon was very pleased with
his repairs and how Chloe had come
through it. Trygve cried as he listened.

She was still in the recovery room, and
the doctor wanted her to stay there until at
least noon. And then they would move her
into intensive care for a week or so, and
eventually to her own room. He said he
might like to give her a couple of transfusions later in the day, and asked if he or

either of his sons were the same blood type. And he was pleased to hear they all were.

"Why don't you go home and rest for a few hours. She's all right now. And then you can come back this afternoon, when we move her to ICU. It's going to be a long haul, you know. She's going to be in the hospital for at least a month, or more. There's no point wearing yourself out in the first few innings." Trygve smiled at the image, and a quick nap held a lot of appeal, but he hated to leave Page, with Allyson still in surgery, and no one to keep her company. In the end, he decided to stay, and stretched out on a couch in the waiting room. She would have done the same for him, and he felt an obligation to stay with her.

Noon came and went, and at two o'clock, they finally moved Chloe to the ICU. She was still all doped up, but she recognized him, and she seemed to be out of pain, which was remarkable given all they'd done to her, and the mountain of apparatus that seemed to be attached to her body. But he was relieved that the doctors were both pleased and hopeful.

"How is she?" Page asked when he returned. She had just called Jane and talked to Andy. He was worried about her being gone, and even more so about his sister. But Page was still trying to underplay it. It was too soon to explain the situation to him, and she hadn't even told Brad yet. He still hadn't called, but Jane was waiting to hear from him so she could give him the message.

"She's pretty stoned," Trygve explained with a smile. "But she looks okay, if you don't look at all the stuff hanging off her. She's got all sorts of tubes and rods hanging out of her hip, more rods and pins in her legs. She'll get casts eventually but not yet. She's a mess, but I guess we've got to be grateful."

"I've always wondered about that," Page said, looking and sounding exhausted. "In situations like this, people are always telling you to be grateful. This time yesterday, Allie was a perfectly normal, healthy fifteen-year-old girl, nagging me about borrowing my pink sweater. Today, she's in brain surgery, fighting for her life, and I'm supposed to be grateful she's not dead. I am . . . but compared to yesterday, this is the shits. You know what I mean?" He laughed, it was perverse, but he understood it. People used to tell him that about Bjorn, too, that he should be grateful he wasn't more retarded. Why did he have to be retarded at all? What was there to be grateful for? A lot maybe. Things could have been worse, it turned out, with very little effort.

He finally went home at three that afternoon, just to shower and change, and see his boys. He was going to bring them by to see Chloe in the late afternoon. Nick had said that Bjorn was very worried about her, and very agitated, and Trygve thought it might be better for him if he could see her. He worried a lot about people dying, which was typical of young children, and in his case, the fact that he was eighteen didn't change that.

Trygve told Page to call him if she needed anything, and she continued her vigil alone, and thought about calling her mother. But she just couldn't face it. And she still hadn't told Brad. It didn't seem fair to tell her first. She sat there for an hour, willing Brad to call her.

She hadn't heard anything about Allyson since four o'clock, when they had come to tell her that she was weathering the surgery well, and her condition was as stable as could be expected. She was going to need several more transfusions, too, and Page was relieved to know that she was the same blood type. She went ahead and let them take a pint of blood from her, and it was right after that that Brad finally called. He called the number at the desk at the E.R., and they let Page take it in a separate office.

"My God, Page, where are you?" Jane had only told him to call her at the number she gave him. "It sounded like they said Marin General."

"They did." She fought back her fatigue, looking for the right words to tell him, and not finding them for a moment. "Brad . . . baby . . ." She started to cry and could go no further.

"Are you all right? Did something happen to you?" For a crazy instant he wondered if she had been pregnant and hadn't told him, or had fallen off a ladder again. What else could it be? He couldn't even begin to imagine.

"Sweetheart . . . Allie had an accident." She paused for breath and he immediately questioned her.

"Is she all right?"

Page shook her head as the tears coursed down her cheeks. "No . . . she isn't . . . she was in a car accident last night. I'm so sorry to tell you this. I tried everything I could to reach you, but you'd canceled your golf game."

"I . . . oh . . . yeah. He was busy or something. Who'd you call?"

"Dan Ballantine. He called the guy in Cleveland, and left a message for you. You didn't leave me the name of your hotel, or the number."

"I forgot." He sounded annoyed and curt, which surprised her, as though he was irritated with her for having Dan call Cleveland. "So how is she? And what do you mean, a car accident? Who was driving her? Trygve Thorensen?"

"No, he wasn't. That's what she told us, but she was out with a bunch of kids. They got in a head-on collision, and . . ." It made her sick to tell him, but she knew she had to. "She has a head injury, Brad, a very serious one. She's critical, and she's in surgery now."

"You let them operate? Without asking me? For chrissake, how could you do that?"

"Brad, I had to. The surgeon told me she'd be dead by six o'clock this morning if I didn't."

"Bullshit. You had a right to a second opinion. You owed that to me, and to Allie." He wasn't sounding rational, but Page knew it was his way of coping. The shock of the news was just too great to withstand in a single moment.

"There was no time, Brad. No time for anything." Except prayers. And miracles. It was all in God's hands now, and the surgeons'.

"How is she now?"

"She's still in surgery. It's been over twelve hours."

"Oh my God." There was a long silence at his end, and Page suspected he was crying. "How did it happen? Who was driving?" What did it matter?

"A boy named Phillip Chapman."

"The little sonofabitch. Was he drunk? I'll sue the shit out of them for this . . ." His voice was shaking as he said it, and Page shook her head.

"He's dead, Brad . . . there were four of them in the car. One had a minor concussion. Chloe is very badly injured too, but she's going to be all right . . . and Allie . . . she may not make it, Brad . . . or if she does . . . you have to come home, sweetheart . . . we need you."

"I'll be there in an hour." That was impossible, they both knew, but he could be there in six, if he got a plane immediately. She was sure he'd be able to pull strings and get a seat on the first plane out, for special circumstances, and she was glad he had finally called. She needed him desperately. Trygve had been a godsend, but Brad was her husband.

"I'll be there as soon as I can," Brad said worriedly.

"I love you," she said sadly. "I'm glad you're coming home."

"Me too," he said, and hung up. And much to her amazement, he walked in at six o'clock, an hour after they spoke, moments after they had told her that so far so good, Allyson had survived the operation. But the true test would be in the next forty-eight hours, or even the next several days after that. Her condition was so severe that she would not be out of danger for quite some time, and there was no way of predicting how complete her recovery would be. All they knew was that she was alive, at that precise moment, and on the scale they were forced to be satisfied with for the present, that was something.

At least she had good news for Brad, but she couldn't understand how he had arrived at the hospital an hour after he had spoken to her from Cleveland.

He spoke to the surgeons, and questioned everyone, but they would not allow him to see Allyson. She was going to be in the recovery room until the next morning.

"How did you do that?" Page asked him quietly, as they drank coffee in the waiting room. She hadn't eaten all day, she just couldn't bring herself to. All she had managed was coffee, and some crackers that Trygve had forced on her that morning. "How did you get here so quickly?" He shrugged and sipped another mouthful of the bad coffee. His eyes never met hers, and so far he had spoken only of Allyson. But suddenly, Page had a very odd feeling. "Where were you?" It would have been physically impossible for him to get from Cleveland to San Francisco, hotel to hospital, in an hour. And they both knew it.

"It's not important," he said quietly. "Allie is all that matters."

"Not really," Page said, searching his eyes, but not seeing anything in them. "We're important too. Where were you?" There was a sudden stridency in her voice, born of fresh terror. She had had enough fear for one night, and now suddenly here was another. "I asked you a question, Brad."

There was a look in his eyes she had never seen before when he answered her. "And I chose not to answer it. Isn't that enough? I got here as fast as I could, Page . . . as soon as I knew . . . that was the best I could do."

She felt an icy hand clutch her heart and squeeze. It wasn't fair. She couldn't lose both of them in one day, or could she? "You weren't in Cleveland, were you?" she said in a whisper, and he looked away from her, and didn't answer.

CHAPTER 5

Brad went home before Page, having determined that there was nothing more he could do at the hospital for Allie. They wouldn't allow him to see her in the recovery room, and he had already spoken to the chief neurosurgeon. He told Page he would see her at home, and quietly left to go home to Andy.

Page saw Trygve again briefly before she left. He had brought both of the boys with him, and she explained that Brad had come home from Cleveland. She didn't mention the rest of the conversation to him, and she seemed distracted as she said hello to the boys, and thanked him for all his help. She told him she was going home for a few hours, as long as Allyson was in the recovery room, and she was planning to come back again sometime before morning.

"Why don't you try and get some rest? You look as though you really need it."

"I'll see." She smiled at him, but agony was written all over her face, and there was greater sadness in her eyes than he had seen in an entire lifetime.

"Take care of yourself," he said kindly before she left, and then she drove home to find Brad explaining to Andy what had happened to his sister. He explained that she had a severe head injury, but that she'd be okay once the doctors fixed her all up and she recovered from her operation. Jane Gilson was gone by then, Brad was alone with him, and Page didn't like what he was saying.

She told him as much once Andy went out to play. He looked worried, but not overly so as she watched him from the picture window. He was playing with Lizzie on their front lawn, and she knew the neighborhood was safe, they knew all their neighbors.

"You shouldn't have told him that, Brad," she said, without turning around.

She still had a lot of questions for him, but she was saving them till after Andy's bedtime.

"Told him what?" Brad said tensely. There was plenty on his mind too. Aside from the disaster with Allyson, he knew as well as Page did that the accident had sparked off a serious crisis in their marriage.

"That she'd be all right." She turned to face him. "We don't know that."

"Yes, we do. Hammerman said she has a good chance of surviving."

"In what state? In a coma? As a vegetable, 'severely impaired,' as he calls it, blind? Just exactly what do you think he's talking about, Brad? You have no right to raise Andy's hopes and reassure him."

"What do you want me to do, show him the X rays of her skull? For chrissake, he's only a kid, Page. Give him a break. You know how much he loves her."

"I love her too. I love both of them . . . and you . . . but it's not fair to give false reassurance. What if she dies tonight? What if she doesn't even survive the operation? Then what?" There were tears in her eyes as she asked, and tears in his as he answered.

"Then we face it when it happens."

"And us?" she asked, surprising him by shifting gears, but Andy seemed happy outside with Lizzie. "When do we face that? What exactly is going on here?"

"It was just bad luck the way things worked out," he said quietly. "If Allie hadn't had the accident, you'd never have known. And you never should have asked Dan to call Cleveland."

"Why not?" She looked outraged, their daughter had almost died in an accident, and she shouldn't have tried to find him?

"Because now he's figured it out, and it's none of his business."

"And me? What am I supposed to figure out, Brad? Just how stupid have I been? How often have you done this?" She didn't know where he'd been, but it was obvious he hadn't been in Cleveland.

"That's not the issue." He looked annoyed again. He hated having to admit any of this to her, but in a way, he had no choice now.

"Yes, it is! It's very much the issue. You got caught with your pants down this weekend, and I have a right to know where you were, and with whom. This is my life you're playing with too. You're not just out there on your own, having fun, and passing through here between golf games. This is for real, and so am I. What about you, Brad? Just exactly what's going on here?" She was shaking with rage, and he looked angry more than guilty.

"You've got the idea. Do I have to spell it out for you?" It broke her heart to hear him say it. She almost wondered how much more pain her heart could take in one weekend. She had wanted him to deny everything, wanted none of it to be true. But it was, and now it couldn't be avoided.

"Is this something new?" she pressed on, but Brad didn't want to tell her.

"I'm not going to discuss it with you, Page."

"You'd better, Brad. I'm not going to play these games with you. Is this someone important to you?"

"Oh for chrissake, Page, why do we have to talk about this now?"

"Because it can't wait. You started this, now I want to know what you've been doing. Is this serious? Has it been going on for long? Has it happened before . . . and why?" She looked at him miserably, her voice a sad whisper. "What happened to us, and why didn't I know what you were up to?" How blind could she have been? Had there been signs? Looking back, even now, she couldn't see them.

Brad sat down unhappily and stared at her, hating every minute of their conversation. He hated confrontations with her, he always had. But he knew now that this one couldn't be postponed or avoided. Maybe it was just as well. She had to know sooner or later.

"I guess I should have said something a while ago, but I thought . . . I thought it would end, and I wouldn't have to."

"Is it serious?" He didn't answer for a long time, and his eyes, when he looked at her, almost made her heart stop. This was no fling, this was a serious relationship, and she wondered with a gulp of terror if, without a warning sound, their marriage was already over. "Well?" Her voice was a croak as she listened to it, and tried to force him to answer. "Is it? Serious, I mean."

"It could be," he answered, sounding confused. "Page, I just don't know. That's why I haven't told you." He looked desperately unhappy.

"How long has it been?" How long had she been stupid and blind, and incredibly foolish? Page fought back tears as she waited for his answer.

"It's been about eight months. It started on a business trip. She works in the creative department, and we went to New York to make a presentation to a client together."

"What's she like?" Page started to feel sick as she asked, but she wanted to know everything now . . . eight months . . . *eight months*? How could she have been so stupid?

"Stephanie's very different . . . from you, I mean . . . I don't know . . . she's very independent, very free, very much her own person. She's from L.A., she came up here to go to Stanford, and stayed. She's twenty-six. She's just . . . I don't know . . . we talk a lot, we like the same things. I kept telling myself I had to stop . . . but I just couldn't." He looked at her helplessly, and she would have felt sorry for him if he hadn't been killing her with what he was saying. She wanted to ask him if she was beautiful, if she was great in bed, if he really loved her. But how much more could she ask? And how much more could she bear hearing?

"What were you planning to do about her, Brad? Leave me eventually?"

"I just don't know. I knew it couldn't go on like this. But I've just been so confused." He ran a hand through his hair as he looked at her. "It's been driving me crazy."

"And where was I during all this? Why didn't I see what was going on?" She stared at him, unbelieving. It was all too incredible, and too awful. Her worst nightmares had come true. Allyson was nearly dead, and Brad was in love with another woman. "What's happened to us, Brad? Why have we gotten so involved with our own lives? Why are you always out of town, or playing golf, and I'm always driving car pools? Is that what happened? We just drifted away from each other while I wasn't looking?" She wanted to understand what had happened to them, but for now, she just couldn't. Too much had happened.

"It's not your fault," he said gallantly, and then shook his head again, visibly confused. "Maybe it is your fault . . . maybe it's both our faults. Maybe we just let something happen that never should have. Maybe we got caught up in all the unimportant bullshit. I wish I knew. I just don't have the answers." He hadn't in eight months, which was why he hadn't left her, or told her.

"Would you stop seeing her?" she asked him openly, and he hesitated for a long time, and then slowly he shook his head, as she felt the air go out of her body. "And what am I supposed to do? Just look the other way while you go on fucking Little Miss Creative?" She was suddenly overwhelmed with anger as she looked at him, and out of nowhere came an almost uncontrollable desire to hit him, with words if not her fists, and Brad looked as though he understood it. He had reproached himself a lot of the time, for the past eight months, particularly when Page was good to him, or did something nice for him, or wanted to make love. He had spent the last months feeling unbearably guilty whenever he was with her. And yet he couldn't stop seeing Stephanie. He wasn't ready to give up either of them. He told himself that he was in love with both of them, but the truth was, he wasn't. He still loved Page, but he wasn't in love with her anymore. He hadn't been for a while, he didn't know why, but he knew he wasn't. He loved her, and respected her, she was a terrific mother to their kids, and a great wife to him. She was a great friend, and a great person. She was everything any man would want . . . and yet, she didn't set his heart and his mind on fire the way Stephanie did, and nothing he could do or say would change that.

"What am I supposed to do now? Just disappear? Make life easy for both of you?" She suddenly panicked, wondering if he expected her to move out, or if he was planning to now that she knew about the affair. And what about Andy? She started to cry, just thinking about it, what lay ahead, and now all of it compounded by their anguish over Allie. "What do you expect of me?" she said, looking and sounding as distraught as she felt. He wished he could reassure her, but he couldn't.

"I don't expect anything. Let's just get Allyson through this, and concentrate on surviving. Why don't we deal with this afterward? We just can't do both things at once." It was a rational suggestion, but Page was too unnerved to be reasonable at this point, and he understood that.

"And then what? You move out when Allie wakes up . . . or after the funeral?" she asked, bitter and frightened again. She was bordering on hysterical, but he made no move to console her. He just couldn't. He was too upset himself, and he knew that anything he tried to do would just make it

worse now. Now that she knew about Stephanie, he felt he needed to keep a certain
distance.

"I don't know what we do, Page. I've
been trying to figure it out myself for
months, and I haven't gotten anywhere.
Maybe you can come up with an answer."
He wasn't ready to divorce her yet, and he
wasn't sure what to do about Stephanie,
and Stephanie was willing to wait till he
sorted his life out. She wasn't pushing him
to do anything. But his passion for her was
propelling him toward a solution. And he
didn't want to live a lie forever, or be consumed by the guilt he felt toward Page, particularly now that it was out in the open.

All Brad knew was that he loved them
both, although very differently, and he had
allowed himself to fall into an impossible
situation. It would be even more impossible
now that Page knew, and he could already
see how crazed it was going to make her. At
least for the past eight months she hadn't
suspected anything when he said he was going away on business trips, and sometimes
he did, of course, but more often than not,
he didn't. He had allowed himself to get
involved in a terribly difficult situation. And
everyone had the potential for getting badly

hurt, Page, Brad, Stephanie, and his own children.

"I just don't think we can deal with this right now, Page. I think we have to keep it together till Allyson gets well, or at least until she's out of danger."

"And then?" She kept pressing him for answers he didn't have, and making both of them unhappy, but given the circumstances, he really couldn't blame her.

"I don't know, Page . . . I just don't know yet."

"Let me know when you figure it all out." She stood up and looked at him. He was suddenly a stranger. The man she had loved for so long, and slept with so trustingly, had been cheating on her for almost a year now. In a part of her soul, she hated him. In another, she was terrified she would lose him.

"It sounds pathetic to say I'm sorry, I guess . . ." he said very quietly. He knew he owed her a lot more than that, but suddenly he just didn't have it to give her.

"I think 'inadequate' would be more the word I'd choose. I think you owe me a lot more than 'sorry,' Brad. Don't you?" Tears glistened in her eyes as they looked at each other from across the room. There was hatred in her face, and anger, and more pain than he'd ever seen there.

"I always thought you'd be okay. You're so strong, and you're always so busy. I thought maybe you wouldn't even miss me." Had she pushed him away? Was it her fault, or his? Had she stopped paying attention? She accused herself, and him, of everything, as she listened to his explanation.

"I guess we're both pretty stupid," she said caustically. "Or at least I was."

"You deserve better than this," he said honestly, and he did too. He deserved to be where he wanted to be, and not here crawling around, apologizing to Page. And yet he knew he owed it to her. But it was a hideous moment in both their lives . . . that . . . and Allyson's accident made it a time, he realized, that might easily destroy them.

"We all deserve better than this," Page said softly, and then left the room to check on Andy.

As she moved around the kitchen, she felt like a robot. She put a pizza in the microwave for Andy and called him inside five minutes later. She was still shaking and felt sick, and every time the phone rang, she was terrified it was the hospital calling to tell her about Allie. Her mind seemed to ricochet between the horror of Allyson's accident and the shock of what Brad had told her.

"How's it going, champ?" she said sadly to Andy as she put his dinner on the kitchen counter for him. Brad was still in the other room, and Page felt as if her whole life had been ended.

"I'm okay," he assured her. "You look tired, Mom." He was always so concerned, so kindhearted and thoughtful. She used to think Brad was that way too, but in the past hour she had seen a duplicitous side of him she had never known was there, and wished she had never seen. She wondered what they would do now.

"I am tired, sweetheart. Allie's pretty sick."

"I know. But Dad says she's going to be okay." The gospel according to Saint Dad. And if she died? Like all the other miseries in their life, they would have to face them later.

"I hope so." Andy looked at her strangely as she said it.

"Don't you think so too? . . . that she'll be okay, I mean . . ."

"I hope so" was all she could say to him, and after he finished his pizza, she put him on her lap and held him. He was still small enough to sit there easily, and it was a comfort to both of them. She needed him right now, more than anything, more than ever.

"I love you, Mom." Everything about him was so open.

"I love you too, sweetheart." Her eyes filled with tears as she said it absentmindedly, not thinking about him, but about Allie, and Brad, and everything that had happened.

She put him to bed after a bath, and read him a story. And then she lay down quietly for ten minutes in their bedroom. She closed her eyes, and tried to fall asleep, but there was too much whirling around in her head, too many terrible things, too much pain, too many questions . . . about Allyson . . . about Brad . . . about their marriage . . . and life and death, and the meaning of everything. She heard a sound and opened her eyes, and saw Brad standing in the doorway.

"Can I get you anything?" He didn't know what else to say to her. Too much had happened, too much had been said and revealed for them ever to be the same people they had once been to each other. It was devastating to think about it, and impossible to pretend it hadn't happened. "Have you eaten?"

"No, thanks." She had absolutely no appetite, and for good reason.

"Do you want anything from the kitchen?" She shook her head and tried not to think of what he'd said, but all she could think about now was the woman at the agency, and the eight months he had spent with her. And before that? Who had there been? How long had he been cheating on her? Had there been others? And was it that she was unattractive to him, or did she just bore him?

She realized then that she was still wearing her gardening sweater from the night before, and her oldest jeans, her hair was a tangled mass after her hours in the hospital. She was no competition for a twenty-six-year-old Stanford grad with no responsibilities and no obligations. She wondered what they had done over the weekend.

"Where did you go with her?" She pushed him for more information before he left the room.

"What difference does it make?" He looked annoyed that she was pressing him, and seeing his irritation made Page angry.

"I just wondered where you were when I

didn't know where to find you." What kind of places did he go with her? Page felt totally shut out of his life, and as though he were a total stranger.

"We went to John Gardiner," he surprised her by answering. It was a tennis ranch in the Carmel Valley. She nodded. But he had been back in Stephanie's apartment in the city by the time he called her. Which was why he had come to the hospital so quickly. He had waited as long as he could, so Page wouldn't suspect where he'd been. But after half an hour he hadn't been able to stand it any longer.

"You should eat something," he said then, as though to move on to another subject. He was anxious not to discuss his life with Stephanie with her. But Page seemed to want to know all the details, as though in hearing them, she would understand what had happened.

"I'm going to take a bath and go back to the hospital," she said quietly. There was nothing for her to do at home. Andy was in bed. And she wanted to be with Allie.

"They said you couldn't see her," Brad said calmly.

"I don't care. I want to be there."

He nodded, and then remembered something. "What about Andy? Will you be back before morning?"

She shook her head. "You can get him ready for school tomorrow. You don't need me for that." Or did he? Was that the only use he had for her now? To take care of his children?

"No," he agreed, his voice sounding sad finally, "but I need you for other things . . ."

"Oh?" She sounded detached as she looked at him. "Like what? I can't think of a thing now."

"Page . . . I love you . . ." It just sounded like words suddenly.

"Do you, Brad?" she asked from the depths of her sadness. "As far as I can see, I've been kidding myself for a long time . . . and maybe you have too . . . maybe it's just as well we found out now." Although she didn't feel relieved at what she'd discovered, only wounded, hurt to her very soul.

"I'm sorry . . ." he said softly, and made no move to approach her, which said it all. There was a world between them.

"So am I," she said, and stood up, looking at him, and then without a word, she walked into her bathroom. She turned on the tub, and closed the door, and once she lay in the bath, the tears ran down her face, as she thought of Brad and Allie. Now she had two people to cry about, she reminded herself. It had sure been a great weekend.

CHAPTER 6

Page spent Sunday night at the hospital, curled up in a chair in the waiting room. But she didn't even notice how uncomfortable the chair was. She scarcely slept, worrying about Allie. The noises of the hospital kept her awake, the smells, and the fear that at any moment her daughter might slip away. It was a relief when, finally, at six the next morning, they let her see her.

A pretty young nurse took Page to the recovery room, and spoke pleasantly to her on the way there, about what a beautiful girl Allie was, and what lovely hair she had had. Page listened with one ear, and found

163

her mind wandering as they walked the endless halls. She was too distracted to really listen. But she was grateful for the nurse's attempts to be comforting. She couldn't imagine how they could even glimpse Allyson's beauty now. She was so battered, there were even bandages on her eyes from the repairs they had had to do there.

Several sets of electric doors opened on the way, and Page tried to force herself back to reality. For a minute, she had been thinking about Brad and all he had told her. But she knew that seeing Allyson would require her full attention. But what she saw when she approached the gurney Allyson was lying on was far from encouraging.

If anything, she looked worse than she had before surgery. The bandage on her head looked frightening, her head had been shaved, her face was deathly pale, and she seemed to be surrounded by monitors and machines. She seemed a million miles away, in her coma.

The operating room nurse had saved a long silky blond lock of hair for Page, and the recovery room nurse handed it to her as soon as she saw her. It brought tears to Page's eyes again, as she clutched the lock of hair in one hand, and gently touched Allyson with the other.

Page stood quietly next to her for a long time, gently touching her hand, and thinking of how life had been only two days before. How was it possible that everything had gone so wrong so quickly? It made you no longer trust anyone or anything, surely not the fates, or destiny. How cruel they had been . . . as had Brad. . . . As Page thought of it, she almost couldn't bear the pain of losing Allie. It reminded her of how she had felt years before when Andy was born, and they had thought they might lose him. She had spent hours staring at him, willing him to live, his tiny body filled with tubes, struggling in the incubator. And miraculously, he had made it.

Page sat down next to her, on a small stool, and spoke softly into the bandaged ears, praying that she would hear her. "I won't let you go, sweetheart . . . I won't . . . we need you . . . I love you too much . . . you have to be a brave girl and fight now . . . baby, you have to! . . . I love you, sweetheart . . . no matter what, you'll always be my baby." Allie smelled of medical things, and the machines beeped now and then, but there was no sound, no move, no gesture of recognition, as Page knew there couldn't have been, but she needed to talk to her, to feel her near her.

The nurses let her stay with Allyson for a long time, and then finally, when the shift changed at seven o'clock, they suggested she go to the cafeteria and get some coffee. She went to the waiting room instead, and sat there dazed, thinking of Allie as she had been, and as she was now. She didn't even hear anyone come in, until someone touched her arm, and she looked up and saw Trygve. He was clean, and shaven, and he was wearing a crisp white shirt and jeans, his thick blond hair was neat, and he seemed rested and healthy. But as he looked at her, he seemed worried. It was Monday morning, the weekend had taken a brutal toll on her.

"Have you been here all night again?"

She nodded. She looked terrible, even worse than she had the day before. But he understood only too well how desperately she wanted to be with Allie.

"I slept in the waiting room." She tried to smile at him, but she looked wretched.

"Did you sleep?" he asked, sounding like a stern father.

"A little." She smiled at him. "Enough.

They let me see Allie this morning, in the recovery room."

"How was she?"

"About the same, I guess. But it was nice just being with her." At least she was still there with them, at least Page could still reach out and touch her. She couldn't bear the thought of it, and all she wanted now was to be back in the recovery room with her again, telling her how much she loved her. "How's Chloe?"

"Asleep. I just checked on her. They're keeping her pretty blitzed, so she's not aware of the pain, and I think that's probably the best thing for her."

She nodded at him, as he sat down next to her. "Are the boys okay?"

"More or less. Bjorn was pretty shook up when he saw her. I asked his doctor about it before he came, and he thought it was important for him. He doesn't really understand things sometimes unless he sees them. But it was hard for him. He cried a lot last night, and he had nightmares."

"Poor kid." She was sad for him. How difficult life was sometimes. How unfair. It was so hard to understand it.

"How's Andy?"

"Scared. Brad was telling him Allie's going to be fine, and I was less reassuring. I don't think it's fair to mislead him."

"I agree. But Brad's probably having trouble coping with it himself. Denial is easier sometimes."

"Yeah. Maybe," she said, sounding as disenchanted and disillusioned as she felt.

"This is a dumb question," he said, "but are you okay? I mean . . . considering what's happening. You look beat."

"I am. I'll get used to it, I guess . . . eventually . . . or something."

"When was the last time you ate?"

"I don't know . . . last night . . . yesterday . . . I made Andy pizza for dinner last night and took a bite . . . something like that."

"You can't do that, Page. You have to keep your strength up. Your getting sick isn't going to help anyone. Come on." He looked down at her sternly as he stood up. "Get up. I'm taking you to breakfast."

She was touched, but the last thing she wanted just then was food. All she wanted was to curl up in a ball and forget the world, or maybe just die, if Allie did. She felt as though she were already in mourning. She was in mourning for what Allie had been, and might never be again . . . for what she had had with Brad, and would never have again. She was in mourning for a lot of things. Herself. Her child. Her marriage. And a life that would be different now. Forever.

"Thanks, Trygve. But I don't think I could eat just now."

"You'll have to try," he said quietly but firmly. "I'm not leaving here until you come and eat. Otherwise, I'll call the doctor, and they can feed you intravenously, if you like that better. Come on," he said, grabbing her hand and pulling, "get off your ass and come to breakfast."

"Okay, okay. I'll come," she said reluctantly, and smiled as she followed him down the hall to the cafeteria, which smelled really awful.

"I'm not sure this is the best idea," he said apologetically, "but it's all we've got, so this is it." He handed her a tray and prodded her into taking oatmeal, scrambled eggs, bacon, toast, jelly, and a cup of coffee.

"If you think I'm going to eat all that, you're crazy."

"If you eat even half of it, you'll be in much better shape. I learned that as a kid when we lived in Norway. You can't starve yourself in cold weather . . . or stressful times. Sometimes I went for days without wanting to eat when Dana and I split up, but I forced myself. And I always felt better for it."

"It seems so redundant somehow. Eating in the midst of disaster."

"Things look worse when you don't eat, or sleep. You're going to have to take care of yourself, Page. Why don't you go home today and sleep for a few hours? Brad can sit here while you go home."

"I think he probably wants to go to the office. But maybe I'll take a break and pick Andy up at school. This is going to be hard for him. I haven't even thought about who's going to pick him up, drop him off, take him to baseball."

"I can do some of it for you. Nick'll be back in college after vacation ends in a few days, Bjorn's in school all day, and Chloe'll be okay here. Whenever you get stuck, just let me know, and I'll take Andy wherever he needs to go." He smiled at her, he had always liked her.

"That's really nice of you."

"It's no big deal. I've got the time. I do most of my work at night anyway. I can never get any writing done in the daytime."

They chatted for a little while, while she

fought with the oatmeal and wrestled with the eggs, and finally managed to eat a little breakfast. He did everything he could to distract her, talking about his writing, his Norwegian relatives, and asking her about her painting. He told her how much he liked the mural at school, and she thanked him. She really appreciated his support, and the fact that he was there made the hospital seem a little less daunting. But her mind kept wandering back to Allyson and Brad, and Trygve knew she was having a hard time paying attention.

He explained that he had to take Bjorn for an evaluation for a new school that day, and she promised to look in on Chloe, which she did, but Chloe spent most of the day sleeping. She stirred uncomfortably every time the shots wore off, and the nurse would give her another shot of Demerol to keep her comfortable. She never even realized Page was in the room as she stood and watched her.

They moved Allie to intensive care at noon, and it was easier to keep track of both girls then. Brad stopped by at lunch, and he cried when he saw Allyson. He stopped and talked to Page when they left the room. He felt awkward seeing her again, now that she knew everything. And he could see how hard it had hit her.

"I'm sorry, Page. I'm sorry you have to deal with me on top of everything else." He looked grim, and Page didn't look much better.

"I guess I had to face it sooner or later, didn't I?" she asked bleakly. But this certainly wasn't great timing.

"It's just too bad it happened the way it did. It's bad enough worrying about Allie." It was, but after being caught in a lie about his whereabouts, it was inevitable that the whole story had come out, and she had decided that maybe it was best she knew, instead of deluding herself about her marriage. That was one of the worst things about it, knowing that she had thought everything was fine, when in fact it wasn't. She wondered if he had told Stephanie that he told Page everything, or enough at least, and if she was pleased that Page knew now. Page wondered about a lot of things, about them, about her, and about why their marriage hadn't been enough for him. But she also knew that she would probably never know the answers to her questions.

"I wish I knew why it happened," Page said softly, as they stood in the hallway, with people eddying around them. It was hardly the place for an intimate discussion, but it was all they had. The waiting room was filled with anxious, frightened people, worrying about loved ones in the ICU. The hallway seemed to have more air, and it was as good a place to talk as any. Maybe the reasons for their marriage falling apart didn't even matter, just that it had happened. She looked up at him then with an odd expression. "Did it strike you both funny that I was the fool in all this, that you two were off having a good time, and I was the idiot staying home with the kids, driving car pools?" He had talked about how different Stephanie was from her, how she was so "independent," and "her own person." Why wouldn't she be? She had no kids, no husband, she didn't owe anything to anyone. She was free to have fun with Brad, while Page stayed at home carrying out her obligations. The thought of it really made her livid.

"Nobody ever tried to make a fool of you, Page," he said in an undervoice as a group of residents walked by them. "I was perfectly aware of how awkward the situation was. I just didn't know what to do about it. But no one ever thought you were the fool in this. If anything, you were the innocent victim."

"At least we agree on that much," she said sadly.

"The big question is what we do now." He looked nervous as he said it.

"Is it? It's beginning to look pretty obvious." She tried to sound flip, but her eyes told a whole other story, a story of shock and despair and disappointment.

"Nothing is obvious. Not to me, at least." And then he looked suddenly worried. "Are you leaving me?" He almost sounded surprised at the idea, and she smiled a small bitter smile as she looked at him. He was amazing.

"Are you kidding? Are you implying that you'd be surprised, or that I shouldn't, or that you're not planning to leave me anyway?"

"I never said that I was leaving," he said stubbornly. "I said no such thing. I said I didn't know what I was doing."

"That's an understatement apparently. Well, neither do I. But I certainly think leaving is a fairly appropriate option for either of us, given the situation. And just exactly why are you hesitating? What are you saying here? That you want to go on being married to me, or that you're not sure of this girl, or you're just too damn scared to make a move? What is it, Brad?" She was starting to raise her voice, and he was looking extremely uncomfortable in the hallway.

"Lower your voice. The whole hospital doesn't have to know our business."

"Why not? I assume everyone else does. Everyone at work must, they must all think you're pretty hot stuff, and you've probably run into at least some of the people we know while you were with her. I guess, as they say about these things, I was the last one to know."

"I wish you had never known . . . or at least not the way it happened . . ."

"It could have happened anytime. Someone could have said something. Andy could have gotten hurt instead of Allie, when you were supposedly 'away,' or I could have gotten sick. Or I guess I could have just run into the two of you. But what exactly are you saying to me now? That this is just an affair? Last night you gave me the impression it was serious, and you had no desire to end it. Did I hear you wrong, am I crazy?"

She wanted to believe that she had misheard him, but another part of her suddenly knew that she would never feel the same about him again. The anger might go away one day, but she could never imagine trusting him again. And maybe after all was said and done, maybe by then, she wouldn't even love him. It was hard to know now, and all she could do was wonder about his intentions.

"You're not wrong," he said, looking annoyed again. "I didn't say I would end it. But I think it's too soon for you to make a decision about us, and this is an impossible time, with all of this happening to Allie."

"Oh, I see." She began to steam again, but this time, she kept her voice down. "You don't want to stop seeing your little friend, but you just don't want me asking you to move out, or move out yourself, because this isn't a convenient time. I'm sorry, I hadn't understood that. No problem, Brad. Stay as long as you like. Just be sure you remember to invite me to the wedding." There were tears stinging her eyes, and angry words on her lips, but they both knew they were not going to resolve the situation in the hallway outside ICU, where their daughter lay in a coma. There was too much going on, and this was far too explosive a situation.

"I think we just have to cool it for a

while, and see what happens to Allie," he said calmly. It was a reasonable suggestion, but Page was still too angry to hear it. "Besides, it would be too hard on Andy right now, if we did anything drastic." It was the first really sensible thing he'd said, and Page had to nod in agreement.

"Yeah, I guess you're right." And then she looked up at him, her eyes full of anguished questions. "So you just go on with . . . this thing . . . and we talk about it later, is that it?"

"More or less," he said, squirming a little as he met her eyes. He knew he was asking a lot of her, and that in her shoes, he couldn't have done it. But he expected her to.

"Sounds like a pretty easy deal for you. And I turn the other way? Is that it?" Page asked, wondering how he could ask that of her.

"I don't know what to do, Page. You have to figure that out." This time he said it almost harshly. He was not willing to jeopardize his relationship with Stephanie, and yet at the same time, he seemed to want to hang on to his marriage, at least until he had decided what exactly it was he wanted. It sounded like a sweet deal for him, and it made Page furious to be asked to agree to it. But right now, she had no choice and she knew it. She couldn't cope with separating from him, and Allie's accident, and Andy's reactions to all of it, not to mention her own. But no matter what she did, she knew that she would be thinking about what was coming at her in the future. And for the moment, none of it looked pleasant or easy.

"If you're asking me for permission, I'm not going to give it to you," she said icily. "You have no right to expect that from me. You didn't have my permission before, and you did what you wanted. But I'm not going to make it easy for you now by saying it's fine with me. It's not. And sooner or later, you're going to have to live with the consequences of your actions." In some ways, it was lucky for him that they had more important things to deal with right now, and he could get by without having to face what he had done to their marriage. But eventually, no matter what happened to Allie, they'd have to deal with it, and they both knew that. It was what was frightening Brad, and depressing Page, as they stood outside the ICU at Marin General.

He looked at her for a long moment, not sure what to say to her, and then glanced at his watch. He needed a reprieve desperately. This was all too much for him, the emotions were running too high, and the reality of it was terrifying. Their lives had changed in the blink of an eye, and he still hadn't fully absorbed all that had happened.

"We can talk about this some other time. I have to get back to the office."

"Where will you be if I need you?" she said coldly. He was removing himself from her in every way he could, from Allie, from the hospital which was so upsetting to both of them, and from having to face her now that she knew about his affair. He was simply leaving, and going back to the office to hide . . . and to Stephanie, to console him. Page suddenly found herself wondering what she looked like.

"What do you mean, 'Where will I be'?" he said unpleasantly. "I just told you. At the office."

"I just thought I'd ask, in case you wander off somewhere." He knew exactly what she meant, and his face got red as he fought back a flash of embarrassment and anger. "If you do, leave a message at the desk in ICU as to where I can find you."

"Obviously," he said coldly.

She wanted to ask him if he'd be home that night, but suddenly she found she didn't want to ask him anything. She didn't want to hear the lies, didn't want to argue with him anymore, or insult him, or listen to the contempt and defensiveness in his voice. She felt totally drained by their conversation.

"I'll call you later," he said, and sped away, as she watched him disappear down the hall. She felt so many things as she looked at him, angry, sad, confused, hurt, betrayed, furious . . . furious . . . frightened . . . and so lonely.

She went back to Allyson then, and at three o'clock she drove to Ross Grammar School to pick up Andy. It was a relief to follow her old routine again, to be with him, to be there for him, and take him to familiar places. She stayed with him all afternoon, and then dropped him off at Jane Gilson's for dinner. Brad was supposed to pick him up later, on his way home from the office.

"I'll see you in the morning," she said, kissing him, grateful for the sweet smell of his flesh, the softness of his hair, the two little arms around her neck as he kissed her. "I love you."

"I love you too, Mom. Kiss Allie for me."

"I will, sweetheart."

She thanked Jane Gilson again, who admonished her, as Trygve had, not to overdo it. "What do you think I ought to do?" Page asked irritably, "stay home and watch TV? How can I be anywhere else but there, given her condition?"

"I know, just be reasonable. Try not to wear yourself out completely." But it was too late for that, and they all knew it. Page's engine was running on fumes, but she had no choice now. She had to be there for Allie.

She was back at the hospital by seven-fifteen. She sat with Allyson for as long as she could in ICU, and then she went to sit in the hallway. She sat in a stiff chair, and leaned her head against the wall with her eyes closed. She just sat there for a long time, waiting for them to let her come back in again. You weren't supposed to stay in ICU constantly, the staff had too much to do, and most of the patients were too sick to enjoy the visits.

"That looks uncomfortable," she heard Trygve's voice in an undertone next to her, and she opened her eyes slowly and smiled to see him. She was exhausted by then, it had been an endless day, and Allyson had not improved or regained consciousness after the operation. They didn't really expect her to regain consciousness. But there were important signs they looked for to indicate further complications to the brain. Even though she was in a coma, they tested her constantly. And so far, things were no better. "How was your day?" he asked, as he sat down in the chair next to hers. His hadn't been easy either. Chloe was in a lot of pain, in spite of the medication.

"Not great." And then she remembered the messages on her machine. They had used up the tape, and it amazed her. "Did you get as many calls from kids today as I did?"

"Probably." He smiled. "A bunch of them came down here after school, but they wouldn't let them into ICU. I think a few of them tried to see Allie, too, but of course the nurses wouldn't let them."

"It'll probably do them good . . . once they're better" . . . if . . . when . . . or maybe never. "Word must have traveled like wildfire at school." And everyone was devastated about Phillip Chapman.

"One of the kids told me that some reporters showed up at school, to talk to the other kids about Phillip, about what kind of boy he was. He was a big star on the swimming team, got terrific grades, the perfect kid. I guess it makes it a better story." He shook his head, thinking, as Page did, that either of their daughters could have died just as easily as Phillip.

There had been a big article in the paper that day, about the accident, with photographs, and stories about each of the four young people involved. The main focus of it of course had been on Laura Hutchinson, her devastation over the death of Phillip Chapman. She had refused an interview, but there was a lovely photograph of her, and several quotes from one of the Senator's aides. They had explained that Mrs. Hutchinson was far too upset about the whole event to make any official comment. As a mother herself, she understood only too well the grief of the Chapmans, and the anxieties of the parents of the injured children. The article essentially cleared her name, and without actually saying so, somehow managed to imply that while the young driver hadn't been legally drunk, the group had in fact been drinking. The feeling one got in the end was that the accident was

Phillip's fault, although the writer never actually came right out and said it.

"It was very well done," Trygve said quietly, as they talked. "They never actually accused him of being drunk, but they somehow managed to convey that impression, while saying of course that Mrs. Hutchinson is a mature, upstanding citizen, and an excellent mother. How could she possibly be responsible for the death of one boy, and the near death of three others?"

"You sound as though you don't believe them." Page sounded worried. She didn't know what she believed anymore. The hospital had said clearly that Phillip was not drunk, and yet the accident had to be someone's fault, or maybe it really didn't matter. Knowing whose fault it was wouldn't whisk Allyson out of the ICU like magic, or repair Chloe's legs. It wouldn't change a thing. The only thing it might change was the eventual lawsuits, and Page couldn't even think about that now. The whole idea of suing someone wouldn't do the kids any good, or bring Phillip back to life. The idea of suing made her sick. It was all much too confusing.

"It's not that I don't believe them," Trygve answered her, "it's that I know how reporters write. The innuendos, the lies, the way they cover themselves, or develop a story to coincide with their opinions. Political reporters do it all the time. They only report what works with the story they have in mind, and their point of view, or that of their paper, it's not necessarily the whole truth. It's designed to fit a preconceived picture. And that could be happening here. Also Hutchinson's aides were pushing a lot of propaganda to cover her and make her look good. Maybe it wasn't her fault, but it could have been, and they wanted to be damn sure she looked like Mrs. Goodie Two Shoes, Mrs. Perfect Mother and Driver."

"Do you think it might have been her fault?"

"Maybe. Maybe not. But it certainly could have been, just as much as it could have been Phillip's. I spoke to the highway patrol again, and they still maintain that the evidence is inconclusive. If anything, the cars seemed almost equally to blame. The only difference is that Phillip was a kid, he hadn't been driving as long as she had. Boys are assumed to be wild behind the wheel, but not all of them are. And from everything the kids have said, the Chapman boy

was a very responsible guy. Jamie Applegate said he had half a glass of wine, and
two cups of black coffee. I've driven on a lot
more than that. Maybe I shouldn't have.
But he was a big kid, half a glass of wine
shouldn't have knocked him flat, not followed by two cups of coffee and then later,
a cappuccino. But Mrs. Hutchinson said she
didn't have a drink all night. So she was
older, sober, better known, more respectable, more grown up, and without further
evidence, Phillip somehow begins to look
guilty. It isn't really fair. I think that's what
bothers me. Kids always get a bad rap, even
when they don't deserve it. It seems particularly unfair to his family. Why should he
get blamed, if no one knows for sure whose
fault it was?

"I spoke to Jamie today, and he swears
that they weren't drunk, and that Phillip
was paying attention. I wanted to blame
him at first . . . I wanted to be mad at
someone, and he was the obvious choice.
But I'm not so sure he is anymore. And I
have to admit, I wanted to kill the Applegate kid at first too, for conspiring with
Chloe and getting her to lie to me, for getting her into that car in the first place. But
he seems like a decent kid, and I've spoken

to his father twice on the phone. Jamie is just beside himself over it. He keeps wanting to see Chloe, but I think it's too soon. I told him to wait a few days, and we'll see."

"Are you going to let him see her?" Page was impressed with his sense of fairness. And intrigued by his suspicion of Laura Hutchinson. The truth was that it was probably just what it appeared. An accident. With no one to blame, and too many who had paid too dearly for a moment's distraction, a glance in the wrong direction, the merest move of the hand on the wheel, and tragedy resulting. She wasn't really angry at anyone. She was just desperate for Allyson to survive it.

Trygve nodded in answer to her question about letting Jamie Applegate see Chloe. "I'd probably let him see her. If she wants to see him. I'll leave it up to her when she feels better. She may not even want to see him again. But he's so overwrought over the whole thing, it might do him good to see her, when she's a little better. His father says he's convinced they're all . . . ah . . ." Before he spoke, he realized the harshness of his words, and he didn't want to upset Page any further. "He's afraid that they might die, and he feels guilty for surviving. He said as much to me, he kept saying it should have been him instead of Phillip . . . and instead of Chloe . . . and Allie. Apparently, he and the Chapman boy had been best friends for years. He's in a terrible state." And then he glanced at Page again, and gently asked her a question.

"Are you going to the Chapman boy's funeral tomorrow, Page?" He hated to ask her.

She nodded slowly. She hadn't been sure before, but now she thought she really should go. She owed it to them. They had lost their boy. And she had almost lost Allie. But almost was not the same, and her heart ached as she thought of the sorrow they must be feeling.

"It must be awful for them," she said softly, as Trygve nodded.

"Will Brad go, or do you want me to drive you? I think it's in the afternoon, so the kids can go too. It might be easier not to go alone." He was dreading it too, as she sighed, thinking of the sheer horror of it, and the pain. She could only pray that they wouldn't have to go through it with Allie.

"I don't know if Brad will go, but I doubt it." He hated funerals, and she knew that, unlike Trygve, he was very vocal about blaming Phillip for the accident. She doubted that he'd be willing to go to the funeral with her, and with their current situation, it was even less likely.

"I don't know how you begin to survive that," she said in a whisper, as she tried not to think about it. And then she looked at Trygve again with grief in her eyes. "I'm not even sure how you survive this. I'm beginning to feel like my whole life is coming apart, and it's only been two days. I don't know . . . what does one do? How do you learn to get through something like this, and not let your whole world fall apart?" There were tears in her eyes as she spoke to him. He felt like an old friend, or an older brother.

"Maybe you don't keep it from falling apart. Maybe it does, and you pick up the pieces later."

"Maybe so," she said sadly, thinking of Brad. Trygve seemed almost to read her mind with the next question.

"How's Brad taking it? It must have been quite a shock when he heard in Cleveland."

For a moment she was tempted to tell him that he'd never been in Cleveland, but that didn't seem fair. She just shook her head and was silent for a long moment. "He hasn't taken it well at all. He's upset and frightened and angry. He blames Phillip for the accident. But in a way, I think he blames me too, for not knowing what she was doing. He hasn't exactly said it, but he implied it." It was also a way of deflecting the guilt from him. It was a relief to him to blame her for something. "The worst thing," she turned to him, her eyes suddenly brimming with tears, "is that I'm not sure he's wrong. Maybe it *is* my fault. Maybe if I'd paid more attention, if I'd been suspicious, or questioned her, if I hadn't believed her . . . this would never have happened." She began to sob openly then, from exhaustion and emotion, and he put an arm around her shoulders.

"You can't let yourself think that. We had no reason to suspect them. They'd never done anything like this before, and you can't play cop constantly. We trusted them, that's not a crime, and their lie wasn't so terrible either. Other kids have done the same thing. It was just the result that was so terrible, but who could have known that?"

"Brad thinks I should have."

"So does Dana. But it's just talk. They need someone to blame, so we're it. You can't take it to heart. He's upset. He doesn't know what to say probably, or who to rail at."

"Maybe," she said, and she was quiet for a long time, as she remembered the statistics she'd often read about what accidents to children, or their deaths, did to destroy a marriage. If there was a crack in it somewhere, it would surely break. And their marriage apparently had a crack in it the size of the Grand Canyon. "Actually," she said quietly, surprising him with her next remark, "things aren't going too well with me and Brad." She wasn't sure why she was telling him, but she had to tell someone. She had never felt as alone or as miserable in her life, and there was no one else she wanted to talk to. She knew she had to call her mother one of these days to tell her about Allie, but she wasn't ready to do that yet. She needed time to adjust to what was happening herself, before she took on her mother in New York. It was just more than she could handle right then. Everything was, except being at the hospital, sitting with Allyson, or talking to Trygve. "Brad and I . . ." She started to say the words, and then found she couldn't.

"You don't have to explain, Page." Trygve tried to make it easier for her. "No one would have an easy time with this. I was just sitting here thinking that Dana and I would never have survived it." In fact, he still couldn't believe that even after he'd called her, she had decided not to come to see her daughter. She had accused him of negligence, but she didn't want to fly all the way to San Francisco to see Chloe. She just hoped she'd be well enough to meet her in Europe in the summer. She was definitely not a woman he admired, or even a decent mother. He could only wonder how he had stayed married to her for twenty years. Sometimes he felt like a total fool, when he thought about it, but he also knew that for the past several years he had stayed with her so as not to disrupt the children.

Page tried to explain what was happening to them. "Our problem doesn't have anything to do with the accident. It just happens to have come to light right now, in the midst of all this." She was cryptic, but it was obvious that she was deeply upset about something that had happened with her husband. Maybe an affair, he thought, he had a lot of experience with those, and their impact on a relationship. But that didn't seem likely. Brad had never seemed the type to be unfaithful.

"You can't judge anything in a crisis."

"Why not? What if it's real? What if nothing is the way I thought it was for all these years? What if it's all been a lie?"

"If it is, you'll know it later. Don't judge anything right now. Neither of you is in any condition to think straight."

"How do you know that?" she asked worriedly. She had a lot to think about, and in some ways the hospital was a great place to do it.

"I have a lot of experience with difficult relationships, and things that aren't what they seem. Believe me, I know what I'm saying. But I also know that everything is upside down right now. You can't hold each other accountable for what you do or say, or the way you react. Look at you, you're exhausted, you haven't eaten decently or slept in two days. Your child almost died. You're completely traumatized. Who wouldn't be? So am I . . . so is Brad . . . so are our other children. . . . Do you really trust your own reactions right now? Hell, I'm afraid to order groceries, I'd probably order bird food for the dog, and dog food for the kids. Listen . . . give yourself a break. Try not to think about anything right now. Just try to get through this."

"I didn't realize you did marriage counseling." She smiled, and he laughed.

"I only know it from worst case. If anything good happens, don't consult me."

"Was it that bad?" Somehow they felt
like old friends now and he still had his arm
around her shoulders.

"Worse." But he was smiling as he said it.
"I think we probably had one of the worst
marriages in history. I think I've finally recovered, but it's made me damn scared to
try it again." She remembered what Allyson
had said on Saturday afternoon, that he
never went out with anyone, and Page was
sorry for him. He was a very attractive man,
intelligent, and a nice one.

"Maybe you just need more time," she
said sympathetically, and he laughed out
loud.

"Yeah, like another forty or fifty years.
I'm in no hurry to make the same mistakes
again, and make myself and my children
miserable. I'm taking it very easy in the
meantime. They deserve a lot better than
they had, and so do I. It's just not easy to
find it."

"Maybe once you stop being scared,
you'll find it more easily," she said gently.

"Maybe, but I'm not holding my breath.

I'm happy like this, and so are my kids.
That means everything to me, Page. It's a
lot better to be alone, than to be with the
wrong woman."

"Maybe. I don't know. I've been married
to the same man since I was twenty-three. I
always thought everything was perfect, and
suddenly the bottom dropped out of everything. I don't know what to think, or who
I'm married to. Things have gotten very
confused." And all in a matter of days,
hours, minutes.

"Remember what I said," he warned
again, "don't judge anything in the midst of
a crisis."

"Maybe not," she said quietly, surprised
that she was willing to tell him so much
about her life. But what she had learned
from Brad had shaken her to the core, she
needed to talk to someone, and she trusted
Trygve. She wasn't sure why, but she did,
implicitly. In the past forty-eight hours, he
had been there as no other friend would
have. Even Brad had let her down. But
Trygve had been there, and crisis or not, she
knew she wouldn't forget it.

It was almost midnight by then. They had
talked for a long time, and gone into ICU
several times, to check on Allyson and

Chloe. Chloe was asleep, and Allyson was still unconscious. Trygve was thinking about going home, when the resident came out to find Page, and explained that Allyson was having complications. The brain swelling that they had feared had begun to occur, and she was experiencing a lot of pressure on the wound, and her skull. This was the "third injury" they had warned her about, and the resident explained that they were afraid of blood clots.

Trygve volunteered to stay at the hospital with her, the head of the surgical team came, and Allyson began to experience further difficulties. With the swelling, her blood pressure had risen, and her pulse had slowed, and the doctor didn't like the way she was looking. By one o'clock, it looked as though she might not make it. Page couldn't believe it was happening. She had been stable only an hour before . . . but on the other hand, two days before that, she had been normal. Life had a way of changing a hundred and eighty degrees without a moment's warning.

By the time the rest of the surgical team came, Page had tried to call Brad several times, but the answering machine was on, and he didn't pick up. Finally, in desperation she asked Trygve to call Jane Gilson, and have her go over and wake Brad up. She could stay with Andy so Brad could leave. But when Trygve came back from the phone, he only shook his head and delivered Jane's message. Brad had never come to pick Andy up at all. The boy was sound asleep in her bed, and she had no idea where Brad was. He had never called her.

"He never called?" Page looked stunned. How could he do that now, with everything happening, and after all he'd said? What was he thinking of? His sex life, or his daughter?

"She said she never heard from him. I'm sorry, Page." He took her hand in his, and knew then that what he had suspected was probably right. Brad Clarke probably was having an affair, or maybe he was just getting drunk, to take the strain off. And his timing was certainly lousy. Trygve felt sorry for Page, who seemed to be carrying this responsibility all alone. But nothing surprised him anymore. He had seen and lived it all with Dana. "Don't worry about it," he reassured her, as they waited for the doctors to evaluate Allie. "He'll turn up. And there's nothing he can do here anyway. None of us can." But he could have been

there, as she was, and Trygve was for Chloe.
"Not everyone can handle this, you know. I
used to get sick at the thought of hospitals."

"So what changed?"

"My kids. I had to do it for them, because
Dana never did. Brad has you, so he knows
Allie's in good hands." He smiled gently at
her, making excuses for Brad that he didn't
deserve, and Page knew it. And who was
there for her? If Trygve hadn't stuck
around, she would have been alone. She assumed that Brad was probably with his girlfriend. But she still didn't know where to
find him.

The doctors came back and talked to
them again eventually. Allyson had stabilized somewhat again, but she was still
clearly in danger. The swelling of her brain
was not a good sign, and could have been a
sign of further injury, or a result of the surgery on Sunday. It was difficult to tell, but
they didn't want to raise false hopes. They
felt there was a good chance now that Allyson might not make it.

"You mean now?" Page said, looking terrified. "Tonight?" Was that what they
meant? That she was about to die . . . oh
God no . . . please . . . when they allowed her to, she hurried in to see her, and

sat silently next to the bed, as tears poured down her face, and she held the girl's hand, as though by keeping a firm grip on her she might keep her from drifting off, or finally leaving them after all she'd been through.

They let Page sit with her that night, and she never moved, she just sat there holding her hand, watching her face, and praying.

"I love you," she whispered from time to time. "I love you," as though she were determined for Allie to hear her. And when the sun came up, the swelling of her brain had gotten no worse, and her breathing continued mechanically on the respirator. She hadn't improved, but she was still with them. Everything could change again in a matter of moments, and they suggested that Page stay in close touch if she went home, but they assured her that they felt that for the moment, Allyson was out of immediate danger, and she was heavily sedated to combat the effects of the operation.

It was six-thirty in the morning when Page left ICU, after gently kissing her child, and as she walked out into the hall, every inch of her body was stiff and aching. And she was amazed when she saw Trygve waiting for her there. He was asleep in a chair, but he hadn't moved in hours. He had

wanted to be there with her in case Allyson
died, and Brad had never called. He was a
damn fool, Trygve thought, but he would
never have said it to Page. He was just
grateful, with her, that Allie had made it
through the night, and survived yet another
disaster.

"Come on, I'll take you home. You can
leave your car here. I'll bring you back
later."

"I can take a cab if I have to," she said
appreciatively. She was too tired to walk, let
alone drive, and she followed him out to his
car in the parking lot, relieved that Allyson
had survived another night. If only she
would live, Page thought to herself as she
slipped into the front seat of his car. If only
they could will her to make it.

"You were very brave," Trygve said softly
as he leaned over and kissed her cheek. He
gave her shoulders a squeeze and patted
her hand, and then started the car.

"I was so scared, Trygve . . . I wanted to
run and hide," she confessed. It was all so
much worse than anything she had ever
dreamed, worse than anyone's worst nightmare.

"But you didn't. And she made it. Just
take it step by step," he said wisely, as he

drove her home. When they got there, he glanced over at her, and saw that she was sound asleep, and he hated to wake her. He shook her gently, and she stirred, and then looked at him with a slow smile.

"Thank you . . . for being such a good friend."

"I wish we had become good friends some other way," he said ruefully, "like the swim team, or your mural." And then he remembered. "You still want to go to Phillip's funeral today?" he asked quietly, and she nodded. She was sure by then that Brad would not go with her.

"I'll pick you up at two-fifteen. Try and get some sleep between now and then. You really need it."

"I'll do my best." She touched his hand, and got out, and he watched her let herself into the house with her key. There was no one there, and it was seven o'clock in the morning.

Trygve waved and drove away, as Page gently closed the door, wondering what she would say to Brad when she saw him. There seemed to be nothing left to say, except good-bye. Or had they already said it?

CHAPTER 7

It was seven o'clock in
the morning as Page stood in her living
room, trying to decide whether to go to bed,
or go next door to pick up Andy at Jane
Gilson's. She was bone tired, and desperately in need of sleep, but she knew that
Andy needed her too, so she washed her
face and combed her hair, and then listened
to her messages on the phone machine in
the kitchen. There were none from Brad,
which suddenly made her furious. How
could he do this now, with Allyson barely
clinging to life? And what was wrong with
Stephanie that she would let him?

Page went next door to pick Andy up

then, and found him eating breakfast with
Jane. The television was on, and Jane was
making him fresh waffles, and singing.

"Lucky you!" Page said tiredly as she
kissed the top of his head and smiled at
Jane. Her friend saw then that the dark circles under her eyes had deepened.

"How's Allie?" Andy asked immediately,
and Page hesitated for a moment. She had
to fight back tears before she answered.
Suddenly, she couldn't say the words. She
had almost died that night, but thank God
she hadn't. Jane saw her choke on her
words and touched her shoulder as she
went to get her a cup of coffee.

"She's okay," she told Andy, and then
turned to Jane and spoke softly while Andy
helped himself to more waffles. "Things got
kind of rough last night. Her brain swelled
after the surgery, and she had a lot of trouble breathing."

"Is she gonna *die*?" Andy's eyes looked
huge as he listened, and Page shook her
head. At least she hadn't died, and they
were still praying she wasn't going to.

"I hope not."

He was silent for a moment as he absorbed what she had said, and then he
asked her another difficult question.

"Where's Daddy? He never came for me last night."

"I think he got tied up at the office, and you were sound asleep when he got home. He didn't want to wake you."

"Oh." Andy looked relieved. He had sensed their fighting the night before, and he didn't like it. Allie's accident had changed everything. Suddenly nothing seemed secure to him, and the people he loved were all frightened and upset and angry. "Can I see Allie today?"

"Not yet, sweetheart." There was no way Page would let him see her. With no hair, her head and eyes wrapped in bandages, tubes and machines everywhere, and the smell of death and fear heavy around her. It was a terrifying sight for anyone, especially a child of seven. "When she's better. When she wakes up . . ." she said, fighting tears again. She had to turn away this time, so he wouldn't see, and Jane put an arm around her shoulders.

"You need sleep more than anything. Why don't you go to bed, and I'll take Andy to school today." But Andy looked crestfallen at the suggestion. He had no idea how tired she was, or how frightening things were at the hospital. And he wanted his mother near him.

"I'm okay." Page took a deep breath, and then a long sip of her coffee. "I'll be back in a few minutes, and I can go to bed then." Page had already promised herself that she was going to go to bed until Trygve picked her up for the funeral. The hospital knew where to reach her if there was a problem. And she needed sleep desperately, she felt as though she couldn't walk another step. She had to fight to stay awake all the way to Ross Grammar School, and she drove home by inches. The moment she got back, she checked the phone machine again. Still no call from Brad. And it was too early to call him at the office.

It was hard to believe that he had dared to stay out all night, without even calling. But what would he have said? Sorry, I'm spending the night with my girlfriend. But it amazed her that things had gone so far in just a few days. Their whole married life, and their relationship, seemed to have crumbled.

Page was in bed by eight-fifteen, and although she tossed and turned in the daylight at first, thinking about Allyson and the terrors of the night before, by eight-thirty her body had overwhelmed her brain, and she was sound asleep in her bed with all her clothes on. She lay in a deep sleep until just past noon, when she was awakened by the persistent ringing of the phone. She leapt out of bed once she realized what it was, terrified that it was the hospital calling about Allie.

"Yes?" Her voice was barely a croak, but it wasn't the hospital. It was her mother.

"Good Lord, what's wrong with you? Are you sick?"

"No, Mother . . . I . . . I was sleeping." There was so much to explain, and it would be so difficult to get it across to her mother.

"At noon? That's unusual. Are you pregnant?"

"No, I'm not. I was up late . . ." with your granddaughter, who almost died. . . . Suddenly, Page felt guilty for not calling her sooner.

"You never called me back over the weekend. You said you would." She loved to complain, she relished the role of the injured party. She always claimed that Page neglected her, but the truth was she was much closer to Page's sister, Alexis. Page's older sister lived in New York, and spent a lot of time with their mother.

"I've been busy, Mom." How did you even begin to say the words? She closed her eyes as she struggled with her own emotions. "Allyson had an accident Saturday night."

"Is she all right?" Her mother sounded stunned. Even she couldn't hide from those words, or the force they carried with them. She was a basically intelligent woman who hid that fact from everyone, and lived in a dream world.

"No, she's not. She's in a coma. She had brain surgery on Sunday. We don't know what's going to happen. I'm sorry I didn't call you, Mom. I just didn't know what to say, and I wanted to wait until things were a little better."

"How's Brad?" Page thought it was a strange question.

"Brad? He's fine, he wasn't in the accident. She was with a bunch of kids."

"This must be very hard on him." It was so typical of her mother, to focus on him, not on her daughter, or whether or not Allie would survive, but on Brad. If she didn't know her so well, she would have thought she hadn't heard her correctly.

"It's hard for all of us. Brad, me, Andy
. . . Allie . . ."

"Will she be all right?"

"We don't know yet."

"I'm sure she will. These things look terrible at first, but people survive accidents all
the time." Oh God. How typical. Always es-
caping reality, at any price. Things hadn't
changed. But maybe, without seeing her, it
was hard to understand Allyson's condition.
"I've read some extraordinary stories of
head injuries, and people in comas, and
they just walk away from it. She's young.
She'll be fine." Her mother sounded so certain. Page only wished she could believe
her.

"I hope so," Page said wanly, staring at
the floor, wondering how anyone could
communicate with her mother. Nothing had
changed since she was fourteen. Her
mother still heard and believed only what
she wanted to, and not another thing, no
matter what you told her. "I'll keep you
posted."

"Tell her I love her," Maribelle Addison
said firmly. "They say people in comas hear
everything. Do you talk to her, Page?"

Page nodded, as tears started to roll
down her cheeks. Of course she talked to

her . . . she told her how much she loved her . . . she begged her not to die and leave them . . . "Yes," she whispered hoarsely.

"Good. Well, tell her that her Grandma and her aunt Alexis love her." And then, almost as an afterthought, "Do you want us to come out?" They did almost everything together. But Page answered in a single breath. That was all she needed.

"No! . . . I'll call if I need you."

"You do that, dear, I'll call you tomorrow." It sounded like a date for a bridge game. It was amazing, she was totally positive, completely confident that Allyson would be fine, and not frightened of the possibilities for a single moment. As usual, she offered no comfort, no solace, no support for her youngest daughter.

"Thanks, Mom. I'll call if anything happens."

"You do that, dear. Alexis and I are going shopping tomorrow. I'll call you when I get home. Give my love to Brad, and Andy."

"I will." They hung up then, and Page sat staring at the floor for a long time, trying not to remember what it had been like to live with her . . . with them . . . all the lies and the misery . . . and the endless hiding from reality. Alexis was perfect for it. She played the same games their mother did. Everything was lovely all the time, no one ever did anything wrong, and if they did, it was never mentioned. The waters were always calm, their voices were never raised, and inside they were all drowning. Page had almost drowned. She couldn't wait to leave home. She had moved out as soon as she had started art school. They hadn't wanted her to, and refused to pay for it, but she had done free-lance work, and worked as a waitress in a restaurant at night just so she could afford it. She would have done anything to get out. Her survival depended on it, and she knew it.

She was so engrossed in her own thoughts that she never heard him come in, and he never saw her. Brad was halfway across the room when she stirred, and they both jumped when they saw each other.

"For chrissake! . . ." he said as his eyes met hers. "Why didn't you say something?"

"I didn't know you were here. Home for lunch?" she said coolly. She was still sitting on the bed in her rumpled clothes, and her uncombed hair. But she looked better and more rested than she had earlier that morning.

"I just came by to drop off some things."
He looked vague as he walked into the
bathroom and put a shirt in the hamper.

"Yesterday's laundry? How soon would
you like it? Or did you come home for a
clean shirt so you can stay out again tonight?" Her voice dripped anger and
venom. "Don't you think you could at least
call? Or are we dropping all pretense of being married?"

"You weren't here anyway. What's the
difference?" He looked and sounded so callous suddenly, and she wanted to strike
him.

"You could have called ICU, or Jane.
Andy was waiting for you. He thought you'd
had an accident too. Or do you no longer
care about him either? Allyson almost died
last night." She let him have it with both
barrels. And he looked appropriately
stricken.

"Is she okay?"

"She's holding on. But barely."

He looked at her miserably then. He had
just wanted to forget it all for one night. It
had been such a relief to be away from the
hospital, and Page, and even Andy.

"I guess I just forgot to call." It was a
terrible excuse, and he knew it.

"I wish I could forget too. Maybe you're lucky," she said sadly. She couldn't walk away from any of it, and she wouldn't have wanted to. And three days before, she wouldn't have walked away from him either. Now everything was different. "You can't just blank out on this, Brad. It's really happening, and you have to face it. How would you feel if she'd died last night?"

"How do you think I'd feel?" He looked grim as he watched her.

"Andy needs you too. And maybe you need to be with Allyson. If something happens . . ." She couldn't have been anywhere else, but Brad didn't agree with her.

"Sitting with Allyson won't change anything," he said defensively. "She's going to live or die, whether I'm there or not. It just upsets me, and maybe trying to drag her back at any cost isn't the answer."

"What are you saying to me?" Page looked horrified. "Are you saying we should let her die?" Page wanted to scream just listening to him. What had happened to him? What was he saying?

"I'm saying I want Allie back. *Allie.* The girl she used to be, and would have become if this hadn't happened. Beautiful and strong and intelligent, and capable, able to do anything she wanted. Do you really *want* her to live if she's going to be less than that? Do you really want a brain-damaged child to nurse for the rest of your life? Do you want that for her? Because I don't. I'd rather let her go now if that's what she's going to be. And sitting there, watching her, while her brain swells, and a respirator breathes for her, isn't going to make a damn bit of difference. We've done what we could. Now all we can do is wait. And waiting here or waiting there doesn't make any difference to her." But what if it did? What if she knew they were there with her?

Page looked sickened by what he was saying. "Andy needs you as much as she does. Or is that too much for you too?" She was giving him no mercy, but right now, in her eyes, he didn't deserve it. He was failing all of them, and for totally selfish reasons.

"Maybe it's all too much for me. Has that ever occurred to you?" he asked, taking a step closer to her again. He hated seeing her now, it always turned into an argument or a reproach, or a series of accusations.

"It occurs to me that you're indulging yourself, and making some terrible decisions. Time hasn't just stopped because you want it to, Brad. This isn't 'time out' while you sort out your sex life. Allie needs you, no matter what you think of her condition or her future. She needs you even more because of that. And Andy needs you. The poor kid is terrified, he's watching his family fall apart in front of his eyes, he knows his sister may die, he doesn't know where you are, and all of a sudden he's living with the neighbors."

"Then maybe you need to come home at night," Brad said, and was startled when Page stood up and walked several steps closer to where he stood.

"Let me tell you something, Brad. I'm not leaving Allie more than I have to until we know if she'll make it, or until she dies. And if she does . . ." Tears filled Page's eyes as she said the words, but her voice didn't waver. "I'm going to be there with her, holding her hand, and holding her as she leaves this world, just as I did when she entered it. I'm not going to be at home, or with you, unless you're at the hospital too, or even with Andy. But at least I'm not with some floozie somewhere, trying to pretend this hasn't happened." She turned away from him then. She couldn't stand the look on his face, which told her that he had already left them.

"Page." She turned to look at him then, when she heard the tears in his voice, which surprised her. He sat down heavily in a chair, and dropped his face into his hands. "I can't stand seeing her like that. It's like she's already gone . . . I can't stand it." Page couldn't understand what made him think he had a choice. She couldn't stand it either. But she knew she had to. For Allie.

"But she's not gone," Page said quietly, wanting to comfort him, but afraid to come any closer. There was so much between them now, so much pain and loss and disappointment. She no longer trusted him, or believed in him. She hardly knew who he was now. "She still has a chance, Brad. You can't let go of that till she does."

"She'd be better off dead than a vegetable, Page, and you know it."

"Don't say that!" she said vehemently. She had never given up easily, and she couldn't understand his attitude now. It was as though he wanted the easy way out, even for Allie, even if it meant losing her, or giving up. Page just couldn't do that.

"I don't know . . ." he went on, looking and feeling guilty for everything he was feeling. But he just couldn't help it. "When I saw her, I just couldn't imagine her pulling out of this, and I don't want her to be a vegetable for the rest of her life . . . the things they talk about . . . about comas . . . and spasticity . . . and loss of motor skills . . . and brain . . . forebrain . . . brain stem . . . how can you listen to all that and still think she's going to be normal?"

"Because there's still hope for her. Maybe it won't be easy . . . maybe she won't make a total recovery . . . hell, maybe she won't even live . . . but if she does . . ." Her eyes filled with tears again. ". . . But if she does . . . we have to help her."

He looked at Page in despair, crying softly. "I can't . . . I can't do this, Page . . ." He was desperately scared, and Page knew it. She came to stand next to him then, and put her arms around him, as he leaned his head against her. She gently stroked his hair, and wished neither of them had come so far on the road to destruction. But it couldn't be erased, just like the accident couldn't be erased for Allie. "I'm so scared," he whispered as he leaned his head against her breasts. ". . . I don't want her to die . . . but I don't want her to live like that, Page . . . I can't even stand to see it

. . . I'm sorry about last night . . . I shouldn't have disappeared like that . . . but I just couldn't face it." She nodded, understanding what he felt, but it didn't make it any easier for her. He wanted to run away from it, and he had. But it left her all alone, to face the nightmare that was happening to Allie. "What if she dies?" He looked up at her with anguished eyes, and she took a deep breath as she thought of it, and tried to face it.

"I don't know," she said softly, "I thought she would last night . . . but she didn't. We have another day . . . another hour . . . we just have to pray." He nodded, wishing he had her strength. He still wanted to run away, and Stephanie made it so easy for him to do that. She felt sorry for him, and she let him escape the horror of what was happening to his child. She let him think that he couldn't help anyway. He had told her Page was good at handling it, and she had urged him to let her. But when he saw Page struggling with the pain of it, he felt consumed with guilt, and he knew he was wrong to fail her.

And as he leaned against her, he felt a deep ache of longing for her, and a stirring that he knew would bring them closer. He put his arms around her, and tried to pull her down on his lap so he could kiss her. But she stiffened instantly and looked down at him in outrage.

"How could you?" After all that had come to light since the accident, she couldn't imagine being physically close to him again. Surely not now. And very probably never.

"I need you, Page."

"That's disgusting," she said, and meant it. He had Stephanie. What more did he want? A harem? Before she had known, it was different. But now she just couldn't. He kissed her anyway and there was a frantic quality to his passion. But it did nothing to soften Page's feelings toward him. If anything, she felt more distant. Suddenly he had become a stranger. He belonged to someone else, and not to her now.

She pulled away firmly, and he was out of breath, as she took a step backward. "I'm sorry," she said, and walked away from him, leaving him looking angry and feeling foolish. He knew it was wrong to be doing this, to be hurting her, and clinging to Stephanie, but just as she had said, he was making all the wrong decisions.

He came to find her a little while later in

the kitchen. She was making herself a cup of coffee, and she didn't turn around when she heard him walk into the kitchen behind her.

"I'm sorry. I got carried away. I guess it's inappropriate, given everything that's happened." It was particularly incredible to realize that only a week before they had been making love, as though nothing were wrong, and she had had no idea that he had a lover. But now all of that had changed. And given the importance of his relationship with Stephanie, she didn't want him to touch her. It might have been different if he'd been consumed with regret, and promised to end it. But there was no such promise offered. If anything, it was ending between them. He seemed to want it that way. And now everything was out in the open, just as he had disappeared the night before, in spite of their needing him, or a possible emergency, or even just because of Andy's feelings. Stephanie came before all of them. The realization of that had hit Page like a ten-ton stone, and she couldn't ignore it.

"I think you ought to give me her number. If anything happens, and you're there, I should know how to reach you." She said it without turning around and looking at him, and he didn't see the tears in her eyes when she said it.

"I . . . it won't happen again, I'll stay home with Andy tonight."

"I don't care." She wheeled to face him then, and the look on her face frightened him. She was so hurt, and so angry, and so determined. Their brief moment of closeness was clearly over. "It will happen again, and I want the number."

"Fine. I'll leave it on the pad."

She nodded and took a sip of the hot coffee.

"What are you doing today?" He assumed she was going back to the hospital, and was surprised to discover that she wasn't.

"I'm going to the Chapman funeral. Do you want to come?"

"Not likely. The little bastard almost killed my kid. How can you go?" He looked incensed and she looked at him with barely concealed contempt and disapproval.

"The Chapmans lost their only son. And nothing proved it's his fault. How can you not go?"

"I don't owe them anything," he said coldly. "And the lab tests showed he was drinking."

"But not much. And what about the other driver? Couldn't it be her fault?" Trygve had wondered as much, and so had Page, but not Brad. It was so much easier to blame Phillip Chapman.

"Laura Hutchinson is a senator's wife, she has three children of her own, and she isn't going to run around drunk driving, or being negligent." He sounded absolutely certain.

"How do you know that?" She wasn't sure of anything anymore, not the Senator's wife, not even her own husband. "How can you be so sure that it wasn't her fault?"

"I'm sure, that's all, and so were the police. They didn't give her a blood test, they obviously didn't think she needed one, or they would have. And they've laid no blame on her." He clearly believed that.

"Maybe they were impressed with who she was." They argued about everything these days, and Page was only grateful that Andy wasn't there to hear it. "Anyway, I'm going to the funeral. Trygve Thorensen is picking me up at two-fifteen to take me."

Brad raised an eyebrow at her. "How cozy."

"Don't give me that." Her eyes blazed at him, her fatigue and anger showing. "The

two of us have been sitting at that hospital
that you hate so much for the past three
days, waiting to see if our daughters were
going to make it. And Phillip Chapman was
driving the car his daughter was in too, but
it's not keeping him from showing a little
sympathy to the boy's parents."

"What a great guy he is. Maybe you two
can become 'friends,' since I no longer
seem to appeal to you." He was still piqued
by her rebuff, although he understood it.
But he was irritated by her praise of Trygve.

"Actually, he is a great guy, Brad. He's a
good friend. And he's been there for me.
He sat there and held my hand last night,
when no one knew where you were, and the
night of the accident when you were at the
'John Gardiner' with your little friend. He's
been terrific. And you know what else, he's
smart enough to keep his dick in his pants,
and think about his kids, and not his sex
life. So if you're looking for me to feel
guilty or embarrassed, don't bother. I don't
think Trygve Thorensen gives a shit about
me as a woman, and that's just fine, because
I'm not looking for a boyfriend. I just need
a friend to be there for me, since I no
longer seem to have a husband."

There wasn't much Brad could say, and

he walked into the bathroom and slammed the door. And without another word to her, he slammed out of the house ten minutes later. She wanted to strangle him, she was so mad, but a part of her was sad too. Everything had gone so wrong between them so quickly. It was almost impossible to understand it. The pressure they were under was excruciating, but so much else seemed to be wrong too, and she never knew it. The accident had uncovered everything, and brought its own problems along with it.

She showered and dressed for the funeral then, and Trygve came to pick her up at exactly two-fifteen. He was wearing a dark blue suit, white shirt, and dark tie, and he looked serious and very handsome. Page was wearing a black linen suit she had bought in New York the last time she visited her mother.

The service was at St. John's Episcopal Church, and somehow Page hadn't been prepared for the hundreds of kids who would attend, their shining young faces stricken by the loss of their friend, their hearts open for all to see, their grief overwhelming. There was a wonderful photograph of him with the swimming team on the program that the ushers handed out.

And then Page realized that the ushers were Phillip's friends from the swim team. She saw Jamie Applegate there too. He looked devastated as he sat between his parents. But they seemed supportive of him. And his father had an arm around his shoulders.

They played all the music that the kids loved too, and Page felt tears instantly fill her throat as she heard it. There were at least three or four hundred young people in the church, and she knew Allyson would have been there too, if she hadn't been in the hospital in a coma.

And then, looking very dignified, and overwhelmed with grief, Phillip's parents walked in and took their seats in the front pew. There was another much older couple with them, Phillip's grandparents, and just seeing them made one cry. The power of his loss was so obvious just from their faces.

The minister spoke very movingly about the mysteries of God's love, and the terrible pain we feel at the loss of a loved one. He spoke of what an extraordinary young man Phillip had been, how admired by everyone, what a bright future he'd had before him. Page could hardly stand listening as she sobbed, trying not to think of what they would say if Allie died. It would be much the same thing. She was loved and admired by all. And the pain of her loss would be beyond bearing.

Mrs. Chapman cried openly through the entire ceremony, and the school choir sang "Amazing Grace" at the end of the service. And then everyone was invited up to the altar, for a moment of special prayer, and a last tribute to their friend. Mostly, the young people went, in groups or alone, crying, and holding hands, as they placed flowers on Phillip's casket. Everyone in the church was sobbing by then, and Page felt overwhelmed as she looked around her at the devastated young faces. It was then that she saw Laura Hutchinson, crying softly in a pew a few feet away. She seemed to have come alone, and she seemed as moved as everyone. Page stared at her for a long time, but she could see nothing more than a deeply affected mourner. Surprisingly little was said. Everyone looked dazed. It was just too painful.

And then, as they walked outside afterward, Page and Trygve noticed the reporters. They were following Laura Hutchinson at first, but she disappeared quickly into a limousine without speaking to them. And then they took photographs of the young people's faces, as they stood crying on the sidewalk. And then suddenly, they seemed to close in on the Chapmans. And Phillip's father became enraged and shouted at them through his tears that they were heartless bastards, as friends gently led him away. But even then, the reporters didn't leave, but they backed off slightly. It was still a hot story.

There was a reception after the service, in the school auditorium, and the Chapmans had invited a few friends to go home with them after that. But Page didn't want to go to either place. She couldn't bear it. She just wanted to be alone somewhere, to recover from the powerful blow of what she had felt at the service. She looked up at Trygve then, standing quietly at her side, and saw that he had cried as much as she had.

"Are you okay?" he asked gently, and she nodded but started to cry again. "Yeah. Me too. Come on, I'll take you home." She nodded again and followed him back to the car, and they sat there for a long moment in silence. She hadn't had the courage to say anything to the Chapmans as they left, but they had signed the guest book in the front of the church. She read afterward in the paper that there had been over five hundred mourners.

"Oh God, that was rough." She finally spoke, trying to catch her breath, as Trygve looked at her, feeling drained by his emotions.

"It's awful. There's nothing worse. I hope I never live long enough to see the death of one of my children." And then he was sorry for what he had said, knowing that Allyson's life still hung in the balance, but Page understood it. She didn't want to go through it either.

"I saw Mrs. Hutchinson. It was pretty ballsy of her to be there. I would think the Chapmans would be upset by her coming."

"Yeah, but the press would be favorably impressed. It shows how much she cares, how human she is. It was a smart move," he said wryly.

"That sounds pretty cynical," she said bluntly. "Maybe she's sincere."

"I doubt it. I know politicians. Believe me, her husband told her to be there. Maybe the accident wasn't her fault, maybe she is totally innocent. But in the meantime, this makes her look good."

"Is that what it was all about?" Page looked disappointed.

"Probably. I don't know. I just keep feeling that she was negligent somehow, that it wasn't the kids' fault, or maybe I just want to believe that." So did the Chapmans. Trygve started the car, and they followed a long line of cars back toward Page's house, on the way to school, and then she remembered that she needed to go to the hospital anyway for her car. And she wanted to see Allie more than ever after what they'd just been through. She wanted to reassure herself that Allie was still there, after the misery of being at Phillip's funeral, and sharing all that anguish.

"Do you mind dropping me off?" she asked, smiling sadly at him. It had been a terrible afternoon for both of them. Page had called the hospital several times that afternoon to see how Allyson was, but there had been no change since that morning.

"No problem. I want to see Chloe anyway. It makes you grateful they're alive, doesn't it?"

Page nodded, thinking of what Brad had said in the heat of the moment about not wanting Allie to be less than perfect. But he seemed to believe it. "I'd rather have Allie

in any state than lose her. Maybe that's
wrong of me, but that's how I feel. Brad
says he'd rather lose her than have her be
limited in any way."

"That's a pretty elitist view of life, and
awfully black and white. I agree with you,
I'd rather have whatever I could get, than
nothing." Page agreed with him, but oddly
enough, not about her marriage. She was
much less willing to compromise there, but
in her eyes that was different.

"He can't seem to face what's happening.
He's running away from it," she said quietly, trying not to get angry again thinking
of his disappearances, as recently as the
night before.

"Some people can't handle this kind of
thing."

"Yeah, like Dana . . . Brad . . . so
how come we get stuck with it? Are we so
brave? Or just stupid?" Page smiled at him.

"Probably both," he grinned, "no choice,
I guess. When there's no one else there, you
do what you have to." He looked at her
honestly. He had spent enough time with
her now to ask her a straight question. "It
doesn't make you mad?" He was intrigued
about her, and her willingness to accept
what was obviously a less than perfect mar-

riage. Brad had scarcely been around since the accident, and Trygve knew it.

"Actually, it makes me furious," she admitted with a smile. "We just had a knock-down-drag-out fight about it at lunchtime."

"At least you're human. It used to make me mad too, when Dana was never around when I needed her, or the kids did."

"In this case, there are some other complications."

Trygve nodded, trying not to ask any further questions. And then finally, he couldn't resist, and asked her anyway.

"Serious complications?"

"It looks that way," she said honestly. "Possibly terminal."

"Then it came as a surprise?" he asked gently.

"Actually, yes. I've been married for sixteen years and up until three days ago, I thought our marriage was terrific," she said as they approached the hospital. "Apparently, I made a mistake. A big one."

"Maybe not. Maybe this is just the hard part. Every marriage hits a rough spot, now and then."

She shook her head, thinking about it. "There was a lot I didn't know. I've been kidding myself for a long time, and I didn't know it. But now that I do know it's hard to pretend it's not happening. I just can't do that. The timing is pretty rotten." She looked grim as she explained it to him.

"Remember what I said before, some people go off the deep end when faced with a crisis."

"I think he's been off it for a long time. He just happened to get caught with his pants down." She smiled ruefully, and Trygve laughed at her expression, and the way she'd said it.

"Bad luck for him." Trygve smiled. Page was amazed at the ease with which she spoke to him. She seemed to be able to tell him anything. Things she certainly wouldn't have told her sister or even Jane Gilson, who was an old friend, but not a real confidant. After the rigors of her early life, she had never gotten close to anyone except Brad, which made his betrayal all the more painful. And now, much to her surprise she could tell Trygve things she might even have hesitated telling Brad before all this happened.

They were at the hospital by then, and they headed for ICU, still subdued by the aura of the funeral, but it was almost a relief for both of them to see their children.

Chloe was stirring a little bit, but doing fairly well, and Allie was the same. For the moment, her condition was stable.

Page left before Trygve this time. She went home around five o'clock to pick Andy up at Jane's. The car pool had taken him to baseball, and he would have been home by then. And by the time she drove to her house, she couldn't wait to see him.

It had been an agonizing afternoon, and the grief of Phillip's funeral took her breath away every time she thought of the young people crying for him, or the faces of his parents. They had looked inconsolable as they left the church, and Page's heart had gone out to them. She could still hear the high school chorus singing in her head as she rang the bell at Jane's house.

"Hi, how are you?" Jane looked at her, and then frowned as Page walked in. "Or shouldn't I ask?" Maybe things had gotten worse. Page looked drawn and pale and desperately unhappy.

"I'm okay," she said quietly. "I went to Phillip Chapman's funeral."

"How was it?" Jane asked as Page sat down on the couch and looked exhausted.

"About as bad as you'd expect. There

were four hundred sobbing kids, and half as many parents."

"Just what you need right now. Did Brad go with you?"

Page shook her head. "Trygve Thorensen took me. We saw the Senator's wife, looking appropriately grief-stricken and very proper. Frankly, I thought it took a lot of guts for her to be there. Trygve thought she did it for PR, and was playing to the reporters, to make sure everyone knows how innocent she is."

"Is she?" Jane asked honestly.

"I'm beginning to think we'll never know. Probably no one was at fault, it was just a lot of bad luck and bad timing."

"I'll say . . . there were reporters there?"

"TV cameras, and some photographers from the newspapers. I guess it's big stuff because of Mrs. Hutchinson, and it tears your heart out seeing those kids." Not to mention the parents.

"The piece in the paper I read yesterday seemed to imply, more or less, that it was the Chapman boy's fault. Is that just talk, or is it real? Was he really drinking?"

"Apparently not enough to matter. And I hear Mr. Chapman is planning to sue the paper to clear Phillip's name. As I said, there's no evidence either way to prove whose fault it might have been. Neither his, nor Mrs. Hutchinson's, but he's a kid, and he had half a glass of wine . . . and two cups of coffee." She and Trygve had talked it to death, and the story still stayed the same. It was an accident. It was no one's fault apparently. And she didn't blame the Chapmans for wanting to clear their son's name. He was a great kid, and he deserved to die with his fine reputation, if only for their sakes.

By then Andy had spotted her and he came running to meet her. He was wearing his baseball uniform and he looked so cute, she almost cried when she saw him. He looked so normal and healthy, it reminded her of only days before when she had taken him to his game, and everything seemed so simple. Allie wasn't in a coma then, and Brad hadn't confessed that he was cheating.

"And how was your day, Mr. Andrew Clarke?" she asked, beaming at him as he threw his arms around her.

"Great. I scored a home run!" He was pleased with himself, and she was happy to see him.

"You're terrific."

He was thrilled to see her too, and then he looked up at her worriedly. "Are you going back to the hospital now? Am I staying here?"

"No, you're coming home with me." She had decided to take a night off, for his sake. She knew how badly he needed it, and she wanted to be there for him. And as long as Allie's condition didn't change, she felt she could do it. She had decided to make dinner for him, more than just frozen pizza, and she wanted to sit down and talk to him, so he didn't feel so neglected.

"Can Dad do a barbecue?" She didn't know if Brad was coming home or staying out again, and she didn't want to promise anything, so she told him he couldn't. "Okay. We'll just have regular dinner then." He seemed delighted at the prospect, and they went home a few minutes later.

She made hamburgers and baked potatoes for him, and a big green salad with avocados and tomatoes in it, and she was surprised when she heard Brad come in just as they were sitting down to dinner. She hadn't really expected him, but she had made enough to feed him too, just in case he did come home.

"Dad!" Andy shouted excitedly, and Page

could see in his little face how desperately he needed contact with them. He was deeply worried.

"What a surprise!" Page said, not quite under her breath, and Brad shot her a dark look.

"Let's not start that, Page," he said irritably. He had had a long day too, and he had made a point of coming home for dinner, for his son's sake. "Have you got enough?" he asked curtly, glancing at the table set for two, and the dinner she was serving Andy.

"No problem," she said, and served him a full plate a moment later. Andy was telling his father about the game, and his home run in the fourth inning. He rattled on about his friends at school. He was like a little sponge soaking up whatever moments they had for him, whatever time they could spare from his desperately injured sister. Watching him made Page aware again of how frightened he was, and how much he needed them right now. In his own way, he was as scared as she was. And in some ways it was worse for him because he hadn't seen his sister.

"Can I go to the hospital to see Allie this weekend?" he asked as he finished his baked potato. Page was pleased to see that

he had eaten well, and he looked more relaxed than he had at the beginning of dinner. But she still didn't think he was ready
to see his sister. Her condition was too
frightening, the danger still too acute. And
if she died, Page didn't want him to have
that as his last memory of Allie.

"I don't think so, sweetheart. We need to
wait until she feels a little better." She also
knew that you had to be at least eleven to
visit the ICU, but their doctor had already
told her he'd make an exception for Andy.

"But what if she doesn't feel better for a
long time? I need to see her." He started to
whine, and Page glanced at Brad, but he
wasn't paying attention. He was flipping
through the paper with a deep frown and an
unhappy expression. Stephanie had been
furious when he told her he couldn't have
dinner with her. He was almost used to it
now. Someone was always angry at him.

"We'll see," Page said about Andy's visit,
as they cleared the table. She served them
both ice cream with chocolate sauce for
dessert, and made herself another cup of
coffee. Neither of them had noticed it, but
she had hardly eaten. And after a few minutes, she glanced over at Brad. "Brad . . .
why don't you read that after dinner?" She

hated it when he read during meals, and he knew it.

"Why? Did you have something to say to me?" he snapped, and she bristled, as Andy watched with a frightened look. He had never seen them fight that way before, and for the past few days they had done nothing but, and he was worried.

After dinner, Brad went to his desk to look for something. And Andy went to his room, looking forlorn, followed by Lizzie.

Page cleaned up the kitchen, cleared the table, set it for breakfast, and then listened to her messages. There were at least a dozen more, inquiring about Allie. And several of the young people at the funeral had asked when they could see her. Mercifully, the hospital was turning everyone away, and whatever flowers came for her were being sent to the children's ward, because there were none allowed in ICU. Page was glad she didn't have to see any of Allie's friends. She knew she couldn't have coped with their fears too. And the last call on the machine was from a reporter who said he wanted to ask her some questions. She didn't even bother to write his name down when she jotted down the others.

She called a few of the young people

back who had left messages on the machine, but as always it was exhausting trying to explain it all to them, or telling the story again and again to their mothers. She had thought about putting a special recording on her message machine, telling everyone how Allie was, but the news was still so frightening, and the hope so slim, that Page couldn't bring herself to do it.

She went in to check on Andy finally, and she found him sitting on his bed, crying and talking to Lizzie. He was explaining to the dog about Allie's accident, and that she was gonna be okay, but she was still asleep, her eyes were bandaged, and her head was pretty swollen. It was a summary of sorts, though not entirely accurate, but it was close enough, and Lizzie wagged her tail as she listened.

"How's it going, sweetheart?" Page asked tiredly as she sat down next to him on the bed. She was grateful for the time at home with him, but it was also obvious how upset he was, and how little she could do to relieve it. She was happy that she had decided to spend the night at home with him. He really needed both of them, it was a good thing Brad had come home too, although he certainly wasn't being pleasant.

"How come you and Daddy fight all the time now?" he asked unhappily. "You never used to do that."

"We're upset . . . about Allie . . . sometimes when grown-ups are sad or scared, they don't know how to show it, so they crab at each other, or they yell. I'm sorry, sweetheart. We don't mean to upset you." She stroked his head as she tried to reassure him.

"You sound so mean when you talk to him." How could she explain to him that his father was cheating on her, and their whole marriage had gone out the window. She couldn't, and she wouldn't. "It's hard being at the hospital with Allie."

"How come, if she's just sleeping?" None of this made any sense to him. It was all so difficult, and so complicated, and the grown-ups he loved were acting so strangely.

"I worry about her a lot. Just like I worry about you." She smiled, and his brows knit again.

"And Daddy? Do you worry about him too?"

"Of course I do. I worry about all of you. That's my job." She smiled at him, and a few minutes later she ran the tub for him.

And after his bath, she read him a story. He went to say good night to Brad, but he was on the phone, talking to someone, and he waved him away brusquely. Brad's nerves seemed to be on edge, not only with Page, but with Andy. Coming home for dinner hadn't been easy for him, and he wasn't entirely glad he'd done it. And he knew there'd be hell to pay with Stephanie when he saw her. Now that things were out in the open with Page, Stephanie was less willing to be patient.

Page put Andy to bed, and tucked him in, and he asked her to leave the light on in the hall, which he seldom did. Only when he was really frightened of something, or very sick, but they were all a little of both at the moment.

"Okay, sweetheart. I'll see you in the morning." She kissed him again, and was grateful for him, as she walked back to the kitchen to put away the dishes.

She caught a glimpse of Brad sitting in the living room, but she didn't speak to him. There seemed to be nothing left to say anymore. And she had guessed correctly that he was talking to Stephanie on the phone when he'd been interrupted by Andy.

She emptied the dishwasher, finished

cleaning up, returned a few more calls, and made herself another cup of coffee.

It was ten o'clock when Brad wandered in looking anxious and unhappy. It had been another difficult day for both of them, with their earlier exchange, the Chapman funeral, and dinner together had been far from easy. She was going through the mail, which she hadn't seen in two days, and looked up to see him.

"I guess things aren't going too well," Brad said unhappily, as she glanced at him. He was wearing jeans and a T-shirt, and for an instant Page remembered all the feelings she'd had for him for so many years, and wondered if through it all, he had really been a stranger. They had had two kids and shared sixteen years, and suddenly he had turned out to be someone completely different from the man she thought she lived with.

"You might say that," she said sadly, as she poured a last cup of coffee. Her nerves were so on edge anyway, the caffeine no longer seemed to make much difference. "I think Andy is becoming aware of it." Who wasn't? The air between them was palpable with grief and anger and disappointment.

"It's been a rough week."

"Yeah. A doubleheader."

"What's that supposed to mean?" Brad asked with a puzzled expression.

"Allie, and our marriage."

"Maybe it's all part of the same thing. Maybe once she's okay again, we'll be able to work things out." It seemed odd to hear him say that, particularly since he'd been adamant about not giving up Stephanie. She wondered what he was saying. Was there hope for them? Had he changed his mind? Had something happened? She couldn't figure him out anymore, and wasn't sure she cared to.

"Maybe we could still work it out," he said again, but he didn't sound convincing as he said it. "If we want to."

"Us and Stephanie? Is that what you have in mind, Brad?" She said it bitterly, sounding exhausted. "Let's not start this again, or tease each other with false hope. Let's just get Allie back to life again, and then we can turn our attention to this. But right now, to be honest, I just don't have the stomach for it."

He nodded. He couldn't disagree with her. And suddenly, Stephanie was pressuring him. It was almost as though she felt upstaged by Allyson and she was suddenly making demands he'd never before had to contend with. She wanted to spend more time with him, to be with him constantly, to have him spend the night when she knew he shouldn't. It was as though she was trying to prove something, as though she was trying to say that he belonged to her and not Page now. But the pressure on him, from both of them, was driving him crazy.

But before he could say anything to Page in answer to what she'd said to him, they heard a terrifying scream from Andy's bedroom. They ran to him as fast as they could, and Brad got there first. Andy was hysterical and still half asleep. He had had a terrible nightmare.

"It's all right . . . it's all right, champ . . . you're okay . . . it was just a bad dream . . ." But neither of them could calm him. He had dreamed they'd all had an accident, and everyone had been killed except him and Lizzie. There was blood everywhere, he said, and broken glass . . . and they had had the accident because his Mom and Dad were fighting. Brad and Page looked guiltily at each other over his head, and eventually he settled down again, although Page discovered he had wet his bed, and she had to change it. He hadn't done that since he was four, and it worried her even more. He was deeply disturbed even at an unconscious level.

"I guess you don't need a shrink to figure that one out," Brad said softly as they went to their bedroom.

"He's been very upset about Allie. It's very frightening for him. He hears us talk about how serious it is, and he still hasn't seen her. For all he knows, she's already dead."

"That's not all that's bothering him, and you know it," Brad said.

"I know," she admitted quietly. "We have to be more careful." It was obvious that he had heard them fighting.

"I hate to say this," he looked at her unhappily, "but maybe I should move out for a few days, or until we're all a little calmer and can handle what's happening." Page was shocked by the suggestion.

"Would you move in with her?" They both knew who she meant, but Brad didn't answer.

"I can stay at a hotel, or rent a furnished place in the city at 2000 Broadway." But Page also realized that it was the perfect opportunity for him to be with Stephanie, and not have to deal with his wife's re-proaches and accusations. Given the circumstances, she wasn't even sure she blamed him, though it would certainly be difficult to explain to Andy.

"I don't know what to say," Page said, looking at him, saddened by his suggestion. They had come a long way in a short time, to a place she had never dreamed they would get to. But as she looked at him pensively, the phone interrupted them, and she grabbed for it instantly in case it was about Allie. It was in fact the hospital. Allie's brain was swelling more, and the pressure was becoming too dangerous for her now. If there was no improvement, they wanted to operate in the morning. And they wanted her or Brad to sign the papers again in case they had to. They felt comfortable waiting through the night, unless something changed, but in all likelihood they felt she'd need surgery the following morning. It was her second brain surgery in four days, but Dr. Hammerman said there was no choice. Just like the first time they had operated, if they didn't, she wouldn't make it.

"They want to operate again?" Brad looked at her grimly and Page nodded. "And then what? Again and again . . . for chrissake, how often?"

"Maybe as often as they have to . . . until she gets well again . . . until her brain goes back to normal."

"And if it doesn't?" He repeated his earlier concerns but Page didn't want to hear it. For her it didn't change anything.

"If it doesn't, she's still our daughter. I'm going to sign the papers, Brad. She has a right to everything they can do for her." She would have fought him to the death if he tried to stop her, but in spite of what was happening to them, he was a reasonable man, and he wanted what was best for Allie. Page looked at him angrily, but the fight went out of him as he watched her.

"Do whatever you have to, Page." He went to their bedroom then, and lay down on the bed, thinking about Allyson, and how wonderful she had been. It was almost hard to remember now, looking at the creature she'd become, lying in the hospital, broken almost beyond recognition. "Are you sleeping there tonight?" he asked, as Page walked in, and took her nightgown out of her closet. But she shook her head and looked at him.

"I thought I'd sleep with Andy."

"You can sleep here." He smiled hesitantly. "I'll behave myself. I still can, you know." They exchanged a rare smile. But they had come to a sad crossroads in their life when it became an issue of who would sleep where, and whether or not he would move out. She felt, once again, as though she were living in a nightmare.

She lay in the narrow bed holding Andy for a long time that night, and the tears seemed to flow endlessly until her ears filled with them and the back of her throat, and her pillow was drenched. She had so much to mourn, so much she had taken for granted, and it was all gone now.

Andy was surprised in the morning when he found his mother sleeping with him, but he didn't question it. He got up and got dressed, and she made breakfast for all three of them. He never mentioned his nightmare again, but he was quiet when she dropped him off at school. Brad had said he would meet her at the hospital later that morning. She had to be there by eight-fifteen to sign the papers. They wanted to operate on her by ten, and this time Brad had promised that he'd be there.

CHAPTER 8

Page met the chief neurosurgeon outside ICU. There had been no improvement since the night before, so she signed the papers, and then went in to see her daughter. Allyson was still deeply comatose, all of the machines and monitors were on, but Page still managed to have a quiet moment with her. At that hour, there were no other visitors in ICU, and the nurses left them alone. They could monitor Allyson from the desk, where they could keep an eye on her monitors through their own screens and computers. Page sat quietly next to her, holding her hand and talking to her, touching her cheek from time to time, and she kissed her gently when they took her away at nine-thirty.

It was a long, lonely wait then, knowing that she was being prepared for surgery, and that if the operation was not successful, she clearly wouldn't make it. The pressure on her brain would cause extensive damage eventually, and the fractures and wounds could not heal with the ongoing trauma of the pressure.

Dr. Hammerman had told her that the operation would take eight to ten hours, and would once again be performed by the same team. It was almost routine, but in truth, it wasn't. It was terribly frightening. She had to fight to let herself think of the outcome. She couldn't allow herself to think of what might happen in the operating room, or if they came to tell her Allyson had died. She just couldn't bear it.

She looked anxious and pale when Brad finally arrived. He was half an hour later than he had said, but he had come, just as he'd promised.

"Did they say anything?" he asked anxiously.

"Nothing new," she said softly. And then, "She looked so sweet just lying there, before they took her. I keep wanting to wake her up, but she doesn't." Her eyes filled with tears, and she turned away from him. She no longer wanted to burden him with her feelings. She had lost her trust in him, and the openness they had always shared. It was as though he were someone else now. It was strange how you could lose someone so easily, how everything could change in a matter of moments. But she tried not to let herself think of that either, as they waited.

It was a long day, as they waited in the ICU waiting room, on uncomfortable chairs, amidst a constantly changing group of strangers. She and Brad said very little to each other all day. He was very quiet, and unusually patient with her, almost as though he felt obliged to be polite to her. They reminisced once or twice about Allie a little, but it was just too painful. Most of the time, they sat quietly, lost in their own thoughts, saying nothing to each other.

They finally went to get sandwiches in the cafeteria at four in the afternoon, and there was still no news. They told the nurse where they were going, and they ran into Trygve in the lobby. He wished them luck, and then went upstairs to see Chloe, and they didn't see him again after that. The Clarkes stayed to themselves in the small airless waiting room, watching the clock, and waiting to hear from the surgeon.

He finally came in at six-fifteen, and by then they both looked like they were ready to collapse from the endless tension. It had been yet another day filled with terror for them.

"How is she?" Brad leapt to his feet and met the doctor's eyes head-on, but the doctor nodded in satisfaction.

"She did better than we expected."

"What does that mean?" Brad challenged him instantly, as Page sat tensely and listened. She thought that if she stood up, she might swoon, so she didn't move, she just sat there.

"It means that she survived, her vital signs are good. She gave us a little scare early on, but she rallied. We relieved as much pressure as we could. It was somewhat worse than we had suspected. But there's still every reason to believe she could make a full recovery, or close to it. We just have to wait and see how she does now, and of course how long she remains in the coma. Actually, we want her pretty subdued now, and she's being medicated accordingly. She needs that to allow her brain to repair, but in a few weeks we'll need to reevaluate her position."

"A few weeks?" Brad looked horrified. "You expect her to stay in a coma for a few weeks?"

"It's possible . . . and not unlikely. In fact, longer than that wouldn't rule out a successful result, Mr. Clarke. This kind of injury requires a lot of patience." Brad rolled his eyes and the surgeon smiled, and then looked down at Page. "She did fine, Mrs. Clarke," he said gently, "she's not out of danger yet, by any means, but we're one step further, one more day, she survived one more enormous trauma. It's an encouraging sign. Of course we still have to wait to see the extent of her recovery, what lasting impact the trauma may have had, if any. But we're still a long way from there." They still had to wait and see if she even survived it. She could still die very easily, and they all understood that. "She'll be in the recovery room overnight again. You may want to go home. We can call you there if there's any problem."

"Do you expect there to be?" Page asked in a choked voice, and the surgeon hesitated for an instant before he answered.

"No, but we have to be realistic. This is

her second major surgery in four days, she's withstood a great deal of trauma, both in surgery and from the accident. This adds further jeopardy to her status, until she stabilizes of course. She's doing well, but we're watching her very closely."

"More so than after the last operation?" Page asked, and he nodded.

"She's weaker than she was. But we're hopeful about the outcome."

"Hopeful." Page had come to hate the word, and she had understood what he was saying. Allie was doing well, but the operation might have been too much for her. She could still die at any moment.

He left them after a few minutes and Brad sighed and sat down, and looked at her. They were like two people who had almost drowned and were lying breathless on the beach after the terror of it.

"It knocks the shit out of you, doesn't it? I feel like I climbed Everest today, and all I did was sit here," Brad said miserably.

"I'd rather be climbing Everest," Page said sadly, and he smiled at her.

"So would I. But she did okay. That's all we can ask for right now." He thought of all the things he had said about not wanting her to survive if she was going to be seriously brain damaged, and suddenly he knew he didn't care. He just wanted her to live . . . just for another hour . . . another day . . . and maybe in the end, they'd get lucky. "Do you want to come home?" he asked, but Page shook her head.

"I want to stay here."

"Why? They won't let you see her, you know. And they said they'd call us if there's a problem."

"I just feel better being here." She couldn't put it into words, but she knew she had to be there. It had been that way when Andy was in the incubator too. There were times when she knew she had to be near him. And she felt that way now. Whether they let her see Allie in the recovery room or not, she wanted to be there, in the hospital, near her. "You should go home to Andy though. He must be worried." After his nightmare the night before, they were both more concerned about him than they had been. That afternoon she had even called his pediatrician, who said that the anxiety and the nightmares were to be expected. Allie's accident was as traumatic for him as for them, possibly even more so. The doctor had also told Page how sorry he was about Allyson's condition.

"Are you sure you don't want me to stay here with you?" Brad asked quietly before he left her, but she shook her head and thanked him. It had been difficult sitting there with him all day, there was so much she wanted to say, so many questions she wanted to ask him. How long had it been this way? Why had he lied? . . . why wasn't she enough? . . . didn't he love her? It was pointless though, and she knew it. She forced herself not to say anything. But her stomach hurt all afternoon. He looked as handsome as he always had, except that he was no longer hers, he was someone else's. And when she looked at him, it was like looking at a stranger. They had been polite to each other all day, and she'd been glad he was there, but they didn't really dare talk to each other anymore, not about anything that mattered.

"Tell Andy I love him," she said as he left. He nodded, waved, and was gone, and told her he'd call her in the morning. And then she went back to her vigil in the quiet room, realizing that Brad had neither touched her nor kissed her when he left. Somehow, the connection between them had been broken.

Trygve stopped in to see her briefly in the

waiting room with Bjorn, but he could see she wasn't in the mood for conversation. She looked worried and sad, and Bjorn wanted to know where her daughter was, and if her legs were hurt like Chloe's. She explained to him that Allie's head was hurt and not her legs, and he said he had had a headache once too, and he was very sorry to hear it about Allie.

They left Page some sandwiches, and Trygve squeezed her arm as they left, and looked at her. She looked very small and thin and very tired. "Hang in there," he said softly. She nodded, as tears filled her eyes, but once she was alone again, she felt more peaceful. Sometimes people's kindness made it worse. She cried every time they said how sorry they were about Allie.

It was a long night as she lay on the couch in the small room, and she had more time to think than she had had in a long time. She thought about Brad and how happy they had been . . . about when Allie had been born, and how sweet she had been. She closed her eyes and saw herself in their house in the city. It had been a mess when they bought it, but she had fixed it up, and it was beautiful by the time they sold it. She thought about the house in Marin, and when Andy was born, so terrifyingly tiny. But again and again, her thoughts went back to Allyson. It was as though the child she had been were standing in the room . . . the things she had said . . . the way she had looked . . . and Page was not surprised when the nurse came to get her just after midnight. It was as though she knew. She had felt Allyson in the room with her, and when the nurse opened the door, Page was instantly on her feet and knew that she was needed.

"Mrs. Clarke?"

"Yes?" It was like something in a dream, she couldn't believe this was happening to her, but it was. She couldn't deny it.

"Allyson is having complications from the surgery."

"Has the surgeon been called?" Page's face was very white as she asked her.

"He's on his way now. But I thought you might like to see her. She's still in recovery, but I'll take you up if you like."

"I'd like that . . ." And then, she looked at her honestly. "Is she . . . is she dying?"

The nurse hesitated, but only for a moment. "She seems to be fading . . . she's not doing well, Mrs. Clarke, I think she might be." And so did the recovery room

nurses. They had called the surgeon immediately but they didn't even think she'd be
alive by the time he got there.

"Do I have time to call my husband?"
She was surprised at the sound of her own
voice. She felt strangely calm, as though
now she knew what to expect. She had been
waiting for this, without knowing. She had
been there when Allie had been born, and
now she would be there when she left. Her
eyes filled with tears, but she felt calm as
the nurse shook her head and walked to the
elevator with her.

"I think you'd better get upstairs. We'll
call your husband for you if you like. We've
got the number." She hated for him to hear
it from a nurse, it would have been kinder
to call him herself, but she didn't want to
miss Allie. This wasn't a moment that
would come again, and she wanted to say
good-bye to her. She knew now that no
matter how far away she seemed, Allie
would hear her.

They put a gown and mask on her just
outside the recovery room and she followed
another nurse inside, and then she saw her.
She lay surrounded by machines, her head
swathed in bandages as it had been before,
but suddenly now she looked very small and

peaceful. "Hi, sweetheart," Page whispered as she stood next to her. She was crying but she wasn't sad suddenly, she was just happy to see her. "Daddy and I love you so much . . . I want you to know that . . . and so does Andy. He misses you, and so do I . . . we all do . . . we miss you a lot . . . but I know that you're always with us . . ." A nurse brought her a stool then and she sat down, and took one of Allie's hands in hers. It seemed very frail and clawlike. Her fingers were rigid and her arms were stiff, which was part of the reaction from her brain being so disturbed. It was also part of why Page hadn't wanted Andy to see her. The results of the accident were just too upsetting.

"We called your husband," a nurse whispered to her, as Page quietly held Allie's hand and stroked it.

"Is he coming?" Page asked calmly. She didn't feel frightened anymore, she just felt peaceful, and closer than she ever had to Allie. They were together now, mother and child, bonded forever, in a moment that meant as much, in its own way, as her birth had. In some ways, this was no different. It was a beginning, and an end. They had completed the circle. Sooner than they'd planned. But they were still there together.

"He said he didn't want to leave your son." Page nodded, knowing he could have called Jane, but he was afraid to come and she understood that. She accepted it now. Brad did not want to face this moment. The nurse touched Page's shoulder then and gave her a little squeeze. She had seen a lot of this, but it was never easy, particularly with children.

"Allie?" Page whispered to her then. "Sweetheart . . . everything's okay . . . don't be scared . . . and I'll always be here if you need me." She had wanted to tell her that. Allyson had always been reluctant about new places, and now she was going to one, and Page couldn't be there to help her. But she would be with her in spirit, just as Allyson would stay with her mother.

"Mrs. Clarke?" It was Dr. Hammerman, she hadn't heard him approach her. "We're losing her," he said softly.

"I know." She was crying and didn't even know it. She looked at him with a smile and a look in her eyes that tore his heart out.

"We did everything we could. The damage is very great. I thought maybe she'd make it this afternoon, but . . . I'm

sorry . . ." He stood nearby, not to in-
trude, and kept an eye on the monitors. He
checked her pulses himself, looked at several tapes from the monitors, and consulted
with the nurses. He didn't think she would
last more than a few minutes. And he felt
very sorry for the mother. "Mrs. Clarke?"
he asked finally. "Can we do anything? Is
there anything you'd like? A priest?"

"We're fine," she said, remembering perfectly the first moment she had held her.
She had been so firm and round, a perfect
little ball with a bright pink face, and a fuzz
of blond hair. Despite the ordeal her birth
had been, Page had laughed and held out
her arms the minute she saw her. Thinking
of it made her smile now, and she turned
back to Allyson and told her the story, as
she had a thousand times, as two nurses
wiped their eyes and went to attend to another patient.

The surgeon continued to keep an eye on
her, and it was an hour after he arrived
when he checked the monitors again, and
found that nothing had changed. She had
not improved, but she was no worse. From
somewhere deep within, Allie was fighting.

Page just went on sitting there, holding
her hand, and talking quietly to her. In her

heart, she had opened the doors, and let her go. She had no right to hang on to her, if she wasn't meant to keep her. She was like an angel now, and just being near her made Page feel happy.

"I love you, sweetheart." She couldn't say it often enough, it was as though she needed to tell her a thousand times before she left them. "I love you, Allie . . ." A part of Page still expected her to wake up and smile, and say, "I love you, too, Mom," but she knew she wouldn't.

Dr. Hammerman kept a close watch on her, and now and then he felt her hands, adjusted a machine, checked the respirator, and then he left them. Page had been there for almost two hours by then, and she was almost sorry Brad hadn't come. He needed to say good-bye to her too. She was startled when Dr. Hammerman approached her, and spoke to her in a whisper.

"Do you see that machine?" He pointed to one of the monitors as Page nodded. "Her pulse is getting stronger again. She gave us quite a scare . . . but I have to tell you, I think she's turning around on us." Page's eyes filled with tears and all she could think of was the time Allyson had fallen in a swimming pool and almost drowned. By the time she got her hands on her all she wanted to do was spank her for the terrible fright she had given them. She looked at her now, grinning through her tears, wishing that she were well enough to shake or spank or kiss or hold or cry with.

"Are you sure?"

"Let's watch her."

Page continued to sit next to her, and talked to her, she reminded her of the swimming pool and how scared they had been. Allie had only been four or five. And then she gave her mother another scare, riding her bike into traffic in Ross when Page was pregnant with Andy. She told her that story too, and reminded her again and again how much she loved her.

And as the sun came up slowly over the Marin hills, Allyson seemed to almost sigh and settle into a peaceful sleep. It was as though she had been somewhere and back, and now she was very tired. Page could almost feel her move into a different space. There was no longer that ephemeral feeling of her leaving them. She had settled in again, and decided not to desert them.

"My business is filled with miracles," Dr. Hammerman said with a slow smile, and the nurses stood nearby whispering and watching. They had all been sure the Clarke girl would be gone before morning. "This young lady has a lot of fight. She's not ready to give up yet . . . and neither am I."

"Thank you," Page said, her emotions overwhelming her. It had been the most extraordinary night of her life. She had been terrified, and yet not afraid at all. She had known Allie was leaving them, and yet she was happy for her, and relieved, even though it was sad for them. She had almost felt her leaving this place, and then returning to them. And as she looked at her, and kissed her daughter's fingertips, she knew that nothing would ever frighten her again. She felt more peaceful than she had in years. They had been blessed, and as Page finally left the hospital to go home, she was awestruck by the power of the blessing. She had felt the hand of God near them all night, and she had felt safer than she ever had before, and as though Allyson were safe forever.

Page was more grateful than she had ever been, and completely at peace as she drove home to Ross in the early morning sunlight.

CHAPTER 9

For the rest of the day, Page felt as though her life had been transformed. She had never felt as light or as happy. It was impossible to explain, or to describe, but it was as though she would never be afraid again, or unhappy. The miseries around her didn't matter anymore, she felt overwhelmingly calm, and at peace with the world around her.

Even Brad could see a change. She didn't look tired or upset, and although she had been awake all night, she looked refreshed and almost luminous as she made them breakfast.

He was deeply relieved that Allyson had

269

made it through the night, and he was immediately moved by what Page told him. He
took Andy to school, and told Page he'd see
her at dinner that night. And after he left,
she called her mother, and told her the latest news of Allyson. Her mother offered to
come out again, and once again seemed to
miss the point about everything, but for
once it didn't bother Page. She still felt
peaceful and happy when she hung up and
promised to call again in a few days. She
had never felt as close to Allyson, and she
knew without a moment's doubt that Allie
was safe and in God's hands. For once Page
didn't feel as though she had to be at the
hospital every moment.

She took a shower and went to bed, and
fell into a deep sleep, and she awoke in
time to dress and stop at the hospital briefly
before she picked up Andy. Allyson was
back in the ICU by then, and Page felt as
though they had taken a long voyage together the night before. She sat down next
to her and took her hand in her own, and
spoke softly.

"Hello,   sweetheart . . . welcome
back . . ." She knew that somewhere Allie
would know what she meant, in her heart,
in her soul, wherever it was that they had

been together. "I love you an awful lot . . . you fooled me last night. I'm glad you did though." She could almost feel Allie smile, it was a warmth deep in her heart. It was as though she could feel her now, as though they could communicate without words but only with feelings. "I need you here, Allie . . . we all do . . . you've got to hurry up and get well now. We miss you." She sat and talked to her for a while, and felt perfectly at ease when she left her.

Trygve was just on his way into the hospital when she was leaving, and he noticed the change in her. There was a fresh bounce in her step, her hair looked great, and she was smiling broadly for the first time in days.

"My God, what happened to you?"

"I don't know . . . we'll talk about it sometime."

"How is she?" He looked concerned.

"Better. The same. She came through the surgery yesterday, and after a little scare last night, they say she's stable, that's something." But there was much more to tell, it was just too much to try to say in a hallway. "Chloe's asleep, by the way, I just saw her. But she was awake when I came in. She was complaining a lot, which must be a good sign, and she looks better."

"Thank God. Are you coming back?" he asked with interest.

She shook her head. "I don't think so. I want to pick Andy up and take him to baseball. And I thought I'd try and stay home for dinner, unless Miss Allyson pulls our chain again." But Page felt absolutely certain she wouldn't. Whatever happened, she knew that another moment like that would never come again. Something like that happened once in a lifetime.

"I'll see you tomorrow then." He looked disappointed. They kept each other company in ICU, and brightened the difficult moments.

"I'll be in after I drop Andy off at school in the morning." She smiled and left him then, and went to pick up Andy.

They had a nice time that afternoon, and he did well at the game, although not as well as usual. He was still upset, but even he responded to Page's calm, and he cuddled up next to her in the car with an ice cream. It reminded her suddenly of Saturday. It was hard to believe that only five days before, their lives had been normal. It had been five days since the accident, four since the bottom had fallen out of her life with Brad, and it felt like a lifetime.

He didn't come home for dinner that night, but this time he called and said he had to work late at the office, and it would be "easier" to stay in the city. She knew what that meant, but at least he had called her and she wouldn't worry, and she could give some excuse to Andy. She was surprised by how little it bothered her. She was happy to be at home with her son, and relieved that there had been no additional crisis with Allie.

She put Andy to bed and called Jane, who had gathered a very disturbing piece of information. She had talked to a friend of hers in the city that day, a woman who had known Laura Hutchinson for years. She said she'd had a drinking problem ever since she was in her teens. She had gotten treatment for it years before, and as far as the friend knew, she hadn't slipped since then. "But what if something's changed?" Jane asked in a worried tone. "What if she's drinking again, or drank that night?" They would never know. Page listened to what Jane said, and mulled it over. It was all gossip, all conjecture, all wanting to blame someone. But none of it would change what had happened.

"She's probably clean," Page said in a spirit of fairness.

"If she isn't, you'll be reading about it one of these days in the tabloids," Jane said. "The papers certainly seemed interested in her when it happened."

"I hope for her sake that's not the case," Page said quietly. "I hope she's fine. I don't think gossip helps anyone."

"I just thought you'd be interested in hearing her history," Jane said. She'd been very excited by the information. What if it had been the older woman's fault, and not Phillip's?

"It's not really fair to judge her by a problem she had that long ago," Page said to her friend. "Anyway, thanks for the information."

"I'll let you know if I hear anything else." And then they exchanged the usual information about Allie. There never seemed to be time to talk about anything else these days, and afterward Page paid some bills and caught up on some mail. It was the first time all week that she had taken a few moments to catch up on things, and it felt good to do that.

The next morning she took Andy to school, and then went back to the hospital to see Allie. In the past two days, she felt as though she had accomplished some things. She had spent some time with Andy, which he had needed desperately. And she felt calmer than she had before. She knew now that if this was going to be a long haul, she'd have to keep her wits about her, and her strength up.

Allie was still holding her own when Page got to the hospital shortly before nine o'clock in the morning and the nurses all smiled cautiously when they saw her. They all knew how close Allyson had come to dying the night of her surgery, and suddenly it made every moment, every day, more of a gift and infinitely more precious.

"How is she?" Page asked hesitantly. She had called several times since the night before, and they had assured her that nothing had changed. She was still stable.

"About the same." The nurse smiled at her. She was a woman about the same age as Page with a good head, a warm heart, and a great sense of humor. Her name was Frances. "Dr. Hammerman saw her an hour ago, and he seemed satisfied with her progress."

"Has the swelling gone down any?" It was impossible to see under the enormous dressing, but she seemed to be resting more peacefully, and her color was a little better.

"A little bit. The surgery seems to have reduced the pressure." Page nodded and sat down next to her, she took Allie's hand as she always did, and began speaking to her softly. There was no visible change since the day before, but Page still felt better about everything. She was better able to accept what was happening, and she was even less angry with Brad. She couldn't explain why, but she knew she had changed after her experience the other night with Allie.

When Trygve showed up at ten with a bag of croissants for her, he noticed the change in her again too.

"You look happier than you have all week," Trygve said with a smile. "It's nice to see it." People had a remarkable way of adjusting to anything. He felt better himself, after six days of visiting Chloe. She was being moved out of ICU that afternoon, and in a few more weeks she'd come home. It had been a long week, but at least they had all gotten through it.

Page waved when they left the ICU, and when she left the hospital later that day, she stopped in to see Chloe. She was less groggy now, although she was still in considerable pain. But her room was filled with flowers, and a few of her closest friends had come to see her. Trygve was standing outside the room, taking a breather and leaving the kids to visit without him. It was the first time Chloe had seen friends since the accident. Until then she had only seen her father and brothers. Jamie Applegate had called and asked to see her too, and Trygve had asked him to wait another day until the weekend. Jamie had been very polite to him, very concerned, and he was very anxious to see Chloe. The largest bouquet of all, which arrived the moment she moved into her room, was from Jamie and his parents.

"Things are looking up." Page smiled at him. It was nice to see him looking relieved and more cheerful.

"I'm not so sure." Trygve smiled ruefully. "Maybe phase two won't be so easy. She wants her music, her friends, she wants to go home next week, which is impossible, and she wants me to wash her hair." But they both knew how thrilled he was to be having these problems, and not those related to her survival.

"You're very lucky," Page said with a quiet smile. She would have liked to have the same problems he did.

"I know," he said gently. "I hear you almost lost Allie the night of the surgery." One of the nurses had told him the whole story.

She nodded, not quite sure how to explain it to him without sounding crazy. "It was the strangest experience I've ever had. I knew what was happening. I felt it before they even called me. I was sure she was about to die, and so were they . . . I've never felt closer to her . . . I remembered every day, every hour, every minute . . . I thought of things I'd forgotten for years, and then suddenly I could feel things change . . . I could feel her come back from a great distance. And I've never felt anything as powerful, or as peaceful. It was incredible." She still felt awed by it, and he could see it in her eyes as she told him.

"You hear about things like that . . . thank God she came back," he said, looking at Page, almost wishing he could have been there with her. The nurse had also told him they'd called Brad, and he had never come to be with her.

"She surprised us all," Page said with a warm smile.

"I hope she continues to do that."

"Me too," Page said softly.

"How's Andy holding up?"

"Not so great. He's been having night-mares," she lowered her voice not to em-barrass him, even though he wasn't there, but he would have hated anyone to know, "and wetting the bed. I think he's really shaken up over all this, but I don't want him to see her."

"I agree." Allie still looked terrible. No matter how stable her situation had become since the second surgery, she still looked terrifying to those who saw her. Even Chloe had been shocked the first time she had been aware of it, and she had sobbed when she understood it was Allie. At first, she hadn't even known it. "It would be too trau-matic for him."

"Actually, he's having a hard time with us too." She hesitated for a long moment, star-ing down the hall, and then she looked up at him. "Things are getting pretty rough with Brad, and Andy knows it. He's not coming home much these days. He . . . uh . . . actually, he's talking about moving out," she said almost calmly. There was the smallest tremor in her voice as she said it, but she surprised herself by how smoothly she said the words. After sixteen years, he was leaving her. In fact, for all intents and purposes he had already left her. He had called her that morning and told her not to expect him home for the weekend.

"Poor kid. That's a lot to handle all in one week," Trygve said emphatically.

"Yeah, except I haven't told him. But he knows something's up, and he's very worried."

"I didn't mean Andy when I said 'poor kid,' I meant you. You've really been through it. At first it just sounded like Brad was hysterical after the accident, but it sounds like things are a little more complicated than that." He was sorry to hear it.

"They are. He's been involved with someone else for eight months. He seems to be in love with her. I missed that somehow. Too busy doing murals and car pools, I guess." She tried to make light of it, but she didn't convince him. He stood very near her, and watched her.

"I know what that feels like, and it's not good," he said softly.

She shrugged, wanting to make light of it, but she couldn't. "I didn't even suspect

. . . can you imagine that? I feel so stupid. . . ." And hurt, and cheated, and bereft . . . and lonely.

"We're all stupid sometimes. Those things are pretty hard to face. Everyone in Marin County knew about Dana, and I was still trying to pretend we had a marriage."

"Yeah . . . me too. . . ." Her eyes were damp when she looked at him and he wished he could put his arms around her. But it was different somehow when they were talking about Brad, and not Allie. "It's funny how it all happens at once . . . Allie . . . Brad . . . it's kind of a shock . . . and poor Andy is trying to cope with all of it. So am I, but I'm supposed to be the grown-up."

"Forget that, kick him in the shins if you want to." She laughed at the idea, and the image.

"I think we just about did for most of this week. I can't believe how bad it was, and then when Allie almost died, suddenly I got a different perspective . . . it didn't seem quite as catastrophic anymore, Brad I mean, it's just something we have to resolve . . . and the accident is something I have to live through. I feel stronger now, though I'm not quite sure why."

"You look it. The mind is an extraordinary thing. We always find the resources we need there." She nodded, feeling comfortable and close to him, and he looked at her almost shyly then with a question. "What are you and Andy doing tomorrow afternoon?"

"I'm not sure, he doesn't have a baseball game for once, and I was going to leave him with my neighbor. Brad won't be around but I haven't told Andy yet. I don't want to leave Allie alone all day. I really hadn't figured it out yet. Why? What were you thinking?"

"I was thinking that it would be nice if the two of you came for lunch. Bjorn loves kids Andy's age, and they might get along okay. If they do, you could leave him with me when you go to the hospital, and pick him up again after dinner, or even come back and join us." It was quite an invitation, and she was touched that he had asked her.

"That sounds like a lot of trouble for you. Are you sure you want us? What about Chloe?"

"I promised Bjorn we'd come over tomorrow morning and see her, and then go home and play. Two of Chloe's friends said they would visit and Jamie's going to visit her too. I thought I'd come back again in the evening."

"Sounds like a full day for you." She was hesitating, but his eyes pleaded with her to come. He enjoyed her company, and he liked the boy, and they both needed a break from the grimness of the situation. It had been a rough week for both of them, and he knew she needed a breather as much as he did.

"Honestly, Page, we'd enjoy it . . . and maybe Andy would too." It might also distract him from wanting his father.

"I'd enjoy it too," she said softly. "Okay . . . and thank you. . . ."

The two girls who'd been visiting Chloe left the room, which was his signal to go back in, and he told her to come at noon the next day, with Andy.

"And tell him to bring his mitt. Bjorn loves to play baseball."

"I'll tell him." She smiled and waved, and then she went home and told Andy about the plans, and that Brad had to go away for the weekend on business.

"On *Saturday* and *Sunday*?" he asked suspiciously, but he didn't question her further.

She tried to explain Bjorn to him, and he

wasn't frightened but intrigued. He knew Bjorn, but he'd never played with him before. He said there was a boy like him at school, but they had put him in special classes.

But she and Andy were both surprised by how smoothly it all went the next day. Bjorn had helped to make lunch, he had made really good hamburgers and french fries, and Trygve had made hot dogs and potato salad, and sliced tomatoes. Nick had gone back to school at USC, but Bjorn said he made the best hot dogs in the whole family, much better than their Dad's. He said it with great seriousness, and Andy laughed toothlessly, and helped himself to a hot dog.

"What happened to your teeth?" Bjorn asked, intrigued.

"They fell out," Andy explained, looking nonplussed. He understood better about Bjorn now, and didn't think it remarkable that he had Down syndrome. He was intrigued by the fact that he was eighteen though. He was the oldest child Andy had ever played with.

"Will the dentist give you new ones?" Bjorn asked with continued interest. "I broke one last year, and the dentist fixed it." He showed Andy which one, and Andy nodded solemnly, it looked just like the others.

"No, mine will just grow back in. Yours probably did at my age, too. You just don't remember."

"Yeah. Maybe I wasn't paying attention." Page and Trygve were watching them, intrigued. They were getting on splendidly, like two old pals, sitting on deck chairs in the spring sunshine. "You play baseball?" Bjorn asked, looking at him.

"Yup," Andy said with another smile, helping himself to a hamburger this time.

"Me too. I like bowling too. You like bowling?"

"I've never been," Andy confessed. "My Mom says I'm not big enough yet. She says the balls are too heavy."

Bjorn nodded. It made sense to him. "They're heavy for me too, but my Dad takes me. . . . Sometimes I go with Nick . . . or Chloe. Chloe's sick. She broke her leg last week. But she'll be coming home soon."

"Yeah," Andy nodded, looking serious, "my sister's sick too. She hit her head in a car accident."

"Did she break it?" Bjorn looked sorry

for him, it was bad when your sister was hurt. He had cried when he'd gone to see Chloe.

"Yeah, sort of. I haven't been to see her yet, she still feels too yucky."

"Oh." Bjorn was pleased that they had a common bond. They both liked to play baseball, and had sick sisters. "I'm in the Special Olympics. My Dad does it with me."

"That's nice. What do you do there?" Bjorn explained to him how much he loved basketball and long jump, as Trygve and Page walked away and sat down across the garden.

"I'd say it's a hit." Trygve smiled. "Andy is just about the right age. Bjorn is somewhere between ten and twelve, but he has a real soft spot for younger kids. Andy's a nice boy." Trygve had been touched by the warm, respectful way Andy had talked to Bjorn, and it was obvious that he liked him. "You're lucky."

"We both are. They're all good kids. I just wish that two young ladies we know hadn't told a lie last Saturday night and gotten themselves in a hell of a lot of trouble," she said, watching their brothers—it was hard to believe that only a week had gone by since fate had torn their lives apart stem to stern, and then thrown them together. All week she had bared her soul to him, and she had paid no attention at all to how he looked. But now she realized that he was actually very good-looking.

"Sometimes, I wish I could turn the clock back," he said quietly, and then looked at her. She had stretched out on a lounge chair, her hair fanned out on her shoulders, and her face turned to the sun. It felt wonderful to be there.

"I'm not sure turning the clock back is the answer . . . maybe ahead would be better, but very fast, so you get past all the bad parts." She smiled as she said it.

"The bad parts seem to take forever, don't they?" They both laughed, thinking how true that was.

"I wouldn't mind speeding up right now to the part where Allie gets better." She sighed, thinking about it.

"She will," he said encouragingly. She had lived a week past the accident, and as the doctors said, that was hopeful. "But it may be a long haul. Have you thought about that?"

"Nothing but. The doctor said it might be

years before she's 'normal,' whatever that is."

"It might. I don't know about those things, but I know what it was like with Bjorn. He wore diapers until he was six, and he still had accidents until he was eleven. I worried about street traffic constantly, he burned himself on the stove trying to cook something when he was twelve. It took a long, long time to get where he is now, and a lot of patience and hard work, on his part as well as mine, and off and on I had some great people to help me. You may need that too, you may have to start from scratch with Allie." He didn't say it, but they both knew that it was possible Allie would never be normal. She might be even less capable than Bjorn, if she recovered.

"It's pretty frightening to think about . . . but I'd rather have her that way than not at all."

"I know. I understand that." It was very comforting talking to someone who understood, and she hated to leave to go to the hospital that afternoon. But she didn't want to leave Allie alone, and she had promised to take some things to Chloe. She wanted magazines, cookies, and her makeup. She was definitely feeling better, and she said the food in the hospital was disgusting.

The boys were playing baseball on the front lawn when Page left for the hospital, and Trygve waved as she drove away. She felt happy for the first time in ages. No matter what else was happening, at least he was there for her, he had become a good friend, and her time with him was an island of calm in a sea of terror.

Everything was peaceful at the hospital that day. Allie was still deep in sleep, the respirator breathing for her, and her condition listed as critical but stable. Page sat next to her as she always did, talking quietly and telling her what was going on, and reminding her of how much they loved her. When she took a break from Allie, she went to Chloe's room, and found Jamie Applegate visiting her. He had brought a stack of CD's, his own player to lend to her, and another bunch of flowers. And he was extremely polite to Page and asked how soon he could visit Allie.

"Not for a while," she explained. It was too soon for her to have visitors and it would have been too upsetting to him. As a parent she knew that. She promised to let him know as soon as he could, and left the two young people listening to music.

Page went back to pick Andy up late that afternoon, the boys were screaming with laughter playing cards. They were playing slapjack, and they were both cheating, and Trygve was busy making dinner.

"I'm making my famous Norwegian stew, pasta, and Swedish meatballs."

"The meatballs are pretty good," Bjorn volunteered as he flew through the kitchen with Andy at his heels. They were on their way upstairs to watch a movie.

"I don't think Andy'll leave. You'll have to stay for dinner." Trygve grinned and she laughed, and offered to help him. She set the table for him, and cooked the pasta and some mushrooms. The stew actually smelled pretty good, and he let her try one of the meatballs. Bjorn was right. They were delicious. He was a good cook, a good friend, and fun to be with.

"How was Chloe?" he inquired, checking on his stew, and Page smiled.

"Fine. Jamie was there. He's a nice kid. He seems very nervous, and apologetic. But he brought her a stack of CD's and they were listening to music when I left." Her face got more serious then, as she thought of it. "It made me lonely for Allie. Just last week, a week ago tonight in fact, she was trying to con me out of my favorite sweater." The pink one had been destroyed, of course, it had been cut off her in shreds at Marin General. Tonight was the first time it had even crossed Page's mind. She didn't want her sweater back, just her daughter.

"I wish I could do something to make it easier for you," he said as they sat down at the kitchen table with a glass of wine, waiting for the stew.

"You already have. I don't think my life is going to be easy for a long time. At this rate, Brad'll move out sooner or later, and that'll be rough . . . especially on Andy . . . and me too . . . and whatever happens with Allie, that won't be easy either." It could be nightmarish, or at best it would take a long time, and be heartbreaking at times. But that was just the way life was sometimes, and she was willing to accept that. This week had taught her many things, among them acceptance, and patience.

"How do you think Andy will take it if Brad leaves?"

"I think it'll be pretty awful. And I don't think it's 'if' but 'when.' That's becoming pretty clear now."

"Kids surprise you sometimes. I think often they know things before we tell them."

"Maybe so." The boys ran through the kitchen again then, and both seemed to be having a great time with each other. Trygve called them to the table five minutes later.

"Meatball time, guys!" he called, and made them wash their hands when they got there. They said grace at the table, which surprised Page, but it was also comforting to hear it. It was a far cry from her own family when she'd been growing up. They had never said grace, and only went to church on major occasions. It startled her to discover that Trygve was religious.

"I go to Sunday school," Bjorn explained to his new friend. "They teach me about God. He's a nice guy. You'd like him." Page repressed a smile, as she glanced across the table at Trygve and he was smiling too.

The two boys chatted on, and Page and Trygve went outside afterward. It was Bjorn's job to clean up after dinner, and Andy stayed to help him.

"He's a great kid," she said as they sat down in chairs on the lawn. It was a beautiful evening, and there was a deep orange sunset on the Marin hills that they both watched for a long time in silence.

"He is," Trygve agreed. "Fortunately, Nick and Chloe think so too. One day they'll have to keep an eye on him, when I'm gone. I've thought about trying to put him in an apartment eventually, but I don't think he's ready."

It was something she might have to think about now too. If Allie wasn't able to take care of herself, one day Andy would have to be responsible for his sister. It was a problem that had never occurred to her before, but special children had special needs. Suddenly, there were whole new worlds for her to consider.

"It was fun having you here today." Trygve smiled. "We really enjoyed it, Page."

"So did we," she said softly. "You actually gave us a place to relax and have a good time, in the middle of this mess our life has turned into."

"It won't be a mess forever," he said knowingly, wanting to help her through it.

"It feels like it right now. I don't even know which way to turn. So much is changing so fast I can't even catch my breath anymore. And the things I thought were so important last week aren't even part of my life now. It's hard to know what to make of it," she said slowly, and he took her hand in his and held it. He didn't want to frighten her, and he knew this was the wrong time, but something about her kept making him want to protect her.

"You're doing all the right things. You just have to go step by step and move very slowly." But Page laughed at him.

"Believe me, I'm the only thing moving slowly right now. The rest of my life is falling apart so fast I don't even have time to pick up the pieces." He laughed at what she said, and they sat together and watched the sunset.

"Life seems so simple sometimes, but it's never as simple as it looks, is it?" he asked as the sun slipped slowly behind the hills. "We think we have everything worked out, and then the whole damn thing falls apart. The only good thing is that when we get it all put back together again, it's usually better."

"I wish I believed that," she said, looking at him, and liking what she saw there, he was genuine and whole and incredibly decent.

"I'm much happier than I used to be," he said honestly to her. "I never thought I would be, but I am. And I don't even give a damn if I get married again. I'd like to, I'd even like to have more kids, but you know what . . . if the right woman doesn't come along, I'm perfectly happy the way things are now. I'm happy with my kids, my work . . . I used to be half crazed all the time, trying to make things work with Dana . . . and I never quite could. She always managed to make it impossible, and I was always miserable and feeling like I'd failed. I don't feel that way anymore. I like my life. I feel good about myself and my kids. Pretty soon you'll feel that way too. You have wonderful children, you're talented as hell, and you're a great person. You deserve to be happy, Page, and one of these days, with or without a man, you will be."

"Would you sign that in blood, please? It would be reassuring."

"I'd love to. It'll get better, you'll see."

"I can hardly wait," she said softly, and he seemed to watch her for a long time. And then, he leaned toward her and suddenly she wondered if he was going to kiss her. But at that exact moment, the two boys exploded onto the lawn and wanted to play baseball.

"Nothing doing, you guys," Trygve said

firmly. The moment had passed, and Page wondered if she had dreamed it. "Bjorn, it's too late for baseball. Why don't you go inside and watch TV. Pretty soon it'll be bedtime." And then he turned to Page. "Do you want to leave Andy here tonight? Are you going back to the hospital?"

"I thought I'd go home, Brad said he might come over and get him tomorrow. If he does, I'll spend more time with Allie then. Are you going back tonight to see Chloe?" Their whole life had been taken over by trips to the hospital, and it took a lot of rearranging and juggling to meet everyone else's needs at the same time. At times it was utterly exhausting.

"I'll go back in a while," he said softly.

"We should go home," Page said regretfully, and they sat side by side for a while, comfortable in the night air, and at ease with each other. He didn't make a move toward her again, and on the way home, she decided that she'd imagined it. He was very independent, and he had his own life. And as Allyson had said the week before, and he had confirmed since, he seemed perfectly happy without a woman in his life. Dana had burned him very badly.

But now Brad had burned her too. And it

was odd to realize that she was actually attracted to Trygve. She had never even thought of it before, but after a week of being close to him so much, she had to admit that she thought he was not only good-looking, but appealing. She was thinking about him with a smile, in spite of herself, when Andy spoke up from the backseat and took her breath away with his question.

"Who is Stephanie?"

"What do you mean?" Her heart pounded at the question.

"I heard you shouting at Daddy about her the other day. And then I heard him call her."

"I think she's someone he works with," Page said, with absolutely no expression in her voice. Trygve was right. Kids knew more than one thought. She wondered just how much Andy had overheard the night of his nightmare.

"Is she nice?" he persisted.

"I don't know her." Page's voice had no expression.

"Then why did you shout at Daddy about her?" He was pressing her and she was getting angry.

"I wasn't shouting at Daddy, and I don't want to talk about this."

"Why not? She sounded nice on the phone."

"When?" Page felt a blow to her solar plexus. Even though she knew about her now, she didn't like hearing about her from Andy.

"She called yesterday, when you were at the hospital. She told me to tell Daddy she called."

"And did you?"

"I forgot. I hope he won't get mad at me."

"I'm sure he won't," Page said, but her face told its own tale, as she parked in the driveway and they walked into the empty house.

"Are *you* mad at me?" Andy asked worriedly as she helped him undress, and she had to take a deep breath and look at him. There was no point being angry at him for what his father was doing.

"No, sweetheart, I'm not mad at you. I'm just tired."

"You're always tired, Mommy . . . ever since Allie's accident."

"Well, it's been hard for all of us. You too. And I know that."

"Are you mad at Daddy?"

"Sometimes. Most of the time we're just

tired and worried about Allie. We're not mad at you. You have nothing to do with any of this."

"Are you mad at Stephanie?" He was trying to figure it all out, and he was bright for his age, brighter than he knew, as Page sighed at the question.

"I don't even know her." It was the truth. It was Brad she had to be angry at, Brad who had cheated on her, who had lied, who had broken her heart. It was all Brad's fault, not the fault of the girl he'd slept with. "I'm not really mad at anyone, sweetheart. Not even Daddy."

"Good." He smiled at her then, relieved, and she knew that soon they'd have to say something to him, particularly if Brad was going to move out in the near future. "I like Bjorn."

"Me too. He's a nice boy."

"He's the oldest friend I have. He's eighteen, and he's special."

"He is special," she smiled, "and so are you. I love you, sweetheart." She kissed him and put him to bed, and then she lay on the bed in her own room, thinking how life had changed in one brief week, how simple it had all been a week ago, with Allie out for dinner with the Thorensens, and Brad in Cleveland. It had all seemed so simple. And now it no longer was. The teenagers' lies had all but killed them.

CHAPTER 10

Page spent most of Sunday at the hospital, after leaving Andy at a school friend's. Brad had called that morning to say he didn't have time to see him. But after his initial disappointment, Andy had been happy to go to his friend's house.

Trygve visited Page at the ICU waiting room for a few minutes to bring her some sandwiches and cookies, and then went back to Chloe, who had visitors. She was reveling in seeing young people again, and it seemed to make her feel better.

"Bjorn was ecstatic about yesterday, by the way," Trygve told Page as he shared a sandwich with her outside the ICU. He seemed happy to see her, but she was convinced now that her illusion had been just that. He was friendly, but not romantic.

"So was Andy. He had a great time. He would have invited Bjorn over today, except that he had to go to a friend's. Brad called to tell him he couldn't see him."

"Bjorn had to do his homework anyway. How was Andy when Brad canceled?"

"Not great, but he adjusted."

They chatted for a little while, and then he went back to Chloe, and when Page went home that afternoon, she picked up Andy on the way home, and they stopped for ice cream. In a world where everything had changed overnight, the smallest rituals brought them both comfort.

And they were both surprised when Brad arrived shortly after they got home, and said he was staying for dinner. He asked how Allie was, and Page told him the truth. She was still alive, but there was still no improvement.

They ate dinner quietly in the kitchen, just the three of them, and she was startled afterward when she saw Brad packing a suitcase.

"Are you moving out?" she asked, sounding as though she was expecting it, which saddened both of them. In a mere eight days, this was where they had come to.

"I'm going to Chicago on business." He didn't tell her Stephanie was going with him. This time, she had insisted.

"When are you going?" she asked quietly, ready for anything.

"Tonight. I'm taking the red-eye."

"What about Allie?" What if she failed again? Could he live with that? But she already knew the answer to her question.

"I have to. There's an important deal I have to close." He said it calmly, and she couldn't stop herself.

"For real, or like the one in Cleveland?"

"Don't start that, Page," he said harshly, "I mean it."

"So do I." She no longer trusted him, but it was no longer an issue.

"I still have a job, you know. Accident or no, I still have to work. And my work takes me to other cities."

"I know that," she said, and left the room. He kissed Andy good-bye before he left, and left the name and number of his hotel on the pad in the kitchen. He was going for three days and she didn't really mind it. In some ways, his being gone would ease the tension between them.

"I'll be back on Wednesday," he said just before he left, and he said nothing more to her. Not "I love you." Not "good-bye." He just closed the door, and drove down the driveway. He had just enough time to pick Stephanie up on the way to the airport.

"Are you mad at him?" Andy asked nervously. He had heard their tone of voice when they talked, and he hated it. He had put his pillow over his ears so he didn't have to hear them in case they started yelling.

"No, I'm not mad at him," she confirmed, but her face said something different.

She read for a while after he left, trying not to think of all the things that had changed. There were too many to think of. She turned off the light and went to bed, after calling the hospital to check on Allie.

And the next morning, after dropping Andy off at school, she went to see her, and settled in for the day in ICU. Frances, the head nurse, knew her so well, she let her spend hours at Allie's bedside. It was becoming routine now. She had no other life, no other job, no other work, except ricocheting between Andy's needs, and her vigil at the hospital, and her fights with Brad whenever she saw him. It was incredibly claustrophobic.

She felt almost numb as she sat there, watching the machine breathe for Allie. They had taken the bandages off her eyes by then. And for an instant, she had thought she saw an eyelid move, but after watching intently for a long time, she realized that she had dreamed it. One saw things sometimes because one wanted to, but they weren't really there, they were illusions.

She sat back in her uncomfortable chair for a moment and closed her eyes, when Frances came to get her. She was waiting for the physical therapist to come so she could help move Allie's arms and legs. It was important to keep doing that so her muscles wouldn't atrophy, or her joints become too stiff to move. There was a lot to do, even with a patient in a coma.

"Mrs. Clarke?" Page jumped at the voice, startled.

"Yes?"

"There's a phone call for you. You can take it at the desk."

"Thank you." It was probably Brad, checking on Allyson from Chicago. He was the only person who knew where to find her, except Jane, and there was no reason for her to call. Andy was in school. But it turned out to be Ross Grammar School. They explained that they were sorry to disturb her, but it was an emergency, her son had just been injured.

"My son?" she said blankly, as though she didn't have one. Her whole body felt as though it were going into shock. "What do you mean?" Her whole being seemed to fill with panic.

"I'm sorry, Mrs. Clarke." It was the school secretary and Page scarcely knew her. "There's been an accident . . . he fell off the jungle gym . . ." Oh God, he was dead . . . he had broken his back . . . he had a head injury too . . . she started to cry. She couldn't go through this again. Didn't they understand that?

"What happened?" Her voice was barely audible, and one of the nurses was watching her face and saw her turn gray at what she was hearing.

"We think he may have broken his shoulder. He's on his way to Marin General now. If you go down to the emergency room, you'll be there to meet him."

"Fine." She hung up the phone without

saying good-bye and looked around her in panic. "My little boy . . . my son . . . he's had an accident . . ."

"Calm down . . . he's probably fine." Frances took charge instantly and led Page to a chair and got her a drink of water. "Take it easy, Page. He's going to be fine. Where is he?"

"He's on his way here, to the emergency room."

"I'll take you down there," the head nurse said calmly. She arranged to leave the floor and escorted Page to the emergency room. She looked terrible, and she was shaking visibly when they got there. But Andy hadn't come in yet.

Frances left Page in the care of the emergency room staff, and a moment later, Page disappeared and went to a pay phone. It was stupid of her, she knew, but for once in her life, she couldn't manage alone. She had to call him.

He answered on the second ring, and he sounded distracted. He was probably writing. She knew he had an article due for *The New Republic*. "Hello?" It was Trygve.

"I'm sorry . . . I had to call . . . there's been an accident at school . . ." For a moment, he didn't recognize her and he thought someone was calling about Bjorn, and then he realized who it was.

"Page? Are you all right? What happened?" She sounded awful.

"I don't know," she was crying into the phone, and making very little sense as he listened. "It's Andy . . . the school just called . . . he's hurt . . . he fell off the jungle gym . . ." She began to sob, imagining the worst again, and Trygve stood up as he listened.

"I'll come right over. Where are you?"

"I'm in the emergency room at Marin General." It was certainly a familiar place to them both by now, and he drove there at full speed. He pulled in just as Andy was being carried out of a car by a teacher. And he was quick to reach him. The boy looked frightened and pale and as though he was in pain, but he was very definitely conscious, and in no apparent danger.

"What are you doing here, young man? This place is for sick people. You look fine to me." Trygve examined him with his eyes as they chatted.

"I hurt my arm . . . and my back . . . I fell off the jungle gym," he said wanly as Trygve held the door open for the teacher. He looked like the P.E. teacher, in sweats and tennis shoes with a whistle around his neck, and he looked worried about Andy.

"Your Mom's inside waiting for you." He smiled gently, and followed them in, and he saw Page immediately. She looked terrible and she couldn't stop shaking. She started crying the moment she saw him. All the strength she had had for Allie had suddenly left her. Trygve put an arm around her and pulled her close to him, to stop the shaking, as the teacher carried the child into an examining room where a nurse was waiting to check his vital signs and examine the damage. She was cheerful and nice. At first she carefully examined him with her fingers. She could see that he had broken his arm and dislocated his shoulder. But she also looked into his eyes with a flashlight to check for a head injury.

"Wait a minute here," Trygve teased, "you're as big a mess as Chloe. She can't walk, and now you've got a broken arm . . . boy, you two. I'm going to let Bjorn take care of both of you." He grinned and Andy tried to smile through the pain, but the arm hurt a lot. They put him on a gurney to take him to X-ray, and Trygve stayed with Page every minute.

"He's going to be all right, Page. Take it

easy." He reassured her when they were doing the X ray.

"I don't know what happened," she said, still looking deathly pale and shaking. "I panicked . . . I'm really sorry I called you." But it was all she could think of when she'd heard. She needed Trygve to be there with her, just as he had been in those first nightmarish days with Allie, and ever since then. It was Trygve she wanted with her, not Brad, and realizing that surprised her. But she knew she could count on Trygve. And he was happy to be there.

"I'm not sorry you called. I'm just sorry this happened. But he'll be all right." The teacher had gone back to school by then, and Trygve stood with Andy and held his hand when they put his shoulder back in place and set the arm, which was pretty painful. They put the arm in a sling afterward and gave him something for the pain. They wanted him to go home and stay in bed for a day, and after that he'd be as good as new. The cast had to be on for six weeks. It was a pretty nasty break, but at his age they didn't think it would cause any long-term problems.

"I'll drive you two home," Trygve said quietly. He wouldn't have trusted Page with a tricycle at that point, let alone a car. Page agreed, but first she went back to ICU to get her bag and tell them she was leaving. Trygve also stopped by Chloe's room to give her a quick kiss and tell her he'd be back later. He told her what had happened to Andy and she sent him her love, and marveled at the bad luck that seemed to be following all of them lately.

"Tell him I'll sign his cast when I see him."

"I will . . . see you later . . ." Trygve hurried back to the emergency room and carried Andy out to the car. He was already half asleep from the shot they'd given him, and Page had pills to take home for him. He was going to sleep away the day, which was the best thing for him.

Trygve carried Andy into the house, while Page opened doors, and he helped her undress the boy and put him to bed. He scarcely woke up while they did it, and he was asleep before his head touched the pillow. But it wasn't Andy Trygve was worried about, it was Page. She looked awful.

"I want you to lie down, too. You look like hell."

"I just got startled, that's all . . . I didn't know what to expect . . . I thought . . ."

"I can see what you thought." She looked gray. "Come on . . . where's your bedroom?"

She led the way and he waited until she lay down on the bed with her clothes on. "I feel silly . . . I'm fine."

"You don't look it. Do you want a shot of brandy? It might do you good." But she smiled as she shook her head, and then sat up on her bed and looked at the man who had dropped everything and run to help her.

"Thank you for being a good friend. I didn't even think before I called you. I just knew I needed you there."

He sat down in a big easy chair near the bed, and looked at her kindly. "I'm glad you called me. You've been through enough." And then he had a thought, but it was interesting that she hadn't called him to begin with. "Do you want to call Brad?"

She shook her head without hesitation. "I'll call him later. He's in Chicago." And then she thought of something else. "I didn't even think about calling him when they called me in ICU." She wanted him to know that. "All I could think of was calling you . . . it was almost a reflex."

"That's an okay reflex to have," he said

gently, leaning closer to her. He was feeling things he hadn't felt in years, and she was confused by her own emotions as she watched him. "Page . . . I don't want to do anything you don't want . . ." he whispered, but suddenly it was all he could do to keep himself away from her. He felt the power of a magnet as he watched her, and she realized that she hadn't been imagining it the other night in the garden. He had been about to kiss her. As he was now. As he had wanted to for days, as they sat together, night after night, and day after day, in their unhappy vigil.

"I don't know what I want, Trygve." She raised her big blue eyes to his honestly. "Ten days ago I thought I was happily married . . . then I find out it's all a lie, and my marriage is probably over . . . and in the midst of it all, there you are, the only person I've been able to depend on in years, the only friend I have who knows what I'm feeling . . . the only man I want to be with," she whispered, looking at him as he moved closer. "I don't know where I am, or what I'm doing, or what's going to happen . . . I don't know anything . . . except . . . I just don't know . . ." Her voice drifted off in confusion, as she watched

him, but she didn't stop him as he moved
closer.

"Shh . . . you don't have to say anything
. . . don't . . ." he whispered, and sat on
the edge of her bed, and took her in his
arms. All he wanted was to hold her as he
hadn't held anyone in years, and kiss her.
His lips pressed down against hers, and his
tongue gently parted them and moved inside, as she felt her breath catch, and their
bodies almost melt together. She was overwhelmed by what she felt, and frightened at
the same time, but she knew she wanted
him. This was not a game, or a revenge on
Brad . . . this was someone who had been
there for her at the worst time in her life,
who hadn't let her down for a single moment, and whom she felt overwhelmingly
drawn to.

"What are we going to do?" she asked as
he moved away from her again, and sat
looking at her in all her flushed blond
beauty.

"Let's not worry about it right now. At
least I know what to do to get some color
back in your face. You look a lot better."
He smiled, looking very happy.

"Stop that!" She swatted him gently, but
he pulled her back in his arms again, and

this time he kissed her harder. He hadn't felt anything like this since long before Dana, if ever.

"I will not stop. I will never stop," he informed her. "I'd forgotten it could be like this."

"So had I," she said honestly. Brad had always been so self-involved that she realized now how little he'd ever given her, emotionally or physically. Trygve took her breath away, and she giggled as they kissed again. It was a good thing Andy was sedated, but she also knew that neither of them was ready to do anything foolish. She had to settle her life with Brad before she started anything serious with Trygve, and he knew that. But this certainly changed things.

"What am I going to do?" she asked him honestly, swinging her legs back to the floor again, and looking at him like a little kid as he smiled at her. She couldn't ever remember being this happy.

"You'll figure it out eventually. It sounds like things are taking care of themselves. And I'm not rushing you . . . I want you to know that." He tried to look serious, but he found he couldn't. "I'll just stand here panting and making a pest of myself until you decide you can't live without me." They both knew that this was more than just kissing.

She grinned mischievously and this time she kissed him. The whole thing was amazing. "How did this happen?" she asked when they finally parted.

"I'm not sure. Maybe it's something in the air at ICU." Or trauma or pain or fear, or being there for each other. He had made a tremendous difference, and she had made a difference to him too. They had been through the worst that life had to offer, and they had survived it, together, with very little help from anyone else, particularly Brad, who had done everything he could to hurt her.

"Life is amazing, isn't it?" she asked him, awed by what had happened. "I guess we'll just have to take this one step at a time. Brad hasn't figured out what he wants to do yet."

"He probably has, but he hasn't told you. What about you? Do you know what *you* want to do?" Did she want him to move out? A divorce? More time to think it out? He wasn't actually sure what she wanted, he wasn't sure she was either, which was normal. The demise of their marriage was very new to her, and she didn't know what to do yet.

"Every time I see Brad, I realize how impossible it is. He's practically living with that woman. But I'm still married to him. It's hard to change all that in a single moment."

"No one expects you to," he said gently. He understood it all perfectly. He had been there himself. And he was willing to wait patiently while she sorted her life out. He had never met anyone like her.

They were still talking when the phone rang, and Page jumped. She couldn't imagine who was calling, unless it was the hospital about Allie. She couldn't take any more bad news though, and she closed her eyes as she answered. She felt Trygve's hand on hers, giving her strength if it was needed.

"Hello?" she said cautiously, as though she was afraid to hear it. And then she opened her eyes and shook her head. It wasn't the hospital, it was her mother. And her news wasn't good either. She had been thinking about it all weekend, and she and Alexis had decided to visit. It was obvious to them that Page needed help, even though she assured them she didn't.

"We're fine. Honestly," she insisted, "everything's in control, and for the moment, Allyson's condition is stable."

"That could change at a moment's notice. Alexis wants to talk to you anyway. David gave her the name of a fabulous plastic surgeon, if you need it." They would eventually, but it was the least of their worries now. First Allie had to live, and then her brain had to recover something approaching normal function. But Alexis only had one thing on her mind: her niece's looks, and making sure that everything was perfect.

"I really think you shouldn't come out," Page said, trying to sound calm, but she wasn't. The last thing she needed right now was her mother, let alone Alexis.

"Don't argue with me," she said firmly. "We'll be there on Sunday."

"Mother . . . you can't . . . I have no time to take care of you . . . or Alexis. I need to be with Allie, and Andy just had an accident." She wanted to do everything she could to dissuade her.

"*What?*" For once her mother sounded ruffled.

"It's nothing serious, he broke his arm. But I really need to spend all my time with the children."

"That's why we're coming, dear. We want to help you."

Page sighed, listening to her. She didn't know what more to say. "I really think you should reconsider."

"We'll be there on Sunday at two o'clock. Alexis will have David fax Brad the details. I'll see you then." And before Page could say another word, she hung up, and Page sat staring at Trygve.

"You won't believe this," she said miserably.

"Let me guess. Your mother's coming from the East. Will that be difficult for you?"

"Difficult? Are you kidding? How was Samson for Delilah? . . . or maybe David for Goliath? . . . or the asp for Cleopatra? Difficult doesn't even begin to touch it. I've been trying to keep her at bay for a week. And not only is she coming out, but she's bringing my sister."

"Whom you hate?" he asked, trying to catch up on family history all in one lesson.

"Who hates me . . . but most of her energies she spends on loving herself. She is completely narcissistic. She's never had kids and she's married to a plastic surgeon in New York. At forty-two, she has had her eyes done twice, three noses, new breasts, liposuction everywhere, and a full face-lift. Everything about her is perfect. The nails, the face, the hair, the clothes, the body. She spends every moment of every day taking care of herself. She has never taken care of a living, breathing soul in her life, and neither has my mother. Let me explain the scenario to you. They are coming out so I can take care of them, and reassure *them* that there's nothing wrong with Allie, and if there is, it won't hurt, embarrass, inconvenience, or affect them."

"You don't make them sound very helpful," he said, kissing the tip of her nose, and amused at how she described them. His own parents were wonderful, and had been offering to fly out all week. But he had insisted they not come, since they had retired back to Norway. But looking at Page, he suddenly realized she was serious. She actually looked depressed as she stood up, speaking about her mother and sister.

"Helpful is not a key word here."

"Where are you going?" He pulled her closer to him, and took her in his arms again.

"To set fire to my guest room," she said despondently, but in a moment they were kissing again, and she had all but forgotten about her mother.

"I have a better idea." His voice was hoarse and hungry, and he was kissing her neck, as she closed her eyes and savored every moment. How was it possible? In ten days, she had lost the only man she had ever loved, and now suddenly she was in the arms of another, someone who had been so decent to her, who wanted her as much as she wanted him . . . it didn't make sense but it was lovely . . .

"Not yet," she whispered as he kissed her again, and he smiled and looked down at her.

"I know that, silly girl . . . I'm not a fool. We have lots of time. I'm not rushing anything."

"Why not?" she teased him, pretending to be insulted, but he looked at her very seriously, and he meant what he said to her.

"Because I want you for a long time, if you come to me, Page. And I don't want to lose you." He kissed her again then, and it was a long time before they pulled apart, and she reminded him that he had better leave before Andy woke up, and found them kissing in her bedroom.

He promised to come back again later

that afternoon, to check on them. Maybe he'd bring Bjorn. And he promised to look in on Allie for her at the ICU. She didn't want to leave Andy for the rest of the day, and he promised to take care of all of it, and maybe even cook her dinner.

"Anything else I can do for you?" he shouted from his car before he drove away, as she stood outside and waved at him.

"Yeah," she shouted back.

"What?" He stopped the car for a minute to hear her answer.

"Kill my mother!" He laughed and drove away, smiling like a schoolboy.

CHAPTER 11

Brad was very upset when he heard about Andy's arm, and it sounded as though he blamed Page, but he didn't say it.

"Are you sure he's all right? It's his right arm, isn't it?"

"It is, and it's a nasty break, but they said it should heal cleanly. He has to be a little more careful with the shoulder. No pitching this year, and maybe even no more baseball till next year."

"Shit," Brad said, sounding almost as upset as he had been about Allie. But their reactions were no longer appropriate. They were both filled up with fear and disaster.

She understood perfectly why he was react-
ing the way he was about Andy.

"I'm sorry, Brad."

"Yeah . . ." he said absently, and then
remembered to ask. It had been such a relief to be in Chicago. "How's Allie?"

"The same. I haven't seen her since this
morning. I stayed home with Andy." She
didn't tell him that Trygve and Bjorn had
brought dinner for them, and oddly enough
neither did Andy. She didn't tell him not to
tell Brad anything, she wouldn't have done
that to him, but it was as though he sensed
there was already enough trouble with his
parents.

She and Trygve had been very circum-
spect while they were there, but there was
something warm and different now that
passed between them. Just since that morning, things had changed, and it was suddenly very hard to deny their feelings.

They had sat and talked in the living
room for a long time, while the boys played
quietly in Andy's room with the dog. Bjorn
really liked Andy's baseball cards, and his
rock collection from the previous summer.
Bjorn wanted to play slapjack too, but Andy
was too tired.

They were both sorry to see them go, and

Page let Andy sleep in her bed that night, and for once he didn't wet it. He had been having accidents ever since Allie had been hurt. But now he seemed calmer than he had in a long time, and the pain pills let him sleep peacefully until morning. And while he slept, Page lay in bed and held him for a long time, stroking his hair, and thinking about him . . . and Brad . . . and Trygve. She didn't know what she was going to do. Trygve had become a dear friend and she was very attracted to him. But Brad was her husband of sixteen years. She still couldn't bring herself to believe she would lose him, and yet in a way she already had, and she knew it. But she had never cheated on him before, and no matter how attractive Trygve was, or how difficult her situation, she didn't want to do anything she'd regret later, or start their relationship in a way that might spoil it.

But when Brad came home from Chicago on Wednesday night, he was distant and cool, and he acted as though he scarcely knew her. He stayed away Thursday night, never called, and was chilly with her on Friday night when he came home briefly. It was impossible to pretend that the marriage wasn't over. The mark of Stephanie was all

over him. He was wearing different ties,
new suits, and had had a different haircut.
But no matter how far Brad went, she
didn't want to go to Trygve on the rebound.
She wanted more than anything to sort out
her situation with Brad, and what they were
going to do, before she did anything, but he
wouldn't even discuss it. The only thing he
would discuss with her now was how furious
he was about her mother's visit.

"How can you let her come out here right
now? And your sister on top of it! Did you
hire a hairdresser to stay with us, or are you
going to call 911 and have one sent over
anytime she needs it?"

"All right, Brad. I'm not happy about it
either." They were discussing it on Friday
night before he went out for dinner, supposedly with clients. "How can I tell them
not to come? Allie's in critical condition,
and they want to see her." It sounded reasonable, but she also knew that her mother
and sister were not reasonable people. Brad
had always hated them, and they really
weren't fond of him either, although her
mother pretended she was, but she wasn't.
He knew too much about the past, her
mother had always held it against her that
she had told him. "I did everything I could

to discourage them, but she just announced that they were coming."

"Then you just announce to them that they can't stay here." She could see from his expression that he meant it.

"I can't do that, Brad. They're my family," she said uncomfortably. She had managed to run away from them finally, but she still couldn't bring herself not to see them, or keep them away completely.

"Horseshit, you can do anything you want and you know it."

She started getting angry then. He didn't do a damn thing to help her, all he did was issue ultimatums. "Like you do, Brad? Are you afraid they might interfere with your social life, now that you've become so open about it?" The war was on again, it had actually been very restful while he was in Chicago.

"I've been busy at the office."

"Like hell you are. And I'll bet you were real busy in Chicago." But he wheeled on her then with an angry look that warned her not to push him any further. He was in the wrong, but he still didn't want any pressure from her. It wasn't fair, and he knew it, but he wasn't ready to do anything to change that.

"That's none of your business," he said in a taut voice.

"Why not?"

"Things are moving too fast for me." They were moving too fast for her too. They had moved with the speed of lightning in the last two weeks, but it wasn't her fault. "I want things to calm down before I make any major decisions." And then he turned to her and said something that surprised her. "I've decided that I'm not ready to move out yet." She didn't say anything as she looked at him, wondering if he'd had a change of heart, or if he was fighting with Stephanie now too, or just scared of too many changes.

"Does that have anything to do with geographics, or our marriage?" she asked, her heart giving a little leap of confusion. No matter what he had done to her in the last two weeks, he was still her husband, and maybe she still loved him.

"I don't know," he said unhappily, but making no move toward her. "Moving out is such a big step, it scares the hell out of me. Maybe I've been a fool . . . I just don't know. But I don't think I could go back to the way things were either." They both knew that nothing would ever be the same again. She would never trust him, and they both suspected he couldn't give up Stephanie. He wondered about that most . . . but leaving Page meant leaving Andy. In the past week, he had thought about that a lot, and the pain of it almost killed him. Stephanie didn't seem to understand that. She said Andy could visit them, but it wasn't the same thing, and Brad knew it. "I just don't have any of the answers." He looked at Page unhappily. "I don't know which way to turn." He sat down on the bed and ran a hand through his hair, as Page watched him. She was leery of him now after he had hurt her so much, and was continuing to do so daily.

"Maybe we should wait and see." Maybe some of it was a reaction to the accident, but she knew now that a lot of it wasn't. "Want to try seeing a counselor?" Page asked hesitantly, not sure she wanted to herself, but Brad's answer was quick and certain.

"No." He shook his head. Not if it meant giving up Stephanie. He wasn't willing to do that. He didn't want to leave Page yet, but he didn't want to lose Stephanie either. Stephanie was more important to him. She seemed to embody youth and hope and the future, almost like Allie. But even he knew that his life was a mess, and everything he touched confused him.

"I don't know what else to suggest. Other than an attorney."

"Neither do I." He looked at her honestly. "Can you go on living like this for a while, or is it too hard on you?"

"I'm not sure. I couldn't do it forever. Or maybe even for very long. Not much longer."

"Neither can I," he said, looking tired. Stephanie was pushing him like crazy to leave Page, and marry her, and he knew he needed to make a decision.

And in a way, everything he'd shared with Page was being destroyed moment by moment. Their marriage, their child, their relationship, their trust. In an odd way, to him, Page seemed like the past, and Stephanie the future. But when they lay in bed that night, the past began to stir him.

Andy was asleep, and their door was closed. Page was reading quietly in bed, ignoring him, and suddenly he was kissing her as he hadn't in months, with a passion and a fire she scarcely remembered. At first, she resisted him, but he was so forceful and so aroused, that before she knew what had happened to her, Brad had her nightgown pushed up and pressed himself against her. And much as she didn't want to make love to him again, she found her resistance melting. He was, after all, still her husband, and only weeks before she had thought that she still loved him.

And then slowly, exquisitely, he entered her, and as he did his passion died instantly along with his erection. He tried to cover it for a while, and then to revive the flames, but it was obvious that his confusion and his pain had affected more than just their marriage.

"I'm sorry," he said hoarsely as he lay on the bed next to her, furious at what had happened. She was still breathless, and bitterly annoyed at herself for giving in to him. In the context of what was happening to their lives, it seemed wrong to sleep with him, even though he was still her husband. And she didn't want to be part of a team sleeping with him, or open herself up to getting hurt by him again, as he had already hurt her.

"You can't lie to your body, Brad," she said sadly. "Maybe that's your answer."

"I feel like a fool," he said angrily, as he stalked across the room, his handsome form

looking better than ever. But she had to
deal with reality now, and no matter how
much she had once loved him, it was over.
For now, at least, and maybe forever.

"Maybe you'd better make up your mind
before we screw things up worse than they
are," she said reasonably, and he nodded.
This was ridiculous, and not good for anyone. And it seemed odd to him that in the
past year, he had frequently gone straight
from Stephanie's bed to hers, with only a
few hours breather, and it had never been a
problem. But now that she knew, it changed
everything. He was almost sorry he had told
her, except that he had needed the freedom. He owed Stephanie something too,
and he hadn't been doing her justice either.
He was surprised how much he liked living
with her, and how easy she was to be with.
She wanted him to move in with her now,
and she had recently threatened to leave
him if he didn't. But what he really wanted
was to put Page away for a while, like in a
closet, or a deep freeze, spend a year with
Stephanie, and then come back to find everything the way it had been. It would have
been nice if he could do that.

"Maybe I should move out," he said miserably, sitting next to her on the bed again.

Suddenly all he wanted was to see Stephanie and prove that he wasn't impotent. His little episode with Page had scared him.

"I'm not pressuring you to do anything," Page said quietly, her long, lean body naked under the thin nightgown, but he wasn't looking. She felt stupid for letting him make love to her, and suddenly she longed for Trygve.

"I think whatever we do, it should be fairly soon. I don't think I can take a lot of this . . . and neither can Andy. Your coming and going and disappearing acts are a little wearing," she said sadly.

"I know." But in the past two weeks nothing in their life had been normal. In his own way, he was as traumatized as Page and Andy, and he was not making great decisions. "Let's just see what happens."

She nodded, and went to take a long bath, trying not to think of Trygve. She didn't want their relationship to be a result of Brad's rejecting her, or the trauma of the accident either. If anything happened with him, she wanted it to be because they genuinely had something good to share, and could have a good life, or a good time, or were meant to be together. She wanted it to be right . . . and nothing like what had happened with Brad. She knew it was going to be hard to trust anyone now, even Trygve.

Brad was asleep when she went back to bed, and gone the next morning when she got up. He left a note, saying he was playing golf, and he wouldn't be home for dinner. He didn't say what club he was playing at, or with whom, and she knew instantly that it was a lie. He was with Stephanie, the night before had frightened him, and he was running away to her for reassurance. She threw the note away and sighed just as the phone rang.

"Hi, Page, how's life?" It was Trygve who was calling about Andy. He knew he couldn't play baseball with his broken arm, and he wanted to know if she'd like to leave him to play with Bjorn when she went to see Allie. Unless Brad wanted to be with him, of course, but he suspected correctly that that might not happen.

"My housecleaner is here today, and she could keep an eye on both of them. I want to spend some time with Chloe," Trygve explained.

"He'd love that," Page said, grateful for his help again. Whatever else happened between them, he had been a remarkable friend to them, and she would never forget it. "I'll tell him. What time do you want him?" It was ten o'clock then, and she wanted to be at the hospital by eleven.

"Just drop him off on your way. I'll tell Bjorn, he'll be thrilled. He was upset at my going over to see Chloe without him. But he gets so restless after a little while when I take him. He plays with everything, and he drives the nurses crazy." She laughed at the image, but knowing Bjorn now it wasn't cruel, it was touching.

Andy was thrilled with the invitation, and the woman who cleaned house for Trygve once a week promised to watch them. She seemed very nice, and Page felt comfortable leaving Andy there. The boys disappeared immediately to Bjorn's room to watch a video, and Page gave Trygve a ride to Marin General.

"How's it going with Brad?" he asked gently on the way, "or should I mind my own business?" It was a little bit more his business now too, he had a vested interest in all of this suddenly, but he didn't want to pressure her and she was looking unhappy. She was still uncomfortable about the night before, and sorry it had happened. In an odd way she felt slightly guilty toward Trygve.

"It's difficult. I think we're in the last throes, but he's afraid to admit it."

"What about you? Are you ready to move on?" He had a stake in this now, and wanted to know what she was feeling.

She glanced at him as she drove, she wanted to be honest with him. She liked him too much not to be. "I don't want to move too fast . . . or do anything stupid . . . I don't want . . ." She struggled for the words, but he already understood, and he was comfortable with it. He wouldn't have expected anything different. "I don't want to do something on the rebound. Or something we'll regret that will hurt us later."

"Neither do I," he said calmly, leaning over to kiss her cheek. "I'm not going to push you, or do something we'll both regret. You have all the time you need. And if you can work things out with Brad again, then I'll be sorry for me, but happy for both of you. Your marriage comes first . . . and after that, I'm here if you need me."

She pulled into a parking space at the hospital, and turned to look at him, grateful for all he'd said. The funny thing was that in spite of what she'd once felt for Brad, Trygve was everything she wanted. "How did I ever get so lucky?"

"I'm not sure I'd call it that," he laughed ruefully. "We've paid a hell of a price for all this, you and I. Bad marriages, maybe mine more than yours, but yours doesn't seem to be such a peach either . . . the accident . . . our kids almost died . . . maybe we've earned this." She nodded. It was true. The accident had changed everything, but maybe in the end, it would bring them blessings too. It was hard to know yet. "I love you, Page," he said softly then, and leaned toward her and kissed her. He put his arms around her and pulled her close to him. They sat there quietly for a long time, feeling at peace in the May sunshine. It had been exactly two weeks since the accident. It was hard to believe it.

They went inside to see their daughters then. She chatted with the nurses now and then. And he came to bring her lunch in the ICU a few hours later. He walked her slowly to the waiting room, and handed her a turkey sandwich and a cup of coffee. He was telling her about his latest article, which he'd finished the night before, and it sounded intriguing. But more than anything, it amazed Page how he took care of her, how he thought of everything, how he was there for her and Andy, and his own family. He seemed to nurture everyone, and she needed that very badly.

"How's Allie today?"

Page shrugged in answer, looking discouraged. She had worked with the therapist for over an hour, they had massaged her limbs and done everything they could. But it was obvious that she was losing weight and there was no improvement. "I don't know . . . it's been two weeks, and it seems like forever. I guess I expected some kind of miracle by now, even a small one." It had been ten days since her last brain surgery, she had stabilized, and the pressure had gone down, but she was still in a deep coma.

"They told you it could go on for a long time. Months maybe. You can't give up yet," he said gently. It was so much easier for him, with Chloe so alive, so damaged, but so clearly out of danger. She might face future surgeries, and they would have to teach her to walk again, but the real danger was over. Now she had to adjust to the long grind of rehabilitation, and face the fact that her dreams of being a ballerina were over. No small thing, but she was in much better shape than Allyson, who still might die at any moment. It seemed so cruel to him that she might live for weeks, or even months, and still die in her coma. It was more than any parent should have to bear, and he hated to have Page go through it.

"I'm not giving up," Page said, picking at the sandwich he had brought her. He knew that if he had left her there, she wouldn't have eaten it, which was why he had stayed with her. Besides, he wanted to be with her, although he claimed he needed a respite from Chloe and her friends. Chloe's high spirits were definitely returning. "I just feel so helpless," Page said bleakly.

"You are. But you're doing everything you can, and so are the doctors. Give it time. It could go on like this for weeks, with no sign, and then she might wake up, and be relatively okay."

"They said that if there's no sign of improvement at all after six weeks, she might remain in the coma."

"But she could come out of it later than that too. It's happened before with kids her age . . . three months, isn't that what you said?" He encouraged her, but her eyes filled with tears as she shook her head. So much was happening, so much to endure, so much to cope with, and at times she just felt like she couldn't face it.

"Trygve, how am I going to get through this?" She leaned her head against his chest and cried. It was easy to escape into thinking about him, or being angry at Brad, or worrying about Andy's arm. But the most important thing that was happening, the thing that all of them could barely face, was that Allyson might be dying.

"You're doing fine," he said gently as he held her. "You're doing everything you can. The rest is in God's hands."

She pulled away to look at him then, and he handed her a paper napkin to blow her nose with. "I wish He'd hurry up and fix it."

Trygve smiled. "He will, give Him time."

"He's had two weeks, and my life is falling apart."

"Just hang in there. You're doing great." One thing she knew for sure was that she couldn't have done it without him. Brad was God knows where doing God knows what. She knew he had come to see Allie at least once every day or two, but he couldn't take the anguish of the ICU for longer than a few minutes. He still couldn't face it. He couldn't face the sameness, the lack of change, the machines, the monitors, and the fact that they might lose her. He was leaving Page to cope with it alone. He had been a lot better about it when they had had Andy. But they had been younger then, and Andy had been so tiny and sweet. The incubator was filled with hope, and the ICU was filled with dying.

Page and Trygve sat talking for a long time, and he teased her that she was upset because of her mother's arrival the next day, and actually she didn't deny it.

"Why do you hate her so much?" he asked, he had wondered about it. It wasn't like her.

"Old news. I had a fairly rotten child-hood."

"Most people did. My father, good Norwegian that he was, thought an occasional caning was an important part of life. I still have a scar on my behind from one particularly vigorous session."

"How awful!" She looked horrified.

"That was the way in those days. And he'd probably do it again now, if he had children. He can never understand why I'm so liberal with my kids. Actually, I think he and my mother are a lot happier now that they're back in Norway."

"Could you ever see yourself living there?" she asked, intrigued, trying to forget her worries about Allie. He was right. There was nothing she could do but wait, hope, and pray. And see what happened.

"No, I couldn't," he said in answer to her question about Norway. "Not after living here. The winters are endless there, and it's dark all day long. It's kind of primeval. I don't think I'd survive anymore out of California."

"Yeah, me too." The idea of moving to New York again made her shudder. Although she would have liked the opportunity to pursue her artwork there. But she could do it in California too. She just hadn't bothered. Brad had always made her feel that it was something she should do for friends, or in their kitchen. Not something she should ever work at. Somehow he felt that what she did wasn't important. She'd promised to do another mural for the school, but spending every spare moment at the hospital, she didn't have time now.

"You ought to do something here," Trygve said later, looking around them. The waiting room was a dismal place, and the hallway was worse. "It's so depressing. One of your murals would give people something to think about while they wait. They make you happy just looking at them," he said admiringly.

"Thank you. I enjoy it." She looked around the room, thinking of what she could do there, but hoping she wouldn't be there long enough to do it.

"Am I going to meet your mother while she's here?" he asked comfortably, and Page rolled her eyes while he laughed. "She can't be that bad."

"Actually, she's worse, but she can be pretty subtle about it when she wants to. She refuses to face anything disagreeable. Or discuss it. This is going to present quite a challenge for her."

"At least she sounds cheerful. What about your sister?"

Page could only laugh. "She's very special. They both are. I didn't see them at all for the first few years after I came out here, and then my father died, and I felt sorry for my mother, so I invited her out. That was a mistake. She and Brad fought like cats and dogs every day, subtly of course, it's all very passive aggressive, but it gives me a stomachache to be around it. And of course she thought I had no idea how to bring up Allie."

"At least she can't complain about that now," he said encouragingly.

"No, but she won't approve of the doctor. David, my brother-in-law, will probably have heard that he's a quack and about to be sued for malpractice. The hospital will be all wrong. Not to mention the really important stuff, like how bad the hairdresser is at I. Magnin."

"They can't be that bad."

"They're worse." But behind the humor he sensed that there was more. Page was too grown up, and too at ease with herself to dislike them as much as she did, if there weren't more to it. But it was also obvious that she didn't want to share it with him, and he didn't press her. She was entitled to her secrets.

He went back to Chloe eventually, and she to Allyson, and Page finally came to Chloe's room at five o'clock, and sat down and chatted with her. Chloe was still in a fair amount of pain, and her extensive casts and pins and contraptions looked pretty miserable, but she was handling it well, and she was happy to be alive. She was very worried about Allie. Trygve had told her pretty honestly that she still might die. She wasn't out of the woods yet. Jamie was there that afternoon too, and asked for news of Allyson as soon as he saw her mother.

"How is she?" Chloe asked the moment Page came into the room.

"The same. How about you? Driving the nurses wild, flirting with the residents, ordering pizzas all night long? The usual stuff?" Page grinned and Chloe laughed at the description.

"That and more," Trygve teased, and Chloe laughed. She was a real teenager and it did their hearts good to see it.

"Good." Page only wished that Allyson were doing the same things. But surely so did the Chapmans about Phillip. She could only imagine how they must feel only two weeks after the accident, and her heart ached whenever she thought of them. However awful things were with Allyson, there was still hope. But there was no hope for the Chapmans.

Jamie said that he had seen them a few days before and Mrs. Chapman was still in pretty bad shape. Mr. Chapman had told him he was suing the paper for the article that seemed to blame Phillip. Jamie mentioned too that a reporter had come to see him again, to ask him what it was like to be the only one who'd escaped unscathed. But for the most part, the press interest finally seemed to have faded.

They left Chloe at six o'clock, when the pizza Trygve had ordered for her arrived. Jamie stayed to share it with her, and Trygve drove Page back to his place.

"Do you want to stay for dinner?" he asked hopefully.

"I'd love to, but I should probably go home in case Brad shows up. He probably won't, but if he does, Andy will be upset to miss him." Trygve didn't press, and despite Andy and Bjorn's protests, Page took Andy home, but Brad never came home until the next morning. And then, in spite of all Page's promises to herself, there was the usual explosion.

"What was all that bullshit the other night about wanting to stay here, and not being sure of what you wanted? Who are you kidding with that shit?" She was livid. She was tired of living like this, while he pursued his own life with another woman.

"I'm sorry. I should have called. I don't know what happened . . . I just didn't." He did know what had happened, of course, but he couldn't tell Page. He had gone away overnight with Stephanie and there was no way he could call her from their hotel room. Stephanie hadn't left him for a single minute, and she had been furious on Sunday morning when he had insisted on driving back. But not as furious as Page had been when he walked in at noon, having never called her. She and Andy had been just about to leave for the airport. "Look, I'm sorry," he said helplessly, feeling like a moron. He was ricocheting between two worlds and two women, and not handling either very well.

"Why don't you just ask me if Allie is still alive," Page said cruelly. It wasn't like her to be so unkind, but she had really had it with him.

"Oh my God . . . is she? . . . oh Page . . ." His eyes filled instantly with tears as Page watched him coldly.

"No, she didn't die. But she could have, and where would I have called you, Brad? As usual, you never even called us."

"You bitch!" He slammed the door to the bedroom, and Andy started to cry. They were always fighting.

"I'm sorry, sweetheart." She bent down and held him, and Brad didn't come out of the bedroom again. She didn't pursue him either. They left for the airport, and Andy was very quiet on the way. So was Page, she was thinking of the way Brad had looked when he came home. He looked young, and refreshed, and happy, until he saw her. But it was Andy she was worried about as they drove to the airport. He looked heart-broken as he stared out the window.

Her mother and Alexis were among the first passengers off the plane. Her mother looked trim as usual, with beautifully done white hair, and a navy suit that showed off her slim figure. Alexis looked striking in a pale pink Chanel suit, her blond hair per-fectly done, her exquisite artificial features made up like the cover of *Vogue*. She was carrying a black alligator Hermès bag and matching tote, as she carefully kissed the air near Page's cheek and said a cautious hello to Andy.

"You look wonderful, dear," her mother said happily, looking past her. "Where's Brad?"

"He's at home. He didn't have time to come, but he said to tell you he was sorry." She had no idea if he'd even be there when they got back. There was no predicting his appearances these days, and covering that up during her mother's visit wasn't going to be easy. But she didn't want to discuss the demise of her marriage with her, and her mother wouldn't want to hear it.

They waited for their luggage at the baggage claim, and fortunately all of it arrived safely. A porter staggered under the mountain of bags they had brought. Alexis's were all matched Gucci cases.

"How's Allyson?" Alexis asked cautiously on the drive home, and Page started to explain her current status, still deep in her coma. But her mother cut her off almost as soon as she spoke, and told her how divine the weather had been in New York, and how great Alexis's apartment looked these days, since she'd redone it.

"That's nice," Page said quietly. Nothing had changed. They were the same pair who had come out before. The only mystery was why she always expected two different people. All her life she had expected her mother to be someone else, someone homey and warm, who cared and really listened. And she always hoped that Alexis would turn out to have pigtails and freckles and a heart. But they never changed. Her mother spoke of only pleasant things, and Alexis hardly spoke at all, she was too busy being perfect and looking pretty. Page had always wondered what she and David talked about, if anything. He was a lot older than her sister was, and he was always in surgery . . . much of it obviously spent on redoing his wife, which seemed to be a full-time occupation for him.

"How has the weather been here?" her mother inquired as they crossed the bridge where Allyson's life had been destroyed. Page couldn't drive across it anymore without feeling nauseous and dizzy.

"The weather?" she said blankly. Who knew? She was in ICU all the time, or fighting with Brad. Who had time to look at the weather? "I think it's been fine. I haven't really noticed."

"And Andy, how's your arm? What a silly thing to do!" his grandmother cooed, as Andy showed Alexis all the places where people had signed. Bjorn had even drawn a picture of a little dog, Andy always grinned when he said it looked just like Richie Green's hamster. But he loved Bjorn, and he was proud of their budding friendship. He loved telling his friends at school that he had a friend who was eighteen. And of course no one ever believed him.

Page was surprised that Brad was waiting for them at home. And he was very cordial to both Alexis and their mother. He carried in their mountain of bags, and set her mother's up for her in the guest room. Her mother was going to sleep in the large double bed, and normally Alexis would have slept in it with her, but this time she had asked if she could sleep in Allyson's bedroom. Page didn't really want her to, right now it felt like something of a shrine. Nothing had been touched since the night Allyson left to go out to dinner with Chloe.

But Brad said it was fine. And Page forced herself to overcome her reservations. It was foolish for them to sleep in the same bed, when they had another empty bedroom. It just underlined even more starkly the fact that Allyson wasn't there, and it made Page uncomfortable to have someone else in her space, but it couldn't be helped, and she knew she was foolish to resent it.

Alexis asked her for a drink. She wanted cold Evian without ice, and her mother said that she would love a cup of coffee and a little sandwich while she unpacked her things. It was typical of Page's experience with them, and she went to the kitchen, without saying a word, and made whatever they wanted.

It was four-thirty by then, and Page was

anxious to get to the hospital. She hadn't been all day, and she was sure that her mother and Alexis would want to see Allie. She mentioned it as the two women joined her in the living room, and her mother complimented her on the new couch, and drapes, and new paintings.

"You do such nice work, dear." Like Brad, her mother treated her artwork like a charming hobby, and always had. Page's brief experience with the stage had horrified her, and she was relieved that she had never tried to do that sort of thing in California.

Page glanced at her watch uncomfortably. It was after four-thirty. "I thought maybe we'd go to the hospital. I'm sure you want to see Allie." But the two women exchanged a glance, and Page realized that she had been foolish again. The hospital was not on their agenda.

"We've had such a long day," Maribelle Addison said quietly, leaning back against the couch. "And Alexis is just exhausted. She's recuperating from a terrible cold," her mother explained as Alexis nodded. "Don't you think it would be better to go in the morning?" she asked, looking wide-

eyed as Page struggled for words for a moment.

"I . . . uh . . . of course, if you'd prefer . . . I just thought . . ." How stupid of
her to think they would want to see Allie.
They were probably scared to death of seeing her. Why on earth had they come, she
wondered, except that it was a diversion for
them, and they deluded themselves that
they were doing something nice for Page,
which of course they weren't.

"I think tomorrow would be much better,
dear. Don't you think so, Brad?" she asked
as he came into the room, looking dazed.
Stephanie had just called him at home right
in the middle of the day and issued an ultimatum. And she was insisting that he take
her out to dinner that night to discuss it.

"I . . . uh . . . I think you're right,
Maribelle. You're probably both tired, and
seeing her is pretty upsetting." It annoyed
Page to hear what he said. She went to get
her bag without a word, and told them
she'd be back at six o'clock to fix dinner.

"Will you be here to keep an eye on
Andy?" she asked Brad before she left, and
he nodded.

"I have to go somewhere when you get
back though. Is that okay?"

"Do I have a choice?" she said sotto voce.

"I really need to pick up some papers in the city."

She nodded and didn't say more, and told her mother she'd see her in a little while. Alexis was lying down on Allyson's bed, resting.

Page fumed all the way to the hospital about how stupid she had been to let them come out, and then she laughed at herself. What a mess it all was. Allyson was in a coma, Brad was having an affair, Andy had broken his arm, and now she was stuck with her sister and her mother. It was the classic definition of a nightmare.

She saw Trygve leaving the hospital on her way in, and he stopped for a moment to talk to her. He had dropped in to see her at ICU, but figured he had missed her.

"How's Mom?" It was obvious from his eyes that he was happy to see her.

She laughed, suddenly amused at the absurdity of her situation. "So predictable it makes me laugh. You wouldn't believe them."

"Where are they now?" He was surprised not to see them.

"My mother is admiring my new couch.

And my sister is resting. Actually, she looks like she's gotten even more anorexic. She arrived dripping Chanel, and carrying alligator hand luggage."

"How impressive. And they couldn't make it to the hospital?"

"Too tired," Page explained. "Alexis is getting over a cold. And Brad told them they were right, it would just be too upsetting."

"Oh my God."

"You got it. I guess tomorrow will be the big day, unless Alexis needs to get her nails done."

"And what happened to you? How did you escape? Why aren't you at the hairdresser all day long instead of painting murals and driving car pools?"

"Just stupid, I guess. I never got the message."

"Maybe your dad was okay," he said, that would explain it, but she shook her head and looked away.

"Not really." And then she looked back at Trygve. "I'm just an aberration, I guess. The best news of all would be that I was adopted, my sister used to say I was, but unfortunately, she lied. It would make things easier now anyway." He was laughing at the way she described them.

"Nick always used to tell Chloe that. That she was adopted. Kids love to torture each other with that stuff."

"In my case, it would have been a blessing." She glanced at her watch and saw how late it was, and she knew she had to get home to cook dinner. "I'd better get in to see Allie."

"The therapist was there when I went by. Everything looked pretty normal."

"Thanks for checking." She hesitated then, and as he leaned toward her she didn't move away. Their lips brushed and their eyes held. "I'm glad I saw you," she whispered as she left.

"So am I," he shouted after her, and waved.

She found Allyson in the usual state, and everything status quo. She sat with her for an hour, and told her Grandma had come for a visit with Aunt Alexis. She told her all the latest things Andy had said, and reminded her again and again how much they loved her. She told her anything and everything that she could think of except that her marriage was falling apart, and Brad had a girlfriend.

Page kissed her gently on the forehead when she left, and stood back to look at the bandages for a long time. Brad was right, she just didn't see it anymore. But it was very upsetting.

She felt subdued on the drive home, and exhausted when she opened the door. She could hear her mother's voice, and Alexis was on the phone to David in New York, complaining about the service on the airplane. Not a word about Allyson, and only Andy asked her how she was as she started to make dinner.

"Are you sure she's gonna be okay?" he asked worriedly, pressing her today of all days, but he looked anxious.

Page stopped to look at him, and pulled him closer to her so she could hug him. "No . . . I'm not sure . . . I hope she will be. But we don't know yet. She might . . ." She couldn't bring herself to say the words to him, but she knew she had to. "She could still die . . . but she might not. She might be okay, or she might be like Bjorn when she wakes up. We just don't know yet."

"Like Bjorn?" He looked startled, he had never fully understood that.

"More or less." Or she might not be able to walk . . . she could be blind . . . or

not like Bjorn at all. She could be totally
retarded.

"What are you two talking about?" her
mother asked, interrupting them as she
wandered into the kitchen.

"We were talking about Allyson."

"I was just telling Andrew she was going
to be fine." She smiled at both of them and
Page wanted to kill her. It was not fair to do
that to him, and she wouldn't let her.

"We hope she will, Mother," Page said
firmly, "but we don't know that for sure. It
all depends on when, and if, she comes out
of the coma."

"That's like sleeping, except you don't
wake up, you just stay asleep," he explained
to his grandmother, as Brad joined them.
Page saw that he was wearing a suit, and
she struggled not to comment on it as she
saw him.

"I'll be back later," he said quietly to
Page, as she raised an eyebrow in question.

"Will you? I won't hold my breath."

"Thanks," he said, and ruffled Andy's
hair as he left. "Good night, Maribelle," he
called over his shoulder.

"Good night, dear." And then, after he
was gone, "He's a good-looking man," she
said to Page, "you're a lucky girl." She

wanted to tell her that she used to think so too, but she no longer did. But she went back to cooking dinner and said nothing.

Predictably, dinner was a painful meal. Alexis chased a tiny piece of meat and some salad around her plate and basically ate nothing. She said as little as she ate, and her mother dominated most of the conversation, talking about her friends, her apartment in New York, and Alexis's fabulous garden in East Hampton. She had three Japanese gardeners, and did none of it herself, and she seemed a lot less excited about it than their mother. She wasn't excited about anything, except Chanel. And none of them had mentioned Allyson even once by the end of the evening.

They both went to bed when Andy did, explaining that they were still on New York time, and it irked Page terribly to hear sounds coming from Allyson's room. She closed her own bedroom door so she couldn't hear it. It seemed a sacrilege, and a terrible intrusion.

She lay on her bed quietly for a long time, thinking about them, and how unhappy her life had been with them. They had made it a living hell for her until she left. Seeing them always brought the memories back again. Tears squeezed slowly out of her eyes as she thought of it. And then she forced her mind back to the present.

It was after midnight when Brad came in. She was still awake, but the lights were off and she was in bed. She turned over in the dark and looked at him, and he looked tired and unhappy. She was surprised to see him.

"Did you have a nice time?" she asked. They both knew where he had been. It was a lot to absorb, and she was struggling with it. But from the look on his face, so was he. He stood looking at her for a long time before he answered. He was trapped between two worlds, and both were causing him pain at the moment.

"Not really. This isn't the peachy keen situation you think it is."

"I guess not . . . for either of us."

"I know how hard it is for you," he said softly. He sounded like the old Brad for a moment, but he didn't come any closer. "Maybe I should have gone on lying to you . . . I don't know . . . maybe it was time you knew. We couldn't go on like this forever." The trouble was that she could. She had had no idea what he was up to.

"I'm trying to do the right thing for everyone now. And I'm just not sure what that is." She nodded. There was nothing she could say to him. Their lives hung in the balance.

"Maybe you should just concentrate on Allyson, and forget about it for a while. Maybe right now isn't the right time to be making decisions."

"I know that." But Stephanie was feeling miserable, and wanted him to prove something to her. It wasn't fair, but that's how she was handling it, and he didn't want to lose her. She had never met Allyson, or Page, they meant nothing to her. All she wanted was Brad, and she wasn't going to let him dangle her any longer. For almost a year she had been perfectly happy sleeping with him whenever they could, having a good time on occasional business trips, and a rare stolen weekend. But she was twenty-six and she had decided that it was time for her to get married and have kids. And Brad Clarke was the man she wanted.

Page lay quietly for a long time, and eventually he came to bed, but he didn't lay a hand on her. Everything was working perfectly again . . . with Stephanie at least, but he knew that he and Page could ill afford another fiasco. And he had no desire at all to try it.

It was three in the morning before she fell asleep, and she felt like hell the next morning when she got up at seven to wake Andy and make breakfast. Andy had dragged Lizzie to bed with him. Brad was already up and dressed by then, he skipped breakfast and left early for the city. He said he had a breakfast meeting, and she didn't question him. At least he had been at home all night and she hadn't had to explain to her mother why he wasn't. Who knows, maybe they wouldn't even have noticed.

She dropped Andy off at school, and then came back to the house for Mother and Alexis. She did some paperwork, paid some bills, but by eleven o'clock they still weren't ready. Alexis had to do her exercise routine, and her hair was still in electric rollers. By then she had bathed and put her makeup on, but it would still be another hour before they were out the door, she es-timated, when Page asked her.

"Mother," Page said anxiously, "I want to be with Allie."

"Of course. But we all have to eat. Maybe you should make something here." But she was going to get caught in that trap with them, until it was too late to go at all. They had come out to see Allyson, not to go to restaurants, or drive Page crazy. It was exactly the way she had known it would be with them, and she just wasn't willing to do this.

"We can eat at the cafeteria if you get hungry."

"That's awfully hard on Alexis's stomach, dear. You know how grim hospital food is."

"I can't help that." She glanced at her watch unhappily. It was five minutes to twelve by then. She had wasted half the day, and Andy would be coming out of school at three-thirty. "Would you rather go by cab yourself, after lunch, or maybe with Brad tonight if he goes?"

"Of course not, we'll come with you." The two women from New York consulted at length in Allyson's room, and emerged finally at twelve-thirty.

Alexis looked exquisite in a white silk Chanel. She wore black patent leather shoes and bag, and a wonderful straw hat that looked totally out of place but very pretty. Her mother was wearing a red silk suit. They looked like they were going to have lunch at Le Cirque in New York, not to ICU at Marin General.

"You both look wonderful," Page said pleasantly as they got into the car. She was wearing the same jeans and loafers she had worn off and on for two weeks. She just took them off long enough to wash the jeans, and she had worn all her old tired sweaters. They were comfortable and warm in the drafty halls of the hospital, and she hadn't cared how she looked in more than two weeks. Seeing her mother and sister all dressed up somehow amused her, but it didn't surprise her.

Her mother commented on the warm weather along the way, and asked her where she and Brad were going for vacation that year. She hoped they could come East. It would be so wonderful if they ever decided to rent a little house on Long Island.

They parked in the hospital parking lot, and Page showed them inside, wishing once again that they hadn't come. Their presence there at all seemed like an intrusion. Allyson was their granddaughter and niece, yet Page felt so possessive of her, as though in the state she was in, Allie belonged to her and Brad and no one else. It wasn't fair, but these people didn't deserve her.

The nurses in ICU all said hello to them, and Page led them quietly to Allie's bed. She saw her mother's face grow pale, and heard her gasp when she first saw her. She offered her mother a chair, but she only shook her head, and for a moment Page felt sorry for her, and put an arm around her shoulders. Alexis hadn't even dared to approach the bed. She had stopped halfway there, and watched from the doorway.

They said not a word for the ten minutes they were there, and then her mother glanced worriedly at Alexis. She was deathly pale beneath her makeup.

"I don't think your sister should stay," she whispered. Neither should Allie, Page wanted to whisper back, but she nodded. Why was their concern always for each other and no one else, why couldn't they feel anything real or express it? For a moment, her mother had felt their pain, had seen Allie as she really was, and then she turned away and sought refuge in Alexis. It was the way it had always been. She had never been willing to see Page's pain, she had only been interested in saving Alexis. And Alexis had been lost long since. There was no one there. She was just a Barbie doll in expensive clothes and perfect makeup.

They walked back into the hallway again, as Maribelle put an arm around her older daughter. Not around Page, but around Alexis.

"I forget how she looks sometimes," Page said apologetically. "I see so much of her . . . I'm not used to it, but I know what to expect. One of her teachers came the other day and she was terribly upset. I'm sorry." She looked at both of them, and even though she was disappointed by them again, she meant it.

"Actually, she looks fine," her mother insisted, still looking pale. "She looks as though she might wake up at any moment." In truth, she looked as though she were dead, and the respirator made it even more gruesome to watch, which was why Page hadn't let Andy see her, despite his protests.

"She doesn't look fine," Page said firmly. "She looks frightening. It's all right to say that." She didn't want to play the game then, but her mother just patted her arm and continued.

"She's going to be just fine. You have to know that. Now," she smiled at her two daughters as though to forget what they had just seen, "where are we going for lunch?"

"I'm staying here." Page looked annoyed at them. She was not just passing through, and she was not going to spend the next week playing tea party and bridge game with them. If they had come to see Allyson, they were going to have to face the music. "I can call you a cab if you like, and you can go to lunch. But I'm not going."

"It would do you good to get away. Brad doesn't sit here all day long, does he?"

"No he doesn't, but I do." There was a grim set to Page's mouth, but no one noticed.

"What about lunch in the city?" She tried to tempt her, but Page only shook her head. She wasn't going.

"I'll call you a cab," she said firmly.

"What time will you be home?"

"I have to pick Andy up and take him to baseball. I should be home by five."

"We'll see you then." She told them where a key to the house was hidden in case they got back before her, but she knew they wouldn't. After lunch, they'd be going to I. Magnin.

She went back to ICU to sit with Allyson, and Trygve stopped by to see her midafternoon. He looked around, surprised to see her alone. He had expected to meet her mother and sister.

"Where are they?" He looked confused and Page shook her head ruefully.

"The Bride of Frankenstein and her

mother have gone to the city for lunch, and a little shopping."

"Did they see Allyson?" He looked amazed.

"For about ten minutes. My mother turned pale, my sister stood in the door and turned green, and then they decided to go for lunch in town to forget about it." She was still annoyed, but it was so typical of them, though Trygve couldn't know that.

"Don't be so hard on them. This kind of thing isn't easy."

"It's not easy for me either, but I'm here. They thought I should go to lunch with them."

"It might do you good," he said gently, but she shrugged. He didn't know them.

He stayed around for a little while, and then she picked Andy up at school, took him to baseball practice, and went home. And just as she had thought, her mother and Alexis came in at six, laden with shopping bags, a bottle of perfume for her, a little French sweater for Andy, and a lacy pink peignoir for Allyson that there was no way she could wear in her present condition.

"It's beautiful, Mother, thank you." She didn't explain the impossibility of it to her, and her mother seemed not to care. They had found a fabulous designer sale at I. Magnin.

"It's amazing what you find out here," she said, totally unaware of Page's expression.

"Isn't it though," she said coolly. It was almost as though the reason for their trip had been forgotten.

Page made dinner for them again that night, but Brad didn't come home or call. She made an excuse for him, but later she found Andy looking forlorn and sat down on her bed to talk to him. Having her own mother there made her nervous and edgy.

"You and Dad are mad at each other again, huh?"

"Not really," she lied, she just couldn't cope with telling him about that too. Allyson was enough for the moment. "He's just busy."

"No he's not. I heard you shouting at him . . . and he yelled at you . . ."

"Moms and dads do that sometimes, sweetheart." She kissed the top of his head and fought back tears as she held him.

"You didn't use to." And then, "Bjorn said his mom and dad used to fight a lot, and then his mom left. She went to England, and now he hardly ever sees her."

"That's different," though she was no longer sure why. In truth, it wasn't very different. "Does he miss her a lot?" She felt sorry for him. It had to be particularly hard on a child like him, with limited understanding.

"No," Andy said honestly, "he said she was mean to him. He likes his dad a lot better. I like his dad too," he volunteered, "he's nice." She nodded, and then he looked up at her with tears in his eyes, and she almost panicked. "Is Daddy going to leave and go to England?"

"Of course not," she said, relieved that he hadn't asked her how she felt about Trygve. "Why would he go to England?"

"I don't know. That's what Bjorn said his mom did. Do you think he'd leave us though?" She wanted to say more, but knew she couldn't. It was just too much for him, too much for all of them at the moment.

"I don't think so." It was the first time she had ever lied to him, but she knew she had to.

And when she put him to bed, her mother asked her if she'd mind making her a cup of peppermint tea, and taking some camomile and a bottle of Evian to her sister.

"Not at all," she said, smiling to herself. They were so predictable . . . the wicked stepmother and sister . . . and she, as always, was playing the role of Cinderella.

CHAPTER 12

The rest of the week was much the same. Page continued to spend her days at the hospital while Andy was in school, while her mother and sister did the rounds of the boutiques and department stores in San Francisco. They cruised through Hermès, Chanel, Tiffany, Cartier, Saks, and did a fair amount of damage at I. Magnin. They had their hair done at Mr. Lee, lunch at Trader Vic's, Postrio, and the restaurant at the top of Neiman-Marcus. And about every other day, they began their day with a five-minute visit to Allie.

After the first time, Alexis said she felt her cold coming on again, and didn't want to cause Allyson complications, so she waited in the lobby. But Page's mother bravely went upstairs, and would stand chatting with Page at Allie's bedside, for roughly four or five minutes. Mostly, she talked about what they were going to do that day, and tried to talk Page into going with them. And at the end of the week, she insisted she take Page and Brad out to dinner.

Page tried to broach it to him one of the rare times she saw him that week. It was Friday afternoon by then, and she was beginning to wonder when Alexis and her mother were going to leave, their presence had worn thin right from the beginning. And Brad was using the opportunity of their being there to disappear now on a daily basis. He hadn't been home for dinner once all week, coming home way past midnight and leaving early in the morning before they got up. And one night, he had stayed away all night without calling.

"She wants to take us to dinner somewhere," Page explained, trying not to lose her temper, or confront him for the nights he had spent out without calling. "To tell you the truth, I'm not sure I could stand it."

"She seems all right this time," he said calmly.

"Really?" Page snapped at him. "When did you figure that out? In the four seconds it took you to hang up their bags, or the ten minutes you haven't spent with them since then. How the hell do you know how she is? I haven't even seen you since Sunday."

"Oh for chrissake . . . stop it. What do you expect me to do? Baby-sit your mother? She came here to see Allie." Which was something he was doing less and less too, with the excuse that he was busy.

"She did not come here to see Allie," Page said unpleasantly. "She came here to see Chanel, Hermès, and Cartier. And they've had a lovely visit."

"Maybe you should have gone with them," he snapped back at her, "you might be in a better mood. And God knows, you might look a little more like your sister." He was sorry the moment he said the words, but there was nothing he could do to unsay them.

She laughed bitterly at him. "There isn't a single real piece or part left on my sister's face or body, and if what you wanted is that piece of plastic nothing, then be my guest." She raged at him, but she was hurt by his

comment. She had spent three weeks at Allie's bedside, and she knew she looked a
mess, but she didn't have the time, or the
energy, or the heart, to look any different.
She didn't care how she looked right now.
All she wanted was for Allie to wake up
from her coma.

In the end, Brad agreed to go to dinner
with them on Saturday, and they went into
the city, and had dinner at the Fairmont, at
Mason's. Page had pulled her thick blond
hair straight back, in a ponytail, and worn a
plain black dress, and no makeup. She
looked the way she felt, bleak, unhappy,
and Alexis, on the other hand, was wearing
a white silk Givenchy dress which showed
off her rail-thin figure, and the deep dé-
colletage showed off her implants nicely.

"You look terrific," Brad said pleasantly,
and she smiled at him. But there was no
seduction there, no interest on her part.
She was interested in how she looked, and
what she wore, and very little else. And her
husband understood that. There was no
woman there, just a form and a beautifully
made-up face with perfect features.

Alexis and her mother were talking about
staying another week, and at the mere mention of it, Page looked frantic. She had al-

ready waited on them for seven days, and brought them camomile, mint tea, Evian, cold packs, hot packs, breakfast, lunch, dinner, fresh sheets, more pillows, and she had had to go out and buy an electric blanket for her mother. They did not answer the phone, pour themselves so much as a glass of water, they couldn't figure out how to work the TVs in their rooms, and neither of them was comfortable with Andy. As usual, they were totally useless.

They had seen Allyson a total of three times in a week, all told for probably less than fifteen minutes. It was exactly as Page had predicted it would be to Trygve.

"I think you should go home after the weekend," Page said firmly, and her mother looked horrified at the suggestion.

"We couldn't possibly leave you alone with Allyson," she insisted, and for once, Page was speechless.

Brad was pleasant to both of them, and particularly Alexis, who said very little to any of them. And once they were back at home again, and the sitter had left, Brad told Page quietly that he was going out for the rest of the evening.

"At eleven o'clock?" She looked startled, but she shouldn't have. He hadn't been there all week, and this seemed to be his style now. In the past three weeks, the entire fabric of their marriage had unraveled. She just looked at him and nodded.

"I'm sorry, Page," he tried to explain. "I'm caught between a rock and a hard place."

"Yeah," she nodded again, and unzipped her dress, "I know. So is Allie."

"That has nothing to do with this." But they both knew it had everything to do with it. It had blown them apart, and it was more and more obvious that they weren't likely to recover.

She walked into the bathroom then, and when she came out, he was gone. She went to bed, and lay awake for a long time. Lately, she had more and more trouble sleeping. She thought of calling Trygve, but that didn't seem fair. She didn't want to bounce from one to the other.

And in the morning, over breakfast, her mother told her how lucky she was to have Brad. Page said nothing, and drank her coffee. She said he had turned out to be a fine man, and a very good husband.

Page went to see Allyson alone, and left Andy with them, despite their protests that they wouldn't know what to do if he had a problem.

"What if he has to go to the bathroom?" her mother said, panicking. It was hard to believe she'd had two children, and been a physician's wife, and been so completely helpless.

"He's seven years old, Mother. He can take himself. He can even make you lunch, if you want it." She was amused to think that her seven-year-old son was more capable than they were, but he was, by a long shot.

She talked to Trygve for a long time that afternoon and admitted to him how tired she was, and how discouraged. It was hard for her, having her mother there, it was demoralizing her, and he could sense it.

"What is it about her that upsets you so much?" he asked, she was so funny about them sometimes, and so deeply depressed about them at others.

"Everything. Who they are, who they aren't, what they do, what they don't do. They're rotten people, both of them, and I hate being around them, or even having them around my children."

"They can't be that bad." He was surprised at the force with which she talked about them, and it was obvious that something about her family had upset her deeply.

"They're why I came out here. Actually, I came out for Brad. But I would have left New York anyway. I didn't want to be anywhere near them. And this was perfect for me." It was definitely part of why she had married Brad, and it had seemed fine at the time, although now things had turned out to be different. "He's being pretty outrageous right now too, and I'm getting tired of it. It's hard on me, it's upsetting Andy. It's just not fair."

"I know," he said quietly, "Andy said something about it to Bjorn the last time he was over. He said that the two of you fight all the time, ever since the accident, and he thinks his sister might be sicker than you're telling him."

"My mother's been telling him Allie is going to be fine. And that drives me crazy too." She looked at him then and he could see how tired she was. She was beyond exhausted. Three weeks of the kind of agony she had lived through was too much for anyone, without taking a serious toll on them, and it was taking a toll on her and he could see it.

"Maybe it's time for them to leave." Enough was enough, if this was what it did to her, but he was in no position to help her get rid of them. He was an invisible friend, and they knew nothing of his existence.

"I said that to them last night, but my mother says she couldn't possibly leave me alone with Allie." She laughed at the absurdity of it, and he put an arm around her shoulder and kissed her.

"I'm sorry you have to go through all this. What you're going through with Allie is enough without all this bullshit."

"I don't know . . . I guess I needed to be tested or something. I think I'm flunking." She said it with tears in her eyes and he pulled her closer still and kissed her again in the ICU waiting room where no one would see them.

"I think you're doing fantastically, better than A plus."

"Shows what you know," she said, and blew her nose. And then she leaned against him and closed her eyes, wishing things would get just a little better. "I'm so tired of it all . . . Trygve, will it ever end?" But right now there was no easy end to any of it, and they both knew it.

"A year from now, you'll look back at all this and wonder how you survived it."

"Will I even live that long?" she asked, grateful to have him to lean on, and he spoke gently and firmly as he held her.

"I'm counting on it, Page . . . a lot of us are." She nodded, and they sat for a long time in silence before she went back to Allie.

The phone was ringing when she got home that afternoon. It was a friend from the city whom she hadn't seen in months. Allyson and her daughter had gone to dancing school together two years before, and the girls weren't close friends, but they liked each other. She had heard about the accident and wanted to know if she could do anything to help, but Page told her there was nothing.

"Let me know if there is," she persisted, and then hesitated for an instant. "What's happening with you and Brad, by the way? Are you . . . getting divorced?" Page was shocked by the question.

"No. Why?" But her blood ran cold as she said it. The woman knew something. It was obvious from the way she had asked the question.

"Maybe I shouldn't be saying anything . . . but I see him over here all the time with some young girl . . . I don't know, she must be in her early twenties. I thought she was a friend of Allie's at first when I saw him with her, and then I realized she was older. She lives in the next block, and I got the impression he was living with her. Actually, I saw them jogging together this morning before breakfast." How nice for him. And how nice for him to embarrass her with everyone. It was a small community and now people were seeing him with the girl . . . Allie's age? . . . oh God. She felt two thousand years old as she explained that she was a good friend, and they worked together on projects at all hours, and it was nothing.

She knew she hadn't convinced her friend, but she wasn't about to admit to anyone that Brad was involved with someone else. And she was angry that the woman had called her. It was a mean thing to do, and she had to have known when Page said they weren't getting divorced that there was trouble.

"How was Allyson?" her mother asked as she walked into the kitchen.

"The same," Page said distractedly.

"How did you manage with Andy? Did he find the bathroom?" She smiled and her mother laughed.

"Of course. He's a wonderful boy. He made me and his aunt Alexis lunch and served it in the garden." God forbid they should do anything for themselves for a single moment.

She found Andy playing in his room, and he looked up when he saw her. He looked worried and sad and it tore at her heart when she saw his eyes. All of their lives had changed brutally in the past three weeks, and none of them understood it. They were all like drowning people. She sat down on the bed, and reached a hand out and touched him.

"How was Grandma?"

"Funny," he said, smiling up at her, as she longed to hold him. "She can't do anything. And neither can Aunt Alexis, her nails are too long to do anything. She can't even open a bottle of Evian. And Grandma asked me to wind her watch for her. She says she can't see it, and she couldn't find her glasses." He knew them well, and then he looked up at Page with a worried expression. "Where's Daddy?"

"He's in the city, working." She lied, as always.

"But it's Sunday." He was no fool, but she didn't want to tell him the truth, and he sensed it.

"He works hard." The bastard.

"Will he be home for dinner?"

"I don't know," she said honestly, and then he climbed up on her lap and she held him. She wanted to tell him that she would always love him, no matter what happened with his father, but she didn't want to say too much, so she just told him how much she loved him.

She went to cook dinner after that, and Brad surprised them and came home, and it actually started out to be a very pleasant dinner. Brad did a barbecue for them, and he was very quiet and polite. He avoided Page's eyes, but he made an effort to be nice to her mother, and he had Andy help him make the hamburgers and steaks and chicken. Alexis explained that she wasn't eating meat today, and she had Andy open a bottle of Evian for her.

And it was only when Page stood alone next to Brad that she turned to him and told him about the call from the woman she knew in the city.

"I hear you went jogging today before breakfast." He didn't say anything at first, he just looked at her, it had never occurred to him that anyone would tell her.

"Who told you that?" He sounded furious, and guilty.

"What difference does it make?"

"It's none of your fucking business," he said in total fury.

"This is our life you're throwing in the trash, Brad . . . mine and Allie's . . . and Andy's. You think he doesn't know what's going on. Try looking at his face once in a while. He knows. We all do."

"Great! What did you do? Tell him? You bitch!" He threw the cooking utensils down then, and stormed into the house, and Page struggled with the barbecue for a while until she burned herself, and Andy went running to get Brad. He was crying by then, he had heard them arguing and then he had seen Page burn herself. He didn't want her to get hurt, or his parents to shout, and he had heard them saying something about him. Maybe it was all his fault they were arguing, maybe his Dad was mad that Allie was hurt, and not Andy. He looked devastated as Brad prodded the steaks angrily, and finally finished the dinner. And all three Clarkes were extremely quiet as they sat down to dinner. But as usual, neither Maribelle nor Alexis appeared to notice.

"What a marvelous cook you are," Maribelle complimented him. The steaks were good, but the atmosphere was poisonous. "Alexis, you really ought to try one of the steaks, they're too good to be true." But Alexis shook her head, happy with her lettuce leaves, and Page and Andy were picking at their dinner. Page still had an ice cube held to the two fingers she had burned, and there was already a nasty blister.

"How's your hand, Mom?" Andy asked her worriedly.

"It's fine, sweetheart." Brad said not a word and never looked at his wife. He was convinced now that she had told Andy about his affair, and he was so mad he wanted to kill her. He started arguing with her again in the kitchen when they cleaned up, and neither of them saw Andy standing on the other side of the counter.

"You told him, didn't you! You had no right to do that!"

"I did no such thing!" she shouted back at him. "I wouldn't do that to him. But you might as well tell him yourself, you're never here. What is he supposed to think? And what if someone tells him the way they told me?"

"It's none of his goddamn business either!" He slammed out of the kitchen again, and Page was crying as she put away the dishes. Brad had gone back outside and was putting out the barbecue, when her mother walked into the kitchen.

"What a lovely dinner, dear. We're having such a good time here." Page stared at her unbelievingly, not even sure what to say, it was all so surrealistic. But her family always had been.

"I'm glad you liked the dinner. Brad makes a good steak." Maybe he'd come back to cook steak for them after he remarried.

"You're a wonderful couple," she said, beaming at Page, who finally put down her dish towel and looked at her mother.

"Actually, Mom, things aren't going too well. I'm sure you noticed."

"Not at all. Of course you're both worried about Allyson, but that's natural. I'm sure in a few weeks you'll all be back to normal." It was amazing for her to even acknowledge that much.

"I'm not so sure of that anymore." And

then she decided to tell her the whole truth. Why not? If she didn't like it, she'd just pretend she didn't hear it. "He's involved with someone else, and it's putting an awful lot of strain on us at the moment."

But her mother only shook her head, refusing to believe it. "I'm sure you're mistaken about that, dear. Brad would never do a thing like that. He'd never do anything to jeopardize your marriage."

"Yes, he is," Page went on doggedly, suddenly determined to make her believe it.

"All women think things like that from time to time. You're overwrought with this problem with Allyson." *Problem? You mean like the fact that she's been in a coma for three weeks and might die? Oh that problem.* . . . "You know, your father and I had our little arguments at times too, but they never amounted to anything serious. You just have to be a little more understanding." Page stood staring at her mother then, unable to believe what she was hearing. She was willing not to discuss what had happened in their family, but she was not willing to pretend it had never happened.

"I can't believe what you're saying," Page said hoarsely.

"It's true . . . hard as it is to believe,

your father and I had our difficult moments."

"Mom, this is me . . . Page . . . do you
remember what we went through?"

"I have no idea what you're talking
about." Her mother turned away and
started to leave the kitchen.

"Don't do this to me!" Page said, crying
as she looked at her. "Don't you *dare* do
this to me after all these years, with your
pious, holier-than-thou lies . . . ! 'Little
problems.' Do you remember who you were
married to? . . . what he did for all those
years? How can you say that to me! Look at
me dammit!"

Her mother turned slowly and stared at
her blankly, as though she were unable to
understand what had gotten into her daughter. Brad had just come in from the garden
then, and he saw them, and the look on
Page's face, and instinctively knew what had
happened.

"Maybe you two should discuss this some
other time," he said quietly, and Page
turned to him in fury.

"Don't you tell me what to do and what
not to do, you sonofabitch. You're out fucking your brains out night and day, and now
you want me to take this shit too? I'm not

going to let her do this to me anymore."
She turned back to her mother then. "You
can't play these games with me . . . you
let him do what he did! You *helped* him!
You let him into my room and locked the
door, and told me I had to make Daddy
happy . . . I was thirteen years old! *Thirteen!* And you *made* me sleep with my father! And Alexis was only too happy to turn
her back on me, because he'd been doing it
to her since she was twelve, and she was
happy it was me and not her anymore! How
dare you try and pretend that didn't happen! You're lucky I let you in my front door
and I'm willing to see you."

Maribelle looked at her, deathly pale,
and Brad could see that she was shaking.
"Those are terrible accusations, Page, and
you know they're not true. Your father
would never have done a thing like that."

"He did and so did you, and you know
it." She turned away from them then, with
her back to them, and sobbed, but Brad
didn't dare approach her. She turned back
to face her mother then with a look of outrage. "I spent years trying to get over it,
trying to heal myself of what you'd done
. . . and I could have lived with your telling me how sorry you were, how terrible

you felt . . . but how can you try to pretend it never happened?"

Alexis wandered into the kitchen with absolutely no idea of what was going on. She
had been calling David from her bedroom.

"Do you mind making me some camomile?" she asked Page sweetly, who let out
a groan of disbelief as she leaned against
the counter.

"I don't believe you. The two of you.
You've spent so many years hiding from the
truth that you can't face anything. You can't
even open a fucking bottle of water for
yourself. How can you live like that? How
can you do this to yourselves?"

Alexis looked suddenly terrified as she
looked around at them. "I'm sorry . . . I
. . . never mind . . ."

"Here!" Page tossed a bottle of Evian at
her and she caught it. "Mom was just telling
me how Daddy never fucked either of us
when we were kids. Remember that, Alex?
Or have you had a memory lapse too? Remember when you shoved me at him so he
wouldn't do it to you anymore? Remember
that?" She looked at both of them miserably. "He did it until I was sixteen and
threatened to call the police on him, which
neither of you would ever have had the

courage to do. How could you do that for him? How could you help him?" She was sobbing by then. "I could never understand that." Especially once she had children, and Brad felt sick listening to her. He knew about it, but he had never heard her talk about it so bluntly, or confront them with it.

"How could you say a thing like that?" Alexis looked terrified. "Daddy was a doctor."

"Yeah," Page said through her tears. "I used to think that made a difference too, but it didn't, did it? It took me years to even go to a doctor after that. I always thought I'd be molested or raped. I didn't even go to the doctor half the time when I was pregnant, I was so afraid of what would happen. He was a great guy, our Dad, a wonderful man, a terrific doctor."

"He was a saint," Maribelle Addison said protectively, "and you know it." Alexis had moved instinctively closer to her, and the two women were huddled together, and it was clear that they were never going to admit what had happened.

"You know what's sad?" Page said, looking at them. "You disappeared after all that, Alex. You married David at eighteen, and you got a new identity, new face, new boobs, new eyes, new everything, so you didn't have to be Alexis anymore. You could be someone else so you could pretend it never happened." Alexis made not a sound as she listened. It was too threatening to her, now more than ever.

"Come on," Brad said quietly to Page, sorry that it had happened. Too much had happened to her lately. "Don't do this to yourself."

"No?" She turned to look at him. "Why not? Do you think I can pretend it never happened, like they do? Maybe I should do that with you too, pretend you're not out every night screwing around, pretend everything is wonderful and perfect. What a nice life . . . except that I would kill myself if I tried to do that. I haven't lived this long, and come this far, and suffered this much in order to pretend I believe in a lot of bullshit."

"Maybe other people can't handle that much honesty. Did you ever think of that?" he said sadly.

"A lot."

"They need places to hide in."

"I can't live like that, Brad."

"I know," he said softly, "I always loved

that about you." But he had said it in the past tense and she had heard it.

Her mother and sister escaped from the kitchen then, and Page stood there for a moment trying to catch her breath as he watched her. "Are you all right?" He was worried about her, but he also knew that he couldn't give her what she needed. He didn't have it to give her anymore. That was just the way it was. And for once, it was honest.

"I don't know," she said honestly. "I guess I'm glad I said it. I've always wondered if she has denial and she believes all that shit, or she just lies, to cover up for him, like she did then."

"Maybe it doesn't matter. She's never going to admit the truth to you, Page, and neither is Alexis. You know that. Don't expect it." She nodded. It had been a terrible night, but in some ways it had freed her. She went outside to sit alone for a while, and then she decided to go to the hospital to see Allyson. It was late, but all of a sudden she needed to see her. She told Brad before she went out, and she was sitting quietly in ICU a few minutes later. This time, she didn't say anything. She just sat there, thinking of everything Allyson had been before the accident, and missing her. It had been three weeks now.

"Mrs. Clarke, are you all right?" One of the night nurses noticed her at nine o'clock. She looked shaken and pale, and she was sitting so still, just staring at her daughter. Page nodded, and just sat there, until Trygve came by half an hour later.

"I wondered if you were here." He spoke softly amidst the whirring and puffing of the machines. "I don't know why, I just had a feeling you were. I've been thinking about you." He smiled, but then he noticed her eyes. She looked terrible, and she looked as though she'd been crying. "Are you okay?"

"More or less." She shrugged with a tired smile. "I kind of lost it tonight."

"Did it help?"

"I'm not sure. Not really. It won't change anything, but I got a lot off my chest."

"Then maybe it was worth it."

"Yeah. Maybe." She didn't seem sure as she looked at him, and he saw again that she looked ravaged. Allyson was the same, so he knew she hadn't had bad news about her. It was everything else.

"Want to come have a cup of coffee?" She shrugged again, but she followed him out as the nurse watched them. She felt so sorry for her. It had been a long haul, and so far there wasn't much hope her daughter would get any better. She hated cases like that, they were so hard on everyone, especially when it involved kids. Sometimes, she thought to herself, it was simpler if you lost them. But she never would have said that to the parents.

He handed her a cup of coffee from a machine, and she still hadn't said anything. He was getting more and more worried about her. They sat down in the ICU waiting room and her eyes looked huge in her face, and bluer than he had ever seen them.

"What's happening?" he asked gently as she took a slow sip of the hot coffee.

"I don't know . . . I guess it's all getting to me . . . Allie . . . Brad . . . my mother. . . ."

"Did something happen?" He was trying to figure it out and she wasn't giving him any clues, but he wanted so much to help her.

"Nothing that hasn't happened before. My mother was playing never-never land, just like she always does, and I went nuts, I guess." She smiled at him and looked a little embarrassed. "Maybe it wasn't the right thing to do, but I didn't have any choice at the time. I told her that Brad and I were in trouble, which was dumb of me, and she talked about my father." She wasn't sure how to tell him, and he was afraid to ask her. "My father and I . . ." she began, and then stopped and took another sip of coffee. "We . . . uh . . . had a pretty strange relationship." She closed her eyes for a long moment then, and started to cry as she explained it to him. She hadn't really wanted to tell him, and yet she wanted to now. She wanted to be honest with him, and she knew it was safe to tell him anything.

"It's all right, Page," he sensed easily how miserable she was, "you don't have to say anything if you don't want to."

"No," she looked up at him, through her tears, "I want to. I'm not afraid to tell you . . ." She took a breath and went on, "We . . . uh . . . he . . . uh . . . molested me when I was thirteen . . . actually he slept with me . . . he . . . uh . . . had intercourse with me, when I was thirteen . . . it went on for a long time . . . until I was sixteen . . . and my mother knew it. Actually," she seemed to choke on the words, "she forced me to . . . he'd been sleeping with Alexis for four years before that . . . my mother was afraid of him. He was a very sick man, and he used to beat her, and she let him. She said we had to 'keep him happy' so he wouldn't hurt us . . . she used to bring him in to me, and then lock the door behind him." Page was sobbing as he took her in his arms.

"My God, Page . . . how awful . . . how sick . . ." He would have killed anyone who had done that to his daughter.

"I know. It's taken me years to get over it. I left when I was seventeen. I worked as a waitress to pay for an apartment. My mother said that was a terrible thing to do, that I had betrayed them . . . I had broken his heart, she said . . . when he died, for a while, I actually thought I'd killed him.

"Eventually, I met Brad in New York, and we got married and came out here. I found a good therapist, and I made my peace with it. But she's still trying to pretend it never happened. That's what got me so upset. I don't understand how she can do that. I've never understood any of it . . . how she could know he was doing that, and still pretend that he was decent . . . she called him a saint tonight, and it made me sick."

"No wonder you lost it," he said soberly as he listened. He was stroking her hair, and holding her as she talked, just as she did to Allie. "I'm amazed you even see her."

"I try not to most of the time, but with Allie's accident it was hard not to let her come out. I knew I shouldn't, but I always think I can play the game with her. The trouble is I just can't. Every time I see her it reminds me of when I was thirteen . . . she hasn't changed . . . and neither has Alexis."

"How did she get out of it?"

"He left her alone once he started with me," she sighed, and leaned closer to Trygve, knowing she was safe there. "And she got married at eighteen. I was only fifteen then. She ran away with a forty-year-old man. She's still married to him. I don't think he expects much. I think he's gay, and has had a lover for years. He's kind of like a father to her. And I think her answer was to become someone new, new face, new body, new name. David operates on her constantly and she loves it. And she's willing to play the same games as my mother, they both pretend it never happened."

"Did she ever get therapy?" He was intrigued. It was amazing that Page had survived it.

"I don't think so. She would certainly never mention it to me. But I think if she had, she'd say something. That would make us both survivors of our own little holocaust. But she's still playing the games with them. Actually, I don't think there's much of her left anyway. She's anorexic, bulimic, she's never had kids. She hardly even talks. She's just a showpiece for him, and she looks great in clothes. He spends a lot of money on her, and that keeps her happy." Page grinned at him then. "We're very different."

"Sounds like it. You look pretty good in clothes though."

"Not like that. All she cares about is her face and her body. She's constantly purging herself, starving herself, she's obsessed with being clean, and being the perfect beauty."

"Sounds like she still has a problem."

"How could she not?" Page said sadly. But she felt better now that she'd told him.

"I had a feeling the other day that there was a reason why you disliked them so much, if you really did. I was never entirely sure if you were just kidding."

"I wasn't. It's always a tough call for me. Do I see them and still preserve my sanity by not playing the game with them, or do I stay away from them? It's easier not to see them, but sometimes I have to."

He nodded, feeling drained just from listening to her, when one of the nurses came and told her there was a call for her. It was probably her mother, she assumed, wanting something. She was certainly not going to refer to their encounter in the kitchen. That much Page knew for sure. But it wasn't her mother, it was Brad, and he sounded frantic.

"Page . . ." He sounded breathless. "It's Andy."

"Is he hurt?" Terror ran through her again. Everything seemed so dangerous these days, so lethal. It was as though she was constantly waiting for more bad news, or some disaster to befall someone she loved. "What is it?"

"He's gone."

"What do you mean? Did you look in his room?" That was ridiculous. How could he be gone? He was probably asleep in his bed with Lizzie, and Brad hadn't seen him.

"Of course I looked in his room," Brad shouted at her. "He's gone. He left a note."

"What does it say?" Page glanced nervously at Trygve and held a hand out to him. He took it in his own and held it tightly.

"I don't know . . . it's hard to read . . . something about how he knows it's all his fault that we're fighting, and we're angry at him, and he wants us to be happy." Brad sounded like he was crying. "I just called the police. You'd better come home. They said they'd be here in a few minutes. He must have heard us fighting. Oh God, Page, where do you think he is?"

"I have no idea," she said, feeling help-less and panicky. "Did you look outside? Maybe he's hiding in the garden."

"I looked everywhere before I called the police. He's nowhere around the house."

"Does my mother know?" Not that she would be any help, and Brad sounded irri-tated when he answered.

"Yes. She said he probably went to a friend's house. At ten o'clock at night, at his age, that's not likely."

"That sounds about right. Let me guess. And she and Alexis went to bed, and my mother told you it would probably all be fine in the morning."

He laughed in spite of himself. "At least there are never any surprises."

"Some things never change."

"Could you please come home?"

"I'll be right there." She hung up and looked at Trygve. "It's Andy. He ran away . . . he left a note about not wanting us to fight anymore, he thinks it's all his fault." Her eyes filled with tears as she said the words, and he held her. "What if something really awful happens? Kids his age get kidnapped every day." That was all she needed now. She couldn't have stood one more disaster.

"I'm sure the police will find him. Do you want me to come too?" But she shook her head.

"I don't think you should. There's nothing you can do, and it'll only complicate things." He nodded in agreement and walked her quickly to her car. He kissed her before she left and squeezed her arm gently.

"It's going to be all right, Page. They'll find him."

"God, I hope so."

"Me too." He waved and she drove away. It had been quite an evening.

The police were there when she got home, and they took all the information down, about who his friends were, when he went to school, what he was wearing. They went outside and looked everywhere with flashlights. Page gave them two pictures of him. And not surprisingly, her mother and Alexis never came out of their bedrooms. The secret of their game was never to face, or admit to, anything unpleasant. And they played it well. Despite the commotion in the house, and lights flashing outside, there was no sound whatsoever from their bedrooms.

The police drove around the neighborhood, they left and came back again to see if he'd turned up, and just as they drove away again, the phone rang. It was Trygve.

"He's here," he said quietly to Page. "Bjorn was hiding him in his bedroom. I explained to him that that wasn't a good thing to do, and he said that Andy said he never wanted to go home again, he was too sad there." Page's eyes filled with tears as she listened, and she signaled to Brad.

"He's at Trygve's."

"Why there?" He looked surprised. The girls were friends, but there were no children Andy's age.

"He and Bjorn are friends. He went there because he was too sad here." Andy's parents exchanged a long sad glance, and Page went back to talking to Trygve. "I'll come and get him now." She was grateful that they had found him.

Trygve sighed at the end of the phone, he was relieved as well, and slightly embarrassed at what he had to tell her. "He says he doesn't want to come home."

She looked startled by what he'd said. "Why not?"

"He says his father wishes that he was the one who was gone away and not Allie. He said he heard you two fighting about him tonight and his Dad was really angry."

"He was angry at me, not Andy. He thought I had told him about Brad's girl-friend, but I hadn't."

"He doesn't understand that. And he told Bjorn that he thinks Allie's dead, and you're all lying to him. He says he's sure of it. I'm sorry, Page. I thought you ought to know that."

"I guess I should have let him see her."

"That's a tough call. I'd have done the same thing you did. I didn't have any choice with Bjorn, and Chloe was in better shape. Besides, Bjorn is older, and his case is a little different."

"We'll come and get him."

"Why don't you let Bjorn and me bring him home? He's having some hot chocolate. I'll bring him home when he's finished."

"Thank you," she said gratefully, and went to tell Brad what had happened.

"I guess we have to say something to him," Brad said unhappily.

"I think we have to face it ourselves. We can't go on like this for much longer." She sighed deeply then. "And I guess I'm going to have to take him to see Allie." She went to call the police then, to tell them that Andy had turned up at a friend's, and they told her they were glad to hear it.

And half an hour later, he came home with Bjorn and Trygve. He walked into the house looking very sad and very pale, and Page burst into tears when she saw him. She pulled him into her arms and told him how worried they had been, and how much they loved him.

"Please don't *ever* do that again. Something terrible could have happened."

"I thought you were mad at me," he said, crying, glancing up at Brad too, who was fighting back tears of his own, as Trygve and Bjorn stood with them in the kitchen.

"I wasn't mad at you," Page explained, "and neither was Daddy. And Allie isn't dead. She's very, very sick, just the way I told you."

"Then why can't I see her?" he asked suspiciously, but this time Page surprised him.

"You will. I'm going to take you tomorrow."

"You will? For real?" He beamed from ear to ear, he still didn't really understand what he would see there, that she would not talk to him, would not even look like the sister he loved and remembered. But maybe he needed this, maybe he needed reality too, just as she did.

"He thought Allie was dead," Bjorn explained for him.

"I know," Page said, thanking him for taking care of Andy.

"He's my buddy," Bjorn said proudly.

She took them both into Andy's room, and Bjorn helped her put him to bed. She kissed Andy then, and Bjorn went back to the kitchen to find his father.

"Is Daddy going away?" Andy asked her worriedly, once she had put the lights out.

"I don't know." She didn't know what to say. "When I know anything, I'll tell you. But whatever happens, it has nothing to do with you. No one's mad at you. It just has to do with me and Daddy."

"Is it Allie's fault?" He was looking for someone to blame, but sadly enough, there was no one.

"It's no one's fault," Page continued to explain. "It just happened."

"Like the accident?" he asked, and she nodded.

"Yeah. Like that. Sometimes things just happen."

"You kept saying you were tired, that's why you and Daddy were yelling."

"We are tired, but there's other stuff too. It has nothing to do with you. Just grown-up stuff. Honest." He nodded, none of it was good news, but it was easier to cope with the truth than his fears. He had been so sure that it was his fault. "I love you very, very much . . . and so does Daddy."

He nodded, and put his arms around her neck and kissed her. "I love you too. Will you really let me see Allie?"

"I promise." She kissed him again and started to leave the room and he asked her to send Brad in. And when he went in, she said good night to Bjorn and Trygve. She thanked them again for finding him, and Trygve smiled at her as they left.

"Good night, Page," he said quietly, and she felt as though their bond to each other had deepened. She had no secrets from him, and their families seemed to be becoming slowly intertwined. Brad felt something too. He glanced at her as he came back into the kitchen.

"Something going on between you two?" he asked bluntly, and she shook her head.

"No. But that's not the issue."

"I know. I just wondered. I like him. I figured maybe you did too. He's a decent guy."

"We've spent a lot of time together at the hospital in the last few weeks. He's a good father, and a good friend."

Brad looked at her quietly across the kitchen. "I guess I haven't been there much for you . . ." His eyes filled with tears and he looked away. "I can't stand seeing her like that . . . so broken . . . so changed . . . she doesn't even look like Allie."

"I know. I try not to think about it, just about what has to be done for her." He nodded, admiring her, he just couldn't face it.

"What are we going to do about us?" he asked, and then opened the door to the garden. "Why don't we talk out here so no one hears us."

She followed him and they sat on two chairs.

"It doesn't work this way, does it? I thought we could get away with it for a while, until I figured out what's happening. But I'm never here, you're always mad, and I feel pulled in a thousand directions. And every time I get home, I see Andy looking at me, or the hurt or anger in your eyes, or I realize I can barely make myself go see Allie . . ." And Stephanie was pushing him to move in with her, and he wasn't sure he was ready to do that either. "Maybe I should stay somewhere for a while. In a way, I'd rather be here. But it doesn't work for anyone." She thought long and hard about what he was saying. At first, she had wanted him to stay at home too, but not the way things were now. It was nightmarish this way, and they both knew it. They had to face it. It was over.

She caught her breath before she said the words, and once they were out, she couldn't believe she'd said them. If anyone had told her a month before, she wouldn't have believed them. "I think you should move out," she said in barely more than a whisper.

"You do?" He looked surprised as he stared at her. But in a way, it was a relief to hear her say it.

"I do." She nodded slowly. "It's time. We've been kidding ourselves for the past few weeks. I think it was over long before I knew it. You would never have told me what you were doing, about . . . your other life . . . unless you were ready to let go of this one. I just didn't understand that when you told me."

"Maybe you're right," he said unhappily. "Maybe I should never have said anything." But he couldn't take it back now, he couldn't undo what he'd done, and in truth, he didn't want to. "I wish I knew the answers, Page."

"So do I." She looked at him, wondering how they had come to this. Was it all because of the accident, or was that just the catalyst? Things had to have been ready to fall apart before, or this would never have happened. "I always thought we had such a perfect life," she said, thinking back on it. "Even now, I can't see where we went wrong . . . what we did . . . or should have done . . ."

"You couldn't have done anything," he

said honestly, "I was fucking up for a long time. You just didn't know it."

"I guess not," she said, suddenly grateful that she hadn't known sooner. They had had sixteen years that she cherished now. She still couldn't believe they were over. "What'll we tell Andy?" She looked worried again. It was amazing, sitting here, discussing this, like a party they were going to give, or a trip, or a funeral. She hated every minute of it, but it had to be done, it was better to face it. "We have to say something to him soon."

"I know. We tell him the truth, I guess . . . that I'm an asshole."

She smiled at him in the dark. He was an asshole at times, but she still loved him. In some ways, she would have liked to turn the clock back, in others she knew it wasn't possible. Even after only three weeks of destruction, it had gone too far now. The whole foundation of their marriage had been undermined long since, and the entire structure had finally caved in. In truth, it had been a long time coming. And the fact that she hadn't known it was happening didn't lessen the power of the collapse. Everything around them was falling.

"What do you think you'll do?" she asked

quietly. "Move in with her?" It sounded like he already had, part time at least, from what her friend said.

"I don't know yet. That's what she'd like. But I need some time to catch my breath." It wasn't going to be easy for them. Their relationship had been built on lies, and lust, and cheating. It was harder to build on something like that, and he was beginning to understand that. "When do you want me to go?"

For an instant, she wished he could still be everything she had always thought he was. But he wasn't. "Before we destroy Andy and each other," she said, sounding calmer than she felt. "It's been getting worse pretty quickly."

"You've been pretty angry, and you've been right," he admitted. This was the most civilized conversation they'd had since the accident. It was sad that they had only come to their senses in time to end it. "I'll try not to aggravate things while I get organized. I'm going to New York tomorrow. I'll be back Thursday. Maybe I can figure something out by next weekend. How much longer do you think your mother will be here?" It was a little difficult ending their marriage and moving out with his mother-in-law in the guest room. But he was surprised by Page's answer.

"I'm going to ask them to leave tomorrow morning. I'm not going to have her here anymore. It's not good for me . . . or for Andy." She was cleaning all of it out, him, her mother, Alexis. In their own ways, they were using her, and hurting her, and she had understood that night, as she sat talking to Trygve, and when Andy had run away after that, that it was time to stop it.

"I respect you a lot, you know," he said softly in the night air. "I always have. I don't know where things went wrong. Maybe I wasn't ready for all you had to give." He was twenty-eight when they got married, but he had never really given up the idea that he could do whatever he wanted, and now there was a hell of a price to pay for it.

"You'll feel better when I'm gone," he said sadly. "You can get on with your life then."

"I'll be lonely too. This isn't going to be easy for anyone," she told him honestly, and then she looked at him in the dark night. "What are we going to do about Allie?"

"There's nothing we can do. That's what

gets to me so badly. I don't know how you sit there night and day. I'd go crazy."

"I'm getting there. But what if she never comes back?" she whispered.

"I don't know. I try not to think about it. What if she does, and she's not the same? You know . . . like that kid . . . Bjorn . . . I don't think I could stand it, knowing what she used to be. I guess we just have to accept whatever comes, don't we? At first, I thought we had more choices. But now I realize we don't. . . . Or maybe we did then, we could have chosen not to operate, but then we'd have killed her. We did all the right stuff, and nothing's happening. But I'll tell you one thing, if she stays in the coma indefinitely, you can't sit there for years . . . or it'll destroy you. You're going to have to work that out eventually." But it was still too soon. The accident had happened a little over three weeks before. And there was still a strong possibility she could come out of the coma.

"Don't let your life turn into that, Page . . . " he said, pleading with her ". . . you deserve so much more than that . . . more than I had to give you."

She nodded, and turned away, trying not to think of what it would be like when he left. She looked up at the sky then, and saw stars, as she wondered how their life had gone so wrong . . . how they could have come so far . . . how this could have happened to them . . . and to Allie. . . .

CHAPTER 13

Page waited quietly the next morning for her mother to get up, and when she did, she made breakfast for her and Alexis, and served it to them at the kitchen table. And then she told them quietly that they had to leave, that a week had been long enough, and this was not a good time for her to have them out there. She made no reference to the night before, and no apology, and they must have known she meant business, because neither of them argued with her. Her mother said that David was missing Alexis terribly, and she had to get home herself to see about repainting her apartment.

They were the perfect excuses, and Page didn't give a damn what stories they told each other about leaving. She wanted them out of her house by that night, and she had already booked them on a four P.M. flight in first class, much to her mother's amazement. She had also arranged for a limousine that would pick them up and take them to the airport. The limousine would be there at two o'clock, in plenty of time for their flight. And they could have lunch before they left the house, and even visit Allyson one last time, if they wanted to do that.

"Actually . . ." her mother stalled ". . . it takes me so long to pack. And Alexis said she thought she was getting one of her headaches. Of course, if you want us to visit Allyson, maybe we should take a flight tomorrow." There was not a chance of that, as long as Page was alive. She was not letting them stay another moment. She was taking charge of her life again. As painful as it was, she had told Brad he had to move out, and now she was sending them back to New York.

"I don't think Allyson will mind," Page said facetiously, but they took it seriously and said to be sure she told her that they both sent their love.

She stayed with them until they left, and then changed their beds, did two loads of wash, and vacuumed her whole house. She felt as though she was taking care of things, and doing what she could to get her life back in order. Their departure had been remarkably unemotional, considering the fireworks the night before. Nothing more needed to be said now.

Alexis had put on a new hat, her mother wore one of the new suits they'd bought, they kissed the air somewhere around Page's face, and they disappeared into the limousine while Page watched them. And she felt a wave of relief wash over her as she cleaned her house and realized they were gone. It felt particularly good when she cleaned Allyson's room, and the only thing that startled her was the unbelievable quantity of laxatives that Alexis had forgotten. She was a very sick woman, Page knew, but no one else seemed to be aware of that, or maybe they were and they didn't care. She was trying to make herself disappear, as well as everything that had happened to her, and it was a terrible way to do it. In her own way, she wanted to be a little girl again, the little girl she had been before her father raped her.

Page picked Andy up at school at four o'clock, feeling freer than she had in weeks, certainly since the accident, and he asked if they could stop off to buy a bunch of roses. Page suggested that he might like to give them to Chloe at the hospital because Allyson couldn't have them in ICU, and he agreed. He was excited about seeing her, and he talked about her all the way there, and Page reminded him again of what Allie would look like.

"I know, I know," he said importantly, "like she's asleep."

"No," Page explained again, "different. She has a big bandage on her head, and her arms and legs are very thin, and there's a tube in her throat that helps her breathe, attached to a big machine that breathes for her. Sometimes it all looks pretty scary, particularly if you've never seen it before. Okay? You can talk to her, but she won't answer you."

"I know. She's sleeping."

He felt very important to be going to visit her, and he had talked about it at school all day. When they got to the hospital, he could hardly wait to get out of the car, and he held Page's hand as they hurried into the lobby.

They had bought pink roses finally for Chloe, and he bought one beautiful gardenia to give his sister. "She's gonna love it," he said proudly, carrying it himself. But in spite of all her preparations, Page could see he was stunned when he saw her. And for some reason, she looked particularly bad that day. She was pale, and they had changed the bandage and it looked bigger and whiter. It was obvious too that her hair was all gone, and there suddenly seemed to be more machines than ever. There weren't, of course, but it seemed that way to Page, as she watched Andy stare at her. And then he moved slowly forward, and put the gardenia next to his sister on the pillow.

"Hi, Allie," he whispered, his eyes huge, and then he touched her hand, and Page couldn't keep from crying. "It's okay . . . I know you're asleep . . . Mom told me." He stood looking at her for a long time, and stroking her hand, and then he leaned over and kissed her. Everything around her smelled medicinal, except for the gardenia he had brought her.

"Dad's going to New York today," he explained, "and Mom said I could see you again sometime soon. I'm sorry it took me so long to get here." Nothing stirred except the machines, and Page cried silently as the nurses watched them. "I love you, Allie . . . it's no fun at home without you." He wanted to tell her Mom and Dad fought all the time, but he didn't want to hurt his mother's feelings. And he wanted to beg her to come home. He really missed his older sister. "Oh . . . and I have a new friend . . . Bjorn . . . you know, Chloe's brother. He's eighteen, but he isn't really." He turned around and smiled at his mom, and he was surprised to see her crying. "Are you okay, Mom?"

"I'm fine," she said, smiling at him through her tears. She was so proud of him, and she loved him so much. And she was glad she had brought him. She hadn't realized till then how much he needed to see his sister. And even if Allie died now, he would feel he had reached out to her, and said good-bye. She hadn't disappeared in the middle of the night into a vacuum.

He talked to Allie for a little while, and then he turned to Page and said he was ready to visit Chloe. He looked at his sister for a long moment then, and stood on tiptoe to kiss her.

"I'll see you soon . . . okay? . . . try to wake up soon, Al. We really miss you . . . I love you, Allie," he said, and taking his mother's hand, he left ICU with his bunch of pink roses for Chloe.

It took Page a minute to regain her composure, and then she kissed him and told him how proud she was of him. "You're a terrific guy, you know that?"

"Do you think she heard me, Mom?" he asked, looking worried.

"I'm sure of it, sweetheart."

"I hope so," he said sadly. He was still subdued when they got to Chloe's room, but Page was amazed at how well he had done. He hadn't cried, or been visibly frightened. And he was even better with Chloe. Bjorn was there, visiting her too, and eventually the two boys started playing and laughing and running in the halls, and playing tag around the nurses.

"We'd better get them out of here before the nurses throw us out," Trygve said, laughing, and then he glanced more seriously at Page. "How did he do in ICU? Was he okay?"

"He was fantastic. He was so brave, and so sweet. He left a gardenia next to her on the pillow."

"He's a sweet kid. He seems happier to-day, how is he?"

"Okay. Brad and I had a long talk last night. He's going to move out. We're going to have to say something to Andy."

"Nothing's ever easy, is it?" He squeezed her hand, and they went to round up the boys, and then Trygve invited them out for pizza. "Or do you have to go home and cook dinner for your mother and sister?"

"Nope," she grinned. "All gone. I sent them home on a four o'clock flight," she said, looking ecstatic.

"Aunt Alexis is weird," Andy added, listening to them, "she spends all her time in the bathroom."

They had a nice time together that night, in sharp contrast to the night before. The boys played and talked and teased and devoured the enormous pizza, and Page and Trygve had a chance to talk and share a few normal hours, away from the hospital. It even gave her a chance to talk about her artwork. She'd been thinking about getting a studio, after Allie got out of ICU, or if they settled into some kind of permanent routine. But she wanted to pursue her painting more seriously, and maybe even get paid for her murals.

"Good for you," Trygve congratulated her. "You should have done that years ago. They're sensational." And so was she. He liked her better every time he saw her. He took them home eventually and he was sorry when he had to leave, but he had to take Bjorn home. And Chloe would be coming home in another week or two, that was going to keep him pretty busy. But he had every intention of making time for Page too, and going to the hospital if she needed him to. He also wanted to spend a little time with Andy. It was going to be hard for her now if Brad moved out, and hard for the boy. Trygve wanted to be there to help her pick up the pieces. He just hoped that nothing dramatic happened to Allyson now. They had all been through enough, and with everything else going on in her life, he wasn't sure that Page could take it.

CHAPTER 14

Brad came home from New York on Thursday afternoon, but Page didn't see him. He never came home to Ross that night, and the next day when he stopped by to see Allyson at lunchtime, she missed him. The nurses told her he'd come by at noon, but when she went home after picking Andy up from Jane's that night, she found Brad packing. The door to the bedroom was closed. But she saw his car in the garage, and Andy exploded into their bedroom to see him. And then he looked around him, startled. There were two suitcases on the floor, another on the bed, and there were clothes everywhere.

And as Page saw them, she felt her heart ache.

"What are you doing, Dad?" Andy looked confused, and this wasn't the way Page had wanted him to find out. Brad looked around the room, then at her, and they both knew they had no choice. "Are you going away again?" He looked deeply worried.

"Sort of, champ." He sat down on the bed and pulled Andy onto his lap, as Page watched them, feeling a lump rise in her throat. Her life seemed to be full of goodbyes these days, and painful moments. "I'm going to move to the city."

"Me too?" Andy looked stunned. No one had told him they were moving.

"No, you're going to stay here with Mom." He had wanted to say ". . . and Allie . . ." but he stopped himself in time. Who knew if she'd ever come home again?

"Are we getting divorced?" Andy asked as tears sprang to his eyes and his father hugged him.

"Maybe. We don't know yet. But it seemed like a good idea for me to move out. Your Mom and I have been doing an awful lot of fighting."

"Is it because I ran away that night, Dad? Is that why you're leaving?"

"No, it's because it's something I've wanted to do for a while. And things have gotten pretty difficult lately. Sometimes that's the way things happen."

"Is it because of the accident?" Andy needed a reason. But maybe there was none.

"Could be. I don't know. Sometimes things just get rough . . . but that doesn't mean I don't love you. I love you a whole bunch, and so does Mom. We're both going to be here for you, and you'll come and visit me sometimes, and on weekends." Listening to him, Page suddenly realized that there were going to have to be visitation schedules, and lawyers. It was all so complicated, and so official. She hated it to get that way, but this was what would happen now. They would have to divide up everything they had, the furniture, what was left of the wedding gifts after sixteen years . . . the linens . . . the silverware . . . the towels . . . What a miserable thing their life had become, and all in a matter of moments.

"Where will you be, Dad? Do you have a house?"

"I'm going to stay in an apartment. I'm going to get my own phone number, and you can call me. And you can call me at the office." Andy listened to him and then started to cry as Brad held him.

"I don't want you to go," he said miserably as Page cried while she watched them. It was awful.

"I don't want to go either, Son, but I have to."

"Why?" He didn't understand it, and watching them, neither did Page. How had it come to this? How could they have been so stupid?

"It's hard to explain. Things just worked out that way."

"Why can't you fix them?" It was a reasonable suggestion and Brad smiled at Page through his own tears.

"I wish I could." But the truth was he didn't wish he could. He was happy to move on. He wanted his own life, his own apartment, and Stephanie. He was actually excited about moving. And she was thrilled. She wanted to move in with him right away, but Brad thought they should wait a month or two.

It was only when he came back here, when he saw how painful it was for all of them, that he didn't want to leave them. But he was smart enough by now to know that if he didn't move out, he'd be slipping away whenever he could in a matter of moments. He was ready to go, no matter how sorry he was, or how much he loved Andy.

"Don't do it, Daddy," Andy begged, and Page felt nauseous.

"Son, don't. It's the right thing for all of us. I know it."

"What'll Allie say when she comes back?" He was clutching at straws and they all knew it.

"We'll have to explain it to her." Andy ran to his mother then and sobbed as she held him.

It was a terrible night for all of them. Brad decided to spend the night there and he worked through the night going through his papers. And by morning, they all looked as though they were in mourning.

Page made pancakes and sausages for all of them, normally their favorite, but no one could eat them. Andy had had a baseball game scheduled that day, but with his broken arm, he couldn't play. And he wanted Brad to stay and play with him, but by late morning, Brad said he needed to get to the city. He knew that Stephanie was waiting.

"When will I see you, Dad?" Andy asked, panicky, as Brad loaded his bags and boxes into the car, and prepared to leave them.

"Next Saturday, I promise. Just pretend I'm on a trip. You can call me every day at the office." But Andy was beyond words and promises by then, he just stood there and cried and so did Page, as he backed out of the driveway and left them. Other than Allie's accident, four weeks before, it was the worst day she could remember. All that hope, all those years, those two shining people, the family they had built, gone forever.

Andy stood outside crying in her arms for a long time, and then finally they went inside, and sat together. It felt as though someone had died. They had lost two people they loved. And Page could hardly believe it when her mother called at lunchtime and thanked her for the lovely visit.

"Alexis and I had such a good time. And it was so good to see Allyson. I'm sure by now she's much better." The glib words left her speechless, and she was in no mood to talk to her. Page told her mother she'd call her back sometime, hung up, and went back to Andy. He was lying on her bed, crying into the pillow. He felt terrible, and she had to admit, she didn't feel much better. Somehow, seeing Brad leave made it all so real, and so painful.

"I know you feel rotten, sweetheart. But we have to make the best of it," she said through her own tears. And then Andy rolled over to see her.

"Did you want him to leave?" Was it her fault? His? Andy's? Allie's? . . . whose? . . . Andy didn't understand it.

"No. I didn't want him to leave, sweetheart. But I know he had to. Things had gotten pretty bad."

"Why? Why were you fighting?"

"I don't know. We just were." It was so hard to explain to him. She didn't completely understand it herself, how could she explain it to a child of seven?

Trygve called them late that afternoon, and she told him what had happened. He invited them over for one of his stews, but at first Andy didn't even want to see Bjorn, and then finally he relented. He got in the car halfheartedly, and took the teddy bear he slept with.

"Bjorn has one too," he explained to Page. "He calls him Charlie."

And when they got there, Bjorn could see that his friend was in bad shape. They sat outside and talked for a long time, while Andy told him what had happened.

"How is he?" Trygve asked, worried about them both.

"Upset. It was worse than I thought when the actual moment came. It was awful."

"I remember only too well." It still hurt to think about the day Dana had left. Everyone had cried for hours, even Dana. "God, you've all been through the wringer."

"Who hasn't?" She looked over at him, exhausted again. It was a permanent state these days. "How's Chloe?"

"Raising hell at the hospital. She's supposed to come home next week, if we can rig up ramps for her, and she'll have to sleep downstairs in Nick's bedroom." But listening to him, Page thought about how lucky he was that she was coming home at all. In four weeks, there had been no change in Allie's condition. It was not beyond hope yet, but soon it would be.

They had a nice dinner together that night, and talked about the menu for his Memorial Day barbecue. He gave her his latest article to read, it was part of a series for *The New York Times* he'd been working on for a while. They had a good time, but he didn't press her about anything. He knew she was hurting over Brad, and the last thing he wanted to do was upset her.

"I didn't expect to feel so awful when he left," she explained after dinner, as they sat outside in deck chairs, fighting the mosquitoes.

"Why not? After sixteen years, you'd have to be numb not to. I was pretty numb actually by the time Dana left, but it still knocked the hell out of me. I grieved for a long time. You may too."

"I don't know what's happening to me anymore. My life is such a mess."

"No it's not. It just feels that way right now. You have a lot on your plate. What's happening with Allie? What does Hammerman say?"

"That a lot is still possible, but if she doesn't come out of the coma in a month or two, eventually it won't be. I'm beginning to worry that she's going to stay this way, Trygve." He didn't say anything for a moment as she thought about it, and looked at the stars in silence.

"I hope not." And then he remembered something he'd forgotten to tell her. "I heard something interesting last week, but I knew you had your hands full and I didn't want to upset you."

"What was that?"

"Someone saw Laura Hutchinson drunk at a party. I mean really drunk. She had to be taken away, and it was all done very quietly. Very hush-hush. Things like that make me wonder how often that's happened before and what really happened that night. If the rest of us get drunk, we fall on our faces and make asses of ourselves, and it doesn't matter if we don't do it very often. Someone with a problem . . . in a delicate situation . . . it would be handled very differently, wouldn't it? It would all be whisked away like a bad smell so no one would know it.

"I've always wondered if she was drunk that night. She was so apologetic to everyone, so distraught, so attentive to the Chapmans, from what I heard." She had made an enormous donation to Redwood High School in Phillip's name, and everyone knew it. "I always thought it sounded like she felt guilty."

"Maybe. Or maybe she just felt terrible about Phillip's death, whether she was responsible for it or not. She wrote to me, and told me how sorry she was about Allie," Page said without suspicion. She had wanted to blame Laura Hutchinson at first, but she had gotten over that.

"We heard from her too, but I never answered. What can you say? Oh, no problem . . . it's fine, you almost killed my daughter, and may have turned her into a wheelchair case, but we really appreciate the letter." He looked angry, as he said it, and then he looked at Page pensively.

"You know . . . I had this crazy idea. I don't even know what I'm searching for, but I have an old friend who's an investigative reporter. He works for one of those disgusting tabloids, but he might have some interesting sources."

"What are you looking for?" she asked with interest.

"I'm not sure. Something. Maybe I'm like you . . . maybe we're both looking for a needle in the haystack. But looking back at it, I think there was more than we knew that night. Maybe he can find out something. Maybe Laura Hutchinson still has a drinking problem, and if so we have a right to know it."

"Why don't you ask him," she said softly, as Trygve nodded, and then he looked at her and smiled. "The Chapmans would be interested in the information too." They had just filed suit against both of the local papers.

"We're a couple of troublemakers, you and I," Trygve said quietly.

"Maybe she deserves it," Page whispered sadly.

Without saying more, he nodded.

CHAPTER 15

The next two weeks whizzed by, painfully at times, but pleasantly too. The first week that Brad was gone was incredibly painful. Andy cried every night, twice he had to be picked up from school, too upset to stay, once she was afraid he'd run away again, but she found him sitting alone with his teddy bear in the garden. And it was hard on her too. He wanted something she didn't have to give him anymore, a Daddy.

Brad was true to his word, and took him out the following Saturday, but it was terrible when he brought him home again. They had gone to Marine World. And Andy didn't want him to leave, but Brad said he had to. He would have taken him home with him, but he thought it was too soon to introduce him to Stephanie. She was at his apartment most of the time now, and Brad didn't want Andy to associate her with the pain of the separation.

The second week went a little more smoothly. Andy went to see Allie again, they had dinner with the Thorensens a couple of times. Andy saw Brad again, on Saturday. And Chloe came home from the hospital on Sunday, six weeks after the accident that had almost killed her.

Trygve drove her home, and Bjorn was waiting for them with big signs everywhere, and bouquets of flowers he had picked from their garden. He had baked a cake for her with Trygve the night before, and he made her lunch himself that day, peanut butter and jelly sandwiches, his favorite, and the S'Mores he had learned to make at camp. It was a wonderful homecoming for Chloe. Even Nick had come home from college for the long weekend. And he had given up his room to his sister.

Page and Andy had come by to see her too, after she'd settled in. She was lying on the couch in the living room by then, not looking very comfortable, but extremely happy. She still had quite a lot of pain, but she was trying not to overdo the pain medicine. She didn't want to get hooked on any of it, and she tried to cope with it by distraction.

Jamie Applegate had come to see her that afternoon too, and he looked suddenly awkward when he arrived. He had visited her a lot in the hospital, and he'd gotten used to seeing her there, but seeing her at home for the first time suddenly reminded him of how dishonest they had been when they had snuck away for the date that had injured her and Allyson, and killed Phillip. It seemed to bring back all of it, for both of them, and they talked quietly for a long time, in the living room, while Bjorn and Trygve and Page and Andy sat in the kitchen.

It was a happy, easy day. For the moment, the worst was over. She might have to be operated on again, the doctor thought it was likely that she would. But she would never be in danger again, or in as much pain, or as severely incapacitated as she still was now. Now it was a matter of repairing the damaged limbs, but not of surviving. She looked pretty and young as she lay on the couch in the living room, covered by a pink blanket Page had given her. It was cashmere, and soft, and she fingered it unconsciously as she and Jamie talked about Allie and Phillip.

"It seems weird, doesn't it?" Chloe said sadly as she looked at him. "I can't call her . . . you can't call him . . . it makes me feel so lonely sometimes," she said sadly, her big eyes looking up at him as he nodded. Chloe had helped him a lot, she talked about the things that he wouldn't have dared to say, about the accident and what she was feeling. Because she was a girl, it seemed okay to her, and it somehow gave him permission to vent the guilt and the anguish he felt for surviving the accident unscathed by the cruel hand of fate that had touched the other three. He was still having trouble with it, and seeing a therapist from time to time to help him get over the inevitable guilt he felt. He had even gone to a group of people who had survived plane crashes, and fires, and accidents, but lost members of their families and friends. It had been a great relief to talk to them, and he had told Chloe all about it.

"So what are we going to do today?" Jamie asked eventually. They had become close friends in the past six weeks, and he thought he knew everything about her. The kind of music she liked, her favorite actors and actresses and movies, the friends she really loved, and the people she hated, the kind of house she wanted to live in when she grew up, how many children she thought she'd like to have, where she wanted to go to college. They talked about everything, from the trivial to the important.

"I don't know," she said, teasing him, "I thought maybe we'd go dancing." She hadn't lost her sense of humor through it all, and he took her hand gently and looked at her, after she said it.

"We will one day. I promise you that, we'll go in a great big limousine, like to a prom, and we'll go somewhere and dance all night," he promised with a look of determination. He was serious, and she was touched by the intensity of his feelings. She liked him a lot too, he had come to mean a lot to her in the past weeks. In an odd way, he had almost come to take the place of Allie. If anyone had asked, she would have said they were best friends now. In a way, they were more than that, and they both knew that too, but they didn't say it in

words. They had just come to count on each
other. In a funny way, not unlike Page and
Trygve.

"What are you two up to in here?"
Trygve asked as he wandered through the
room to check on Chloe a little while later,
and see if she wanted anything to eat or
drink, or if she was getting too tired and
needed to be put to bed for a while. But she
seemed happy on the couch, talking to Jamie.

"We're just talking," Jamie said easily. It
meant a lot to him that Trygve had let him
spend time with Chloe since the accident,
and had given him a chance to get to know
her better. At first, he'd been worried that
that was only in the hospital, and they
wouldn't want him in their home. But that
was obviously not the case, and he was im-
mensely relieved to be there that afternoon,
and share the homecoming with Chloe.
"Can I do anything to help?" Jamie asked
nervously, and Trygve just told him to keep
an eye on Chloe, and make sure she didn't
try to hop off the couch. And if she needed
to go to the bathroom, to call him.

When Jamie did call him eventually for
that, it was Trygve and Page who got her
there, and she was pretty independent after

that. But it was obvious she was going to need a lot of help getting around the house, and managing even the smallest task. Coming home from the hospital was not going to be the end of the challenging part, but only the beginning.

Page said as much to him when they went back to the kitchen for another cup of coffee.

"I know." Trygve nodded solemnly. He had figured all that out, and knew how difficult it would be, and how limiting for Chloe. Now that she was back from the hospital, she would expect to have her freedom again, and to be able to move around, but her homecoming wasn't magical. It was going to be a long, slow haul back to the free and easy life she remembered. "I've got someone coming in to help a few hours a day, just so I can get out, or get some work done. And Bjorn is a big help to me, but it's going to be difficult for a while. I don't think she had realized that herself before she left the hospital, but I did." He smiled, and Page thought again of how much she admired him, and what a nice man he was. They were all depending on him, even she was.

Eventually, she and Andy left before dinnertime and went home and had a quiet evening together. They rented videos, ate popcorn, slept in the same bed, and she had cooked him his favorite dinner.

The next day was Memorial Day and Trygve organized a barbecue, and invited four or five of Chloe's friends, Jamie Applegate naturally, and of course Page and Andy.

"They're nice kids," Trygve said, as he sat down next to her with a glass of wine, still wearing his apron. He looked tired. He'd been up a lot in the night with Chloe.

"They are, and they're so happy to have her back." Page smiled at them, wishing Allie were there too. Being with Chloe was always bittersweet for her, but Trygve knew that.

"What an experience this has been. For all of us," he sighed. "Sometimes it feels like none of us will ever be the same again. No one it touched was left the same." Least of all Phillip and Allie. "What about you?" He looked at her with a gentle smile. "How are you doing?" He had seen less of her during the two weeks since her separation. And he had missed her terribly. But he knew how traumatic it had been for her when Brad left, and he wanted to give her time to adjust. She had noticed it and she was grateful for it, although she'd missed him too, and the warmth of their friendship and flirtation. He was always sensitive to her needs, without her having to say anything about it.

"I'm okay," she said quietly. It had been even harder than she'd expected.

"I've missed you," he said, watching her.

"Me too," she said softly. "I didn't think it would be like this. It's lonely, it's sad. In some ways, it's a relief. It got so bad at the end it was like a constant pain. This is better, but it's sad anyway. I feel pretty brave and new sometimes, and at other times, I feel so . . ." She looked for the right word. ". . . unprotected." She had been married for so long that it felt odd to be alone now.

"You're not unprotected though. You're as safe as you were before. You're the one who was taking care of everyone. Brad wasn't." It was true, and she had only just begun to understand that. He had scarcely even been to see Allie in the past two weeks. Only once or twice a week. But at least he was seeing Andy.

"I guess I'm starting to figure that out. It's odd though. After sixteen years of marriage, you're back where you started, minus some towels, and some silver, and the better toaster." She smiled. It was worse than that, of course, but somehow the things Brad had taken had irked her.

"That hurts, doesn't it?" He laughed. "Dana took exactly half of everything we owned. One out of every pair of lamps we owned, half the kitchen chairs, half the pots and pans, half the silverware. Now nothing I own matches, and every time I go to cook an omelet or have guests to dinner I swear, because whatever it is I'm looking for is in England."

"I know." She grinned painfully. "In the beginning he said he didn't want anything. Now it turns out Stephanie must not be as well equipped as he first thought. Every few days I come home and find something gone, and a note explaining that he's taken this or that 'against his share.' I don't know when he comes to the house, but I'm never there. And yesterday he took half the silver flatware my mother gave me."

"You'd better watch out. Those things get nasty."

"I guess so . . . pot holders . . . cooking pots . . . skis . . . it's weird the stuff that it boils down to in the end, isn't it? It's all so petty. Kind of like a garage sale for the emotions."

He smiled at the comparison, but it was true. And then he asked her something he hadn't dared to. "What are you and Andy doing this summer?"

"Summer? Oh God . . . that's right, it's June this week . . . I don't know. I don't suppose we can leave Allie."

"What if there's no change? Don't you suppose you could get away, as long as it's not too far?" He was looking hopeful, and she smiled at him. He had brought up an interesting question. What if there was no change? Could she go away for a few days? Did she dare? Would she have to begin to lead a life that assumed Allie might stay in a coma?

"What did you have in mind?" she asked cautiously, still thinking of her daughter.

"A couple of weeks at Lake Tahoe. We go there every year, and Bjorn would love to have Andy with him," he looked away and then back at her again ". . . and I'd love to have you there with me . . ."

"I'd like that," she said softly. "We'll see. Let's see how Allie is by the time you go. When do you go?"

"August."

"That's two months away. A lot could change by then." Either she would have made some progress, or she'd be locked in her coma forever.

"Just keep it in mind," he said, looking at her with eyes full of meaning.

"I will." She smiled as their hands met and touched for a moment. All the electricity they'd shared briefly was there. But during the trauma of the separation, he'd backed off so as not to pressure her or confuse her. But he had missed her.

They left late, and Andy fell asleep in the car on the way home. It had been a nice weekend.

Trygve called her after she had put Andy to bed, and she was lying in her own bed, feeling lonely.

"I miss you," he said, and she smiled. Now that Chloe was home from the hospital, they would see less of each other unless he came to the hospital specifically to see her. He knew her routine now. "I always miss you," he said, sounding husky and sexy. Most of the time she tried not to let herself think about him right now. She had wanted some time to mourn Brad and their marriage, but she missed Trygve's company too. He was a good friend, an attractive man, and fun to be with. "When am I going to see you again?" he asked. "I'm not sure we can carry on in the ICU waiting room for the rest of our lives." They both remembered the endless hours and the recent kisses they had shared there.

"I hope we won't have to meet there forever," she said sadly.

"So do I. But in the meantime, how about a real date one of these days, without kids, without nurses, with real food, and no pepperoni pizza." She laughed at the thought, it was an appealing idea. No one had asked her out in years. The thought of it made her feel young and attractive.

"It sounds incredible." She had only been out once, with her mother, since the accident six weeks before, but maybe now she was ready. "You mean I don't have to cook?"

"No," he said emphatically, "and no Norwegian stew, and no Swedish meatballs. No peanut butter sandwiches. No S'Mores. Real food. Grown-up stuff. How about the Silver Dove on Thursday?" It was a romantic spot in Marin, and if anything happened, they would be close by if they were needed.

"It sounds wonderful," she said, feeling happier than she had in weeks. He always managed to make her feel special, even in her gardening sweater and worst shoes, he made her feel like a beauty.

"I'll pick you up at seven-thirty."

"Perfect." She could either leave Andy with Jane, or get a sitter. And then suddenly she laughed, thinking of something.

"What's up?"

"I was just thinking it was my first real date in seventeen years. I'm not sure I remember how you do that."

"Don't worry about a thing. I'll show you." They both laughed, feeling young again, and they chatted for a while, about other things than their children for a change, his latest article, her plans for the mural at school, and his house at Tahoe. He told her also that he'd spoken to his investigative reporter friend, who was doing a little initial digging about Laura Hutchinson, and her drinking. It might not turn up anything, and it still would never prove anything about the accident. But somehow Trygve was haunted by his suspicions.

"I'll see you tomorrow," he said finally, sounding husky again, and she wondered what he meant when she hung up, but the next day he turned up at ICU with a picnic basket and a bunch of flowers.

She had been working with Allie and the therapist, trying to stretch her muscles. Her legs were pointed out straight now, her feet rigid in their position, her elbows flexed, her arms locked, her hands tightly clenched. It took endless exercising to even help her move or bend or stretch. And her body, like her mind, seemed not to be responding. It was depressing, working with the therapist, and Page was happy to see him.

"Come on, let's go outside." He could see how tired and down she was. "It's a gorgeous day." And it was, the sun was hot, the sky was blue. It was everything one expects of June in California. And the moment she got outside, she felt better.

They sat on the lawn outside for a long time, with the nurses and the medical students and residents. Everyone looked as though they were in love and lazy.

"It's spring," Trygve announced, lying on the grass next to her, as she sniffed happily at the flowers he'd brought her. Without thinking, she touched his cheek gently with her fingers, and he looked up at her with a look she hadn't seen on a man's face in years, if ever. It made her realize suddenly what she had been missing. "You're beautiful . . . very, very beautiful . . . in fact," he beamed, "you even look Norwegian."

"I'm not," she smiled, feeling young and foolish with him, "Addison is English."

"Well, you look Scandinavian to me." He looked at her seriously. "I was just thinking what gorgeous children we could have. Do you want more?" he asked curiously. He wanted to know everything about her. Not just how she felt about Allyson, or how strong she was, or how good a mother. He wanted to know the rest of it, the things they hadn't had time to explore as they sat in anguished vigil for their daughters.

"I used to want more children," she answered him, "but I'm thirty-nine. It's sort of late by now, and I've got my hands full with Andy, and now Allie."

"It won't always be that way, and you're getting into a routine with her." She had to, for her own survival. "I'm forty-two, and I don't feel too old. I'd love to have a couple more, and at thirty-nine, you could have half a dozen."

"What a thought!" she laughed, and then thought about it again. "Andy would like that. We were talking about it that day coming home from the baseball game, and then that night, Allie had the accident . . . it sure changed everything, didn't it?" He nodded. Six and a half weeks later she was no longer living with her husband, and Chloe was no longer a ballerina . . . not to mention Phillip, who was dead, or Allie, whose life had been changed forever. "Anyway . . . yeah . . . I'd like more kids. One anyway. I'd have to see after that. And I really want to pursue my artwork. Actually, I was thinking about what you said the other day, about doing a mural in ICU. I talked to Frances," their favorite head nurse, "and she was going to ask someone about it."

"Actually, I'd love to do something like that at my place. Would you take me on as a client?—A paying client that is!"

"I'd love it."

"Good. How about a consultation tomorrow night, after dinner? You can bring Andy."

"You won't get tired of me if you're seeing me on Thursday too?" She looked worried and he laughed.

"I don't think that I'd get tired of you, Page, if I saw you day and night forever. In fact, eventually I'd like to prove that." She blushed as he said it, and he pulled her down next to him and kissed her. "I'm in love with you, Page," he whispered, "very, very, very much in love with you. And I'm never going to get tired of you. Do you hear me? We're going to have ten children and live happily ever after." He was laughing and kissing her, and she lay on the grass happily in his arms, feeling like a kid again. It was too good to be true, and she only hoped it would last and he meant it.

They sat up again finally, and she thought about going back to the ICU. It exhausted her to think about it. The exercises, the movements, the therapy, the respirator, the silence, the total apathy, the depth of Allie's coma. Sometimes it was hard to make herself go back there, but she always did. She never failed. The nurses could set their clocks by her, she came back at night and sat with her for hours, stroking her hand or her cheek, and speaking softly.

"I'll come up with you," he said with an arm around her shoulders. She was carrying the picnic basket with the flowers he'd given her, and she looked relaxed and happy as they went upstairs arm in arm, talking quietly, and laughing.

"Have a nice lunch?" a new nurse asked as Page strolled by on her way back to Allie's bed. The smells of the ICU were familiar now, the sounds, the lights, and noises.

"Lovely, thanks." She smiled up at Trygve as she said it, and then went to stand next to her daughter again as he watched her. She was tireless, the most devoted mother he had ever seen, talking to her and moving her limbs, unclenching her fingers, always speaking to her gently, talking about things, telling her little stories. She was telling her about their lunch, and how pretty it was outside, when suddenly Allyson let out a soft moan, and moved her head slowly toward her mother. Page stopped speaking and stared, her eyes riveted by the motion. And then, Allie lay as still as she had before, as the machines purred beside her. But Page looked up and stared at Trygve in amazement.

"She moved . . . oh my God . . . Trygve, she moved . . ." The nurses had seen something from their station, and two of them came running. "She moved her face toward me," Page said with tears streaming down her face, as she bent to kiss her. "You moved your face, sweetheart . . . I saw it . . . and I heard you . . . oh baby, I heard you." She stayed next to her, kissing her, as Trygve cried as he watched

them. One of the nurses went to call Dr.
Hammerman, he was in the building, and
he appeared five minutes later. She described what she had seen, and Trygve confirmed it. The nurses added what they had
seen, and showed him the tape from Allie's
machines. The motion and the sound had
showed up in her brain waves.

"It's hard to say what this means," he
said cautiously. "It could be a good sign, or
it may not mean anything. It certainly gives
us room to hope that she may be moving
closer to consciousness, but Mrs. Clarke,
you have to understand that a gesture and a
moan don't necessarily mean her brain
function is normal. But not to discourage
you . . . this could be a beginning. Let's
hope it is," he said conservatively, but nothing could take away Page's joy as she
watched her daughter. She did not move
again that day, but she did the same thing
again when Page was with her the next
morning. She called Brad at his office to let
him know too, and they told her he was in
St. Louis and finally she tracked him down
in his hotel that night, and he was pleased,
but not as excited as she had hoped. Like
Hammerman, he reminded her it might
mean nothing.

"She hears me, Trygve, I know it," she told him that night, still excited. She and Andy had had dinner with them, and the following night he was taking her to the Silver Dove. "It's like calling down a deep dark hole. At first you don't know if anybody's there, and all you can hear is the echo. I've been calling down there for almost seven weeks, and I haven't heard a sound except my own voice . . . and all of a sudden someone is calling up to me, I know it." He hoped she was right, but like the others, he was afraid to get her hopes up.

And for the rest of the week, every day Allie stirred a little bit, but she never opened her eyes, or spoke, or made a sign that she understood what was being said. She just moaned and moved her head occasionally. It might mean a lot eventually, or it could mean nothing.

But Page was still excited the next day when he picked her up to take her to dinner. Andy was at Jane's and she had said she would pick him up when she got home, if it wasn't too late. And if it was, Jane had said she didn't mind keeping him until morning. He was in bed in one of her children's rooms, in his pajamas, and Page

would just scoop him up in his sleep whenever she got there. And Trygve had left a
sitter at home to help Chloe.

"You look incredible." Trygve stared at
her in open admiration. She was wearing a
strapless white silk dress and pearls, with a
pale blue shawl around her shoulders. It
was exactly the color of her eyes, and her
hair hung loosely down her back, not unlike
Allie's. "Wow!" he said, and she laughed as
she got into his car, and they headed for
Corte Madera.

He had reserved a quiet table for two,
and she was surprised to realize there was
dancing. It was the most romantic spot
she'd seen in years, and she felt special and
spoiled as they took their seats and he ordered wine, and they looked at the menus.
He ordered duck, and she ordered sole
Florentine, they both had soup to start, and
he ordered chocolate soufflé for dessert. It
was a wonderful dinner, a lovely place, a
perfect evening. They danced afterward,
and she felt his body close to hers. It surprised her to realize how strong he was, and
how supple. He was a terrific dancer.

They left the restaurant at eleven o'clock,
and Page smiled happily at him. They had
hardly drunk any wine, but she felt drunk

on the excitement of the evening. "I feel like Cinderella," she said blissfully, "when am I going to turn into a pumpkin?"

"Never, I hope." He smiled and drove her home. He played music in the car, and walked her slowly to the door, feeling like a boy again himself. And it was different suddenly when he kissed her at the door. Suddenly they both felt shy, and yet as he held her, he felt swept along by the tides of mounting passion.

"Do you want to come in for a minute?" she asked breathlessly, and he smiled as he answered.

"Are you timing me? Is that my limit?"

She laughed and unlocked the door, and they both stepped inside but got no further. She never even turned on the light. They just stood there, kissing in the dark, as he touched her body hungrily, overwhelmed by her beauty and his passion.

"I love you, Page," he whispered in the dark. "I love you so much . . ." He had waited two months for this, through the storm that had battered them and their families, but in truth he had waited years for this, maybe an entire lifetime.

They stood together swaying in unison as they whispered to each other and kissed, until he couldn't stand it anymore, and neither could she. Without saying anything, he led her to where he knew her bedroom was, and then stood there in the dark, and undressed her, and she didn't stop him.

"You're incredible," he said as the dress fell away from her. "Oh Page . . ." He devoured her with his lips, his hands, and slowly she undressed him, until at last they stood naked together in the moonlight. He lifted her gently onto the bed, and caressed her with his lips until she moaned in pleasure, arched toward him, and then led him toward her. Their union was a powerful one, throbbing, arching for what they had both longed for, until at last they both exploded in unison, and lay spent in each other's arms, stunned by the force of what they felt for each other. It was a long time before either of them spoke as Trygve gently stroked her hair and she kissed him.

"If I'd known that two months ago," he whispered finally, "I'd have taken you home with me the night of the accident," he said, and she laughed with pleasure.

"You're silly . . . but oh how I love you." The amazing thing was that she did. He was right for her in ways that Brad never had been and she'd refused to see it, not just sexually, but they were both so compatible, so artistic, so at ease, so in tune with each other and their children. They were both nurturers, and they nurtured each other now with the gratitude of people who know they have been lost for a long time, and are found at last. Trygve felt like a starving man who had been fed at last as he held her.

"Where were you twenty years ago when I needed you, Goldilocks?" he teased and she thought about it for a minute.

"Let's see, by then I was working off-off-Broadway and going to art school when I could afford it."

"I would have loved you."

"I would have loved you too." But she had still been very shaken by her experience with her father. "It's amazing, isn't it?" she mused. "We could have lived in the same community for years and never really known each other. And now, here we are, and our lives have changed completely."

"Fate, my dear." It blessed, and it destroyed, and it had done both to them. But at last, this was the blessing.

They lay talking for hours, and then finally, reluctantly, he got up. He had to go home to Bjorn and Chloe and send the sit-

ter home. But it was too late for her to re-
trieve Andy at Jane's. It was three o'clock in
the morning.

"You mean you'll be here all alone all
night?" he asked, horrified, as she nodded.
"What a waste! I can't stand it." In the end,
they made love again, and it was four in the
morning as she kissed him in her bathrobe
in the doorway.

"What time do you take Andy to
school?" he asked between kisses. He
looked sated and happy, and so did Page.
They looked like passionate young lovers,
barely able to tear themselves from each
other.

"Eight o'clock."

"What time do you get back here?" he
asked, sounding desperate.

"About eight-fifteen."

"I'll meet you here at eight-thirty."

"My God, you're a sex fiend." She
laughed.

He pulled away from her for an instant,
"Did I forget to warn you? That's why Dana
left, you know, the poor thing was worn
out." They both laughed and he kissed her
again. The truth was, of course, that he and
Dana hadn't even slept with each other for
the last two years, and he had begun to

wonder if he had lost it. But whatever he had lost, he had just found again, and then some.

"What are you doing tomorrow?" he asked more seriously.

"Going to the hospital."

"I'll come have breakfast with you, and take you there." She nodded, and he kissed her one more time, and then tore himself from her arms and forced himself to walk to his car. But he ran back for one more kiss as they both laughed, and then finally he went home. And true to his word, he was back at eight-thirty in the morning. She hadn't really thought he'd meant it. She had picked up Andy and taken him to school. She was doing laundry and singing to herself when Trygve arrived. And instantly, she found herself smiling.

"Good morning, my love," he said, coming through the door with an armload of flowers. He was the most romantic man she'd ever known, and the kindest. "Ready for breakfast?" But they never made it to the kitchen. He started kissing her again, and five minutes later they were in her bed, still unmade from the night before, and just as inviting.

"Do you think we'll ever get anything

done from now on?" he asked, lying on his side, admiring her for the thousandth time that morning.

"I doubt it. I'll have to give up doing murals."

"I'll forget writing." But their schedules were so flexible, their lives so free, their hunger for each other so enormous, it was fun to realize how much time they had to indulge it. "Do they have day care at Andy's school?" he continued to tease, and then kissed her again. But this time she chased him out of bed. It was eleven o'clock and she had to go see Allie. Now that she had started to show some improvement, however small, Page didn't want to miss a moment with her.

He stayed with her at the hospital for the first hour, and then went home to work, and to check on Chloe.

"What about tonight?" he asked hopefully, and she grinned at him in the ICU, and shook her head.

"Andy will be home."

"Tomorrow?" he persisted.

"He'll be out with Brad for the day," she giggled mischievously, and the nurse smiled. It was nice to see something pleasant happen for a change.

"Perfect," he said in answer to her announcement that Andy was spending Saturday afternoon with Brad. "Lunch? Caviar? An omelet?"

She leaned close to him and whispered in his ear so no one would hear them. "How about a peanut butter sandwich and a roll in the hay?" She laughed and he smiled wickedly at her.

"Excellent, my dear, I'll arrange it at once. Chunky or plain?"

"You're crazy!" she said.

"I love you," he answered, as he kissed her and left the ICU. It was utterly mad but she loved him too, and as Page turned her attention to Allie's lifeless form, she couldn't stop smiling.

CHAPTER 16

Brad told Andy about Stephanie on a Saturday in June. He had introduced them to each other over lunch, at Prego's on Union Street in the city. Andy looked her over suspiciously, and she chatted uneasily with him. She was wearing tight white jeans and a red T-shirt. And even he would have had to admit that she was pretty, with long dark hair and big green eyes, but it was obvious that Andy didn't like her from the moment he met her. He spoke to her in a surly tone, and he was rude to her several times over lunch, saying unflattering things to her, immediately followed by high praise of his mother's looks and virtues.

"Andy," his father frowned at him over dessert, "I want you to apologize to Stephanie." He glowered at him, and Andy stuck out his chin and pretended not to listen.

"I'm not going to," he said in dark tones to his ice cream.

"You've been very rude to her. You just told her that her nose is too big." Brad would have smiled at the offense, except that he could see that Stephanie was clearly insulted. She had no children of her own, and she was not amused by him. She didn't think he was cute, she thought he was a rude little boy, and thought that Brad should probably give him a good spanking. He was a brat, and had been horrible to her during the entire lunch. He had also told her that her pants were too tight, and her chest was too small. He had announced in no uncertain terms that his mother had a much better figure, was smarter, nicer, a good cook, and Stephanie probably couldn't cook anyway, and she'd painted a mural for his school that everybody admired. He'd gone on and on, singing his mother's praises, and pointing out all of Stephanie's flaws, both real and imagined.

What he had done too, without knowing it, was point out that Stephanie knew nothing about kids, and had a very limited sense of humor.

"I hate her," Andy growled just barely audibly, staring at the table.

"In that case," Stephanie answered him this time before Brad could, "we won't take you out to lunch again. We may not even take you out on Saturdays if you hate us," she said spitefully, and Brad looked uncomfortable. He wanted to support her, but he needed to support Andy too, as long as he behaved himself within reason.

"Of course we'll take you out on Saturdays," Brad said calmly, looking at each of them, and trying to reach out for Andy's hand to reassure him. He knew how frightened and upset he was, but he also wanted him to get to like Stephanie. It meant a lot to him, and if they started a war with each other, things weren't going to be easy. "I'll always see you on Saturdays, and weekends, and whenever else I can. But it would be more fun if the three of us could be together."

"No, it wouldn't," Andy said, looking at him, and acting as though Stephanie had already vanished. "Why do we have to take *her*?"

Stephanie fumed, but Brad answered, "Because I like her. She's my friend. You like to take your friends places too. It's more fun that way."

"Why can't I bring Mom?" Mainly because that wouldn't be fun at the moment. But Brad didn't say that.

"You know how difficult that is right now. You didn't like it when we fought. And Stephanie and I don't fight. We're good friends, and we have lots of fun. We could go to movies, and baseball games, and the beach, and do all kinds of things."

Andy looked her over contemptuously. "I'll bet she doesn't know anything about baseball."

"Then we'll teach her," Brad said calmly, looking at both of them. They looked equally miserable, angry, and unhappy. He was forcing things, and it was not going well, and he knew it. Maybe it would be easier to just leave it for a while, and go out with him alone again. But sooner or later he would have to get used to her. They had been talking about marriage again, and Stephanie was determined that he either make a commitment to her, or end the relation-

ship. After more than ten months, and seeing him through the end of his marriage to
Page, she felt as though she'd been patient
enough. And now she wanted to know if
Brad was going to come up with the goods.
If not, she wanted to stop seeing him, and
explore other avenues, none of which
pleased Brad, after all he'd been through,
he didn't want to lose her. She was almost a
security blanket for him now, she was his
buffer against the loneliness he felt without
Page, or Allyson, or Andy. And he loved
her too, but their affair had not been the
easiest of late, with all the trauma he'd
been through, and now Andy wasn't making
things easier for them. Life was definitely
not simple.

"I want you two to give this a chance."
He looked at both of them. "For my sake. I
love you both. And I want you to be friends.
Deal? Will you try?" he asked them both, as
though they were the same age, and from
the petulant look on Stephanie's face, he
could almost believe she was the same age
as Andy.

"Okay," said Andy grudgingly, glancing
over at her with a look of hatred.

"You'd better behave yourself," she
snapped at him, and Brad almost groaned

as he paid the check and gave Andy the candies that had come with it.

"Stop it, you two!"

It was a hellish afternoon. They went down to the Marina green, and walked along the beach in almost total silence. Stephanie said she was cold and wanted to go home. Andy said absolutely nothing, and only answered when his father spoke to him. He said nothing to Stephanie at all, until he was forced to say good-bye to her, when they dropped her off at her apartment. They stopped at Brad's briefly on the way home, and when he went to the bathroom, Andy noticed some of her things on the sink, and a pink terrycloth bathrobe on the back of the bathroom door, which only depressed him further.

"You really weren't nice to her," Brad said gently on the way home. "That's not fair. She means a lot to me, and she really wants to like you."

"No, she doesn't. She was mean to me right from the beginning. She hates me. I know it."

"She does *not* hate you. She's not used to kids, and you probably scare her a little bit. Give her a chance." Brad was almost begging. It had been a hideous afternoon, and he knew he was going to get an earful from Stephanie as soon as he got back to the city.

"Allie's going to hate her too," Andy said confidently, and the words tore at Brad's heart. He was no longer sure that Allie would ever love or hate anyone again. In spite of her recent movements, there had been no real improvement.

"I don't think Allie would hate her," Brad said more to make conversation with him.

"And so would Mom. Besides, she's too skinny and she's stupid."

"She is not stupid." Brad found himself defending her. "She went to Stanford, she has a good job, and she's a very bright girl. You really don't know her."

"So what, she's dumb, and I hate her." They had come full circle, and Brad tried to distract him by talking about other things on the way home, but Andy seemed not to want to talk. He just sat quietly and stared out the window.

Brad dropped him off at the house, and waved at Page as he drove off. He was tempted to stop and talk, but decided that would just be too difficult. He wasn't in the mood, and he was anxious to get back to Stephanie and reassure her. He knew how upset she would be about how rude Andy had been, she was childish about things like that sometimes, and he knew he'd have to make it up to her. He just hoped that eventually they'd get used to each other. If not, things were going to be very rough for him in the meantime.

Andy was very quiet with Page when he came home, and she noticed it immediately.

"Something wrong?" she asked as she tucked him into bed that night. He had scarcely said a word to her all through dinner. Usually he raved about whatever it was he had done with his father. "You feel okay?" She felt his neck and his back but he wasn't hot. He was very cool, but his eyes looked worried, as his head rested on his pillow.

"Yeah." He looked as though he was on the verge of tears and she didn't want to leave him. "Dad said . . . I can't tell you." He didn't want to hurt her feelings.

"Did you two get in some kind of argument today?" Maybe Andy had done something really dangerous and Brad had swatted him on the behind, but it wasn't like him. But Andy only shook his head and continued to look unhappy.

But after a few minutes, he couldn't contain himself anymore, and he started to cry as he lay there.

"Oh sweetheart," she said, and held him close to her as she lay next to him on the bed. "You know Daddy loves you, whatever he said to you today."

"Yeah . . . but . . ." he choked on the words as he clung to her ". . . he has a *girlfriend*. Her name is Stephanie," he said miserably. It was out now. He had told her, and she smiled through her own tears as she held him.

"I know. It's okay. I know all about her."

"Have you seen her?" he asked, looking amazed as he pulled away from her, but his mother shook her head, thinking how sweet he looked as he lay there.

"No, I haven't. Have you?"

"At lunch. She was terrible. She's skinny and dumb and ugly, and she hates me."

"I'm sure she doesn't. She's probably scared of you, and wants to make a good impression."

"Well, I hated her. And Dad says I *have* to try to like her." It was serious then, Page thought to herself. If he was pressing Andy on her, maybe they were planning to get married. She felt a tug at her heart at the thought, but knew that, like Andy, she'd have to get used to the idea that Stephanie was part of Brad's life now, perhaps forever. "Why don't you just try?" Page said gently. "She may be nicer than you think when you get to know her. She must have something good about her, if Dad likes her."

"No, she doesn't," he said, and wiped his eyes. "I hate her." And then, with worried eyes, he asked her a question.

"Do you think Daddy will ever come back to us?" he asked anxiously. That was what it was all about. Stephanie was a threat to Brad's safe return to Andy's mother.

"I don't know," Page said honestly. "I don't think so."

"But if he marries her, he *can't* come back to you." He looked at Page miserably. "I *hate* her."

"No you don't. You don't really know her. And Dad's not marrying her yet. I think you're worrying too much." But she also knew he wasn't wrong. They probably would get married.

"They're going to Europe this summer. That means he won't take us on vacation." He didn't understand that Brad wouldn't have taken them on vacation now anyway.

But it irked her to hear that Brad was taking Stephanie to Europe. He had never taken her, and she had wanted to go for years. She hadn't been since before she married Brad, with her parents.

"We shouldn't leave Allie anyway," Page said quietly. "Does Daddy want to take you with him?" He hadn't said anything to her, but maybe he would eventually. But Andy just shook his head.

"They're going alone. For a month." Page nodded as she listened. He had his own life now, and they had theirs. And she had Trygve.

"Let's not worry about it now, okay? Daddy loves you very much, and so do I. And I'll bet his friend is really very nice, and you'll get to like her."

He growled a little bit about it again as she tucked him in, and the next day he was still grouchy over breakfast. To him, the threat of Stephanie meant only one thing: Brad was not coming back to him, or his mother. And then he looked up from breakfast suddenly and asked Page a question that tore at her heart. She had to turn away so he wouldn't see her crying.

"What are we going to tell Allie about Dad? When she wakes up I mean? How will we tell her?" Page looked out the window and blew her nose as she struggled for an answer. If only one day they'd have a chance to talk to Allie.

"We'll figure something out by then."

"Maybe Stephanie will *die,*" he said angrily, and Page almost laughed when she turned around to face him. He was so emphatic, he was almost comical. She chased him out to the garden then, and her mother called a few minutes later.

She had nothing new to say except that Alexis had developed a frightful ulcer. It didn't surprise Page at all. It was something that happened to anorexics. From starving themselves their stomach acids began eating through their stomach. But of course her mother said it was because Alexis was naturally nervous.

Her mother seemed surprised when Page explained again that Brad was no longer there. It was as though Page had never told her. As usual, she refused to accept what Page was saying to her, and they hung up a few minutes later.

She said something to Trygve about it that afternoon, about how dysfunctional her family had been, and it was hard for him to understand it. His parents were normal to the point of being boring.

"You're lucky," she said comfortably.

They sat together talking and touching hands, and wishing they could kiss as they sat on his front lawn, within clear view of their children.

Bjorn and Andy were playing ball, and Andy was throwing left-handed. His cast was going to come off soon. And Chloe was sitting in a wheelchair, next to Jamie Applegate, poring over some homework.

"Brad introduced him to Stephanie yesterday," she told Trygve as they watched them.

"How did he take it?"

"Not very well. But I wouldn't expect him to. She's a big threat to him. It means it's really over. He said he hated her." She grinned mischievously. "It must have been a great lunch."

"I think kids always have dreams of their parents getting back together." He smiled at her. "I know even mine still secretly think that Dana will come back home and we'll get back together again."

"Would you want her to?" she asked with a look of interest, and he leaned close to her and smiled.

"God, no. I'd leave town . . . with you in my suitcase."

"Good." She smiled back at him and their hands touched briefly.

The two families spent a happy afternoon, and Page and Trygve cooked dinner for them. Chloe set the table from her wheelchair and did whatever she could, and Bjorn and Andy cleaned up afterward. They were a good team and they had a great time together. Chloe seemed to fill Andy's longing for his older sister. Nick was coming home in a few days again too. He had a summer job in Tiburon, at the tennis club, and they were excited about him coming home from college. The only one missing would be Allie.

After dinner, they were sitting in the dining room, talking about her, when Chloe said how much she missed her, and how much she still hoped she'd wake up from her coma. They all wished for that, and it still wasn't too late. But two months was a long time. In another month, the outlook would dim further. Dr. Hammerman still seemed to feel that if she didn't come out of it within three months of the accident, perhaps she never would. It was something Page tried not to think about, but late at night, as she lay in bed, she was haunted by the fear that Allyson might spend the rest of her life in a coma.

"I saw Mrs. Chapman yesterday," Page said quietly. "At Safeway. The poor woman looked awful. She just looked kind of gray, as though all the life had gone out of her." Trygve nodded, thinking of what it would be like. He couldn't even imagine it, and didn't want to. Phillip would have graduated a few days before. And at graduation, there had been a moment of silence for him.

Chloe's eyes filled with tears, and she turned away, thinking of that night, as she often did. Bits of it had come back to her. She had even gone to the therapy group with Jamie because she had a lot of guilt about talking Allie into going with her. That night had changed so much for so many.

Trygve suggested a game of Monopoly then, and the young people played ardently, wheeling and dealing and cheating when they could, squealing with amusement and amassing paper fortunes, while Page and Trygve quietly went upstairs to sit in his study. He put his arms around her there, and kissed her as he'd been longing to all afternoon. He was aching to spend more time with her, to have her spend the night with him, to go away with him. There were a thousand things he wanted to do with her. But he knew it was too soon. He knew Page couldn't leave Allyson right now, and he had his own hands full with his children.

"Do you suppose we'll ever get any time away from them?" he asked with a rueful grin as he held her. "Maybe even for a weekend?"

"It would be nice, wouldn't it?" she dreamed. She liked the idea of Lake Tahoe with him too, but she just didn't feel right leaving Allie. Spending her days at the ICU was her whole life now. She felt bad for Andy too, there was so much she wanted to do with him, that he needed now that Brad was gone, but Allie came first. That was just the way it was for the moment. They all had to wait their turn, including Page herself, and they knew it.

She hated to leave Trygve that night. She loved spending time with him, and the days when they meshed their families were particularly happy. Andy looked a lot happier than he had the night before when she had put him to bed, and he stared at her with a silent question.

"What's up? Did you have a good time today?" she asked on the way home.

"A great time. Chloe beat us at Monopoly, but she cheated. Bjorn says she always does." Andy grinned. "So does Allie." Page smiled at the mention of her. It would have been so nice to see her playing Monopoly. So nice if she could have.

"Bjorn says his dad likes you," Andy said, looking noncommittal.

"What makes him say that?" She didn't comment one way or the other, but her heart was pounding faster as she watched Andy's face. She wanted him to like him. Just as Brad wanted him to like Stephanie, but he didn't.

"He just does. He says he's watched you guys a lot, he thinks you're really nice, and he says his dad says you're really pretty and fun to be with. He says you kissed him once, on the lips. Did you?" It was not an accusation, it was more a question. After the shock of Stephanie the day before, this was a whole new world for him, and he was examining the landscape. But it was a whole new world for her too, and she wasn't sure how much to tell him. Just exactly how much of the truth did she owe him?

"Maybe when I said good-bye to him, something like that. But yes, I like him."

"Like . . . like Dad?"

"No. I don't like him as well. But like a friend, like a very good friend. He's been wonderful to me while Allie's been sick." Andy nodded. He didn't disagree. He just hadn't thought about him that way.

"I like him too . . . and I like Bjorn . . . but I like Daddy better."

"Your daddy will always be your daddy. Nothing's ever going to change that."

"Are you and Dad going to get divorced?" he asked worriedly. That really would mean it was all over. A lot of his friends' parents had gotten divorced, and some of them had remarried. He knew what that meant.

"I don't know." In the month that he'd been gone, neither of them had called a lawyer. Brad had asked her to, and Stephanie was pushing him, but Page just couldn't bring herself to do it. Trygve had offered her the name of his, but she kept saying she was too busy to call. But she knew that one of these days, she'd have to.

Brad reminded her of it too the next time she saw him at the hospital. He came by one afternoon, he hadn't seen Allie in a week, and when she looked up, Page was suddenly startled to see him.

"Hi, how are you?" she said uncomfortably, trying to pretend she didn't feel awkward.

"Fine." He smiled down at her, looking better than ever. He was an awesome looking man, sometimes she let herself forget that. "How's Allie?"

"Not much change. But she's still moving and making little sounds. It's hard to know what it means." But the scans showed movement when Page said her name, she wanted to believe that that meant something too. But who knew? She was still sleeping, and the respirator still kept her breathing.

He stayed for as long as he could. Five minutes was his limit, and then he asked her to come out in the hall of the ICU and talk to him for a minute.

"You're looking good," he said, watching her closely. She looked less tortured than she had, and happier, but there was still something sad in her eyes when he saw her. He wasn't sure if it was because of Allyson, or him, and a part of him still wanted to take her in his arms, and hold her, but he knew he couldn't. Besides, Stephanie would have killed him if she knew. She was ferocious with him, she said she wouldn't put up with any cheating on his part, not even once. She wasn't Page, in a lot of ways, and sometimes Brad really missed her. "Are you okay?"

"Hanging in there." She was happy with Trygve, and hopeful with Allyson, but life wasn't what it had once been, with Allyson still so sick, and a divorce to be gotten through, and it made her sad when she saw him. Her life was reduced to such a small scale now. Hospital and home, and an occasional dinner with Trygve. There were no horizons to look toward anymore, except the constant hope that Allie would come out of her coma.

"I wanted to talk to you, and I haven't had time to phone. I think it's time to call our lawyers." He said it apologetically and he felt like a total bastard when he saw the look in her eyes. She looked like Andy.

"You're right," she agreed. But she hated to do it. It was the final death knoll to their marriage.

"There's no point hanging on. It's just painful for us, and I think it creates false hope for Andy. I think he'll adjust better if he knows this is it. And maybe we will too, who knows? You have a right to more than this too, you know," he reminded her, and she nodded, not disagreeing with him. She had a right to a family, and Allie whole again, and a husband. She had a right to a lot of things. But whether or not she got them was another story.

"You're sure," she asked quietly. "About the divorce I mean." He nodded, and she inclined her head. She understood. She accepted it. It was over.

He wanted to marry Stephanie, to start a new life with her, and maybe this time, do it better.

"It's time," he said sadly. "Do you have someone to call?"

"I have a name, but I haven't bothered to call him. I didn't realize you were this anxious." There was an edge to her voice as she said it. And she was suddenly angry that he had come to tell her this here. Everything terrible had happened to her in this hospital . . . but good things had too . . . there was Trygve . . .

"We'll be divorced by the end of the year," Brad said soberly, as Page mulled it over in silence. "Probably before Christmas." Stephanie wanted to get married on

Christmas Eve, if the divorce came through in time, and it might just, if they hurried.

"I can think of other things I'd rather put on my Christmas list," she said ruefully. And then she looked up at him and took a deep breath. "I'll call the attorney in the morning."

"Thanks. I appreciate it." He hesitated for a moment then, as though he wanted to say more, but wasn't sure how to do it. "I'm sorry, Page . . ."

"Yeah, so am I." She touched his hand, and she went back to the ICU again. But Allie didn't stir all day, not even one little moan or rustle. It was as though she knew her mother was depressed, and she was leaving her alone. Page just sat there all day and watched her. And that night, when she put Andy to bed, she didn't even call Trygve. She needed one last moment to mourn for Brad before she moved ahead into the future.

She felt better the next day, and she was anxious to talk to him. Trygve had sensed that something was bothering her, and she told him about her conversation with Brad. As usual, he was sympathetic. He knew how hard it was, and he didn't think it was a reflection on them, it was just very painful terminating a marriage. He gave her the name of the attorney again, and then she called and made an appointment.

And when she saw the lawyer, he told her what Brad had, that she'd be divorced by Christmas. Trygve picked her up afterward, and they went out to dinner and talked that night. By then, she felt a little better. And as they sat at their favorite table at the Silver Dove, they looked like two beautiful blond Scandinavians. People commented frequently on how much they looked alike, and asked if they were brother and sister. There was something interesting about that, Page had always had a theory that married people looked alike, but she and Brad certainly didn't.

They talked for hours that night, about their lives, and their marriages, and their children . . . and their hopes for the future.

"You're the first person I've known who made me want to get married again." And from the look in his eyes, she knew he meant it. It still seemed too soon to both of them, but the accident had changed everything and made time move so much more quickly. Everything was propelled at a great speed as they fought for their survival.

"I think you know when it's right. I think you feel it," he said with quiet assurance. "I knew almost right away in the hospital. I just didn't understand how I could feel something like that. You were married . . . and then everything changed. Page, when I look at you, I know I could be happy with you for the rest of my life. And I think you know it too." She didn't deny it. She felt that too, but it was very scary.

"How could I be so wrong before, and so right now? Why would I be smarter now?" she said, looking worried.

"I don't think it has to do with smart. I think it has to do with something you know in your stomach . . . your heart . . . your gut . . . whatever you want to call it. I always knew with Dana it was wrong. I knew it right from the beginning, and so did she. She tried to talk me out of it, but I wouldn't let her."

"It's funny," she thought back, "I tried to do that with Brad too. I didn't feel ready. I was still reverberating from everything that had happened with my family, but he wanted to get married and come to California. I was scared, but I thought it was the right thing to do. Maybe I was just very stupid."

"No, it was right at the time. It wouldn't have lasted as long as it did if it weren't." Her marriage to Brad had never been as rocky as his to Dana. "I don't know how to explain it to you, I just know this is right. And I don't want to waste any more time. I feel like I've wasted half my life with the wrong woman." And then he took a breath and forced himself to slow down. "But I don't want to rush you. However long it takes for you. I'll be here."

"My mother's right for once," she said, smiling at him.

"How's that?"

"She always tells me I'm a very lucky woman."

"I'm the lucky one this time." He smiled. "Now I'll have to learn to be patient." He took a sip of wine, and then grinned at her. "Doesn't Christmas sound good to you? I just think . . . Santa Claus . . . mistletoe . . . sleigh bells . . ." He knew her divorce would be final by Christmas.

"You're a lunatic. For all you know, I'm a monster to live with. You don't suppose Brad would have gotten so bored with me if I were fun to live with?"

"He's a fool, thank God. And I'll tell you one thing, I'd sure like a chance to find out for myself . . . without having to run home at four o'clock in the morning . . . or tiptoe around the house so Andy doesn't hear us." Clearly, that had its limitations. He wanted to wake up lying next to her, and go to bed with her every night. He still wanted to go away for a weekend with her, but she still didn't feel right leaving Allie. "Just keep Christmas in the back of your head . . . see what you think of it, maybe after Tahoe."

"Put it on your Christmas list," she said mischievously, and he laughed.

"I'll do that."

CHAPTER 17

In late June, Page started the mural for the ICU at the hospital. She had offered it to them and they had been thrilled by the suggestion. She was doing two, both in Allie's name. One in the long, depressing hall that led up to the ICU, and the other in the dismal waiting room. She had spent long nights researching it, and she had chosen a countryside in Tuscany, and a port scene in San Remo. The one was peaceful and soothing, the other one amusing with lots of little details and vignettes. It would give people lots to look at and discover while they waited.

She showed Trygve the early sketches and

he was very impressed. She thought they would each take her over a month, and then she was going to finish the last one at Ross Grammar School. And after that, in the fall, she was only going to do paid commissions.

"I can't afford not to," she said bluntly. She would only be getting child support from Brad, and a small amount of alimony for two years. His contention was that, with her talent, there was no reason for her not to be earning a living. She was hoping to work things out with her murals and her work for friends, because she didn't want to leave Andy all day long, and she had no idea yet what Allie's needs were, how much time she'd be spending with her, what state she'd be in, or how much she'd need her.

It was becoming obvious now, though, that there was a good chance Allyson would never come out of the coma. She hadn't admitted that to Trygve yet, but he sensed that she was wrestling with the idea, and trying to accept it. She talked about Allie a lot these days, about the happier things she'd done, her accomplishments, her strengths, it was as though she was trying to remind everyone of what she had been, and who, and keep her from being forgotten.

"I don't want her life to have been in

vain," she said sadly to him one night. "I want people to remember her for who she was . . . not for the accident, or the tragedy, or what she is now. This isn't really Allie."

"I know." They talked about it for hours sometimes, and as always, he was there to help her.

He was happy to see her start the murals at the hospital, and she loved doing them. It kept her nearby, and sometimes she would just pop into the ICU to look at Allie, or kiss her. The bandages were off now, and her hair was growing again. It was short, but it looked sweet. It made her look even more childlike as she lay stiffly on her bed, with her head on the pillow.

"I love you," Page would whisper and then go back to work again, her hair tied up in a knot, with her brushes sticking into it, and an old workshirt.

But she also started another very special project at the same time. Suddenly she was moving ahead at full steam, and Trygve was relieved to see it. She was returning to the living. She started an art project at Bjorn's new school, and everyone was in love with her, especially the students. She did papier-mâché with them, and sculpture in clay, pottery, watercolors and drawings. They were so proud of their work, and she was so proud of them. It was the most rewarding thing she'd ever done, she told Trygve one night, as they cooked the kids dinner.

Bjorn was explaining to them what Page was doing at school, and Page beamed at him when he said how much he liked it. She had a warm relationship with him, and now when he went to bed, and she was there, he clung to her and kissed her good night, and asked her to read him a story, just as she did to Andy. She was surprised by his strength sometimes when he squeezed her, or lifted her up, but he was always gentle, and affectionate, and loving.

"He's such a good boy," she said to Trygve after she put him to bed one night, and Trygve was so touched by what she said and did for him, and for Chloe. She worked tirelessly with Chloe, in her therapy when she had time.

"I wish you'd been their mother all along," he said honestly, and she smiled.

"That's what Bjorn said. I'm honored." But it meant a lot to her to be with him now, and share a relationship with him at school. She had the feeling finally that she was doing something important with her art, and even if she wasn't getting paid for it yet, she knew she would be. They had already asked her if she would be open to heading their art program at a later date, and it was something that appealed to her a great deal, and the hours would have worked out perfectly for Andy.

She and Andy spent the Fourth of July weekend with them. She stayed in the guest room, and Andy slept with Bjorn, and Trygve snuck into her room at night, and they giggled like two kids, locking the door so the children didn't catch them.

"We can't do this forever, you know. Sooner or later they'll have to accept what's happening," he said, but neither of them was brave enough to force the issue yet, it was still too soon for Page to sleep in his bedroom openly, and they both knew that. Chloe was particularly possessive of him, and Page didn't want to upset her.

"If Chloe ever catches us, it'll be all over," Page laughed, "she'll shake Allie awake just to tell her what's going on." She smiled at the image, and he kissed her, and they both forgot their children.

They had a family barbecue on the Fourth of July, and they each invited a few friends. Jane Gilson and her husband were there, the Applegates, and four other couples. It was the first any of them had known of the relationship, or the fact that Brad was gone, the first anyone had seen of Page since the accident. It was not quite three months, but it felt more like three years, and a lot had changed in a short time. But people were happy for them, everyone had always liked Trygve.

He was in charge of the barbecue, and she and the children did the rest, and Trygve let Bjorn shoot off a few firecrackers while he watched, and he kept a watchful eye on Andy.

"They're too dangerous," Page complained, but the boys loved it, and nothing untoward happened. Everyone had a good time, and the last guests left at ten-thirty.

Page and Trygve cleaned up, and they were still putting food away, when Chloe came into the kitchen as fast as she could on her crutches.

"You have to come right away." She looked shaken and pale, and Page didn't understand what could have happened. She thought one of the boys had been hurt, and she was instantly terrified as she hurried after her, and Trygve followed in anxious silence. But neither of them was prepared for what they saw when Chloe stopped in front of the television, and they saw a scene of carnage that had apparently happened that afternoon in La Jolla.

". . . wife of Senator John Hutchinson . . ." the voice droned on ". . . in La Jolla earlier today, in a head-on collision . . . killed a family of four, one of her own children seriously injured in the accident, although the child, a girl of twelve, is listed in stable condition . . . Mrs. Hutchinson was arrested at the scene for felony vehicular manslaughter. Tests showed that she was driving while intoxicated. The Senator was not reached for comment . . . Early this evening, a spokesman for the family said that although the early evidence indicates that Mrs. Hutchinson was in fact at fault, it is more than likely that she wasn't . . . However," he looked straight into the camera as though he could see Page's heart beating out of her chest as she listened, "Mrs. Hutchinson was involved in a similar accident earlier this year, in San Francisco, in April. A seventeen-year-old boy was killed, and two fifteen-year-old girls were severely injured, in a head-on collision on the Golden Gate Bridge. No blame was assigned in that accident, which occurred only eleven weeks ago. Investigations into this current accident are under way in La Jolla." He went on to a riot in Los Angeles then, as the threesome continued to stand and stare at the television set. Laura Hutchinson had killed a family of four, and been arrested for drunk driving.

"Oh my God," Page said as she fell into a chair and started crying, "she *was* drunk then . . . she was drunk . . . she must have been, and she almost killed all of you . . ." She couldn't stop crying, and Chloe was too, as Trygve turned off the TV, and sat down with them. The Applegates called them only moments later, and Page wished she had the courage to call the Chapmans. But she knew they'd hear about it very quickly. Trygve had been right in his suspicions.

He turned the TV on again, and flipped the dial, and they saw a similar report on another channel. The news was worse this time. She had killed a twenty-eight-year-old woman, and her thirty-two-year-old husband, their two-year-old little girl, and five-year-old boy, and the woman was eight months pregnant. Five people, not four. And her own daughter had broken an arm, had fifteen stitches in her left cheek, and had a mild concussion. There was film of ambulances, fire trucks, other cars that had been forced off the road. Six or seven other cars had been involved in lesser ways, but no one else had been seriously injured. It made Page feel sick as she listened.

"My God." She didn't know what else to say, but it vindicated Phillip Chapman. She wondered how his parents would feel when they heard it. "Will she go to jail?" She looked at Trygve.

"Probably. I don't think the Senator is going to be able to get her out of this one." He was well known, but controversial, kind of a movie star senator in a way, and having a wife with a serious drinking problem wouldn't have helped him. They had apparently kept it very quiet. But they hadn't kept her out from behind the wheel. And they should have. "She's just killed five people, that's a lot to overlook. I don't think they will. She'll have to stand trial for this." The charge was four counts of felony vehicular manslaughter, since they couldn't bring charges for the murder of the fetus. Efforts had been made to save it with an emergency cesarean, but the baby had died anyway from the impact, and its mother's sudden death. It had been too late to save it.

"She's killed six people," Page said quietly, counting Phillip. Seven if Allie died, and she still could. But Page couldn't bear to think it. "How could she come to Phillip's funeral? How could she do that?"

"It was a smart thing to do. It made her look sympathetic," Trygve explained wisely.

"What a terrible thing to do," Page said, looking shaken. And she lay in bed and cried in his arms that night, it was as though they finally knew who had killed, or almost killed, their children. It didn't change anything, but it made it all so much more real. You knew who was to blame, and what she had done. There was no question in their minds that Laura Hutchinson had been drunk that night on the Golden Gate Bridge when she and Phillip Chapman had collided.

Trygve carefully checked the newspapers the next day, and he turned the news on over breakfast. Page watched somberly with him as the Senator made a statement to the press about how terrible he felt, and how devastated his wife was. They were paying for the funerals, of course, and a full investigation, and full disclosure would be made. He had some serious questions about his wife's car. He believed that the steering col-

umn and the brakes had been defective.
Page wanted to scream as she listened.
They showed him then with his injured
child. She looked glazed and nervous as she
clutched his hand and tried to smile. Laura
Hutchinson herself was nowhere to be seen.
They said she was in shock and under seda-
tion. Page said she probably had the DT's
and was drying out somewhere.

And when they opened the door to go to
the hospital, they ran straight into the arms
of a cameraman and four reporters. They
wanted a photograph of Chloe in her
wheelchair, or on her crutches, and they
wanted to know how Trygve felt about
Laura Hutchinson's accident in La Jolla.

"Terrible, of course. It's a shocking
thing," he said somberly, trying to avoid
them. He had refused to let them photograph Chloe. But as he and Page slid into
his car, she suddenly realized there would
probably be reporters at the hospital too.
And she ran to the ICU as soon as she got
there. She didn't want anyone photograph-
ing Allie the way she was, or turning her
into a ghoulish spectacle, or an object of
pity. This was not the Allyson Clarke that
anyone had ever known, and they had no
right to use her to arouse public outrage.

No matter how guilty Laura Hutchinson was, Page was not going to let them use Allie as an object to torment her.

Half a dozen reporters and photographers were clustered in the hall outside the ICU and they tried to stop her when they realized who she was, and ask her endless questions.

"How do you feel now that you know Laura Hutchinson was probably responsible for your daughter's accident, Mrs. Clarke? . . . how is she now? . . . Will she ever come out of the coma?" They had tried to talk to the doctor too, but of course he wouldn't talk to them, nor would the nurses in the ICU, despite all their pleas and cajoling. They had even tried to bribe one of them to let them in for a quick photograph, but unfortunately for them, the person they had chosen to bribe was Frances. She had threatened to have them thrown out of the hospital, and get a court order against them. And she came out to rescue Page now, while Trygve tried to get them to leave her alone. Page insisted that she had no comment.

"But aren't you angry, Mrs. Clarke? Doesn't it make you furious that she did this to your daughter?" They tried to provoke her.

"It makes me very sad," Page said in a dignified voice as she walked past them, "for all of us, all those who have lost loved ones, or suffered the agony of this accident. And my heart goes out to the relatives of the family in La Jolla." She said not another word, and walked into the ICU with Trygve, feeling as though they just climbed through a tornado. The nurses closed the doors to the ICU that day, and drew the shades, so no one could get photographs of Page or Allie.

Trygve called his investigative reporter friend later that day, and was amazed by what he told him. Laura Hutchinson had had four stays recently in a well known dry-out clinic in L.A., all in the past three years, and apparently none of her stays had been successful. She had gone there under another name, but a source at the clinic itself confirmed that she had been there. In addition the DMV records showed that she had been involved in at least half a dozen small accidents, and one larger one in Martha's Vineyard, where she spent the summers. There had been no fatalities in any of them, except the one on the Golden Gate Bridge, but there had been minor injuries, and in one of them Mrs. Hutchinson herself sustained a concussion. They had all been carefully hushed up, of course, and wherever possible, the records had been sealed. But somehow, Trygve's friend had gotten around that. He said there might have been bribes to close the records on her, and some political favors called. But her husband's lawyers and PR people had done a brilliant job at hiding Laura Hutchinson's record.

It was horrifying to realize that in this year alone, she had injured her own child, and she had killed six people, nearly crippled one, and left another in a coma. It was quite a record.

And by the end of the day, the public outcry over it was enormous. Mothers Against Drunk Driving had given interviews, and made public statements, and the Chapmans had given an interview talking about the young life that Laura Hutchinson had taken, and the reputation she had sullied. Meanwhile, spokesmen for the Senator were continuing to say that her brakes had failed and the steering column had gone out, but they were going to have a tough time selling that one. And through it all, Laura Hutchinson herself was "unavailable for comment."

By the following week, *Oprah* and *Donahue* had interviewed families who had lost children and husbands and wives in similar accidents, and the news showed Laura Hutchinson running into the courthouse in dark glasses, to be arraigned for felony vehicular manslaughter. The maximum possible jail sentence she faced was forty years, which Page felt didn't even begin to touch what she owed them.

Every time Page saw Allie that week all she could think of was Laura Hutchinson and the young woman who had died with her unborn baby in her belly.

By midweek, the press had started to go wild with the story. They continued to interview the Chapmans about how they felt about their son, and to hound the Applegates, Page, Brad, and Trygve. The news camera continued to show up at the ICU, and the producer of the show tried to get her to agree to having Allyson shown on TV in her coma.

"Don't you want other mothers to see what happened to you? They have a right to get people like Laura Hutchinson off the road," a very aggressive young woman explained, "and you have an obligation to help them."

"Seeing Allyson won't change anything." All she wanted was to protect her.

"Will you talk to us at least?" She thought about it at length, and then finally agreed to a brief interview in the hallway, if only to support the case against Laura Hutchinson in La Jolla. She explained what had happened to Allyson three months before, the physical results of the accident, and her current condition. It was fairly straightforward, and for a fraction of a moment, she was glad she'd done it.

Then the same aggressive young woman asked her if her life had been affected in any other way by the accident. Had there been any other complications? And as she asked her that, Page realized that someone must have told her that she and her husband were separated. But she wasn't about to become an object of pity on TV, and she evaded the question.

"Do you have any other children, Mrs. Clarke?"

"I do," she said quietly, "a son, Andrew."

"And how has this affected him?"

"It's been hard on all of us," she said candidly, as the reporter nodded.

"Isn't it true he ran away several weeks after the accident? Would you say that was a direct result of all this trauma?" They had checked the police records and Page was angry at the invasion of their lives. These people were using them to make a point. Trygve had been right not to talk to them in the first place.

"I'd say it's been difficult for all of us, but we're coping." She smiled pleasantly, and then thought about why she had agreed to do the interview. "I'd just like to say that I think that anyone responsible for this kind of tragedy must answer for it, to the fullest extent of the law . . . not that that changes anything for us now," she said as they ended the interview. But if they had been honest in dealing with Laura Hutchinson's drinking problem years before, maybe she wouldn't have been on the road, behind the wheel that fateful night in April.

Page was unhappy when she saw the interview on TV, they edited it so it made her look as though she had said things she hadn't. And they made her seem pathetic. But maybe if people knew what Laura Hutchinson had done to all of them, maybe she'd be fairly punished in La Jolla. This accident would not be admissible evidence because she hadn't been tested for alcohol at the time. But it established a pattern of what she'd done. It was the only reason Page had talked to them, but she was sorry she'd done it.

None of it changed anything for Allyson, but Page felt better knowing that the woman who had done it would be brought to justice. The trial was set for the first week in September.

CHAPTER 18

Trygve and the children left for Lake Tahoe on August first, and Page had promised to join them there with Andy in mid-August. Brad was in Europe with Stephanie by then, and for lack of anything else to do with him, she had put Andy in day camp. Trygve had offered to take Andy to Tahoe with them, and Andy was tempted to go, but he still wanted to stay close to his mother. He was not as secure as he had been before the accident, he didn't like to spend the night at friends' anymore, and sometimes he still had nightmares about Allie.

The accident had been almost four

months earlier. The feared three-month
mark had passed, without a whimper from
Allie. Page had almost come to accept that.
She had wanted so desperately for her to
wake up, for her to be herself again, even if
it took a long time to get her back on her
feet or rehabilitate her. She would have
done anything to bring her back. But she
was slowly beginning to understand that it
wasn't going to happen.

Trygve called her from Tahoe every day.
And she was settling into a routine by then.
She took Andy to day camp, went to the
hospital, visited with Allyson, worked with
the therapist to keep Allie's body moving
and from atrophying completely. Then
she'd work on the mural, sit with Allyson
again. And pick Andy up at day camp, go
home, and cook dinner.

She missed Trygve terribly, more than
even she expected. Once he said he was so
lonely for her that he drove down one night
just to spend the night with her and go back
up in the morning. He was wonderful to
her, and they were very happy together.

She had finished the first mural by then,
and had started on the port scene in the
waiting room by the end of the first week in
August. There were a lot of intricate details

she had done in her early sketches, and she was sitting next to Allyson thinking about them, and checking her drawings. It was a peaceful afternoon and the sun was streaming into the room, as Page felt a little movement of Allie's hand on the bed. She did that sometimes. It didn't mean anything, she knew now. It was just the body responding to some electricity in the brain. But instinctively she looked up and glanced at her, and went back to her drawings again as she munched absentmindedly on her pencil. There was a detail she wanted to do that wasn't clear to her, and she sat and stared out the window for a minute trying to figure out how to do it. And then she glanced at Allie again, and saw her hands move. They seemed to be clutching the sheets this time, and reaching out to her. It was something she had never done before, and Page stared at her, wondering if this was just more of the same, or something different.

And then, almost imperceptibly, she saw Allie's head move. She seemed to be turning it slowly toward her, as though she sensed that Page was there. Page watched her, feeling her breath catch. It was as though she knew that someone was there, as though she herself were back in the room again, and Page could feel it.

"Allie? Are you there? . . . can you hear me?" It wasn't like the time she had almost died, it was much stronger, and much more real, although that had seemed real at the time too, but this was very different. "Allie . . ." She put down her pencil and pad and took Allyson's hand in her own, intent on reaching her if there was any chance at all. "Allie . . . open your eyes, sweetheart . . . I'm right here . . . open your eyes, baby . . . it's okay . . . don't be scared . . . it's Mommy . . ." She spoke very softly to her and stroked her hand, and then weakly, Allyson squeezed her hand, and Page started to cry. She had heard her. She knew it. She had heard her. "Allie . . . I felt you squeeze my hand . . . I know you can hear me, baby . . . come on . . . open your eyes now . . ." And then ever so slowly, as the tears streamed down Page's cheeks, she could see Allyson's eyelids flutter, and then they stopped. As though it were all too much for her, and she was exhausted. Page sat looking at her for a long time, wondering if she had slipped deeper into her coma again. There seemed to be no sign of life now, and then suddenly she felt her squeeze her hand again, but this time it was stronger.

Page wanted to jump up and shake her awake, to scream to someone, to tell them that Allie was still there, that deep inside her child was still alive and breathing, but she just sat there, mesmerized, staring at her, willing her to wake up, as the eyelids fluttered weakly again, and Page cried silently as she watched her. What if it was all a cruel joke, if they told her it was just spasms again . . . if she never woke up again . . . "Baby, please, please open your eyes . . . I love you so much . . . Allie, please . . ." She was sobbing softly and kissing her fingers, as the eyelids fluttered again, and ever so slowly Allyson opened her eyes for the first time in almost four months, and saw her mother.

She looked very groggy at first, as though she wasn't sure what she was seeing, and then she looked Page straight in the eye and said, "Mama." Page couldn't stop crying as she looked at her, she bent down and kissed her cheeks, and her hair and the tears ran down her cheeks into Allie's face, and then Allie said it again, louder this time, as she looked at her. It was a croak, but it was a word, the sweetest sound Page had ever heard . . . Mama . . .

Page sat there for ages, crying and looking at her, and then Frances came, and couldn't believe it.

"My God . . . she's awake . . ." She ran to call Dr. Hammerman, and by the time he came, she was dozing. But she had not fallen back into her coma.

Page explained to him what had happened, and he examined Allie quietly. After a while, Allyson opened her eyes and looked at him. She didn't understand who he was, and she cried as she looked at her mother.

"It's okay, sweetheart . . . Dr. Hammerman is our friend . . . he's going to make you all better . . ." She didn't care what anyone did anymore, Allie was awake, she had opened her eyes and spoken to them. Whatever came after that would be icing.

The doctor asked Allyson to squeeze his hand, and to look at him, which she did. And then he asked her to speak to him, but she wouldn't. Her eyes darted back to her mother's then, and she shook her head. And afterward he explained to Page, in the hall, that she had probably lost most of her language. She had lost most of her large motor skills, and how much brain damage there was remained to be seen now.

"She can learn many of those things again, walking, sitting, moving, feeding herself. She can learn to talk again. We just have to see how much is left, and how far we can take her," he said matter-of-factly. But Page was willing to do anything for her, to work as hard as she had to, to bring her back as far as they could. She was ready to do anything she had to, to help her.

She called Trygve when Hammerman left, and told him what had happened.

"Wait a minute . . . wait a minute . . . slow down . . ." He was on a portable phone at the lake, and he could hardly hear her. He knew the doctor had said something to her about Allyson's motor skills, but he hadn't heard the rest. "Tell me again." She was crying and laughing and he could hardly understand her.

"She talked to me . . . she *talked!*" She almost screamed and he almost dropped the phone when he heard her. "She's awake . . . she opened her eyes and looked at me, and said 'Mama.' " It was the most beautiful moment of Page's life since the day Allie had been born . . . and the day they had

known they wouldn't lose Andy. "Oh
Trygve . . ." All she could do was cry inco-
herently and he was crying too, as his children watched him. They crowded around
him anxiously, wanting to know what had
happened. They weren't sure if it was something terrible, or good, maybe Allie had
died. Chloe was terrified of that as she
watched him.

"We'll come down tonight," he said hurriedly. "I'll call you back. I want to tell the
kids," he said almost hysterically, and severed the connection when Page did. She
hurried back to the ICU to see Allyson, and
he told his children that Allie was awake.

"Is she okay?" Chloe asked in amazement.

"It's too soon to tell, sweetheart," he
said, hugging her. It could so easily have
been her in a coma and not Allie.

The whole family drove down from
Tahoe that night, but Allyson was asleep
again by then. Not in a coma this time, but
just sleeping, like a normal person. She was
being weaned off the respirator, but she was
still in the ICU and would stay there for
some time so they could watch her.

"What did she say?" Chloe wanted to

know everything as they sat around the Thorensens' kitchen table.

"She said 'Mama.' " Page cried again as she told them everything, and Trygve did too as he listened. And then Chloe cried, and Bjorn, because when people cried it upset him. He and Andy held hands as they listened.

It was the happiest day of their lives, and the next morning, Page took Chloe to the hospital with her. Allyson opened her eyes and stared at her for a long time and then she frowned and looked at her mother. "Girl," she said. "Girl." And then she lifted her hand and pointed.

"Chloe," her mother said carefully. "Chloe is your friend, Allie." Allyson looked at her again then and nodded. It was as though in some part of her she knew, but she had lost the words for everything. It was like being on another planet.

"I think she knew me," Chloe said when they left, but she admitted to her father that she was disappointed that Allie hadn't shown more recognition.

"Give her time. She's come from a long way. It's going to take a long time to get her back where she was, or even close to it." If she could even do that.

"How long, Dad?"

"I don't know. Dr. Hammerman told Page it could take years. Maybe two or three years before she's as rehabilitated as she can be." She'd be eighteen years old by then, and in the meantime she had to learn how to sit up, how to walk, how to eat with a fork . . . how to speak English . . . it was awesome.

Page told them more about her progress that night. The therapists were busy with her night and day now. She had a physical therapist, a specialist for large motor skills, a speech therapist, who worked with people with aphasia, or language difficulties common after strokes. She was going to be a busy girl for the next few months. And so was Page.

"What about Tahoe?" Trygve asked her that night. They were all going back up in the morning. And he wanted to take Andy with him, after he visited his sister.

"I don't know," she said, looking worried. "I hate leaving her now." What if she slipped back into the coma again? What if she stopped moving and talking? But Dr. Hammerman said that wouldn't happen now, and in fact, it was safe to leave her.

"Why don't you wait another week, or

two. You weren't going to come until later anyway and then you can commute every few days. I can drive you down if you want, we could stay overnight and go up in the morning. It's tiring but it's not nearly so bad as what you've been doing for the past four months. What do you think?" He was always willing to do anything to make her life easier and better.

"I'd like that." She smiled as she kissed him.

"Why don't I take Andy up with me now? I think he'd love it." And they both knew he'd be disappointed if Allie didn't recognize him at first. It was better for him to be away and distracted.

"I think it would be great for him," she agreed. She wanted all the time she could have to work with Allyson. They had a lot to do now.

"I'll come down and pick you up next week, and if it's too soon, I'll spend a couple of days with you, and you can come up the week after."

"Why are you so good to me?" she whispered as he pulled her closer to him.

"Because I'm trying to seduce you" was the answer.

She had called Brad in Europe the mo-

ment Allie had woken up, and he was ecstatic to hear it. He said he couldn't wait to
see her when he got back. But when he did,
like Chloe, and Andy when he'd seen her
before Tahoe, he was disappointed. He had
expected her to scream "Daddy!" the moment he walked into the room, and throw
her arms around his neck when she saw
him. Instead, she looked at him suspiciously, and then nodded and looked at
Page. "Man" was all she said for a long
time. "Man." She looked at him as though
struggling to remember his face, and then
suddenly as he was leaving the room she
whispered, "Dada."

"She said it!" Page said, beckoning him
back to them. "She said 'Dada.' " He had
held her and cried, but he was relieved
when he left the ICU. He couldn't bear seeing how limited she was. She was sitting up,
but she still couldn't walk, and she struggled
with every word and movement.

But when Trygve came back a week later,
he was impressed by her progress. "Chloe,"
she said, when she saw him, "Chloe." She
knew who he was, and that he belonged to
Chloe.

"Trygve," he explained. "I'm Chloe's
dad."

She nodded at him, and then a moment later, she smiled. It was a new action for her. She could smile, but never at exactly the moment she wanted, there seemed to be a delay. Similarly, when she cried, it always seemed to come late. But Dr. Hammerman said that all of those things would eventually fall into place, with a lot of work, and tremendous effort.

"She looks great," Trygve said to Page, and meant it. It was a hell of an improvement from where she had been a month before, or before that.

"I think so too," she beamed, "she understands a lot more than you think. She just doesn't know how to say it anymore. But I can see it in her face, and she tries so hard. Yesterday, I held her teddy bear out to her, and she called it 'Sandwich.' His name is Sam. But that was close. And then she laughed, and scared herself and burst into tears over it. It's kind of a roller coaster ride, but it's terrific."

"What does Hammerman think?"

"It's kind of early, but he says that from the tests now, and what he's seeing of her progress, he thinks ninety-five-percent recovery is realistic." It sounded incredible to him. A month before they were resigning themselves to her never coming out of the coma.

"It means she'll never balance her checkbook perfectly, her reflexes may not be fast enough to drive a car, or they may, she may not be the greatest dancer in the world, and simultaneous translation may be beyond her. But she can have a normal life, go to college, hold a job, have a family, laugh at jokes, enjoy a good book, tell a story. She'll be like the rest of the world, and like herself, just maybe a hair off what she might have been if all this hadn't happened." It was a lot to be grateful for considering the fact that she had almost died and spent four months in a coma.

"Sounds terrific to me." It was not unlike Chloe. Her dreams of being a ballerina had gone down the tubes, but she could walk, dance, move, live. She had lost something, but not everything. Not like Phillip, or the other people Laura Hutchinson had killed in La Jolla.

Page explained to Allyson about going to Lake Tahoe the next day. She cried when her mother said she was leaving her, but then she smiled again when she explained that it was only for two days. Page hated to leave her, but she would drive down every two or three days to see her. It was a grueling schedule, but Page wanted to do it, and Trygve understood that. She wanted to spend what little time she could with Andy, Trygve, and his family, but not abandon Allie completely.

Page felt like a new person as they drove through the mountains. She felt freer than she had in years, stronger and more alive. She turned to look at Trygve, and she felt like her heart was about to fly out of her chest, she was so happy.

"What are you grinning about? You look like the cat that swallowed the canary." It made him feel good just to see her. He had missed her during the past two weeks, and he hoped the day would come soon when they could be together.

"I'm just happy," she said, smiling.

"I can't imagine why," he teased.

"I can. I've got everything in the world to be thankful for. Two miracle children . . . and a miracle man . . . and three more children I'm crazy about."

"Sounds good to me. There's still room for more though."

"Maybe we shouldn't push our luck. Maybe five great kids is more than anyone deserves."

"Baloney." He was determined to have more children, but after all they'd been through she didn't dare ask for anything more in their lives. Allie's recovery was more miracle than she had ever hoped for.

The time in Tahoe was just what she needed. They finally slept in the same bedroom this time, and in spite of Bjorn and Andy's giggles the first night, everyone seemed to survive it.

It was a peaceful, relaxing time. They rode and fished and went hiking together. They talked about a lot of things, and got to know each other even better than they had. They had campfires and barbecues, and one night they all slept out under the stars. It was the perfect vacation. And Page's trips back to Ross every few days were grueling but worth it. And Allie's progress was amazing.

By the end of the second week, she could stand up and take a few steps with a little assistance. And when Page walked in, she grinned at her on cue and said, "Hi Mom, how are you?" She remembered Trygve's name, and she never forgot to ask for Chloe. She said she wanted to see Andy again too. Page had brought him to visit her before he left for Tahoe. She told her that he was at Lake Tahoe going fishing.

"Fish . . . gooey . . . yuk!" she said, making a horrible face, and they all laughed at her.

"Yeah, pretty bad," Trygve confessed, as excited about her progress as Page was. "They smell bad too."

"Garbage." Allie was struggling for words, and they laughed at her.

"I wouldn't go that far. Next time you'll have to come with us, and you can come fishing for garbage too." Allie laughed at his joke, and he hugged her. She was still beautiful, it was amazing how little visible damage there was from the accident. For her, all the real damage had been inside.

Trygve and Page went back to spend Labor Day weekend at the lake. The air had cooled a little bit, and you could already feel the end of summer. They were sad to see it end, but even as chopped up as the time had been, it had restored them. They all had a lot to do when they went home, especially Page, who had her murals and her art program to work on, and a lot of hard work to do with Allie.

And it sobered them again when they picked up a newspaper and saw that Laura

Hutchinson was going on trial Tuesday in La Jolla.

"I hope they put her away for a hundred years," Chloe said vehemently, more for Allie than herself. And of course for Phillip. She had been only too happy to let Phillip take the blame and imply that it had been his fault. For the rest of time, he would have borne the blame of the accident, when she had been the one. Someone had come forward recently and said that they thought she'd had a lot to drink when she left the party. Why hadn't the police noticed that? Why hadn't they done anything about it? It was too late now. But at least, this time, she was going to have to pay for what she'd done in La Jolla.

"It's amazing how life changes, isn't it?" Page said wistfully as they sat at the edge of the lake at sunset. They were going home the next day, and the kids were all up at the house getting ready for dinner. They were going out that night, to a new restaurant in Truckee. "Five months ago my life was in a whole different place . . . and now look what we've been through, where we've gone. You never know in life what's going to happen." They were richer for it in the end, but at what price. They had paid dearly for everything that had happened.

"I never want to relive that day," Trygve said thoughtfully. "I still remember when they called me . . . and then I saw you at the hospital . . . I thought they were with you."

"And I thought you'd been killed when they said the driver had been killed on the bridge . . . God, what an awful moment." She looked up at him with wide eyes, filled with respect for the power of destiny, its cruelty and its kindness. "I guess we've been pretty lucky." She smiled at him, and took his hand in her own.

"You've been so good to me these past months."

"You deserve even better. Just give it time." She laughed then, as though he'd said something funny, and he had, but he didn't know it. "Have you been doing any thinking about our plans?" He didn't want to push her, but he brought it up from time to time, just to remind her. He still wanted her to marry him when her divorce became final at Christmas.

"Yes, I have." She said it quietly, looking out across the lake as he watched her, and then she turned to him with an odd expression. "Are you really sure that's what you want, Trygve? It's a lot to take on. I've got two kids . . . and Allie's recovery won't be easy."

"Neither will Chloe's. And Bjorn will always be who he is. What about you? For all my pushing, how do you feel about my burdens?"

"I happen to love them very much. I never knew I could love someone else's kids as much." She had even grown fond of Nick in the short time she had come to know him better over the summer.

"I'd say it's a fair match." He smiled, and she nodded, and then he looked serious again. "I used to feel that I really shouldn't get married again because of Bjorn, that it wasn't fair to him. I couldn't imagine anyone loving him as much as I did, and I didn't want anyone to hurt him. And then you came along," his eyes grew damp as he pulled her closer to him, "and you were so wonderful to him . . . he really deserves to be around people who love him. He's such a good little soul, in spite of his limitations."

"So are you," she said, nestling close to him, and she hadn't found his limitations yet.

"How does Christmas sound to you?" He smiled, looking mischievous, and this time she laughed.

"Actually, I was going to discuss that with you," she said, and then lay on their towel and looked up at him.

"Are you serious?" He looked thrilled. She had been reluctant to move too soon before, but now everything looked different since Allie had come out of her coma.

"Maybe. I have to discuss something with you first though." Her face grew serious and he lay down on his side next to her and waited. "There's something I think I should tell you." Something about Allyson perhaps . . . or Brad . . . maybe she was going to tell him that she still loved him and thought he should know that. He had considered that himself, but she seemed to have adjusted remarkably well, better than he had after Dana. "Remember what you said about wanting to have a baby right away?"

She looked worried and he laughed. He knew she was reluctant about that. She said she wanted more, but she was afraid she was too old, and didn't want to be distracted from helping Allie.

"I can wait on that if I have to. I just thought it would be nice. But if you need time . . . we're young enough to wait a while." And if she decided she couldn't handle more, he was willing to accept that, but she was frowning at him now. She was looking worried. "It's not a deal breaker, Page."

"Let me put it to you this way," she said, propping herself up on one elbow. "How would you feel about getting married at Christmas," his heart soared and he laughed out loud, he was ecstatic, but she wasn't finished, "if I was nearly six months pregnant?"

"What?" He sat up and looked down at her, and she grinned at him sheepishly and rolled over on her back and chuckled.

"I don't know how the hell it happened. I think you overworked my birth control or something, about six weeks ago. I thought I was imagining it at first, but I wasn't. I wasn't sure how you'd feel about this, with the kids and all . . . it's kind of a shock for everyone, and it makes for kind of an interesting wedding." She looked like an embarrassed kid as she explained it to him. She felt foolish, but pleased. She always wanted another baby. And they had certainly started this relationship with a bang in every way. It was like being shot out of a cannon . . . and landing in a field of flowers.

"You know, you amaze me." He lay next to her and held her close to him. "I can't believe it." And then suddenly he laughed again. He was thrilled. This was exactly what he had wanted, even faster than he'd wanted it, which was fine with him. "I guess this'll be yet another miracle baby for us." He laughed openly as he teased her.

"What do you mean?"

"Well, there's Bjorn, who's pretty special in his own way. And Chloe is pretty miraculous now too . . . and Andy who was so premature and is fine now . . . and Allie's miraculous recovery . . . and let's see, if we get married in December, and you have the baby in what . . . three and a half, four months after that . . . think of what a miracle that will be! A three-month baby!" He was laughing and she looked sheepish.

"You're awful. Think how embarrassed our poor children will be."

"Then we won't let them. If they can't understand how lucky we all are, and how blessed, and that grown-ups can make a mistake occasionally too, then to hell with them. I'm certainly not going to question a gift like this, or God forbid turn it away when it's been offered to us . . . I'm going to hold it as close to me as I can, and you along with it, and whisper my thanks every night before I go to sleep . . . as miracles go, I'd say we've cornered the market," he said proudly, and without saying another word, he reached down and kissed her, and she held him close to her, thinking how far they had come, how far they had traveled on dangerous shores, and how lucky they were to have each other.

Marriage

Also by Gwen Davis:

a novel by

GWEN DAVIS

ARBOR
HOUSE
New York

Marriage

For Bob, my son: a coming of age

"For one human being to love another: that is perhaps the most difficult of all tasks, the ultimate, the last test and proof, the work for which all other work is but preparation."

—RAINER MARIA RILKE

Marriage

One

THEIR SON was in the hotel room with them, so Chris considered it wise to speak her unrest as little as possible. He had been talking in his sleep, chewing at his fingers, filled with a feverish intuition that his family might be coming apart. He had developed a slight stammer at the mention of "divorce," swallowing before he could speak the word, as though it choked him. Her children were the miracle she'd been sure would never be conferred on her. The daughter, with all the cold strength a woman needed to survive, even at thirteen, would weather whatever happened. But Josh had a marshmallow heart: he was achingly vulnerable. Chris could not bear the thought of bringing him pain. But she wondered how much sacrifice was expected of her, she expected of herself.

From the balcony of their room, overlooking the Sea of Cortés, was a view of Las Tetas de Cabra: Tits of the Goat, the Mexicans called it unpoetically, a spectacular jagged slash of mountains against a sunset sky. "We should never have to leave this room," Harry said. "From here, Mexico is Heaven."

Across the water, the sun sank at a curious speed, unreal, disconnected, filmic. Her eye could not keep up with its course as it plummeted towards the horizon, searing the sea purple. The sky lit with a dying blaze, burning along its

15

edges, outlining the nippled mountain, catching a trailing feather of cloud, and turning it scarlet. "From a distance it's all beauty," Harry said.

Like marriage, Chris thought, but did not say aloud.

She still had nightmares about her own splintered childhood, a terror of inflicting the wrench of divorce on her own children. But the shards of her personal chronicle, parents who hadn't loved her enough to overcome their loathing for each other, didn't seem to be at issue anymore. The problem was her own survival. She clung to the hope that Harry would do something to reassert the charm, the loving-kindness that had won her, so she wouldn't be faced with the agonies of the courtroom, the lawyer's fees. ("What happened to that nice lawyer who was so crazy about you?" her mother asked once. "The one you would have married if you had any taste? I bet he'd give you a break on legal fees." "He's dead," Chris answered. "Then he should really be dirt cheap," said her mother.)

Harry seemed to have no idea the marriage was in trouble. Either that, or he chose not to acknowledge it, not to deal even on a fantasy level. Fantasy was the province of women, who always conjured the best, and the worst. Reality was the domain of men. So he opted to live in reality, taking his disappointments as they struck him in the heart, not anticipating. That he was being unrealistic was something he did not stop to analyze. They were on vacation. Whatever pressures were on them were going to disappear. That was a conviction he had carried with him out of the Bronx. If you made enough to be able to afford to go away, life straightened out. ("Forty-two weeks," he used to say to Chris, in jovial echo of his father. "I should have been in Florida.")

Harry was still a handsome man, standing tall, wide shouldered, with a thick mane of dark silky hair, that which would have given automatic confidence to the bald business men jogging through the smoggy mornings of Beverly Hills, as though there was much to live for besides masculine beauty. He did not try to keep up with them in mileage or manipulation. The athleticism of his young manhood had been stuffed away along with the scrapbooks his mother had kept. The aspirations of his youth had also been closeted, his geniality eroding into forced heartiness, cloaking his anger at a world full of villains who had passed him. He had set great store by success, but like a heartless chorus girl, it had scorned him, saving its favors for scoundrels. Still, he did not dwell on the agony of that, he convinced himself almost daily. As he read of sub-rosa real estate deals, the sly exchanges of favors, the subtle and not so subtle maneuvering of the law by the well esteemed, he simply noted that he hadn't been a big enough crook to flourish in the entertainment industry, and turned to the sports pages.

He had some credentials in the business community, though none he would boast of at the high-echelon parties to which they were still invited because of his wife. He was part owner of one of the more profitable health-food stores in Southern California. But at seventeen he had pitched for the Brooklyn Dodgers, so thought that the whole of existence would take place at the top of the world. That first great the record business. When that, too, failed him (though his colleagues trumpeted vice versa), he had compromised, pic- colleagues trumpeted vice versa) he had compromised, pic- tured himself as a great restauranteur, a Chasen, a Vincent Sardi, men who catered to the celebrated, and became, through style and manner of greeting, as notable as those they entertained. Instead, his fortunes had placed him in a windowless room, balancing books, bartering barley. He did not examine his surroundings too carefully, lest he note how airless they were.

In the same way, he did not study his marriage for signs of

17

disintegration. His children amazed him, lifted his heart, shiny apples on a tree he chose not to notice was being uprooted. He knew that things were not good between him and Chris. But things had been not good before. He took his life axiom from the black baseball player who advised, "Don't look back, someone may be gaining on you." In his one concession to backward glancing, where his marriage was concerned, Harry relied on the past for precedent. No matter what the pressures, the apparent rents, like a witty guest at a dinner party, love had always risen to the occasion, saving what otherwise would have been a disaster.

And now they were in Mexico, where tropical heat would bake away whatever chill had fallen on the relationship, where leisure would restore their humor, and solidity, he was sure. He studied his wife through half-closed lids, so he would not seem to be observing her, as she observed the sunset. She had flowered, under his tutelage, from an insecure fat girl to a lovely woman, giving off an aura of confidence only he knew was a lie. She was slender now, onyx eyes like sculptures on a high pedestal of cheek, skin already burned coffee dark from one day of sun. His affection, his devotion, had chiseled her out of the formless person she had been when he met her. That was a knowledge she shared, but no longer wished to dwell upon.

She was tired of being grateful. Tired of being dependent on other people's good opinion to define herself. She was almost sure of who she was, now, nearly ready to make a life because she wanted to, not because it was expected of her.

"Come here, Josh," she said to her son. "Look at the sunset."

"I saw it last night." He was kneeling on the floor between the two double beds, the sturdiness of his calves roundly bulging his thick white socks, as he pored over an Arizona newspaper, flown in that morning.

18

"It's different every day," she said. "Like the sports pages."

He smiled, and got up grudgingly, coming out onto the balcony beside her, leaning his arms on the carved ebony rail, examining the sunset with grim tolerance, as though he understood her madness imagining such things to be as important as the health and well-being of Vince Ferragamo. She put her arm on his shoulder, tentatively, not really touching hard enough that he would construe it as a maternal embrace, and so shy away from it. Big as he was, with all the gruff of his eleven years, if she narrowed her eyes, close to his profile, she could see him as he had been when he was a baby, held on her shoulder: the same sweetly rounded cheek, heavily lashed deepset angular dark eyes, the amazing burst of chestnut hair, slightly disappointed lower lip, as if he'd known from the start life had a heartbreak in it.

His fingers moved to his mouth, worrying his braces. She reached for his hand. He scowled. She kissed his knuckles, as if carried away by overwhelming affection for him, and not a mother's concern. He could not really deal with either, but seemed to find the first slightly less repellent.

"That's enough," he said, pulling his hand away. "I know you're crazy about me."

"I am."

"You have good taste," he said, in his basso voice. He swallowed, ingesting the bluff. "Only joking."

"It's all right to have a good opinion of yourself," Harry said, as though buttressing in his son the confidence lacking in his own character. He was always giving confidence, as though by some blood exchange, saving other people, transfusing his strength to them, sapping himself. Chris wondered why the realization filled her with such quiet anger.

Once, she had found his self-sacrifice touching, like his incapacity to harm, in a town, in a business that demanded betrayal. Now, it rankled her, clawed at the edges of her impatience. Her own success, which their society thought considerable, had long ago outstripped his. She hadn't intended it to. It had never occurred to her that she was capable of taking care of herself, much less anyone else. She still had difficulty facing that particular truth, had for years fed the myth that he was the head of the family. But it was no longer possible to try to be less, so he could seem more. The humiliation she felt at having outreached him was only compounded by pretending she had not.

The annual season of flood had come to Los Angeles, presaging the annual season of fire, ravaging the hillsides, dispelling any illusion of clemency in the weather, a terrible toll that had to be paid in exchange for a surfeit of sunshine. Torrential rains had swollen the walls of their house, cracked their roof. A marriage already strained, like their house, groaned at the seams. She'd suggested that they take the children away on holiday. To clear her head, was it? To give her the courage to do what she had sworn she would never do, divorce? Inflict on her children what had been inflicted on her? Fortifying them for the kill.

Wasn't that the job of life, to fortify for the death? To give fruits and comforts and bodily pleasures as to an Aztec warrior before his sacrifice. All of it an oiling, a preparation of perfumes, before the rankness of it struck, and they tore your living heart out.

She looked past her son at her husband, tried to find in his pale countenance what had propelled Josh into life. She searched Harry's features for the seed of the rowdy, dark boy. No sign of him. Josh looked as though he'd sprung from her unaided, Diana from the forehead of Mars, burst into life on the strength of his own conviction. With his hair that came from neither of them, the great, thick, dark explosion proclaiming an argument to genes, announcing his independence.

20

The daughter who even now stood below their balcony on the beach, her face turned stubbornly seaward, as though to catch last rays of sun, in some quiet, desperate attempt to match her mother's tan, was like both of them. Part Harry, part Chris. ("I look like my father," she'd say with contained ferocity, when people would compliment her on looking like her mother.) Her hair was silky like his, lighter brown; she had her mother's black eyes. Her legs, which seemed to be half of her, were slim, like Chris's but with a roundness of thigh and fullness of hip t..at came from Harry. She seemed to be a perfect blend, favoring her father only by liking him better, something that Chris tried not to take personally.

But Josh was completely his own person, as proclaimed by his hair. It billowed around his head, concealing his heavy brown eyebrows, framing the Oriental set of his eyes, his high-boned, freckled cheeks. He frowned slightly, as though in concentration at the sunset, pretending he didn't know his mother was staring at him. Softly pointed chin pressing into the tops of his hands, he leaned on the wooden railing. "Why does the sun sink so fast here?" he asked.

"It's a strange configuration of the earth," Chris guessed.

"It thinks it's a tourist's stomach," said Harry.

Sometimes she remembered how much she had loved him.

It had been the worst part of winter when they met, New York pretending it was prancing into spring because the calendar indicated it was almost the equinox. Department store windows foisted thin-fabricked wardrobes on shivering passersby, of whom Chris was not one. She allowed herself not even the luxury of marking the bleakness of sky, the gritty, ash-spattered slush at the edge of the sidewalks. Instead, she lay in her half-furnished apartment, on the bed her stepfather had bought for her, her only conscious movement the press of

21

her thumb on the remote control of her television set, a gift from her mother which she daily threatened to take back. ("You have to get out of that apartment, no matter how you look," Evelyn said. "Maybe you'll meet someone who likes fat girls.")

What had laid Chris so low was an accumulation of sorrows, the most recent being the release of her tenth recorded song to resounding obscurity. Her talent was all that redeemed her from the overweight spectacle in the mirror, she was sure, and now that, too, seemed destined to be unloved, uncelebrated. She was also in a dull kind of mourning for Marilyn Monroe, whom she had never met, but was sure she could have comforted, rescued, made her best friend, since they were so much alike, if only Chris had gotten thin, been fucked a lot, and abandoned afterward, instead of first thing. She was twenty-five years old, and her life was clearly over, like Marilyn's. Each of them had blossomed prematurely, Chris in the brain, as Marilyn in the breast, and been abused by an uncaring world. She drew the blankets over her head, and wasn't conscious of eating, although there were always dirty dishes in the sink.

"You're starting to look like my Aunt Jenny," her stepfather said. He had come with some sandwiches from the delicatessen, not so much to feed her as not to have to eat alone. Sonny took great comfort from corned beef, the fattier the better, to line his heart, cushion it against the slings and arrows of outrageous fortune and Evelyn. He was not a man who thought of suicide, but he wouldn't have minded a nice, quick heart attack, especially if it would have gotten him out of Wall Street, and fights with his wife. To his great regret, he loved her, although he was no longer fool enough to invite her to accompany him to P.J. Bernstein's. When he ate, it was with such joyful self-indulgence that he had no time for manners, and pieces of meat tended to slip from the sides of his sandwich. Once, from across a restaurant, Evelyn had watched Cesar Romero eat a roast beef on rye, meticulously. When he was finished, she'd leaned over and slapped Sonny's face.

"You'd better pull yourself together," Sonny counseled Chris, mustard around the edges of his words. "Take a bath, get dressed. Go somewhere, anywhere."

Of the men in her life, what few there were, she loved him best, capitalist though he was. There was a passion in him for art, for the gentle quests he had never been able to set out on, commandeered as he had been into a pirate's life on the seas of Wall Street. His admiration for what she was able to create had combined with his affection for underdogs. "You can't just give up," he said to her now, as he every morning advised himself.

Usually, when Sonny suggested, Chris listened. So she made an appointment to see a producer who'd called her about some material for a record. He was savvy and sharp, a hustler, obvious even to her who never saw villains until she was already murdered. She gave him a few good ideas, because she had nothing to protect: he seemed interested in what she had to say, unlike the world, unlike her mother, unlike the young men she'd loved before it was fashionable to come out of the closet and tell a girl why it was they never touched her. Then she asked about money. He sent her out to lunch with his two young lieutenants, as if food and the company of men should be payment enough.

Of the two, one was sarcastic and cutting, so Chris paid deepest attention to him, drawn as she was to those who would reinforce doubt. The other she hardly saw. In addition to being uncombed, unkempt, she was suffering from a cold, and kept whisking a finger under her nose in a gesture she hoped was inconspicuous. Halfway through lunch, she felt a pressure against her knee, and saw a package of Kleenex being placed next to her elbow. She looked up and saw Harry.

He was, she observed, a handsome young man, if a little too strong for her taste, a touch too clean-cut, his gaze more direct than those she was used to encountering. His eyes were very light green, openly appraising. She could not imagine their liking what they saw.

She thanked him, took a tissue, blew her nose, and dismissed him even as they sat there. When she called the producer's office the next day, and Harry answered the phone, she did not even remember him.

"You better go out on a date," Sonny was saying from behind his desk. "So you don't turn into my Aunt Jenny." Chris was visiting him in his Wall Street offices, its ticker tape framed by two giant elephant tusks which Evelyn had bought by mistake at auction and had been unable to persuade Parke Bernet to take back. The phone Chris was using was another of Evelyn's errors, an antique French design she had paid too much for, and no longer liked, so insisted on installing somewhere it didn't matter, like Sonny's place of business. There were four other phones to the side of his desk, plain black, workmanlike models equipped with push-button direct lines to key banks and important customers. Chris was not allowed to use them, nor had she a particular wish to use the phone she was on, except that she wanted to display to Sonny she was at least attempting to continue her life, such as it was.

"Hi," Harry was saying, on the other end of the line. "You want to have dinner?"

Coming as the invitation did, as though in answering salute to Sonny's suggestion, she seemed to have no choice. All the way to the restaurant she worried that she would not recognize him. But he was standing just inside the doorway, waiting with a packet of Kleenex, a Benedrex inhaler, cough drops, Vick's Vaporub, and a green carnation.

"Happy St. Patrick's Day," he said, offering it all.

She was never conscious of falling in love. As desperately as she thought she sought romance, she did not recognize it dressed as Harry. It was the first real courtship of her life, most of it taking place that evening, as she exorcised all the uncelebrated teenage years, the proms she had never been invited to, visiting locales tacitly off-limits to the unlovely. They began with drinks at Toots Shor's, continued to "21," where they both pretended not to mind when they couldn't get a table, dined at the Absinthe House, danced at the Harwyn, and, as if there were no need for orchestras, waltzed around the lobby of the Sheraton East. All her life she'd felt clumsy, graceless, envying those light enough to be whirled around by someone they trusted. Now, his hand strong on her back, she was transformed. She could move as easily as any-one, into laughter, past the disapproving glances, Holly Golightly reborn as chubette, the world laid out on terrazoed floors.

At four in the morning, they breakfasted at Reuben's. Harry ran into a friend who fell in love with what a good time they were having, and wouldn't go away, insisting on helping Harry take her home. So they didn't make love that night. In a way she was glad for the unwanted presence, because it was still a time when a "good girl" resisted going to bed, didn't even fall into a man's arms, suck the cleft in his chin, try to disappear into him as she did that first night, with his friend waiting in the hall.

When they did make love, it was not to the strains of music on the stereo. In her mind that would have looked too premeditated, too much of an invitation, the setting of a scene she was not bold enough to seem willing to play. Instead, they watched David Susskind, romanced to his curious tune. Chris pretended utter absorption, so Harry could sneak up on her.

There was still in her a shyness, the innocence she hadn't meant to keep, fostered by a string of unloving, uncaring men. She had not had an opportunity to be wanton, although she suspected it existed in her nature, felt it leaping up when Harry touched her, dancing in her with his tongue. He was so strong he made her feel delicate. Like the small, shy girl she was inside, she averted her eyes when the lovemaking was over, made no mention of how joyful she felt. The erotic was still the domain of men, the celebration of the sensual in women considered immodest, only beginning to peek from the pages of magazines. Nor would she admit, even to herself, how happy she was about Harry. There had to be in him some terrible flaw, she was sure, that he wanted her.

"You ought to get your hair done," he said, a few weeks into their courtship. It was clearly a courtship: he came with Chinese food in white cardboard containers, flowers, over-sized jars of aspirin after dinner with her family.

She got her hair done. "You really look nice," he said. "I bet if you took off a few pounds you'd be a knockout."

Rage welled up in her. As if she hadn't spent the whole of her life trying. As if thin people understood. "Why did you take me out?" she asked angrily, looking for the root of it, the truth, the lie that was underneath. Her parents were sure it was money. Sonny wanted to run a check on him; Evelyn didn't have to. ("He comes from the Bronx," she had said, explaining everything.)

"You have great teeth and great tits," Harry said.

It was a crudity of speech that did not ring true. Everything about Harry was couched in gentleness, including his language, his humor, as he deliberately skirted around his own

26

beginnings, sneaking in side doors, surprising everyone. That he spoke to her now in the *patois* of the street tough was a kind of embrace, like a wolf whistle, something she did not consider herself attractive enough to inspire. The intentional coarseness of it was to let her know she was sexy, she understood that, loved it, even while it embarrassed her, because she didn't believe it.

"You can't fake a hard on," advised a woman friend, as thick-skinned and blunt as Harry wasn't really.

The observation didn't salve Chris's malaise. The friend who made that pronouncement, Chris counted on even less than she did Harry, although she liked her better, since her friend was contemptuous of Chris's affection, more what Chris was used to, warming to abuse.

She decided to go on a diet to spite Harry, planning to become heartless as well as thin, intuiting that both were really out of her grasp. But if either were attainable, she would be able to leave him, to find someone better. The nerve of him, loving her. As if she could believe it.

Sonny was impressed by the physical change in her, a miraculous shedding of skin that sent her spinning into the world younger, quieter, more composed. Lost with the weight was much of her anger, the fifty pounds of chip she had had on her shoulder. But like Chris, Sonny was still not ready to credit Harry, to allow Pygmalion citizenship in the ghetto. Mythic men, sculptors of human character came from Greece, and Cornell, had careers in medicine and law, futures in diplomacy. As little as he loved the sexual ambition of his wife, Sonny could see the wisdom of Evelyn's contention that thin, Chris could get Somebody. "He'll drag you down," he muttered to Chris, watching Harry from across the room, resenting Harry's acting the host, resisting finding him personable, appealing. Sonny had heard enough of Chris's betrayal by those in the music business to know none of them

27

were up to any good, and few deserved her talents. "You hurt my daughter, I'll see you end up in the can," he said, reverting to Brooklyn tough in the presence of this person from Gun Hill Road, when she should have had Harvard.

"I won't hurt her," Harry said. They were leaning with their backs against the wall as people squeezed by them in the small hallway, in their way in and out of the cocktail party Chris was giving. "Don't worry."

"I won't worry," Sonny said, his shoulder lifting in the twitch he had developed even before Evelyn. "*You* worry. In the *can*." He spoke very softly, as people could afford to do who understood what true power was, what volume there didn't have to be in the voice when you had it in the bank.

That Chris seemed happy was beside the point, especially to Evelyn. "What do you see in him? With *that* family," Evelyn narrowed her eyes against the smoke, peering through it to see if any of the people at the party were important. "You could get the young Aga Khan now that you're losing weight."

"I don't know the young Aga Khan."

"We'll find him. It's just a question of being in the right place."

"I like Harry."

"You never had any taste. I remember your liking your father."

That gentleman, too, seemed less than pleased with her choice of Harry. He had come back into Chris's life after a long absence, periodically making a paternal pilgrimage to New York. The visits were usually made under cover of darkness, as though his long-ago war experience had been with the O.S.S., since only maneuvers of that clever a nature could outwit Evelyn. She was still suing him for child support for Chris, from the ages of eleven to twenty-one, and traveled at all times with a subpoena in her purse in case she ran into him, which she had hired several private detectives to make it easier for her to do. She was also employing one of the nastier attorneys in Tennessee, where Walter had moved to escape her, and become governor. ("He should have stayed with your mother," Sonny said to Chris. "He would have been president.") So when Walter traveled, especially to New York, it was with a great deal of trepidation. He considered it testimony of his rekindled affection for his daughter that he was willing to come even secretly to a city guarded by a dragon.

The restaurants he chose to dine in were shadowy places. In one of those, Chris introduced her father to Harry. Walter was visibly unimpressed, directing most of his attention and questions to the young man that Harry worked with, more interested in him, as Chris had been, at their first meeting. She regretted having invited Chuck to join them, which she had done only to put Harry more at ease.

"You'd love Nashville," Walter said to Chuck. "It's the Athens of the South."

"I hear there's a lot of music action," said Chuck agreeably.

"You could start your own record company. Plenty of room in Tennessee."

Chris controlled her annoyance till Chuck and Harry went to the men's room. "Why are you paying so much attention to him?" she asked her father. "Why are you selling *him* Tennessee? Harry's the one I'm dating."

"Chuck seems more your type."

"But I'm going with Harry." The era came with its own euphemisms. In fact, they were living together, Harry having moved into Chris's apartment, albeit not bringing enough clothes to seriously underline the arrangement. Society still considered cohabitation reprehensible, so Chris was more than glad to pretend it wasn't so, giving heavy tips to the elevator man to act as though Harry wasn't coming down in the morning.

"Chuck seems more your type," Walter said again.

Parental disapproval was not enough to sour Chris on Harry. On the contrary, her parents' dislike had usually been the strongest argument in anything's favor. But along with her fear that his wanting her made him suspect, went a terror of making a mistake. No matter how strongly she resisted, because on the other end lay disillusion and divorce (her mother *promised*), marriage was where it seemed to be leading. They had not done anything so straightforward as to ask, or propose, either of them. But they did talk of future, what they would do when he got a better job, and they had a number of blood tests, good only for thirty days. Though they didn't have the courage to follow the tests up with the license, it was hard to pretend they weren't serious. ("My veins are starting to open of their own volition," Harry said.)

Chris decided to run him past her college friends, so they could say he wasn't good enough. To her surprise, they loved him. What distinguished Bryn Mawr women, besides marble-mouthed diction and flagrant self-satisfaction, was enormous affection for the original. Because of that, Chris had earned the esteem of her classmates as an undergraduate, in spite of how social she was not, and terrifyingly enthusiastic she was, racing over turreted Gothic rooftops at night to sing her songs to friends in other dormitories, organizing musical comedies, Shakespeare festivals, celebrations of spring. No one had minded how fat she was. Nor did they seem put off now by Harry's pox of not having gone to Princeton.

She took him to dinner at the home of the first one who had married Yale, a thin-lipped, austere young woman who seemed always on the verge of teaching. The apartment was in Morningside Heights, both bride's and groom's families being seventh-generation Americans, with money so old they lived off interest and never touched capital, a mentality so secure it didn't need to dwell in places others considered fashionable.

Chris noted that to him in the elevator, explaining why such gentry lived where they did. "Genteel poverty."

"I thought it was pronounced Gentile," Harry said.

His impression of the hostess, who greeted them at the door in a green felt skirt to the floor, was that of an upright pool table. But she was gracious in a way he had never been exposed to, so he returned her grace in kind, being totally himself, commenting warmly on her husband's manner of dress, the buttondown shirt, the cordovan shoes, the salt still on them from waves breaking on Plymouth Rock. In like manner, Harry charmed the husband's brother, a banker from Connecticut, asking him for instruction in taking over a bank, since his own family background ran only to robbing them.

Chris was mildly horrified at first at the self-deprecating lack of credentials he paraded. She'd expected him to be choked by the presence of Ivy League and inherited income, but by mid-evening he made it seem deprivation not to come from the slums. He told rollicking tales of his father, a former bartender who now ran The Boom Boom Room, a strip joint off Third Avenue, brandishing hairy anecdote as Hoskins Whitehead, the banker brother, wore his Phi Beta Kappa key.

"The Boom Boom Room," Hoskins repeated, fiilling each boom with a Marblehead rheum, part cannon, part edge of tears, as though something of military glory and mystery had eluded him. "The Ba-OO-OOm Ba-OO-OOm Ra-OO-OOm," he said, over and over, chortling into his Jack Daniels. "How droll."

Harry matched him pretty well, drink for drink. Although he never seemed the worse for it, Chris knew he was not used to collegiate boozing, and worried. But he simply seemed looser, more charming than ever, letting go an occasional burst of laughter so deep it seemed to shake the stately walls. Only when they hit the dark of the dining room with its high ceilings, walnut paneling and formally set table barely discernible in the candlelight, did she note him nodding off, listing to port, his eyes half-closed, as the hostess served. He shook himself awake for the main course, which he ate, but could not see.

"What is this?" he asked, halfway through.

"Shrimp caramel," said the hostess.

"Excuse me." Harry bolted from the table, napkin to his lips, so white Chris could see him blanching even in the darkness.

About three o'clock in the morning, the phone rang in Chris's apartment. It was Harry's father. Although they didn't acknowledge they lived together, Chris and Harry had told certain people she would always know where to reach him, among them Harry's father, providing he wouldn't tell Harry's mother.

"You know a guy named Hoskins Whitehead?" he asked his son.

"Huh?" Harry said.

"He's here with some guy from the House of Morgan. What's that, a restaurant?"

"What do they want, dad?"

"They want to cash a check. Is it any good?"

"Hoskins Whitebread in the Ba-OO-OOm Ba-OO-OOm Ra-OO-OOm," Harry said, after he'd hung up the phone. "I love it. I really love it."

"Apparently it's never too late to introduce the finer things to people of quality," Chris said.

"Shrimp caramel," he mused, imitating the flat stretched-out *a*'s of the hostess's pronunciation. "How do you suppose somebody learns to make shrimp caramel."

"Well, you take shrimp, and put it in caramel sauce. . . ."

"Excuse me," said Harry, and tore from the bed, to the bathroom.

Chris finally managed to find one friend who couldn't stand Harry, a high school roommate who echoed all Evelyn's objections but in words so affectionate Chris had to pay attention. "You're a brilliant, educated, lovely woman. He can't hold a candle to you. It isn't fair to him to make him try. I have someone I want to introduce you to."

He was a lawyer named George Mailey. Suitable, divorced, attractive, and funny. He made Chris laugh in a different way from Harry, filling the air between them with sharp repartee, little ripostes she imagined would have been welcome at the Algonquin. She felt guilty when she was with him, as though she were being unfaithful to Harry, laughing with someone else. Harry was still living in the apartment, but she had informed him she was going to date other people, and considered him free to do the same. She had tried to make it into a fight, because she could feel him closing in on her with his affection, ready to indulge her even in this, not being proud enough to leave her, not giving her enough provocation to throw him out. It was as though he had dedicated himself to her, something she had always prayed would happen but knew never would. She felt perversely contemptuous of him for not beating her, and him a former athlete.

George Mailey took her to appropriate places, for appropriate occasions, black-tie charity dances and concerts, alumni football games, revivals at the Thalia. It was the kind of relationship she should have had, and never had before.

33

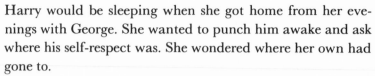

Harry would be sleeping when she got home from her evenings with George. She wanted to punch him awake and ask
where his self-respect was. She wondered where her own had
gone to.

"How can I be with both of them, and feel affection for
both?" she asked the analyst who was helping her sort it all
out. She had started seeing him about the time she met
Harry, so she wasn't exactly sure whose fault it was that she
was losing weight and feeling better about herself. But, of
course, her analyst hadn't told her to get her hair done.

"Well," said Dr. Ehrens. "If you've never had a coat, and
then you can finally afford one, there's nothing wrong with
trying on two."

The tailored coat, which is how she started thinking about
George Mailey, she wore to brunch at the Plaza with Sonny
and Evelyn. They were impressed, impressed enough not to
quarrel in front of him, a courtesy they never extended to
Harry.

But it was the warm coat she wore to dinner with her
father, on one of his surprise visits to New York. She already
knew Walter M. White would prefer someone else to Harry,
so wished to offer no evidence that she had an alternative.

When Chris and Harry got back to the apartment, the
phone was ringing. "You fingered me to your mother!"
Walter was shouting through the receiver, having been
greeted at his hotel by a process server, with a subpoena.

Chris started to cry, shouting denials, but Walter was im-
placable. She hung up the phone and, with Harry watching,
jumped out the window.

"Oh my God," he said, blood drained from his face, finding
her on the small balcony he hadn't known was outside. "I
thought you were dead."

"Don't you see how crazy they are? How crazy I am?" she
wept. "Why do you hang around?"

"Because I like you," he said.

But the more secure she felt with Harry, the more she hungered for George Mailey, tranquility throwing her into a panic, since she knew it couldn't last. The important choices she had to make in life were diminished by the superficial one: who should she take to what event.

A song she had written, and been disappointed over, was featured in a movie. Harry had suffered with her through the double-talk, helping her deal with the people breaking promises, negotiating her a good price. She was invited to the premiere, a black-tie event, with a great deal of trumpeting in a world of vanishing fanfare. Because it was obviously Harry who belonged there, she took George.

He was never wittier, never more appealing. When the triumph was over, and a triumph it was, because there was reality in her career now, her name accredited on the screen, George took her to the Brasserie, and ordered *oeufs aux chevaux*. "An oaf on horseback," he said, sending her into fresh spasms of laughter, cramping her stomach because of all the laughing she had already done and not recovered from. It hurt her now to laugh, she realized with sudden, awful clarity, because he was so witty the laughter felt hollow. Reality was what she needed that night. Harry knew everything there was to know about how important the occasion was for her, what had gone into it. History was what made people rich, gave jokes layers beneath them, fossilized. The evening was empty because Harry wasn't there. She ached for him.

Two days later, they decided to get married. She made a lunch date with George Mailey, loving him even as she told him she was marrying someone else, because he was giving her the chance to play out a drama. She had never imagined that one man would ever want to marry her, much less two. Although George had never exactly asked her, or even hinted,he did look properly baleful as he wished her every happiness.

Chris and Harry were married in the White and Gold Suite

of the Plaza. It was on a Sunday, so Evelyn could not have Walter arrested for failing to pay child support.

She had always assumed that talent in a woman was something she had because she lacked the normal things, the little lights that drew men to her, and settled her down. Drive, Chris imagined, was neurotic, a feverish substitute for doing someone's laundry and cooking his meals. Now she seemed to have it all, fulfillment was visible in her belly. But her ambition did not diminish, nor her creativity. She was chased by melody, tunes martialing around her, orchestrating her walk, words arranging themselves in her head like a slide show, illustrating that inspiration and reproduction could coexist. The only real change was how happy the songs were, not doleful as they'd been, as if from a wellspring of disappointed experience, set with the jade of a sorrowing Dietrich who had seen it all and knew how hopeless it was.

She did not consider herself in competition with Harry, since his career was obviously more than hers, growing in power. He had been made Vice-President in charge of promotion at Request Records, his geniality and savvy about what made people happy helping two albums onto the charts, earning him personal kudos and several bonuses. Her songs were written now out of total joy, a luxury most artists could only imagine. The frenzied edge, her desperation for approval, recognition, and finally the money that would mark her "professional" seemed to erode, slowly vanish. It became easier to sell her songs, with Harry helping her to place them. ("Don't give him *too* much credit," said Evelyn. "They're selling because you're thin. Even pregnant, you're thinner than you were. You could have written the score of *Oklahoma!* before and no one would have bought it, you were so *fat*.")

Chris took time to watch the baby, even before it was born,

filled with wonder as she lay on her back, studying round line of buttocks, rising, shifting. She could not wait to hold it, to give it too much love.

"You aren't going to *nurse* her!" said Evelyn, as she sat beside the hospital bed. "You should see what you did to my breasts, you greedy thing."

"You showed me," said Chris.

"She certainly is funny looking," Evelyn said. "But she has pretty eyes. The rest we can fix."

Evelyn made her way around the hospital room, looking at the cards on the flowers. "Well, maybe you'll be lucky and she'll have your mind. It's the only chance she's got, with that father, with his family. Where is he, the Bronx God?"

"He went home to take a nap."

"As though he was the one who did the work, had the suffering."

"He was up most of the night, timing the contractions."

"That must have been an extraordinary mental effort for him." She turned over a card. "Who are these people? Are they anybody?"

"They're mainly Harry's friends, from the record business."

"Oh," Evelyn said. "Mafia. Well, they can afford flowers. Have you heard from your first father?"

"Not yet. I sent him a wire about the baby, but I don't think he's really forgiven me. He still thinks I told you what hotel he was staying at the night you had the marshal serve him."

"He still hasn't paid me, the son of a bitch. I hear he's very rich. Do you think he's very rich? Why won't he pay your child support?"

"Why can't you forget it?"

"If I forgot it, I might forget him, and I couldn't bear to do that. He was the great love of my life, except that I couldn't stand him. Do you think he really loves Dolores, or don't you think he'd come back to me in a minute?"

"I think he's happy with her."

"Don't be silly. He couldn't be happy with anyone. Neither can you, really. Of course you've deluded yourself that you care for this boy, but breeding will out. You'll grow weary of his grammar, and your in-laws, and eventually you'll see him for what he is. Divorce, like death and taxes, is inevitable. You should have married Karim Khan."

"I love Harry."

"That's now. All the women in our family have a gift for self-delusion. But the day will come, as it's come for me and Sonny."

"Are you getting a divorce?"

"Not right now. He owes the railroad twelve million dollars. I have to stand behind him till he straightens himself out and I can bleed him dry." She moved towards the door, trim, elegant, her dazzling, even-toothed smile more a conscious, practiced signal of her charm than an indication she was joking. "Why don't you name your daughter after your father's father. Then Walter will come to visit, and I can have the marshal waiting."

They named her Caroline. Evelyn considered it "un poquito Kennedy." But that was all right, she said, because had they not been so firmly entrenched in Boston, they could have come from the Bronx.

She was waiting for Chris and Harry when they brought the baby home from the hospital. "She's gotten better looking," said Evelyn, as Chris put the baby in the crib. "In fact, I think she looks like me, but of course I look younger."

"We have to settle her down now," Harry said, guiding Evelyn to the door.

"Are you trying to get rid of me?"

"Of course," he said, and opened the door to the hall, putting her outside, gently, like a cat, closing the door behind her.

The bell rang, persistent, repetitious. He looked through the peephole separating New Yorkers from their terrors, saw Evelyn slightly distorted, like a reflection in an amusement-park mirror, wide-set hazel eyes stretched into a single orb across her face. He put the chain on the door, opened it a few inches.

"Come to dinner tomorrow night," Evelyn said. "We're having steak. I'll make yours overdone, the way your mother cooks it."

Caroline's baby carriage was given them by Sonny, who, debt to the railroad notwithstanding, insisted on buying them the Rolls-Royce of prams. Chris hardly had the muscle to maneuver it, even once she'd completely recovered. So to his wonderful physicality in the bedroom, his willingness to scratch her back, enough to make up for a lifetime of unexpressed affection and concern on the part of close relatives, his intercession with her mother, something, apparently, past divine, since even God had not taken on that one, Harry now demonstrated the virtue of perambulator pushing in Central Park. They would go out early in the morning on sunny days, before he went to work, luxuriate by the boat lake long Sunday afternoons.

Sometimes, in the middle of the night, she would tiptoe into Caroline's room to listen to her breathing. Moving her hand above the small face, Chris would feel the warm staccato rush of air against her palm, reassuring herself that yes, there was a baby there, alive.

Then she would go back to bed and do the same with

Harry. They were all really there. It wasn't a mistake, her being so happy.

But when Caroline was two months old, Request Records was taken over by a Dutch conglomerate. The new owner brought in his own staff, and Harry lost his job.

"How can this have happened?" Harry said. His pale green eyes looked frightened, little arrows of yellow in them.

She had never seen him be anything but confident. Only with his passive acceptance of George Mailey had he ever demonstrated anything but strength, self-assurance. And, in that, there had been a subtle confidence she hadn't recognized at the time, as if quietly waiting would strengthen his chances of getting her back. It was not the same with a career. "People lose their jobs," she tried to tell him, soothing.

She did not understand the pressures of coming from poverty. She had not been there when his first dream died, had no way of feeling the devastation of what it was to have the magic, and lose it. "The Big Right-Hander," his coach had called him in high school, affection and respect in the appelation, as well as a ticket out. There were heroes in those days, real heroes like DiMaggio, a team full of Titans, King Kong Keller, Cliff Mapes, Gene Woodling, a Yankee roster that would be behind eight runs in the bottom of the ninth, and still win the game. After one of those, Harry would run out into the street and pitch into a chalk bullseye on the side of a building, as hard as he could, fast ball after fast ball after fast ball, so high he had to pitch himself out to be able to breathe.

When the talk turned to what everybody was going to do when they got out of high school, Harry kept quiet. There were scouts from the Yankees and the Giants and the Dodgers watching him play, catching him weekends at the Babe Ruth League, the American Legion League. There were priests coming round on Saturday mornings, trying to talk his father into letting him play on the church teams ("How do you think that looks to the neighbors?" his mother said. "A priest"). In the bar where his bartender father hung out in the off-hours, Champ Segal's, home of the first Jewish champion, (lightweight, sure, but an inroad was an inroad), the men bet money on spontaneous ball games made up of teams from various restaurants. His father went home and got Harry.

Sports was all. On game days, after a rain, the boys would pour gasoline on the puddles, burn off the water, get their mothers' brooms and sweep the fields dry. James Monroe, Harry's high school, had one of the few bona fide baseball diamonds in the Bronx. It was there that Harry grew to full stature, six feet two, and stopped crying when he lost, once he was past fourteen.

The Brooklyn Dodgers offered him a contract, and a bonus. Baseball wasn't show business yet: the biggest, the greatest, like DiMaggio, got a hundred twenty-five thousand dollars. What athletes wanted was a chance to play ball, to look graceful on the field. They didn't understand they were stars, that the day would come when so-so players would command million dollar contracts. The bonus Harry got was fifteen hundred dollars. The moon, when all he wanted was a chance to play, and they were paying him.

The Dodgers were in trouble with their pitching staff, so after graduation Harry went straight to Ebbets Field without stopping at a farm club, or going to the minors. It made his head spin. It all came so fast. He was on the mound, pitching to Musial. Striking him out. Stan The Man. Vanquished. He pitched so hard they couldn't get near his fast ball. Pitched so hard his arm started to swell.

Sports medicine wasn't a field then, anymore than big hitters thought of seven figures: a man got better or he didn't play. They sent him for X-rays, but whatever it was didn't show. Breaks they could fix; the rest they didn't have cures for. It was over as fast as it had begun. Faster, really.

He moved his number up and went into the Navy, to give his arm a chance to heal, to see the world, to keep the world from seeing him. His arm got better. He pitched a few innings for the Navy ball team, and his arm swelled again. That, and the waves made him seasick.

So he knew what it was to win very big and then have it all go away. Sometimes it just got pulled from your hands, and there was nothing you could do. Sure, the American dream still existed, threads where once there were tapestries. Threads had been enough to pull him up the first time, to keep him what his mother still referred to as "a good boy." But a good boy in America, with a new baby and a wife whose family brunched at the Plaza, couldn't be out of work.

"You'll get another job," Chris told him. "There are other record companies. They'd be lucky to get you."

"I know that," he said. "You think they'll know that?"

His reputation preceded him, excellent. But he had been fired. Nobody particularly cared why anyone was fired. It became a character defect, the mark of a loser, in a society where people only liked to be reminded they could win. That humiliation, the male equivalent of a Scarlet Letter, Harry wore along with his eagerness. His wide, white smile began to seem slightly forced.

It was a time of great motion in the record industry, much of it illicit. The Beatles were on their way out, Neil Diamond and Elton John were the important new stars. No one particularly wanted a young man who obviously needed a job, decent in the bargain. Potential employers who saw him coming recognized someone in trouble. That panic was an underbelly of themselves, making them uncomfortable in his presence. Little lines of doubt started pulling at the corners of his mouth, even as he tried to communicate a conviction that everything would be fine.

So months went by, without his finding work. He sat long days staring out the window at windows that stared blindly back. Friends stopped calling. Failure was the plague in New York: people feared catching it.

At the beginning of his third month of unemployment, Harry received a call from the past owner of his company, asking if he wanted to go out to Los Angeles to work for a new label. "Is yesterday too soon?" Harry said into the phone.

They moved in the Spring, although it was hard to tell the season by the Hollywood Hills. Winding roads burst with fuchsia bougainvillea, red bottlebrush stalked the sides of the canyons. Clumps of gazanias, brilliant daisylike flowers that opened with the sun and closed at its passing, softened the path beside their driveway. "It looks like summer," Chris said as the cab drove them up to their rented house. "Everything's so brilliant."

Caroline, fat now, growing, struggled in her lap, gurgled satisfied laughter.

"Especially you," Harry said. "You're so damned brilliant. I wonder sometimes how you could have married me."

"Because I'm brilliant," she said, and kissed him, while the baby struck happily at their cheeks, and she knew that they would all be in love, like this, forever.

Palm trees, like fanning sentinels, guarded the beach below the hotel balcony. Brought to Guaymas and planted by the owner of the Playa de Cortés, they added an unreal air of tropicality to the brisk, sometimes chilly locale. The area was rife with contradictions, desert and mountain and sea. The palm trees, exotic, not belonging in that locale, only added to the confusion. Further illusion, Chris considered it. More windowdressing, like the disguises marriage put on to suck you into surrender.

"Well," Harry said. "We might as well get dressed for dinner."

"Do I have to wear a jacket?" Josh's voice was a studied plaint, not quite a whine.

Caroline stood in the doorway to their connecting room, brushing traces of sand from her shoulders. "You would enjoy getting dressed up if you weren't so UG-ly," she sang. "I love looking good."

"Then you better put on a mask," said Josh.

"Mother . . ."

"Stop it," Chris said automatically. "Go get dressed."

"In a jacket?" Josh was a California boy, oppressed if not in OP shorts. But he had discovered to his amazement that he looked good in the dress clothes he despised. So he pretended protest in the hope that his mother would insist, and thus bear full responsibility.

"It gets cool at night," Chris said, a pragmatic argument, permissible. She understood it would not be all right to hug him and tell him he would look handsome. First, because Caroline, as much as she seemed to shy away from her mother's embraces, resented any directed towards Josh. Second, because Josh himself had consistently pulled away from Chris in recent months. She could not tell if it was because of what he felt was happening between her and Harry, or because eleven was the time when boys had to start showing how tough they were. How they didn't need holding, especially from their mothers. He still huddled close to Harry, hugged him whenever he could, as though he were getting ready for the sprint into the big-boys' locker room, where that kind of affection was allowed.

"Should I wear a dress?" Caroline was asking from the doorway.

Not the simple answer that seemed to be called for was being solicited. Caroline hated to be told what to do. She was at the age when instruction from her mother stiffened her already rigid spine. The question was a subtle test: did her mother love her enough to be as interested as she was in Josh, and if Caroline was as perverse as her brother, would her mother love her more? It occurred to Chris as she traced the possible manipulations of her daughter's mind that the UN would do better with a roster full of mothers, who could ferret out whateveryone was really thinking.

"I'd love to see that blue one on you," Chris said.

"I like the red one," said Caroline, and went to change.

She wore the blue, and an aloof, slightly sullen expression so Chris wouldn't think she was happy doing something that pleased her mother. Her shoulders were smooth skinned, browned from the sun, a woman's shoulders, thrown back in an attitude of pride, till she remembered her breasts, and collapsed her shoulders forward, as if that would make the unbecoming part of her disappear.

Chris noted her from behind, walking down the inlaid steps to the courtyard on the other side of Harry from Josh. How ideal they seemed, how strong, how handsome, how much a representation of a fine American family, the mother trailing at a respectful distance. Below, twisted-limbed coral trees, gnarled branches endlessly intertwined, flanked the night-lit swimming pool, an aquamarine flash in the deepening darkness. Some remnants of day still littered the scenery, towels from an afternoon swim, a young woman in a bathing suit lying stretched face down on a chaise while a brown-skinned man massaged her legs. They were both oiled, still glowing from the sun, Chris could tell that, even caught as they were in twilight shadow. She could feel the heat from their skin as they touched, feel the electricity between them. She strained to see their faces.

But Harry was in her way. She could not get closer to the couple without circling around him. And a move in that direction might be interpreted as a wish to join the family flank. Harry's arm was around Josh's shoulder, Josh's arm around his father's waist as he struggled to make the gesture seem effortless, casual. Caroline leaned towards her father on the other side, letting her arm brush against his, permitting the intertwining of fingers. Once, Chris would have yearned to be included. But as much as she wanted to touch her children, she had no wish for contact with Harry.

His hands had begun to feel like an assault, like his gifts. He had given her diamond studs for her ears for Christmas ("Delicate, like you are," he had said, an erotic promise implicit in the delicacy). They were in deep financial stress, like a lot of families in the country. She had had to sell her engagement ring o keep up with the bills. And Harry gave her diamonds for her ears. *The Gift of the Magi* in Beverly Hills. The gesture was so foolish it made her fall in love with him again.

But to wear them, she had to have her ears pierced. There had been enough pain in her life that she felt an aversion to inflicting on herself any that could be avoided. For weeks the studs stayed in their black velvet box in the bedroom. Finally she summoned up the courage and went to a jewelry store on Camden Drive, where the nurse told her what it would feel like was a pinch.

What it felt like was pain. The little automatic gun that shot the gold stud through her lobe jammed. The nurse had to twist her ear unmercifully to work it loose. Chris had visions of her ear being torn from her head, moving through life Van Gogh without any paintings to show for it. The fright was so intense she had refused to have the other one pierced until four hours later, after several margaritas with a political exile who wondered aloud if she had joined some cult that wore one earring.

When she awoke the next morning and saw herself in the bathroom mirror, she felt violated. How could the world consider a democracy a society where a husband could even become a part of your ears? There was no area of woman that was private, sacrosanct. Weakly, she sponged around the wounds with alcohol, the way the nurse had instructed, tried to hide the little gold balls with wisps of her dark, curly hair, tried to see back to what she had been when herself, and could waken unadorned.

She was too frightened of pain and infection to take the studs out. After a month, the nurse had replaced them with the diamonds. Chris had slept on them wrong: now one of her lobes was festering. With the germs in Mexico, in spite of a plastic bag filled with cotton balls, alcohol and Neosporin, she would probably return from vacation without an ear. If she returned at all. She wondered why she had ever thought it wonderful, getting married.

On a metal table by the pool, a congregation of sparrows pecked at the remains of someone's lunch. A pelican sluggishly glided overhead, slack jawed, a contradiction to its own grace. In the arcade below the steps, a bat beat its wings, senselessly circling. It was a quiet busyness, stillness shot with small disturbances that stressed the peace. To be able to hear them at all was a sign of the silence.

By the aquamarine glow of the pool, Chris could see the sweet pumping of Josh's buttocks as he tried to keep up with his father's stride, fine, round cheeks assailing the seat of his pants. She could see it back through time, a feisty little rump that seemed to clock the boy's impatience. She had run behind him once, down a hill near their house when he was just two, seen something so brave about that bottom, like a trumpeting, its movement. More than "world here I come." More like "world, here I already am."

Her daughter's body, too, could still be condensed in Chris's mind, the weight of years pressing back to the squat little round-armed girl with pony tails, her nose squashed against the window, looking out over the driveway till Harry would come home. The clap of pudgy little dimpled hands when he appeared. "Da-da! Da-da! Da-da!" She wondered why both her children had always served such loving attendance on Harry, turned to him as life's sweet highlight. True, as they grew, she had given them over to Harry. But it was not as though she had not herself lavished them with affection, held them, bathed them with all the hugs that had been denied her. But those they had seemed to take for granted and, as they grew older, tolerate. Harry had always been the reward, his arms the fulfillment of promises, the sanctuary.

They stepped past the thick ropes of knotted coral trees, past the heavy hanging limbs of Brazilian pepper. A single star appeared against the sky, proclaiming it evening. From inside the bar came the sound of a trio of guitarists wailing familiar tributes to love, and places with no equal.

"Guantanamera . . ." she started to voice along with them.

"Don't sing," both her children said at once. Her songs they put up with, like her embraces, no pride or appreciation in the cool nod they accorded her career. It was as if their being pleased with her accomplishment might diminish Harry, as if her success were unseemly in their eyes. Or at most, tolerable. About her voice they were not that generous.

"Please, don't sing," Josh exhorted on his own.

"That bad?" she said. "Is it like my kissing you? Pinching your beautiful bum?"

"Cut it out," he said. His head poked in, a sadden turtlelike attempt to disappear into his father's side.

She reached for her daughter; Caroline sighed, accepted

the arm that went around her shoulders. "If it embarrasses you," Chris said, "I could have it taken out. I mean, not just my voice. Everything How much I love you."

"It's okay," Caroline said.

Behind his father's back, Josh reached for his mother's hand. "Just don't sing."

Great ebony beams, pieces of the past, fretted the high ceiling of the cavernous dining room. Carved wooden tables, massive, baronial, with carved mahogany chairs around them, advocated the posture of conquistadors. A giant open hearth, surrounded by painted tiles, offering bluebirds and swans, blazed a little brilliance, a hint of warmth into the room. Smiling waiters in mustard yellow jackets, carrying bud vases of fuchsia bougainvillea to each table, struggled pleasantly to banish the solemnity. Wrought-iron chandeliers hanging heavily from the high ceilings argued the atmosphere back to severity.

None of it seemed to intimidate the Mexican children. They sat at long tables, with several generations of relatives there to celebrate Holy Week, clapped their hands, chased each other in between courses. They seemed very uncomplicated souls to Chris, as evidenced by the ease and matter-of-factness with which the girls, no matter how young, even babies, wore earrings. The boys were already groomed for taking charge, diffident, sligttly contemptuous of their sisters' frivolity, grimly tolerant of their being only girls.

Josh did not look with open interest at the Mexican boys, even those of his own age. As much as Caroline sought the companionship of other girls, it was Josh's manner in recent times to seem unneedful of children. He would come directly home from school, do his homework, and wait for his father, who would arrive at four, to take Josh to Little League or the

49

park. It struck Chris as unhealthy, isolated, too devoted. In a society where sons often didn't know where their fathers were, or, sometimes, who, it shrieked ofexhibitionism, overkill. But she couldn't voice her uneasiness, lest she appear to be jealous, which she was. Caroline, too, was usually in a rage at their closeness. "You only want to be with Josh'" she would pout, and go off with her friends to practire using makeup, jealous for the company of her father, as the mother was for the son.

What could Chris do to win him? Anything she might offer would not be of great interest to him. His was not a dream of visiting the Louvre, winter carnivals at Dartmouth, the hope of Ivy League. His happiest fantasy was a sunny day at Little League, with his father as coach. It made her livid, the Norman Rockwell level of seduction. There was nothing so powerful in woman as to match the lure offather and son at a baseball game. Fucking America.

"Do you want a drink?" Harry asked her, as tte waiter hovered, smiling.

She nodded. He ordered for both of them.

"I'll have a Bloody Mary," said Josh.

"A Shirley Temple," said Harry.

"A fruit punch," said Caroline, who loved Shirley Temples but was too old.

"Are we going fishing tomorrow?" Josh asked his father, beating a tattoo on the table with his breadstick.

"Fishing," Caroline said. "How yucky."

"Nobody invited you," said Josh.

"Of course we did," Harry assured her. "Please come."

"I don't want to smell those yucky fish and watch you getting sick."

"Not me," said Josh. "I don't get sick. It's Dad."

"I won't," Harry said. "Santiago promised to stay in the quiet water."

"Anyway, you'll chicken out," said Caroline.

50

"*Fish* out," said Josh.

"Never," said Harry.

Josh grinned. "Tell us again how you got sent home from the Navy."

"My mother was sick."

"I'll bet." Josh's smile was superior. "It's okay, Dad, I still love you."

The waiter set the drinks in front of them on the table. Harry raised his glass. "Here's looking at you, kid," he said to Chris, Humphrey Bogart.

"Don't do impressions."

"I like his impressions," said Caroline.

"You used to like them," Harry said to Chris.

"No, I didn't."

"You laughed."

"That was because they were so terrible." She reached for her drink, drank a little too fast.

At the front of the room the maître d' bowed slightly to a young couple just entering. The woman was tanned the color of copper; health radiated from her. The man was light haired, dark skinned, hovering slightly behind her like a protective shadow. His palm was close to her elbow as he moved with her, connected by invisible threads. Chris recognized the couple from the pool, dressed now, radiant for evening. She hoped they'd be seated somewhere nearby, so she could watch what it was to be beautiful, young, in tune.

Harry took a handkerchief from his pocket and blew his nose loudly. It shattered her reverie, made her lose track of what the sweetness was, where the couple was going, what was pretty about life.

"Do you know how it offends me when you blow your nose like that?" she said.

"Why?"

"Because you haven't got the courtesy to try and conceal

from me that gross masculine gesture of blowing your nose. All of society tells me how discreet I have to be about female things. My whole life is spent hiding the bodily functions that make me a woman, and you sit right out in the open, blowing your nose."

"I didn't know it bothered you," said Harry, and blew his nose again.

The children were silent, staring down at their drinks. Chris looked around, anxiously searching for the couple, trying to restore a little of wonder to the world around her. But she had lost track of them. She scoured the vastness of the dining room: they were nowhere in sight. Vanished, like beauty, like the plays of Shakespeare in a world of Monday Night Football.

Two

$\mathcal{S}$ UPERMAN HAD not evolved by accident as an American hero. To leap tall buildings in a single bound was the only way a mythic man could do it. Success had to be overnight, while you were young, bringing instant love, instant recognition, instant tables at ringside. Though Harry had not been aware he had that dream, he was no less a victim of it than Chris was. Having lost the hope of heroism in stadiums, he had substituted a no-less-fervent wish for blue-suited success.

The new label for which he was hired had the kind of lightning success and failure possible only in the record business. A group Harry found, The Jujubes, cloned from the Lovin' Spoonful in their sound, scored an immediate hit, putting the company ahead by millions of dollars in accounts receivable. With that first, flush windfall, immediate problems surfaced. Independent distributors wouldn't pay for the first hit until there was a second. By the time there was, the company had already gone under.

As head of A & R, Harry's job had been limited to finding acts, becoming a magnet to attract performers. The Jujubes' success was laid directly at his feet. When the company failed, that, too, according to the talk, was his fault. As victories needed visible heroes, fiascos cried for fall guys. And as he was the least likely to call someone a liar, especially when he hadn't been openly accused, the role fell to Harry.

That his substitute fantasy was vanishing as completely as the first, stunned him. More than a dream was involved. In America, career was the center of a man's life, as hope of romance was a woman's. In the Bronx, it had been even more pointed: you either improved your life, or drowned in it. Harry had a number of uncles with civil-service jobs, good-natured, unimpassioned men remanded to the post office like dead letters, addressees unknown, their lives laid out before them without change, without challenge, without chance of improvement. Those were the good men in the family. The ones with the silk suits and flashy cars, they were discussed in whispers, the sources of their incomes never mentioned, the smiles given to them a little too big, like the checks they laid on poor relatives at weddings and Bar Mitzvahs. Those were the men who lived in Pelham Manor, with guarded, gated driveways.

To be married to Chris, with governors and stockbrokers lined up behind her as fathers, to traffic even as visitor with people who owed millions of dollars, legitimately, made him queasy, frightened him as war games had, when they used real bullets. Brunch at the Plaza with her relatives was usually followed by bouts of colitis. Even the sad emotional history of her family—children who had breakdowns, a half-sister and step-brother in and out of mental hospitals—intimidated him, seemed to him a perverse luxury. In the Bronx, it had been shape up or ship out. No one in his family would have gone mad: they couldn't afford to.

To add to his general feelings of uneasiness, he was aware that Sonny, Chris's stepfather, had come from beginnings as unprivileged as his own, and triumphed. Where was his triumph to come from? Sonny had warned Chris in a moment of rage he couldn't direct at Evelyn that Harry would drag her down, that if she married him, she would regret it. Every time something good had happened to Harry, the first one he wanted to give the news to was Sonny. Who was he supposed to call, now that the walls were closing in?

He began reading biographies of notable men, searching their histories for thwarted promise, early disappointments, looking for a Horatio Alger who vanquished the third time around. Quick success, he started to convince himself, was not quite as inspirational as failure, holding in its ashes, as it did, a phoenix. Comebacks were, after all, what the U.S. of A. loved most. When you were a hit right away, people pulled for you to fail, whether or not they admitted it. There was no clucking tongue louder than over someone once rooted for who fell.

"I'm thinking of going into another business," he told Chris, as though he had a choice.

She was pregnant by then with their second child, in a house bought with the proceeds from her first runaway hit song, a flashy number that pandered to the musical taste of the time, with more wit in the lyrics than most. She was a little embarrassed by the success of it, since it did not touch in style or grace or originality most of her other material. But she was glad for the money, since it got them the house and continued their membership in circles from which they would otherwise have been excluded, tenuous friendships with the locally exalted, those for whom the tour buses slowed down. Faces that were to be caricatured, placed in prominent positions above the red leather booths of the restaurant opened by Harry.

To get it together, Harry borrowed from a number of people in the record industry, who were more than glad to lend him money to assuage their guilt at having refused him a job. There was not enough left after buying the house for the money to come from Chris, and Harry would have been reluctant to take it even if there were. In all, he raised seventy-five thousand dollars, part of it from an architect who became his partner, calling in favors to remodel to specification, at minimum cost. Fifteen thousand of the investment went for a liquor license, which could not be paid for in cash, since the board wanted to be able to trace where the money came from. That was to insure it did not originate with men of the type who offered Harry cigarette machines for the foyer of his restaurant, and twenty thousand dollars—as a bonus—to be allowed to install them. Harry recognized who and what they were, and knowing his life was complicated enough without an undercurrent of criminal support, declined.

That did not stop those would-have-been benefactors from loving the restaurant. Within months of the opening, there was a heavy contingent of what Harry's father would have labeled "wise guys," "buttons," in his personal lingo, men who wore invisible membership, unseen tags in their lapels, who knew the real story better than Mario Puzo. Could name you the original six who started the organization, Meyer Lansky on up.

"Look at that bunch in the corner," Evelyn sort of whispered. "Aren't they brutal looking? So handsome and insensitive."

"Keep your voice down, mother," Chris said.

The restaurant walls were flocked red velvet, "Rodeo Rococo," Evelyn labeled it. ("Harry doesn't know everything," she said.) But the garish decor seemed to have no adverse effect on the patrons, who expressed delight at the availability of genuine Italian food. In California terms, that meant it tasted like New York: a bill of fare Harry had learned from his father, from long Sunday afternoons when the men got together, rolled up their sleeves in somebody's kitchen and made a feast. Harry had always considered him-

58

self more or less Italian, since in his section of the Bronx, the Italians and the Jews seemed the same, except for a feeling of free-floating guilt passed on through the mothers. But through the fathers came a knowledge of clams in red sauce, escarole with oil and garlic. Harry's restaurant was, by consensus, the finest Italian to open in L.A. since La Dolce Vita. It was there the family celebrated their son's first birthday, while Caroline, in a white and yellow dress afloat with satin ribbons, tried to pretend she didn't mind a baby brother, having lived in California long enough to have learned artifice.

A waiter brought Josh his birthday cake. It was spun from marzipan meringue and cream, an indulgence from the chef, who used the excitement of the moment to secrete a side of beef in an empty garbage pail for the owner of the garage up the street, in exchange for four tires. Around the booth where Harry's party was, three busboys and four waiters, a few of them out-of-work actors, sang Happy Birthday and applauded. Out-of-work actors were everywhere in Beverly Hills. Several of them were faithful patrons of the restaurant, a few of them movie stars, who, in between pictures, were, after all, out-of-work actors.

Movie stars gravitated to the place, pronouncing the food delicious and reasonably priced. The atmosphere was warm, congenial, a reflection of its host, a last bastion of gallantry in a cloddish world. Those who patronized were assured of fine service, excellent cuisine, and perfect drinks. Many of those were poured from bottles sneaked in by the bartender, so he could pocket the money. Like the beefy larceny of the chef, such tricks went unobserved by Harry, whose graciousness was matched only by his innocence, assuming those working for him were as glad about the restaurant as he was, with as much affection for its future.

Record executives, a number of them small investors, patronized with regularity. And there was usually in attendance a large contingent of men in white-on-white shirts with white-on-white ties, who kept asking Harry when he would like their cigarette machines, jukes boxes, and cash advance with no obligation, except maybe letting them come up from Orange County to use the kitchen when the joint was closed on Sunday.

It was such a group that captured Evelyn's attention the night of Josh's first birthday. She had flown in, unannounced, surprising Chris in several ways. She did not think her mother would remember Josh's birthday. In fact, Evelyn did not. It was coincidence, which Evelyn did not admit for a moment. The real reason for her arrival was that she had been having more than the usual share of problems with Sonny, some of them not even of her own creation. She had reappraised Chris's move to California as Divine Providence, from a God who was crazy about Evelyn, and knew she needed someplace else to go.

"I understand they're very solicitous to their women," Evelyn said, as Chris cut a piece of cake and put it in front of Caroline. "I think I'm ready for that. A murderer who's tender. I've had enough of these so-called moral men who would secretly love to kill me." She stopped in her musings to astonish over a bottle of champagne the waiter proferred them. "What's this?"

"From Mr. Candella," the waiter said.

"Oh, God, I hope it's the fat one," said Evelyn. "He has such soulful eyes. Which one is Candella?"

"Tony Candella," the waiter said with quiet scorn, having started in the same acting class, knowing it was only a quirk of fate that had made the other a star.

"Where is he?" Evelyn asked.

"Don't rubberneck," Chris said softly. "In the booth behind you."

60

"Dom Perignon," Evelyn said, impressed, as the waiter poured, and Josh, in his high chair, stuck his hand in the whipped cream. "He must really like you." She took her compact from her purse, studied the movie star's profile in the mirror.

"He likes Harry," Chris said, trying not to sell too hard, resisting the impulse to tell her mother how much everybody liked Harry, because he was so attractive and amiable and nonthreatening.

"I wonder why," Evelyn said. "Although he does make beautiful children. Look at that little angel. A boy. Who would have thought you had it in you. What a beautiful baby. My babies were beautiful, but they were *girls*." She remembered Caroline, and reached over to hug her. "Not as beautiful as you, though."

Caroline fixed her grandmother with a stare, and continued eating her cake.

"Tony Candella," Evelyn said. "Why would he send champagne?"

"He and Harry are friends."

"That's his cover," said Evelyn. "I did that with Sonny. I became best friends with his wife, and then it was only a matter of time."

"He's happily married."

"No movie star is happily married. It's a contradiction in terms. He's much more attractive than he looks in pictures."

"That's because he sent Dom Perignon."

"You think I judge a man by how much money he spends?"

"Yes."

"You're right," said Evelyn.

Chris raised her glass and smiled her thanks to Tony Candella, who raised his glass in return. Evelyn caught it in the mirror.

"He's obviously crazy about you," she said. "As long as you

opted for flesh, you might as well go to the head of the class and get a movie star." She put her hands over Caroline's ears, as though it were a new kind of embrace. "Be sure and write him a little note, and give him your home number."

"I love Harry."

"I loved both my husbands. That didn't mean I couldn't do better next time. Harry!" She let go of Caroline's ears, smiling at Harry's sudden reappearance as he slid into the booth next to Chris. "What a wonderful dinner! This really is a delightful place. Maybe you'll be a success after all." There was an argument to that possibility in her tone.

"Tony Candella sent champagne," Chris said.

"Eh!" Harry raised his hand to the man in the next booth, in salute, thanks, greeting. "*Paesano!*"

"I didn't realize the language was catching," said Evelyn. "I would never have ordered the ziti."

In spite of the slightly disdainful perch from which she viewed the world, Evelyn's smile, her obvious energy were so overwhelming, even those who thought they knew better fell victim. She was still a beautiful woman, with wide-set, heavily lashed, darting hazel eyes that took the measure of every man who walked through the restaurant. Her hair was a shade more metallic auburn than it had been in her youth, hardened by tint; her body was a touch more buxom. But her smile had stayed the same, glowing, remarkable, and she flashed it indiscriminately, like a beacon light outside a premiere, to attract the world.

At the moment, it seemed to have an effect she had not anticipated. Tony Candella stood beside their booth, red-gold hair hanging boyishly over his brow, posture tentative, as though he were not sure enough he would be welcome at their table to actually lean towards it.

"Hey, join us," Harry said.

"You don't mind?" Tony asked, an invisible hat in his

hand, in the manner his acting coach had instructed to denote humility. He slipped into the booth beside Evelyn.

"Of course we mind," said Evelyn. "Who wouldn't mind having the Number One star in the firmament sit next to them?"

"Number Four," said Tony, "but gaining. Who is this beautiful creature?"

"My mother, Evelyn Sterne. Tony Candella."

"Your mother? *Pas possible.*"

Evelyn beamed. "You'll be Number One faster than you can imagine."

"Unless you give it up for a career in diplomacy," Harry said.

"I wasn't being diplomatic. I was being truthful."

"In the twinkling of an eye," said Evelyn.

"So, *paesan.*" Tony leaned back comfortably in the booth, his arm flung casually around the red leather behind Evelyn so his fingers touched her arm as he addressed Harry. "How's the business going?"

"Pretty good."

"Pretty well," Evelyn corrected, giving a little smile to Tony to soften how clever she was. To her surprise, he wasn't looking at her.

"Escarole," Tony mused, giving it thick Italian pronunciation, kissing his fingers to the air, as though tasting the dish in the word. "Escarole with oil and garlic. A place where they actually make escarole. How'd you know about that?"

"I was the only one on my block who wasn't Italian."

"And the linguini! Really *al dente.* I tell you, I love this place. I'm never eating anywhere else."

"Don't make promises you can't keep," said Evelyn.

"How about to you, sweetheart." Tony looked at her. "Can I make promises I can't keep to you?"

To Chris's amazement, her mother actually blushed. Josh

63

started patting his hands together, the clap of his palms softened by whipped cream.

"He's applauding your performance," Harry noted.

"Gorgeous boy," said Tony. "The girl is also a beauty. She takes after her grandma."

"But of course I look younger," said Evelyn.

"That's true," Tony assented.

"Thank you for sending the champagne," Chris said. "Would you like a glass?"

"No thanks. I should be getting back to my party." He made a slight movement, but stayed. "I hope you like Dom Perignon."

"We don't mind," said Evelyn.

"What kind of champagne did they use in the locker room?" he asked Harry. "You know, to pour over their heads when they won?"

"I wasn't there for the Series," Harry said. "By then I was seasick in the Navy."

Tony shook his head. "The Brooklyn Dodgers at seventeen. That's *real* stardom. How high can you get? A kid from New York, playing at Ebbets Field."

"He should have died then," said Evelyn, and laughed to let them know she was kidding.

Tony got up from the booth and tousled Josh's heavily ringleted hair. "Happy Birthday, kid." He pointed a finger at Caroline. "You call me when you're eighteen. You, too," he said to Evelyn.

"What a charmer," said Harry, after Tony had reseated himself with his party.

"Oh, I don't know," Evelyn said. "I didn't think he was so much."

Chris choked on her laughter, while Josh batted his hands in the whipped cream of the cake in front of him, lathered his cheeks. Harry leaned over and kissed him, hard, came up with foamy lips. "You birthday boy. You beauty."

"He really is beautiful," agreed Evelyn. "I can't understand how that happened. And they're both so intelligent. Obviously they got that from *you*." She smiled at Chris.

"*My* daddy," Caroline said, and clambered over Chris's lap to Harry, throwing herself into his arms.

"He must have a certain magnetism," Evelyn said. "Although it does escape me. Every time I hear one of your love songs, I wonder who you're talking about."

"You, Evelyn," Harry said. "She's really writing about you. You're the only one any of us knows who's irresistible."

"I suppose that's true," Evelyn sighed. "God, if I could only find a man who could appreciate me. What about the one in the corner. The fat one, with the soulful eyes?"

A waiter came over to Harry, leaned over, and whispered something.

"Excuse me," Harry said, setting Caroline on the seat beside him, and left the booth.

"*My* Mommy." Caroline climbed into Chris's lap.

"Well," said Evelyn. "I'm glad you *think* you're happy. But you must be a little bored, dear. Otherwise you wouldn't be so productive." She opened her compact again, rouged her lips, checking the reflection of Tony Candella in the booth behind her. "He really is a charmer."

"I thought you didn't think he was so much."

"Well, we don't want to put Harry on guard. I could fall in love with him myself if only I weren't a little too old for him, although God knows I don't look it. Give him your home number."

"I'm not interested."

"That's now," Evelyn said. "Extramarital sex is like working. It becomes more appealing the longer you stay at home.

Besides, someone with your brains could manage a career, a household, and adultery."

The adultery did not come till a long time later. Her marriage seemed to Chris completely fulfilling, except for vague longings she could not pinpoint and so dismissed from her consciousness. She was not looking for anything different or better than what she had. In the course of her career she encountered men who effortlessly bobsledded through show business. She found them for the most part slick, except for the occasional one who was, underneath, as unsure as Harry, though never weighted down by his concern, his nice-guy consideration of everybody else, even those that posed a threat to him.

Because of her emergence in the pop field, they were welcome guests at lavish parties, where those invited were graded for quality, along with the hors d'oeuvres. Far below hillside houses where the pretty people gathered, lights glittered like meaningless promises. At some of these parties, Chris would strike up a rare, genuine friendship, finding, in the midst of the envied, souls that touched her with their loneliness, their grey shrouds of loss.

"You're lucky he's out of show biz," Cass Elliott said. The singer had found the one chair in the room large enough to accommodate her body, parts of her overflowing the cushions. Chris could X-ray with her imagination and see the tiny, pretty green-eyed girl cowering inside, as she had never been able to visualize herself in her fat days, which continued in her brain. It was still a surprise to her to see herself in a mirror, a slender, pretty woman, grown up, and small. It could be the same for Cass, she knew it could, if only providence would put someone's arms around her, free her from the label "Mama Cass," nothing big about her but her voice, and her need. She felt sisterly towards her, as if they had come from the same foster home, suffered the same crippling disease, unloved and overfed. Flung out into a hostile world, Cass wore Hershey bars for breastplates.

"You're lucky, period," Cass told her. "A smart, pretty, talented woman married to a lovely guy. I see him, I see lovely. And he cares about you. Do you know how lucky that is? A man who can care about a woman who's an achiever?" she mused, as though all that sat between her and happiness was Gargantuan accomplishment. "You've got a blessing on your head, especially now that he's out of the business. I'd get out myself, only I'm not financially secure."

It was an honesty rarely encountered, much less at a Hollywood party. Coming home from such an evening, such celebrated sorrow, Chris would melt into Harry, try to hide in him, as if to expiate her guilt that she had been the one to find him. Outside in the winter world, all alone, face pressed against the window, she could picture Cass, the Poor Big Match Girl.

Under the circumstances, adultery would have been gluttonous, gratuitous. She acknowledged no leftover unfulfilled needs, no seeds of discontent. She was happy with him. Better than happy. His lips on her breasts felt like ripples of esteem. He had only to touch her, to feel her skin next to his, to grow massive, hard, saluting. With the deprivation of her childhood years, still so much alive inside her, with all she had experienced of love people said they felt, that turned out to be lies, it was reassuring to have proof, a flag of affection. His erections seemed to her a pledge of devotion, an affirmation. More than erotically arousing. A tribute. Sex ennobled her, made her feel good about herself. Prince Charming had come with his velvety wand and magicked her into self-worth.

Even after two babies she felt shy with him, a tenuousness in bed. She kept waiting for him to change his mind about

67

her, and not want her anymore. Having been schooled on rejection, it astonished her when it was not forthcoming. A man was a reward, Evelyn had taught by example, the only thing worth having, besides cash. Only those who were beautiful and worthy were so compensated. Since Chris had never been either in her mother's eyes, she wondered at her windfall. Insecurity was a habit like everything else, too deeply reinforced to lose.

Studying Harry's long, powerful body, marveling at the gentle muscularity of it, she would touch the smooth, nearly hairless chest, stroke his long-fingered hands. Evelyn had stripped him of his pinky ring. ("Men don't wear jewelry, except in the Bronx.") But there were still indentations at the base of his finger, little grooves in his flesh, a memento of flashier times. Chris ministered to them as though they were scars.

So considering how full she was convinced her life was, she was astonished at her ambition. Always she'd assumed that the creative part of her life, the intellectual endeavor, shone the more seductive because of absence of love. Fulfilled by family, to still be ravenous for accomplishment, seemed in direct opposition to everything her training had led her to believe. Even in the sacrosanct atmosphere of Bryn Mawr, with its proud assumption that women were special, the tacit surmise was only *some* women, unsexed, like Lady Macbeth. The blue-eyed blondes with rangy legs were kewpily molded for Senators' wives, hostesses for heads of the Fortune 500. Never had it been impressed on any of Chris's schoolmates that their obligation could be to themselves *and* someone else. Active pursuit of mind on the part of married women was something to return to after the children were grown, your hair had grayed, and you'd tired of tea at the Palm Court.

But once a housekeeper seemed like she might be the one

finally to work out, and stay, and Caroline was enrolled in a nursery school that picked up and delivered, and Chris found a cleaner that did the same, there seemed to be no reason to give herself to home. Josh, fascinating as he was, took naps and played, so couldn't involve all of her. It was not restlessness that set her in motion, she was sure, it was healthy drive. Drive in a woman had not yet become a national issue, shrouded in controversy, a synonym for aggressiveness, acrimonious, unflattering, that most unwomanly word. In an artist, regardless of sex, drive was acceptable, even lauded, considering how many creative people lacked the follow-through. It did not seem enough for Chris to write the songs anymore. She wanted to move them into the marketplace, be present at the sessions that turned them into records, help promote them. She was a lively, articulate interview, and so was a welcome guest on the shows that proliferated in Southern California, as though Johnny Appleseed had danced through the country planting talk-show hosts.

"And how does your husband feel about your success?" asked the lady interviewer whose own husband was in Camarillo.

It was a question that had prongs in it: nobody ever asked a man how his wife felt about his success. It filled Chris with a vague malaise, as if she had somehow betrayed him. To admit that they needed the money she made, that it had enabled them to buy their home, have a housekeeper, would have unmanned him, made her appear a castrater, like everyone said the woman interviewing her was. "It's his success, too," Chris said. "If it weren't for him, my life wouldn't have come together."

"Oh, I could hug you, I could just weep, isn't that beautiful, friends out there, listening?" She clapped her hands, so you could almost hear the rings. There were five of them in all, different stones, overlarge, semiprecious, as she was, each of them set inside a circle of rubies to match the dark redness of her hair. "That's exactly the way I feel about my Joe."

In the minds of her audience, Joe was always just in the next room, rooting for her, a myth she fed by making constant references to him, calling out to him as though he were just beyond the door, instead of fifty miles up the freeway in a room with padded walls. "So he likes your music."

"He loves it," Chris said. "He's my biggest fan." It was true. He was always around her, listening to her compose, hearing the songs as soon as they were done, or sometimes before they were finished, offering praise, encouragement, suggestions to make them more commercial. It was all the more remarkable because she still flourished in fields that had been closed to him. More touching because, once she'd hit, she offered to make him a part of future deals, suggested his becoming her manager. He'd declined. She'd wondered briefly if it was out of nobility of character or his fear that she really didn't carry that much weight.

"Well, you're simply amazing," said the interviewer. "Two children, a darling husband who loves you, and I've seen him, listeners, he's *gorgeous*, and all those wonderful songs. You're an inspiration to us all."

"Thank you, Stephanie," Chris said. "So are you."

When Chris got home, Harry's car was in the garage. The house they in sided a mountain above Beverly Hille, halfway up a twisting canyon, with a heartstopping view of the city and ocean all the way to Catalina two or three times a year when the winds were high. It was on such a day they had seen the house and bid on it. Caroline had her own bedroom; the housekeeper slept with Josh. As feisty and rowdy as he was, he seemed fragile to Chris: she had fears about him. She had always thought males were strong, till she got married.

Harry stood at the far end of the living room, in front of the double door where the view would have been, in the absence of smog. There was something past dejection in his posture. Hispowerful physique, evidence of his athletic past, seemed changed. His shoulders were no longer squared, no longer held proudly. Chris wondered if the curious arc of his stance, the subtle curve of defeat, came from leaning over booths, greeting customers, or was not, more accurately, an accumulated wince, wary apprehension, to ward off anticipated blows, as if shrinking slightly might make Fate take less notice of him. "I'm sorry I didn't catch your show," he said.

"It wasn't anything to write home about."

"I've got something for you to write home about," he said haltingly. "To your mother, especially . . . The restaurant's closing."

"But it's a hit . . ."

"Sure. It's a hit with the chef who's robbing me, and the bartender, and the waiters, and the cops who come in every night and harass the guys from Orange County. And the guys from Orange County who are harassing me for not taking their goddamned cigarette machines . . ."

"Harassing you how?"

"Reporting me to the licensing boards. Too many people in the place. Putting turkey in the chicken salad."

"Why would you do that?"

"I don't. It's called authenticity of advertising. It's just a ruse to show they can run me into the ground. Every day something else. I can't handle it anymore. I can't keep up with the bills. A restaurant is in the food business to sell liquor. My bartender's been pocketing half."

"Fire him."

"I fired him. And the waiters who were in cahoots with him. And the chef who was stealing my meat. I'm in debt up to my mozzarella marinara. I'm closing."

"You can't. You can't walk out on a hit."

71

"It's not such a hit," he said sorrowfully. "These people are fickle. They fall in love with you in the beginning, then they find a new restaurant. It's like a honeymoon. It's passionate, then it's over."

"Not our honeymoon," she said. "I'll give you money."

"You been reading your own publicity? Listening to your interviews with *Stephanie?*" Contempt edged his pronunciation. "I couldn't let you do it even if you could afford to. And you can't, you know. You don't make as much as the world thinks you do."

"But if I invested in the restaurant . . ."

"Then we'd lose it all," Harry said. "Forget it. It's over. I couldn't make it work on my own, I'm not sinking you and the kids."

Dizzied, she sat down on the white couch by the window. "It can't be over."

"There's no way you can win in the restaurant business without people around you can trust. A wife who's the bookkeeper."

Was that it, then? Had she failed him by not being subservient to him? Less than she was? A clerk? "I see," Chris said. "In an enlightened relationship like ours, a woman's place is no longer in the home. It's at the cash register."

"I never wanted you to be anything but what you are. I was just giving you an example. You have to have the right people around you, it's that simple."

"Is it?" Behind her anger at the indirect accusation, nagged the sickening suspicion that the guilt was somehow hers, that some defect in her had drawn misfortune to them, as she had brought divorce to her parents, because she hadn't been good enough to keep them together. She felt the same inexplicable terror she'd experienced when she was five years old and her mother told her they were leaving.

But she'd been a child then, helpless, with no choice but to

72

be a victim, letting herself be boarded passively on the train, never screaming no. Lacking the lure that made women able to manipulate destinies, like her mother could. She had it now. Maybe she only had it for Harry, but somebody finally loved her. Passion wasn't only passion, it was a balm, a soporific to dull the mind till life changed and you got to the good part again. Her arms went around him.

"Cut it out," he said, shaking her off. "You can't make that the solution for everything."

"But it is, Harry." She kissed him with a frenzy that nearly camouflaged her sorrow. "It is." She touched him. "It has to be."

Two double beds heavily graced the Mexican hotel room. Ornate carved mahogany headboards carried into whorls of wood the tortuous curlicues of yellow and maroon on the woven bedspread. Chris had asked for extra blankets. It was hard to escape the chill. The room was unheated. Except for a small green rug between the beds, the ochre tiled floors were uncarpeted. In the open-hearthed fireplace catercornering the room, thin, gnarled wood burned like the brooms of witches, quick, with a threatening crackle and little warmth.

Josh and Caroline had had a fight before bedtime, not unusually. Caroline had frostily refused to sleep in the same room with him. It was a sexual trick she had learned from situation comedies on television, where such a declaration transformed man into hangdog, filled with apology and remorse. None of that was forthcoming from Josh, who whooped with joy and celebrated it as a victory, an excuse to move in with his parents. Chris considered his request a relief, coveting his closeness, welcoming the interdiction on sex, forcing Harry to stay in his own bed. She was almost forty years old, and she lacked her daughter's courage to perform

73

an act that, as a child, she didn't understand. To banish Harry from her room, from her bed. From her life. What would that take? With the room and the world so cold, and love so fleeting.

She had noted a tendency to drink more than usual, excessive even where margaritas floated through a holiday, lilies on a tropical pond. The end of love was a death: it was permissible to mourn. Full-blooded people ate and drank after funerals. It gave strength to continue, a heavy task for the digestive tract. Blood rushed to the stomach, leaving the brain. Not to remember acutely, that was the only salvation in loss. That, and being unconscious.

Harry drank along with her. Like the perfect host he had always been, making guests feel less greedy by indulging himself, he made his appetite apparent, hearty, equal. He did not handle alcohol as well as she. Sometime during the evening his mouth had gone sloppy, his hand and reached for hers, heavy, fumbling. She'd pretended not to notice, and moved her fingers away with a frantic gesture she'd considered subtle, knocking over her glass, spilling the contents of Josh's fruit punch into his lap.

"I'm glad *I* didn't do that," Josh had said.

His pants were hanging out to dry now, on the balcony fronting their room, weighted down with two rocks against the wind whipping up from the sea. He was in his nightshirt, an old-fashioned red flannel that reached down to his ankles, an enlarged game of tic-tac-toe painted in white across the front. Chris had bought four for Christmas in the men's department of Saks. One for each of them, in varying sizes, like the three bears and Goldilocks. She still felt that terrible potential in herself: of the entire group, being the most innocent, wide-eyed, searching, grateful for shelter.

"Where should I sleep?" Josh was asking, voice deep in his chest, the top of his torso already filling the size of a medium man, department-store version. Caroline had shut the door between the rooms, enraged at playing into his hands, giving him a chance for even greater closeness with the parents she was sure preferred him. He stood like a somewhat baffled baby giant between the double beds, his hair, curlier than usual, gold edged from the sun, slightly frazzled by the sea. His cheeks were burned a deep, dark red, as though slashed with Indian paint, freckles dancing across the bridge of his nose. His eyes were dark, chocolatey, almost the color of Chris's, but unique in their shape, deep set, Chinesey, whispering of ancient incarnations.

She supposed her fascination with him was as an extension of herself. Caroline seemed more a continuation of Evelyn, able to twist, take words of affection and send them back as darts. Chris loved her daughter, but she was afraid of her, as though there were some terrible curse between females that would never permit them to express complete and open love generation to generation. Erich Fromm had said that mother love was unqualified, but the love of a father had to be earned. In Chris's experience, it was exactly the opposite. Her father, when around, had loved her no matter how she was. Her mother had made her feel that nothing she did would ever be good enough. Now it was the same with Caroline, as if Evelyn's perverse disaffection had passed through the genes unimpeded and produced a grandchild slightly jaundiced with contempt for her inferiors, of whom her mother was the most prominent.

But Josh was ingenuous, loving, a butterfly spirit beneath the sturdy shell, his words having a curious cadence to them, like music. Chris had told him, when he was six, that he was the nicest boy she knew. "And Daddy's the nicest man, right? And then I'll be the nicest man, and he'll be the nicest old man. Then I'll be the nicest old man, and he'll be the nicest angel. And then, it'll be a tie." The words had come in a rush, breathless, couched in a voice too deep to seem to belong to a child. Chris had held him for an hour, trying to deal with her amazement. Where had those thoughts come from? What could explain the depth of his soul, the spirit contained in that package? He had lain with his head resting in her lap while she ran her fingers through his rope-thick hair; nowhere in Harry's family or hers hair like that. Where had he come from? India? China? God?

He stood before her now by the side of the bed, robust little ankles visible beneath the hem of his red-flannel nightshirt, toes curled slightly under his feet, as though to buffer the cold of the tiles. "Should I sleep with you?" he asked her in his basso voice, something so vulnerable about the misplaced deepness of it, so much more resonant than little-boy voices. From earliest speech he had sounded like a man. As her experience widened, Chris had discovered they were mostly all little boys who sounded like men. But to have it in a definitively smaller package tore at her.

"If you want to," she said.

"Don't feel bad, dad," Josh said, slipping under the covers beside her. "You'll have your chance tomorrow."

"I'm not in any hurry." Harry hung up his trousers with exaggerated care, as though to demonstrate that all the margaritas in Mexico could not interfere with impeccable habits. "I'm not anxious to get kicked."

"You think I kick?" Josh sat up, braced on his elbow, a wide grin on his face, fascinated with his comic imperfections.

"I know you kick."

"You watch me at night, huh? You come in to my room at home and watch me sleeping, right? You can't get enough of me."

"Go to sleep," Harry said.

"Did you set the alarm?" he asked his father.

"I set the alarm."

"I wouldn't want to sleep through our first time on the Sea of Cortés. You think I'll catch a shark?" He was obsessed by sharks. He spoke of them with the same enthusiastic, partisan energy as of the Los Angeles Rams, as though they, too, were his team. "Way to go!" he had cheered all through *Jaws* as Caroline cowered beside him. Chris wondered what strange human perversity it was that turned terror into allegiance.

"Maybe," Harry said. "Maybe one will catch you."

"They couldn't digest me. I'm too tough. Did you bring the Dramamine?"

"I did."

"Maybe you ought to take one now, in case you dream we're on the boat." His grin was slightly derisive, edging the gleam of his braces with superiority.

"Maybe I ought to give one to your mother, so when you rock the bed, she won't get dizzy."

"You think I'll rock the bed?" he asked her, as though it were a test of her love for him, as though everything in life were a test of her love for him, which she had begun to think many things were, including her marriage.

She lay back on the pillow, her full breasts straining the red-flannel nightshirt, size small. It annoyed her to wear it. She felt little like proclaiming herself part of a team. But in the next room Caroline was wearing hers, and Josh was wearing his. She looked over and saw Harry getting into his extra large, and wished she had never gone near Saks Fifth Avenue.

Switching off the light on the side of the lamp, she leaned over to kiss her son. He stretched his lips and made a hillock of his mouth, so it would be easier to kiss, without bringing her too close to the rest of his face.

"Night, mom."

"Good-night," she said.

"See you in the morning." He began his litany of good-nights, recollected parting calls echoing from his babyhood, souvenirs of maids who had come and gone melded with the words of his parents. "Pleasant dreams. Have a good sleep. See you in the morning. *Bonne nuit.*" The last, from the French housekeeper they'd had for eleven days, when he was two.

"*Bonne nuit,*" Chris answered.

"Aren't you going to kiss us good-night, dad?"

"Sure." Harry made his way across the room barefoot, wincing exaggeratedly at the cold, moving onto his toes. He knelt by his son and kissed his mouth. "You want me to sing you a lullaby?"

"I'm not a baby anymore."

"I forgot." Harry kissed him again.

"Maybe tomorrow night," Josh said.

Harry made his way around to Chris's side of the bed. She did not look at him. He touched her hair, kissed it gently, as though there might be in those strands wires transmitting the feelings he had. She was silent. He mumbled a good-night.

"Have a good sleep," Josh said again. "*Bonne nuit.* See you in the morning." Greater than habit or rote, it hovered like prayer, exhortation, sorcerer's dust scattered against the demons that might come in the darkness. The affirmation hung in the air: everyone would still be there when the light came.

For a while, after the restaurant closed, Harry got up every morning and went out looking for work. But there was a motorized sense of shame about unemployment in Los Angeles, some feeling of metaphorical punishment in the vast distances that had to be crossed in order to get to places where people did not want you. Like circles of hell restructured to stretch and loop and intertwine, the freeways led to destinations where old friends ducked out doorways and told their secretaries to say they were in meetings. It seemed easier to stay at home and wait for the call-backs that never came, plighting a troth by telephone rather than playing a mandolin beneath a window, and being answered with the contents of chamberpots.

He put in calls to people in the record business, executives he knew in various branches of the entertainment industry who'd patronized his restaurant. He did not look in the classified, because he was proud, and because when he did look, feelings of anxiety beset him. Most of the jobs either spoke to those just starting out, ambitious young men just out of the colleges he had not been to, or called for skills he had never learned and considered himself too old to start learning. More disturbing than a telephone that didn't ring were pages of notice in small type, of a world that had no need for him.

Chris's craving for him, however, seemed to increase in direct proportion to how few prospects he had, as her fortunes seemed to flourish in inverse ratio to his. She hung on him in the manner of their children, seemingly fearful of making a move without him, pressing on him not only career decisions, but beginnings of songs, titles, phrases, as though her creativity itself stemmed from him. There was a desperation in her approach that matched his own in parrying the world. She was transparent. He understood her as he'd always understood her: her success made his dole more glaring. When they'd met, his prospects had seemed as bright as hers, brighter, really, because he wasn't hiding under a blanket, know-how being enhanced by great personal charm. That he had not changed, but his luck had, baffled and undercut him. The personable quality that had tagged him a winner was quietly being sapped. She touched him and asked his advice too much as if, like in fairy tales, a frog could be made a prince with kisses, and men could be restored by the good opinion of women.

79

He would not consider becoming her manager. The town was too filled with stories of hard-nosed women whose husbands rode their backs, becoming harder nosed than their partners. There were lawyers who married clients and took over their careers, agents who retired from agencies to wed star singers and handle them. Most of the marriages ended in disaster. Harry didn't want that happening. If nothing else, they would be the last couple in "the business" that stayed married. Chris did not point out to him that he was not in "the business" anymore.

She did not expect him to look for work that they both considered beneath him: her vanity, too, was at stake. So, while in Israel, doctors, lawyers, great scholars took pride in the lowliness of their positions, keeping the country going—Nobel-prize candidates bragging at being ditch diggers—in Hollywood civic pride was not at issue. A man with waning self-esteem could not joyously bound into a marketplace ill-suited to him, when there was no economic need. Ingenuously, she pretended he didn't know how much she earned. Like the Maughamian heroine who kept from her husband the truth that the pearls she wore were real, lest he understand she'd been unfaithful, Chris thought to conceal from Harry the extent of her income. And, as other wives veiled their dissatisfaction with the emptiness of their lives by tippling in the afternoon, she began to hide her pleasure at her career, addicting herself to dissembling, parading indifference at success.

She had never been *ipso facto* ambitious, driven by drive itself. Her ambition was an adjunct of her talent, an extension of her creativity: having written the songs, she wanted to hear them sung. Glaring ambition, although American, seemed to her basically anti-social, people possessed by and of it patently out for themselves. In the beginning of her career there had been no one else to be for. But now that she was part of a group, a family, she was for them, veering away, as though there were a stench, from obvious determination, for fear her action would earn her that most dreaded appellation for women, "ball-breaker." She didn't want to break his balls. She loved them. It was he who had given her the confidence to move ahead, his strength that had strengthened her. Draining his own, she began to wonder? Was it some Draconian curse in reverse, that he had fed blood into her, and made himself pale?

She had never wanted to be more than he was, never dreamed of being as much. When they'd met, his future was filled with promise, greater than hers, it seemed at the time. Now that their careers were so out of balance, she practiced a maidenly modesty that bordered on self-negation. Annoying, considering it had taken her all her life to begin appreciating herself. Infuriating in a land that lunched on ego. True, she got praise from Harry, but it seemed slightly edgy now, automatic. She began to resent not being able to express pleasure at her achievement, having to be sensitive always to his feelings. Delight, swallowed, turned as rancid as sorrow.

She felt angry at him for standing between herself and the free expression of her joy. Then she got angry at herself, panicking at how shallow she'd turned out to be, judging a man by how he made *her* feel, as men judged women. Taking stock of what he did, instead of what he was. A wonderful father, a loving, faithful husband. Why was he so faithful, she wondered? Other men with crisis of confidence, and there were plenty in the hills and flatlands around them—it went with the territory, like bottlebrush—boozed in the afternoons and picked up starlets at the Villa Frascati, what few starlets were left, in what few Frascatis were left. His rectitude started to weigh as heavily on her as his unemployment. He was always around. Even as the world began to examine the agony of the housewife trapped in the home, Chris began to focus on Harry. Why was he always there? Was there some hidden perversity in his presence? Was he, in fact, trying to interfere with her creativity, as once he had nurtured it? She began to have difficulty writing with him in the house.

"Why don't you go out to lunch?" she asked him.

"Who with?" There was no irony in the question. Business was all in Beverly Hills, as sports had been all in the Bronx. Without projects, or lies about projects, men had a hard time with conversation. It was not a civilization of ideas. So his question had a certain innocence to it, as if she knew something he didn't know, that perhaps there lurked out there a jolly acquaintance who hadn't occurred to him.

The companion she suggested finally was a psychiatrist, a colleague of the doctor who had helped dig her out from under her debris. Harry resisted going. Nothing internal was wrong, he insisted, it was just bad luck. But seeing the expression on Chris's face, hearing her words spoken through teeth set on edge, he consented. Every job he'd loved had disappeared on him: he could not take the chance of being fired as husband.

"They think I'm crazy," he told her.

"Who?"

"The people in my group." They were seated in a corner of La Scala boutique, their voices lowered to avoid eavesdropping by people who really weren't in the least interested in them. At her latest suggestion to go out to lunch, he had invited her. "They listen to me talk about the people we hang around with, and then they hear me say how miserable I am. They think I'm nuts. I mean, people they'd give their nuts to be around, and here I am saying I'm unhappy."

She did not mention to him that these were mostly her friends, accepting them because of who *she* was. Both she and Harry understood that. At least she thought he understood.

82

There seemed no point in rubbing his nose in it. Once she had dreamed of a man whose life was inextricably entwined with hers, passionate partners who lived only for each other. She wondered if anyone really understood what a suffocating nightmare that became. Tragedy no longer seemed two lovers exiting too soon: it was Juliet left alive and well, and Romeo without a purpose.

"You should have married somebody who could have given you everything," he said.

"I have everything," Chris said. It was true. She did. Her children were strong and beautiful, already displaying signs of wit, and they were solid as she had never been, because their parents were loving and attentive. So attentive. Who else had a father who was always available; it was a blessing, she tried to tell herself.

"You should have married someone who could take care of you."

"Oh, Harry, you do. You take beautiful care of all of us. It's the ideal marriage contract. Fifty-fifty."

"Only you make the money."

"That's now. It'll change." She wondered if it would change, and how, tried to shuck off the feeling of hopelessness that suffused her. "It's temporary."

"Temporary." He shook his head. "You should have married a guy in a stable business. You should have married a lawyer. That nice guy. George Mailey."

She looked away. "Honey, I know you're depressed . . ."

"Depressed?" Harry said, and twirled a piece of salami from the antipasto salad on his fork. "I'm not depressed, I'm dead. I'm walking around and food goes in one end and out the other, and I'm not even a fertilizer, I'm a pollutant. I'm walking around and I'm dead. Maybe I should take that to AIP as an idea for a horror picture. *THE POLLUTANT.* It's about this big bag of nothing, see, only it's a creature, and it keeps growing and growing till it's about six feet two, and around thirty-three years old . . . and there's no way they can control it until they get this cute little scientist, what's his name? Santa Claus . . ."

"Edmund Gwenn," she said.

"Yeah, that's right, Edmund Gwenn. Is he still alive?"

"I don't think so," Chris said.

"There goes the picture . . . Why is he dead?"

"I don't know."

"You should have married George Mailey," Harry said.

"He's dead."

"You're kidding me?"

She shook her head.

"What happened?"

"Heart attack."

"Jesus Christ. How old was he?"

"Forty-four."

"Forty-four years old, with a great law practice. Son of a bitch. What a nice guy."

"He was. He was lovely."

"How come you didn't tell me he died?"

"I only heard about it last week. I figured you had enough on your mind."

"Did you have an affair with him?"

"I thought you weren't interested in confessions."

"I meant before we were married."

"I only went out with him before we were married."

"So did you have an affair? I'm not a necrophiliac or anything, it's just that he was a pretty straight guy, probably the only really straight guy you went out with besides me. I figure if you had an affair with him, he probably wanted to marry you. If you had married him, today you could have been a widow. You would look very good in black as long as it's not something of your mother's."

She laughed and hugged him. "So what are you going to do. Kill youself to make me even lovelier?"

"You can't get lovelier," he said.

She kissed him. "Cut it out," he said. "You got to be crazy. Come to my group. They'll really let you have it. I mean, you straightened out pretty good, considering what a lunatic you were, but there's got to be something still twisted somewhere if you're in love with me. Are you?"

"Yes."

"Why? What's the matter with you? I mean, aside from the fact that you come from a legion of emotional paraplegics. Why do you hang in with me?"

"You're the best man I know." It was true. In spite of the tension she felt, the unresolved conflicts between them, she had never thought anyone else might be better. Oh, maybe the unknown glamor figure across a crowded room or, had he lived, Adlai Stevenson. But the verity was that her circumstances were close to ideal, if she didn't demand from men what tradition did.

"And I thought I had freed you from the family curse," Harry said. "The best man you know. I'm a thirty-three-year-old 'kid' who has yet to support his family in the style to which his wife has made him accustomed."

"That sounds strangely like self-pity."

"Well, of course I feel sorry for myself. If I don't, who will . . . Yeah, I know, you will. Maybe you're too generous. Maybe you should kick me out on my ass."

"Such a cute ass."

"Cut it out. You know how embarrassing it is to have your wife admire your ass?"

"That's because I never had one."

"That's true. It's a shame. With your tits, if you had an ass, you could have been Sophia Loren. But even at your fattest you never had an ass. That's what it is. Ass envy."

She laughed, and hugged him again. "Is everything all right here?" the waitress asked. She was a tiny, round redhead in her early twenties, with buttermilk skin and a slightly crooked-toothed smile, which she flashed more freely since the advent of Ali MacGraw.

"Are you speaking of food and service, or general well-being?" Harry asked her.

"Food and service," she said. "General well-being I can't do anything about."

"Sure you can." Harry smiled. "Maybe you should join my group."

"I'm already in a group. We meet Wednesday nights in the forecourt of Grauman's Chinese and try and put ourselves in Susan Hayward's emotional shoes."

"I'll have a glass of white wine, please," Chris said.

"Another one?" the waitress asked, and went to get it.

"She disapproves of me," said Chris.

"She's probably bitter because you're a hit and she isn't."

"An easy feeling to pick up on."

"Not for me," Harry said. "I couldn't be happier about what's happened to you."

"Really?"

"How could I feel anything else?"

"You're a human being."

"Well, that's where I've got you fooled," said Harry.

It had been Dr. Rady's suggestion that Harry join a group, because a group would insist on getting to the problem and not be gulled by his charm. This turned out to be untrue. The anguish of his adolescence, the buried agonies of his childhood, the subtle destruction wreaked by a long line of guilt producers was something the group could get from anyone.

86

The poor, as Hemingway might have noted, were not different from you and me. A common strain in the childhoods of the poor, as the rich, was lack of love. But that, the group could listen to anytime. What they couldn't hear about were golden evenings where the celebrated mocked their society, election-eve parties with participants wearing Nixon masks, black-tie celebrations to watch the Academy Awards on television, where a man from the Bronx sat next to Zsa Zsa Gabor. Harry was the highlight of their therapy, the darling of the group, taking funny carom shots, talking street-smart common sense to the wimp, and the fat girl and the alcoholic, able to have insight into everyone but himself. When Dr. Rady tried to point that out to him, Harry quit the group. "I'm wasting your money," was how he put it to Chris, the one argument she was powerless against.

He retreated from his role as comic enchanter, no longer practicing even in living rooms that skill that the doctor had pointed out to him as a ploy, a cover to keep from seeing himself clearly. It was as if the accusation of "charmer" had stung as deeply as "ne'er-do-well" might have done. He was quiet now at parties, brooding, only his smile flashing quick and slightly dissociated, the anecdotes, the sense of play stilled. A queasy sadness crept over the marriage, like a fungus, a kind of moist despair, because things weren't the way either of them imagined they would be.

They still received numerous invitations, discontented married couples being more or less the norm, and so, of necessity, not unwelcome. Tennis was an important part of the social scene. Harry had taken it up with a vengeance, more careers having been advanced on tennis courts than anywhere else in town. It provided the rationale that he was not only staying in shape but looking for work.

He became very good at the game. His natural, powerful athleticism combined with his ease of manner to make him a highly sought-after tennis partner, carried them into glittering Sunday afternoons at celebrity estates, where Sunday afternoons flowed gracefully into buffet dinners and private screenings.

"Has Harry found work yet?" Cass Elliott said, sitting poolside at one such party. It was a joke between them, Cass thought, as much as it cut into Chris. Instead of saying "Hello" when she called, Cass would say "Has Harry found work yet?"

To add to that special agony, Chris was having trouble with her publisher. A number of songwriters had come forward demanding an accounting, accusing the company of holding out on its authors. Chris's accountant, denied access to the books, had suggested she turn the matter over to a lawyer. Now she was involved in a suit which the lawyer advised would take several years to come to court. In the meantime, the company was holding back royalties. So, in truth, they could no longer afford Harry's self-delusion that magic would happen and change his life. There was the mortgage, nursery school for Caroline, food, utilities, gardener, housekeeper, gas, car payments, pool service, the thousand natural shocks that flesh was heir to, especially in Southern California.

"We can't afford to be with these people," she said when they got home from a tennis Sunday. "We're not in their league."

"I am," Harry said, his waning confidence having been replaced by a veneer of arrogance, not well applied, so the cracks in it showed. He was still wearing his tennis clothes, his long, well-muscled, sunbrowned legs an advertisement for West Coast living. His tennis gear was piled neatly in the part of his closet once reserved for three-piece suits. He no longer saw the point in that manner of dress. Eastern clothes intimidated westerners, he was convinced, doubtless the reason he hadn't done better on the few job interviews he'd managed to set up. On his next interview, whenever somebody called, and he was sure they would, he planned to wear a turtleneck and a sports jacket, unless it was too warm, when a sport shirt would be appropriate.

Californians did better in California. He understood that now. He had left New York behind him, with its three-piece suits and disdain for anything but winners. He was learning to take his victory in little doses, a few sets at a time, with men who ran great corporations struggling to return his serve. "There isn't one of them who can beat me, unless I decide to be kind."

"I'm not talking about tennis," Chris said. "You can't spend your afternoons and weekends with millionaires and magnates, and then go looking for a simple job."

"I don't want a simple job," he said.

"Oh, Harry, please. Stop kidding yourself."

"I'm not kidding myself. I see how things are. I see very clearly, when I finally get an interview and some punk who's younger than I am looks down his nose at me."

"Then do something else. Anything else. Be a used-car salesman."

"What if I run into somebody I know?"

"The people you know don't buy used cars," she said angrily. She sat dow.. on the bed, trying to control her choler. "I'm *sorry*, I just don't know what you want."

That was less than the truth. She knew he wanted at least a little of what she had. Acknowledgment from her peers. Even to have peers. What slot had he fallen into, what conquests could he speak of, what money came into his account from triumphs of the past, or recognition accorded him? Even her dull days had little buzzes in them, the chance of catching a song of hers on the radio, the stereo that waited to bring her to herself, a telephone call that might mean someone wanted something she had done, or could do. Constant affirmation, where Harry had almost none, except the love of his family.

That success for her had turned out to be, as in the clichés, hollower than the hopes, was something she could not explain to him. She felt the same world that had covered her with congratulations stood poised on tiptoe, necks craned, awaiting the spectacle of her downfall. The quarrel with her publisher, her royalties in dispute, seemed a queasy eruption of her own self-doubt, the conviction she harbored that her good luck had been a mistake.

But at least she had had it.

"If I hang around long enough with these people," Harry said, "something will come up—"

"You're dreaming," said Chris. "Get a job. Any job. Please."

"I don't need *any* job. I said to my doubles partner today, 'I've been thinking of opening a new restaurant.' And he said, 'Why bother? I understand your wife is very successful.'"

She felt sapped, destitute. She had let him down by achieving. As tenuous as that achievement seemed, as easily as it could be taken away, it was more than he had. "I'm sorry . . . but other people work at ordinary jobs. They don't feel degraded—"

"They haven't got whizzes for wives. I don't play tennis with the descendants of Louis B. Mayer to be a used-car salesman—"

"Then stop playing tennis with them," she raged, instantly regretting it. Practically, where would he go? What would fill his afternoons? It seemed the only time he left the house now, to go to his tennis appointments, giving her treasured, greedily hoarded moments where she could collect the love of her children, squirrel it away, like acorns. Where she could be the one to welcome her little girl home from school, play mommy. Growing in Chris like the neglected child she had been was the fear that, like Evelyn, her own needs and desires could not come second. Really didn't have to, because it was easier to let Harry do everything. He was always there . . . first to the door, first to the Band-Aids, last one in the pool is a rotten mother.

"Is that it?" Harry asked. "Is that what you want? For me to stop playing tennis?"

"I want you to like yourself. Harry, you have to get a job."

"Your problems with your publisher will straighten out. You'll write more songs. We don't need some two-bit salary—"

"That's not the point, and you know it. Besides, we could send it to your mother . . ."

"My mother's in good shape! She's not so bad off! You want to talk about bad off, let's talk about *your* mother!"

There was a sudden, terrible banging on the door of their bedroom. For a moment Chris was frightened that Caroline had awakened, or Josh had escaped from his crib to find them raging at each other. The bedroom door was usually locked against the chance of the children finding them making love. This would be worse, more obscene, dirtying their eyes, shattering their spirit, giving them the terrible dreams that Chris had suffered, witches in pursuit, ragged-edged cliffs with nothing to keep them from falling, because it was all a lie, her happy marriage: they were as filled with fury and out of control as her parents had been.

But it was the housekeeper. "It's the boy," she whimpered. "There's something wrong with the boy."

They pushed against each other in their rush to reach him. Josh lay still in his crib, harrowingly still, only a strange, faint clattering, his breath whirring like a rusted metal fan coming out of his mouth. Next to the crib a night light illuminated three little pigs barricaded in their home, while a wolf peered in their window. For a disconnected moment, Chris planned on going shopping in the morning for a lamp of a less disturbing design. It would not do for her baby to have even storybook terrors.

Harry turned on the lamp. The child's eyes were rolled up in his head, whites blazing, as though he were possessed by some spectral phantom, his tongue beating on the roof of his mouth.

"Oh my God," Harry choked, and lifting Josh in his arms, carried him into the bedroom.

Before the birth of her children, Chris had lived with all a pregnant woman's fears, losing her baby, delivering stillborn, an infant deformed, crippled, retarded, the poster nightmares that seemed to glare from every window she'd passed. She had spent much of her pregnancy averting her eyes from billboards for the March of Dimes and Cerebral Palsy. Having birthed whole children ("She's beautiful," the doctor had said in New York; "He's a hundred percent," said the pediatrician of Josh), she went on to the fear of crib death, the litanies of horror that threatened an infant.

A child that died at birth was a part of yourself, an amputation, a lost limb, a sorrow you could never resolve. But a child that had established its own identity took everything. Losing Josh, she would lose him, the laughter, the hugeness, the sweetness, and lose herself, too. It would be an amputation and a separate bereavement both.

She was convinced he was dying, even as she prayed that he would not, beseeched for intercession hands she was not even sure existed. She went into the closet to pray, clinging to the plastic bags, promising her life, her future, whatever there was.

When she dared to leave the closet, she went back into the bedroom, where Harry knelt beside the bed, sobbing openly, crying out to God to save his son. In between wailings, he gave

Josh mouth to mouth resuscitation, breathed air into the chattering lips, never losing the rhythm. The spectacle of that big man in his tennis clothes, weeping, praying, giving breath to the unconscious boy, seared Chris's eyes. She felt deeply chastised, as though a thunderbolt had been hurled at her home, to terrify her into knowing what was important. She went back into the closet, to whisper again to the plastic bags, promising a future of right priorities. No importance whether man had a job. Only let him be a father to a baby who was alive, she exhorted.

They ran tests on Josh in the lab of the children's hospital, while she waited in his room. "He had a very high fever," the doctor reported. "These episodes are not uncommon in small children. It doesn't necessarily have to be *grand mal* or meningitis or anything related to the central nervous system. Sometimes it's just a single, isolated episode, and whatever it is, they outgrow."

She didn't believe him. He was a gentle man, with gray eyes that looked as though they'd wept through the deaths of many children. She'd found him after she'd fled the office of a pediatrician who told her he took care of Paul Newman and Joanne Woodward's children, and wanted to know what her husband did.

At three in the morning, a nurse brought Josh to the room. Chris could hear him calling from down the hall, "Mama." She started to cry because his voice was so deep, and weak, and he always wanted Harry—as though the bonding that should have taken place between her and her son had been surrendered to the father, and she'd lost him. So he hardly ever called for her, and he never called her "mama." She was sobbing now because he wanted her, he was calling for her, it

93

was mama he needed, asked for, in that pitiful little-man voice. She ran to the doorway and tried to stop the tears, so he wouldn't be frightened when he saw her.

A nurse was wheeling him in a metal-sided portable crib, so confining for such a large child that his legs were up in the air, resting on the bottom bracings, his arms pressed against his sides. His thick brown hair was matted with gel from the rubber platelets of the electroencephalogram. The chart on the side of the crib gave his name and said "large three-year-old." Chris started to laugh, crazily, because he wasn't even two yet.

"He only looks three," she told the nurse, smiling and crying. "He's such a big boy." She snatched him up into her arms. "Such a good boy." Covered him with kisses. "Such a beautiful boy."

The tests came back with a slight dysrhythmia that could have been caused by the seizure, the doctor assured them. They had to be patient, keep him slightly medicated, and hope he would outgrow it. They also had to avoid high altitudes and anxious glances at each other, because he was very sharp, and missed nothing.

There seemed to be no lasting damage from the experience, except for the chill that came over Chris's heart when she looked at him and thought what might happen, and the pout that fixed itself to Caroline's lips. Her parents wouldn't tell her exactly why Josh had been to the hospital. They hovered around him worse than ever. It was not enough advantage his being a boy: on top of everything else he'd gotten sick, made everybody run in the middle of the night. And now they watched him twice as hard as they watched her.

After a while, Chris began to convince herself she was lucky Harry hadn't found himself yet. In California, they talked of finding yourself, an improvement over New York, where you found *something*. So much more humanistic, animate, to seek your own *persona*, instead of an object. In California you also looked for the good in every experience, no matter how black it was, a "learning experience" it was characterized as by the self-help groups that proliferated. Josh's seizure had been a chance to see what was important: health, family, being together. So Harry's not "finding himself" was really okay, because if anything happened to Josh, God forbid, Harry would be home to breathe into his mouth, keep him alive till the doctor got there.

They were all right, really. Better than all right. They were blessed. "God had his arm around you," said Stephanie the radio interviewer, at a party at Madame Wu's, when she saw Harry. And that seemed the truth. It became increasingly evident to Chris, the cover of *Time* notwithstanding, that God was not dead, at least in Southern California. Maybe he'd withered from disuse in some places, but here the weather alone could restore him.

It was obviously paradise, fire, flood and earthquake aside. A place where a family could flourish, where children could grow up healthy (God willing), walk to school by themselves, provided they lived in the flats of Beverly Hills. There were sidewalks there, and the highest rated public schools in the nation. Enough reason to move, worth the inflated price of the houses, considering the tuition they'd save on private schools, the anguish spared in a future darkly promising bus- ing. The snobbery implicit in such a move was balanced by the threat found in Caroline's first year of private school at John Thomas Dye: a six-year-old girl had come to spend the weekend, with Louis Vuitton luggage.

So Chris and Harry seriously discussed changing at least the externals of their life. His tennis game was getting him down. He told himself in a moment of pained honesty that he had no real right to play, because there was nothing he was relaxing from. Little knots of tension started forming in his elbow, and his arm swelled when he played too hard, as it had when he'd been pitching. So he stopped the tennis, started to thicken slightly through the middle, and said when they found their home in the flats, he would take up running to get back in shape. She did not look in his eyes when he said things like that, for fear of what she would find there, or not find there anymore.

Three

S OMETIME, IN the middle of the chill Mexican night, Josh raised himself on his forearms and started shouting in his sleep. His face was faintly illuminated by a light from the bathroom. She could see the awful anger, the sweet fullness of his mouth vanished, twisted, nightmare making of it what once illness had. "Get out of here!" he yelled, as though confronting a personal Fury.

It frightened Chris on every level. She had felt each kick, each restless toss and flailing of his arms, as something she and Harry had done to him. A sorrow greater than loss suffused her: she had failed to rescue his dreaming. She touched his feverish face, whispered that it was all right, that everything would be all right. The knot between his eyebrows relaxed, his face reassembled as a child's.

"Okay, okay," he said, quieter now, negotiating with his antagonist. "Back off."

His enemy departed, he lay back on the pillow. She stroked his hair, damp with the sweat of his ordeal. She had promised herself that her children would never weep and suffer in the night, as she had. A pledge had been broken, to her, and them.

Was it penance, punishment? Because she had not loved enough, and consistently? Because the great dream of romance she had seemed to find with Harry had vanished in a blaze of reality? Had her fury at her own disappointment transmitted itself to her son, shattered his sleep, as it had shattered her waking? If there were no loving dreams a woman could have by day, perhaps there were none her children could have by night.

She studied the face, untroubled now, thickly lashed lids like geishas' fans over the angular eyes. She whispered into his ears how loved he was, how special, how fearless he should be, and happy. A twinge of envy went through her at the pink perfection of his lobes, no claimant having driven a hole through them, staking him out as a piece of property, adorning him with diamonds, a camouflage for ownership. That she had consented to the ritual of piercing was beside the point. Harry had appealed direct to her sentimentality, and the covetousness that had come to her through Evelyn. Taken unfair advantage.

From across the room came the heavy sound of Harry's breathing, the crash of unwelcome tides. It grated on her spine: he imposed himself on her even while he slept. She remembered earlier darknesses, when the sound of breath was a reassurance, a lift to the heart, a bulwark against the stored-up fear of isolation, the loneliness. She wondered what had transmuted it, caused snoring to become still another rape, an attack on a woman's sensibilities. First she had been angry at him for blowing his nose; now she resented his breathing. Her aversion diminished them both, diminished everything she'd ever thought they were. She tried to conjure up the funny times, the sweet times, but his snoring interfered with her concentration.

When was the instant it changed, when longing turned to rankling? She could not pinpoint it. Love came with such a fiery spark to the human spirit, even the romance that seemed to grow slowly had at its heart a moment when things burst clearer. When the beloved became the beloved, a presence necessary to bring full joy to things. Part of a history richer for being shared, a joke funnier because someone else understood it, instantly, with no explanation needed. So how could it die? How could it die, and the moment not even be memorable?

Caught like a cat with a ball of wool in her own unravelings, she could not get back to sleep. Dawn tinted the edges of the drapes. She stiffened at the prospect of the alarm, thought of turning it off. But why should she gentle Harry from his sleep, spare him the jolt, the shocking intrusion, when she'd spent so much of the night steamrollered by the sound of him, jackhammered from her peace. She calmed herself, finally, by contemplating the face of her son.

"What are you staring at?" he asked, opening one eye.

"You."

"Why?"

"You're so handsome."

"You'd think you would have gotten used to it by now." He grinned at his own outrageousness.

Caroline had opted to sleep late in the morning: she saw no point in suffering an outing despoiled by the smell of dead fish and the sickening vision of Josh having a wonderful time with their father. At such moments Harry seemed not to belong at all to her, as though it were nature, really, that aligned him with Josh, and not his own lack of consideration, not only for her, but for the fishes, cutting their mouths with hooks, bulging their eyes. She had tried going fishing with them once or twice, and it made her nauseous, as well as jealous. Just as she had tried to play baseball to get more of her father's attention, despising the way she looked in uniform, hating the heat of the sun through the shrouds of Little League, abandoning the pretense, finally, for piano lessons. Now, being thirteen, she was tired of all efforts that had no obvious and immediate reward, so had decided to devote the whole day to her suntan.

When it was time to go, Harry took his Dramamine. He was showered and crisp, six o'clock in the morning though it was. He was always showered and crisp; a holdover from his ball-club days, where showers punctuated all great events, sent you fresh into the next adventure, washed away victory and loss alike. He had come to the locker room with his own ingrained sense of cleanliness, an extension of his mother's preoccupation with the state of her floors, scrubbed on hands and knees, with newspapers placed on them for several days afterwards, so the family could walk on the linoleum itself only a day or two a week, after which she would scrub them again.

Chris had known a sweet southern faggot who gently lusted after Harry, but controlled himself, he said, out of affection for her. "He always looks like he just stepped out of a shower," he once remarked admiringly.

"That's because he did," she told him.

She and Harry never showered together. The shower was Harry's place, his club, a ritual, a cure. Water erotica was saved for the bathtub, a concession to her, like holding hands, soaping for pleasure. As if the greater joy were coming clean.

He stood now by the marbleized sink to the side of the room, Josh at his side, the wall mirror behind giving off two sets of them, the impeccable man in shorts and sweatshirt, and his worshipping son. Josh stood, water glass raised, offering it to his father.

"You trying to kill me?" Harry asked, spilling the contents into the sink, rinsing the glass with bottled water.

"I forgot," Josh said, chagrined.

"That's something you don't forget in Mexico."

Maybe that was how she and Harry could end it, Chris thought. Kiss each other good-bye, and drink the water.

"You sure you don't want to come with us?" Harry paused by the great carved wooden door, his son close to his hip, like a pistol in the holster of a gunfighter, ready.

Why did they have to seem like such a team, Chris wondered. Why were there no real alternatives in a world that pretended there were choices. If she gave up the father, did she have any chance of keeping the son? Would there be even joint custody, or wouldn't he say to her, and the judge, "I'm sorry, but I want to live with my dad."

"It's a small boat," Chris said.

"You're a small woman." The compliment hung in the air, meant to melt her, as it once might have done, the hint of delicacy, a dollop of tongue behind it. For a moment, she thought of Cass, gone now, dead of a ham sandwich. Found alone in a London hotel room, choked to death on her own loneliness, her frenzied lack of self-esteem, trying to fill up the fear with food. Lying in a bed, so desperate to numb herself, she didn't even taste. Couldn't have, or she would have eaten something better than ham on white, she who had seen so much humor in a world with no understanding of rye.

But irony, misery, death, deprivation, the example of her vanished, sad friend notwithstanding, Harry's words did not move Chris anymore. It was no longer enough being slender. She should also have been happy.

"You two have a good time," she told them, desperate suddenly to be by herself, to walk on the littered beach and pretend it was covered with white sands. To act as though her every action stemmed from love, to look for the sunbrowned couple and imagine how it was to feel liquid inside, the way they did, instead of frozen.

"Have fun, mom," Josh said, generously, rushing to kiss her

on the lips, as if she had made the noblest sacrifice of all, letting them be men together, to shout, laugh, spit, do what men do without worrying what women would think. There was pity in the kiss, as well, signaling he understood how out of balance she was, this woman who preferred silence to noise, books to television, dry land to water.

"You, too," she murmured.

"You sure you shouldn't take another Dramamine, dad?" Josh mocked him, grinning.

"Come on!" Harry clouted him gently, a grizzly and his cub. The door closed behind them.

From the balcony, she watched their small boat pulling away from the pier, into the pale gray, lightly whitecapped sea. Bright against the morning bobbed Josh's red sweatshirt, a spot of audacity in a world of conforming shadows. She loved him so much she ached, wondering if the ache wasn't all the more intense because she was no longer feeling it for Harry.

A whisper of chill came up from the sea. She wrapped her robe tighter around herself, reluctant to go inside, to lose sight of him. In the far corner of the beach, nestled against the round, orange rocks that bordered the hotel's portion of strand a bright multicolored catamaran was bulwarked against the wind. Chris caught a glimpse of graceful, sun-browned legs, the long, rounded limbs of a woman, stretching from beneath, subtly intertwined with the muscular calves of a man, lazily relaxed, as though it were after. Envy caught in her throat. It could only be the beautiful couple. Not enough they had so much glow in them they kept the sun on their skin after it had set. Now they were greeting it, before it was even fully risen. Warming the world as lovers did, while they were still lovers.

She dressed hurriedly, afraid they might be gone by the time she reached the beach. She had never really seen their faces, only noted the gentle thrust of their bodies arcing towards each other, drawn, attached, the sweet curve of passionate grace. Their features, she imagined, were perfect, like the rest of them, their voices lightly musical, crystallized bells of laughter punctuating the warm and witty things they said to one another in between love words. She felt slightly giddy, adolescent, as she made her way down the tiled steps to the rear of the building, constructing in her mind the casual greeting she would give them, as though accident had brought her there, and not envy, eagerness, longing. She moved down the grassy path to the sand, deftly maneuvering the boulders bordering the beach below the rise of private bungalows.

She could see the roundness of the woman's hips, curving smoothly under his sunbrowned hand, his fingers gripping her copper flesh. They were naked. It did not slow Chris's movement towards them. Rigid, ladylike training in deportment pulled hypocritically at her lids, so her lashes, at least, were modestly lowered, in preparation for pretended embarrassment. "Oh, I'm so sorry," she would say. "I didn't see you."

She moved swiftly past the flapping red and yellow and blue sail of the catamaran, saw the perfect conic rise of the woman's breasts, burnt rust nearly to the nipple. The man's head lay pressed between. For a moment Chris experienced mortification: she had not intended to interrupt their making love—only wanted to see their bodies, their faces, what it was that kept them feeling. The scent of cocoa butter and almonds lightly assailed her nostrils, as though they had rubbed each other with sweet, exotic lotions, still interested enough to explore, caress. Something past jealousy pulled at her insides. Like holding hands and sitting in the moonlight—romantic fantasies she still harbored from the empty days of her adolescence, that Harry only rarely indulged her in, and then with tolerance—the shadier side of her dreaming included making love on the beach. But Harry, clean Harry, pragmatic Harry, who liked his own soft-sheeted bed, always refused. "It's gritty," he would say, explanation to justify stripping the world of lagoons, sands, tender passion itself.

Respectability blazed up in her, slowly, like a blush. A part of her was dissolute, libidinous, curious about the orgies she and Harry had never attended, fascinated by the X-rated movie they had finally gone to, with a sleek, rich couple who laughed at them as "square" when they nervously declined their postprandial invitation. Her imagination was wanton, as feverishly carnal as her romanticism was starry-eyed. Never had she witnessed anyone else making love. Her eyes were drawn to the couple on the sand, even as decorum led her feet away.

The man's tongue stretched from his mouth as though tasting the woman's sunbrowned belly. But something about the color disquieted Chris. She turned and looked at them full. His face was bloated, blue, grotesque. Blood clotted his nostrils. The woman's eyes were open, staring, so Chris would never be able to know whether the twisted features had been beautiful.

The Mexican police moved into the locale with uncharacteristic dispatch. As their activities were usually limited to rounding up drunks, checking on robberies, extricating from the mangled cabs of trucks men left to die in accidents, it was as though a crime of violence to lovers held in it, besides a mystery, the power to ennoble. Seven policemen stood on the beach, semi-circling the naked bodies that lay on the towel, while the police doctor made his inspection of the corpses.

The officers stood more or less at attention, as much as they could, their stance somewhat Mack Sennettized by the shifting sands beneath their boots, as though the Keystone Kops had bungled South of the Border. Their uniforms were a somber dark khaki against the brightness of the day; guns emphasized the seriousness of their purpose. But with it all, the effect was slightly comic, little grins of excitement pulling at their mustachioed faces as they struggled for sober expressions. It was, obviously, a great event for them, and they seemed eager to make sure it was played as such. The streets of Guaymas were shadowed with black-suited soldiers, loaded automatic rifles black-strapped to their shoulders. On the way to the hotel Chris had asked a taxi driver why they were there. "Because no one listens to the police," he had told her.

So, like understudies seizing on a star's long-awaited illness, the police stood trying to project dignity, importance, what they had always had the hope of showing but seldom an opportunity. They tried to keep gawkers away, chased small children. Word of the tragedy had swept the hotel. Guests were collecting on the pier. From Chris's balcony it looked as though they were expecting a parade.

Below, on one of the ground-floor patios, a trio of maids gathered, chattering in sorrowful Spanish of what a sadness it was. "*Qué lástima*," they murmured. "*Hermoso. Tan joven. Pobrecitos.*" The door to the balcony adjacent to Chris's room opened, and Caroline peered out, her eyes still heavy from sleep, her blossoming body camouflaged by the long red nightshirt. She looked straight out at the sun, nearsightedly, single-purposed, to check if it was shining for her vacation as potently as it would have in Palm Springs, where a number of her classmates were spending their holiday and where she had unsuccessfully agitated for her family to go. One of the things that disturbed her about her mother, besides a career that almost none of the other mothers had, and oversized breasts, was an ability to find out-of-the-way places, where no one ever went who Caroline knew, and for good reason.

"Go back inside," Chris said.

"Huh?" murmured Caroline.

"Inside." Chris watched her daughter reluctantly obey the directive. "And shut the doors," she shouted, trying to take the edge of hysteria from her voice. The spectacle on the beach had struck her as a private horror, a personal betrayal, as if the universe did not care for her enough to sustain even love's symbolism. She had tried to weep for the two dead people, to conduct a masque of mourning. But she had never known them, never seen their faces while they were alive. She felt more anxious now than sad, her only concern to keep her children from seeing, worried that the Mexicans with their relaxed attitude towards time would feel no urgency about getting the bodies out of there.

She went inside and tried to open the door to Caroline's room. It was locked. She pounded, not meaning to, but the wood was thick, and the rooms, uncarpeted, produced an awesome echo.

"What is it?" Caroline said, a sulk in her voice.

"Open the door."

"I'm not dressed."

"I won't look."

The door opened after a moment. Caroline was wearing the bottom of her bikini, a large towel held in front of the breasts she so objected to sprouting. "What is it?"

"I just wanted to say good morning."

"Why'd you make me go inside?"

"There were men on the beach. I didn't want them to see you in your nightgown." It was not Chris's intention to feed her daughter's sense of personal panic at being observed. But it was easier than the truth, less likely to fire Caroline's curiosity, send her rushing to the balcony, to look down, and see them.

"Would you excuse me, please?"

"Why are you putting on a bathing suit? It's so early."

"The sun is out."

"I want to take you to breakfast."

"I'm not hungry," Caroline said. "I want to get a tan."

"You have ten days."

"The sun may not shine the whole time. It isn't like we're in *Palm Springs*." Distaste sailed through the observation.

"The sun is more powerful here than Palm Springs."

"Then how come nobody knows about it? I asked Tracy Lichterman, she's been everywhere in Mexico and she never even heard of Guaymas."

"Well, that's where you'll have it over Tracy Lichterman. Come on. Put on a shirt. I'll take you to breakfast."

"I want to go on the beach."

"You can't."

The black eyes narrowed. Not enough her mother had taken her to the ends of the earth, now she even wanted to blot out the sun. Was there no end to the punishment? What had she done, except be born a younger woman?

"Something's down there," Chris said.

Caroline started towards the balcony.

"I don't want you to look."

"What is it? A whale?" The extent of her hideous imaginings were beached creatures of the sea, a mélange of *Jaws* and Jacques Cousteau.

"Two people are dead."

"Really?" Caroline was full of breath now, an innocent again, as she had been before she turned twelve and declared Chris The Enemy. In a way, it was relaxing to know there was genuine disaster in the world, not all of it instituted by mothers. "What happened?"

"I don't know. The police are down there now."

"Can't I even look?"

"No. Please. Get dressed."

"Will you excuse me?"

"I'll turn my back," Chris said, and did.

"You can trust me, you know," Caroline said. "If I say I won't look, I won't look."

"Say it then."

"I won't look," said Caroline, reluctantly.

They went the back way down the steps to the patio, past the pool, Caroline craning her neck, trees and the people on the pier obscuring her view of the beach. "Were they murdered, or drowned, or what?"

"They didn't look drowned."

"You saw them?"

"I found the bodies."

"Really?" Caroline looked at her with something bordering respect. "Who were they?"

"The man and the woman who were by the pool here last night."

"I don't remember them," Caroline said. "Were they young or what?"

"They were young," Chris said, and wished that she could have added "beautiful." She hoped they were beautiful, even now. It made them mythic, lifted it somehow above the sordid.

She turned her face to the sea, searching it for the little boat bearing her second child, looking for the dot of red that would signify him, anxious for his return, nervous that it would be too soon, that it would not be soon enough. She was afraid he would see the dead couple, that she would not be able to come between him and the sight, that Harry, not knowing what was going on, would stumble onto it, with Josh in his wake. Even if she managed to head Josh off, and forbade him to look, he was not like Caroline. He would not obey her. Josh with his rascally intelligence, foraging through bathroom cabinets, where people kept their secrets. She could not imagine his not seeing, even blindfolded, and wished the police would speed up their business.

"*Señora* . . ." A policeman came over to her. "My captain wishes to make an official report. He have to talk to you."

"I already told them everything I know."

"He wants to talk to you again."

"I'm taking my daughter to breakfast."

"I can go by myself," said Caroline, her face bright, keen, high spots of color on her cheeks, interest in her dark eyes.

"I'll meet you in the dining room," Chris said, and kissed her daughter, feeling a wave of perverse gratitude to the police for making her an object of consequence sufficient so Caroline didn't pull away.

"I told you we should have gone to Palm Springs," she said.

Two officers were waiting for Chris in the manager's office. "What time did you find them?" the older one asked. His face was sloppily shaven, tufts of beard at irregular intervals on his cheeks and chin disputing his posture of importance.

"Six o'clock," she said.

"Why were you on the beach?"

"I was taking a walk."

He looked at her with flat black eyes, dead, like a shark's, with no light behind them. "You knew these people?"

"No. I told you. I saw them around the hotel. But I never spoke to them."

"Was there anybody else on the beach?"

"No."

"What time was it?"

"I told you. Six o'clock."

"You have the custom to walk so early in the morning?"

"My husband and son went fishing. So I was awake." Irritation crept into her voice. It had been a mistake coming to Mexico. Everything she touched now turned to dross. Even spied-on lovers changed to the dark pornography of death;

"snuff" as it was in the parlance of X-ratings, a dirty movie in which someone actually died. Just the sex would have been enough for her. The questioning seemed a disproportionate tithe for her small corruption of voyeurism. She wondered why the police were wasting time with her when they should have been clearing the beach, carrying the bodies off so her children wouldn't see.

Mexico. She wondered if the same cloud that hovered over her marriage had been responsible for directing her to this melancholy place.

"What made you come to Mexico?" the policeman queried.

"I was just asking myself the same question."

"An answer, please, *Señora.*"

"I was in love here once, a long time ago," she said.

All that Chris had kept of herself, all that she had really liked about herself from the beginning, considered as good as anyone else's, was her name. She had no idea why she decided to trundle it with her into her marriage, when the act of subverting her own identity had seemed so desirable.

It was not, she thought, like separate rooms, an affront to Harry, a challenge to his supremacy, a dispute of his claim on her. Her name as originally set was simply more mellifluous, closer to a stage name, easy enough to remember so a certain destiny was implied in her career. Having asserted her own title, in print, on records and songsheets, Chris As She Was, she took the name with her to parties, telling the hostesses that yes, that was how she preferred to be introduced. That it led to a certain confusion, and resulted in Harry's sometimes being introduced as Mr. White, was something that gave her occasional pangs of embarrassment for him, but not enough to have her consider changing. It was her *Name*, that was all, having nothing to do with not wishing to surrender her Self, she was certain.

"Ciao, hello!" Nina Warren gushed when they saw each other at a party. "I'm so excited to see you again. *Eccitazione!*" They had known each other as girls in New York, Nina more girlish by a decade, her adorableness undiminished by a bumpy career and bumpier marriages. She was still all enthusiasm, constantly on the verge of giant breakthroughs, both in her films and her personal life. Her way of speaking was filled with embraces, the affection she could not in fact give anybody, which was generally known but never discussed, except in *McCall's*. "What a trip to run into you! You know, I almost recorded your last song. God, you've grown so as an artist, what about me, do you think I have?"

"Faster than a speeding bullet," Chris said.

Nina laughed, a deep womanly cackle she had picked up from Melina Mercouri, along with a certain frenzied approach to cigarettes, as though if she smoked fast enough, she could become both Greek and formidable. Her features were less symmetrical than they appeared on screen, her smile slightly crooked, as if she were holding a part of it in reserve against the day when someone convinced her she was happy. But her energy was palpable, her charm a personal plea not to notice how flawed she was.

"You're so lucky to be creative. I mean *veramente* creative, instead of all this tinsel and glitter shit." Nina took a less than delicate swig of her white wine, as though to wash her mouth of the phoniness that had lodged in her teeth when she took a bite of Hollywood. "To be able to write, to sing from inside yourself. God, what a blessing. When all I was given was incredible beauty and irresistible talent."

They both laughed. "What are you doing now?" Nina asked her.

"The same. Writing."

"What about real life?"

"Married."

"The same husband?"

Chris nodded. "And the same two children."

"I hope you do novenas. I'm going to Mexico. I'll do some for you. They're very effective there. Maybe I'll do some for myself. The churches are supposed to be primitive, but the people will do anything to get out of the sun. What do you think will happen to me?"

"You'll live happily ever after."

"Do you think so? God, I wish I could get hold of it for just a little while, that fucking brass ring."

"You are the brass ring."

"That's nice, it really is. Do you mean that? Why don't you write me a song about a brass ring that everybody reaches for and never gets. Maybe I can sing it over the titles of my new movie, do you know about it?"

"No."

"We're making it in Mexico. It's a true *tour de force*. Unless Eric Lobler directs it. Then, it will be a *tour de weakness*." Nina threw back her head, displaying the giraffish neck it had taken her several seasons studying the Alexander method to feel secure about, and even emphasize, without displacing anything. "Why don't you come visit me on location? I'd be so glad to have a friend there."

They were far from being friends. But Chris supposed the same eagerness with which Nina performed sent her careening into relationships. And Chris felt flattered to have a star of Nina's magnitude consider her even insincerely a friend. One of the worst drawbacks of being an accomplished woman was how few females there were who could relate to you, with whom you could have a genuine exchange. Most of Chris's close friends lived in the East, where they'd gone to school together and hadn't been afraid to show how smart they were.

But California was parched of peers: Cass was gone; and nobody verbal and funny had come to take her place. Places, Chris thought wickedly. She would enjoy palling around with Nina for a week or two or five. It would be good to pick up on that energy. Lately she'd begun to feel a little weary—she did not examine why. Usually it began in the mornings, when she couldn't remember what she wanted to get out of bed for.

"*Senti*, listen, come to Guaymas—it's just a little fishing village, *molto* sleepy. But we'll have laughs, yes? I don't know anyone on the picture. I've never worked ith Tony Candella. He's my costar. I could certainly use a friend." Nina's expression was wistful, striped with orphaned longing.

"I'll have to ask my husband," Chris said.

"No shit. A woman like you, and you have to get permission." The kewpie melted, and Nina stood naked, brazen, astonished at the traps women set for themselves. "Where is he?" She looked around the room.

"Over there," Chris said. "In the blue sport shirt."

"*Bello*. Handsome. Is he in the business?"

"Not anymore."

"What does he do?"

"He's a very nice man," Chris said, trying not to panic at her inability to give a straight answer.

"Nice," mused Nina. "That's something none of mine were. And you have two children."

"A boy and a girl."

"Then you've done everything right. A family and a career. It's possible then. You must come to Guaymas!" It was a royal command now, a knighting in the insistence. "I need you for inspiration." She threaded her arm through Chris's, pulled her in Harry's direction. "Come. *Viene*. We'll ask his permission together."

A part of Chris had always longed to dance on tabletops. A portion of her had done so in her college days, and the months that came afterwards, when she'd lived in Paris, had too much wine, and sung her songs at the least provocation—sometimes less. There were still elements in her of noise and uninhibited joyfulness, a yearning to frolic in the fountains in front of the Plaza, to go colorfully mad, like Zelda Fitzgerald, trailing scarfs of chiffon as sanity slipped away. She saw Nina as a storybook version of herself, in living color, hauling her in the direction of risks Chris no longer had the courage to take on her own, setting bold, flaming sail towards the Sea of Cortés.

She hadn't known, then, that it was the Sea of Cortés. She knew almost nothing about what was waiting for her, except that it was finally, again, destiny: that arrow that had seemed removed from Cupid's quiver. Adventure. Romance. Tony Candella.

There seemed to Chris to be a certain crisp inevitability to it, a knell of recognition when she heard his name, discovered he would be there, saw that Fate had the same mentality as Evelyn. Her mother did know a great deal, there was no disputing it, even while murmuring Harry didn't know everything.

With what little objectivity she had about passion, Chris knew she wanted nothing less than the Romance of the Century. Like most women, she was caught up in her own yarn, hoping it would turn into an extravaganza. An acquaintance of hers was an astrologer, who told her that men always wanted to hear what the stars had in store for their careers. Women, however, wanted to know about love, unless they were actresses.

As exceptional as Chris might have hoped she was, as cut from an uncommon cloth, she was just like everyone else when it came to romance. That it had seemed to vanish from her life, even though she would not consciously acknowledge it had, annihilated a part of her, flowed through her like a deadening lava, obliterating anticipation, that portion of her that shone most childishly bright. Rekindled at the mention of a name, she had a brief insight, quickly dismissed, into how adolescent she really was.

But why should she have been otherwise? Maturity came with confidence in yourself as a woman, and Chris had never had that. Nor had marriage secured her parcel of Paradise. So she was ready for Tony Candella, eager for him, her heart quickening even as his shadow hit the front door of Nina's bungalow. There they were, in Guaymas, an Arcadian setting no one would have known existed, in a scenario only her mother could have conceived. Not that Chris was influenced by Evelyn.

"Hey," Tony said, whispering over the top of the drink Nina had given him. "What are you doing here, you pretty woman?"

"You two know each other?" Nina asked. Behind her, the living room rainbowed like a gallery of Mexican pastiche, colored piñatas, fans and dolls hanging from walls and ceiling. Nina's entourage had arrived in Guaymas three days before the rest of the troupe, to brighten the place, make it unhotelish, nonsterile, so Nina would not be struck with the realization of how empty and nomadic her life was, and get depressed, delaying the start of production. She was a complete professional in every sense, despising those who alibied and feigned illness to avoid being on time. Nothing would have stopped her from hitting her marks, being on stage when she was due, except a total breakdown, which she had from time to time, so sent her cortege to guard against with *papier mâché*.

"Her old man ran a restaurant I used to frequent," Tony said. "Is he coming down?"

"Maybe in a few weeks," Chris said.

"A few weeks." Tony measured them, nodded. "Then you'll be here for a while?"

"Yes."

They thought that over, between them.

He was handsomer than she remembered, the cragginess of his face deepened by diet and heavy workouts in the gym he'd had installed in his wife's sewing room after she'd left him. To her chagrin, Chris was up-to-date on the saga of his separation, having read all the stories about him while waiting her turn at supermarket checkstands, not stooping so low as to buy the *National Enquirer*, or believe it, but not having the strength to pass it up, especially not once she knew they would be together in Guaymas. It was his wife's fault, more than his, that there was such a glut of information. His wife was the one who had given out vindictive interviews. "The women of the world who think he's so hot should know about him what I know about him," was captioned over her picture. That seemed an agreeable suggestion to Chris.

There was about it all the sweet stupidity of sophomores. In high school she had loved a boy, her passion deepening with each rejection. Finally, he asked her to meet him at midnight at the boathouse. She waited till six in the morning, dragging dejectedly back to the dorm. "What happened?" she asked him at breakfast, teary eyed. "I changed my mind," he said.

So she'd been ready for well over half her life for a fantasy love to fulfill itself, for a brute to prove tender. She admired Tony Candella now from up close as she had from afar. His blue eyes, cobalt, iridescent, had a hollow melancholy to them. The break in his nose seemed more a wound than a former wrestler's imperfection. She was moved with a terrible compassion for him, knowing how lonely he had to be without anyone, when she, with a whole family, felt so alone.

Outside the bungalow, the sun was setting. A makeup

woman squealed a tiny "ooooo" as the sky turned mauve. The rest of the company seemed not to notice, more caught in their own spectacle than the one nature provided. Nina's hairdresser brushed barbecue sauce on chicken breasts crisping on outdoor braziers. A grip announced that the shrimp in Guaymas were the largest and most succulent in the world. Tony Candella mentioned to Chris that at his barbecue the next evening there would be steaks, flown in from L.A.

"Will you be there?"

"If I'm wanted."

"Oh, honey, you're wanted," he murmured. "Oh, are you ever."

She could hardly control her impatience through the day that followed, a vague dread in her inquietude, as with a Hitchcock movie she had once been feverish to see but could not watch in the theater, except through her fingers. She felt as terrified as titillated, not only at the thought of being with Tony, but that the prospect of adultery did not seem more abhorrent to her. In fact, it had barely flashed through her mind as a moral question, and for that she was deeply ashamed.

Was she that selfish? Was she that self-indulgent? Or was it only that she was so disappointed in her marriage. And wasn't that the worst sin of all, to have expected so much? No, no sin. More like patriotism. Loyalty not only to the dictums of America ("He will take care of you"), but to history, fantasy, fairy tale ("He will take care of everything").

What could that bubble be, but broken? How unfair was the weight put on men; no wonder they had heart attacks. But how much heavier was the burden on women, expecting?

So she stood by Tony Candella's pool like an overripe groupie, warmed to her marrow by the fact that he had chosen her, out of everyone, her pulsebeat thudding in her ears, nearly blotting out his words. "People don't know how vuh-nerable I am," he said to her. The mispronunciation moved her even more deeply than the revelation would have, put correctly, implying as it did a longing for the education that had been denied him, a need to be more than he was, while wishing women would let him be less. That she found his lack of schooling touching when it alienated her in Harry was something she did not stop to examine.

All she noted carefully was his face, the sorrow behind it, the vague smell of musk coming from his open shirtfront and the house they stood beside. It was a tile-roofed, white-painted stucco in a desert village six miles from the Playa de Cortés, rented for him by the production company, in accord with his stipulation that he be apart and private and alone, except for his stand-in, hairdresser, makeup man, costume designer, dialogue coach, and chiropractor, all of them ensconced in houses surrounding.

The chiropractor was on salary, hired by the film company although he belonged to Tony by friendship, choice, and need. A symptom of the agonies no one suspected the actor suffered inside was his back going out whenever the world hassled him. The dialogue coach, also on the company payroll, had likewise been hired to soothe the star. He was a friend of Tony's from boyhood, with nearly unintelligible diction. The two would spend long hours Ping-Ponging Midwestern accents back and forth at each other while working on Tony's delivery. He would sit declaiming *Lear*, the words getting stuck on his caps.

They were, in all, an entourage of rather inadequate men, it seemed to Chris. But she did not want to make judgments, there being such charisma about Tony she knew it was his obligation to lift lesser men.

Past the mud red roof of his house the sun arced to rest behind the nippled twin peaks of the Tetas de Cabra. His fingers toyed with the chain around Chris's neck as he searched it for charms. She remembered that Harry had promised her an Elsa Peretti tear and had neglected to deliver. It seemed a symbol of his lack of commitment to his promises, the petty ones as well as the great, sending her out into the world, if not exactly defenseless, improperly accessorized. And all the while she was thinking that, she was filled with a vague sense of self-loathing, at how small she'd become, at how niggardly the diminishment of love had made her.

"Plain," Tony murmured, his fingers having come up with nothing. "I guess that makes it even chicer. As if you were the jewel."

Gratitude welled in her, like tears. First a man had called her tiny, and then a movie star considered her chic. Two words in the world she had least imagined ever being categorized as. Combined with her thankfulness was pity for Tony, at how deep would have to be his insecurity, to admire her.

Behind him, the sun jump-cutted into shadow. "You're missing the sunset," she said.

"I'm seeing everything I need to see," he sort of whispered.

From the barbecue at the far side of the patio, drifted the smokey aroma of burning meat. She could feel his warmth, had to fight back the impulse to stand on tiptoe and rub her face against his red-tufted chest, inhale his whole smell. The fingers that touched her chain moved down, lightly traced her collarbone.

"I wish you were going to be here the whole time," he said. "That would be so . . ." he reached for exactly the right adjective. "Comfortable," he said.

That which was maternal in her overflowed. She had to hold her hands at her sides to keep from hugging him, so great was his need to be allowed to be himself, so deep was her perception of him, she was sure. Even as she congratulated herself on how well she understood him, seeing the little boy in him, she felt a wave of shame: she hadn't even thought about her children. Oh, there was no need to worry. There was finally a maid that she trusted at home, and Harry was there, better at the caring than anyone. But Chris had imagined the motherly in her, having finally been fulfilled, was predominant in her nature. And she hadn't even remembered her children, missed them. Her husband she'd thought of only once, and then with irritation, because he'd neglected her jewelry. Harry, the love of her life, she'd imagined, until her children were born. And them she hadn't thought of at all.

"I have to see to my guests," Tony was saying. "Don't you dare go anywhere." He brushed her with his breath. It was lightly minted, sweet, intoxicating. She could feel his lips more intensely from two inches away than if they had touched her. "And then, when they've gone home . . ."

"Yes?" She made the question mark very clear, keeping her assent in abeyance, not wanting to wait again in vain at the boathouse.

"I was a little afraid of you," he said, vuhnerable. "Afraid you'd shoot me down. We'll have to be very discreet. I wouldn't want to do anything to hurt . . ." He hesitated.

"Harry," she filled in for him.

"Yeah. What a great guy."

Well, he was, there was no doubt about it, even though people couldn't remember his name, and she'd thought about him almost not at all, and forgotten his children. And hers. What was the matter with women? Was it a nature she shared? Love was of man's life a thing apart, she knew from the poet and the astrologer, as she was assured it was women's whole existence. But like this, in varying degrees, so when the greater love appeared, amnesia set in? Or was it guilt that caused absentmindedness? Was she guilty? She hadn't felt anything all day, except anxious, restless, eager.

Half the happily married women in America felt guilty because they wanted a crack at Warren Beatty. So why should she feel guilty, unhappily married as she was, that she wanted Tony Candella to have a crack at her? A Talmudic question, loaded, deceptive at its root, carrying the answer within the query. Why she felt guilty was that she was, she thought, unhappily married.

How had that happened? How had she fallen out of love, when she'd loved him so, when he'd so loved her? The first one who had. The only one who had. How could she be cruel and specious enough to betray him, not with Tony, but with herself? Why didn't she love him anymore? Why didn't he love himself? Were they both victims of the myth? Was he enraged at not living up to the way men were supposed to be? He seemed as angry and frustrated as she was at his not turning out the total protector, the Compleat Hero. Was there such a thing as the Compleat Hero? There had to be, or what was the dream about?

Or did everyone fade if you studied them long enough. Was it inevitable that you be blinded only when staring at the sun; did anything less yield clarification, and with it, disillusion? Was it a risk in seeking heaven, that you were asking for hell?

Lasciate ogni speranza, voi che entrate; abandon all hope, ye who enter here. A fit admonition for the entrance to Hades, not marriage. How could she feel so despairing, with no real sorrow in her life, nothing that would have brought tears to her grandmother's eyes, no death of anything except love. *Lasciate ogni disperazione*: Abandon the despair. She would put the motto above Tony's door, teach him Romance languages, read the classics with him. After.

Could Harry forgive her if she did? Could any woman forgive her if she didn't? She would give herself to Tony for all of them, and in the action, rediscover herself: a woman who knew who she was, because she loved a real man.

Wasn't that how women were supposed to define themselves? Certainly her mother thought so. That might have been the tragedy of her generation, the reason why Evelyn had never fulfilled her clever potential, because she looked to men to fulfill theirs, dragging her along. But was it any less delusive for Chris to think she could realize herself as a woman without a man to relate to? Maybe Gloria Steinem didn't think so, or the sharp-featured ladies with boyish names who intimidated Johnny Carson. But they were pragmatists, and women were not supposed to be pragmatic. Were they? Certainly they weren't supposed to be angry, unless of course they'd been denied the chance to do what they wanted. That had never happened to Chris. She had even been given the chance to do what she didn't want, becoming the head of the household by virtue of having more success than her husband. And now, as in some cosmic reparation, she was being conducted into Everywoman's dream. Except maybe Gloria Steinem's.

"I'd really like to nail her," Tony said later that evening when somebody brought up that woman's name. "Except she'd probably shoot me down."

It did not seem offensive to Chris that before they had actually had their assignation, Tony was speculating about others. In fact, she heard his musings as both tribute to her, because of the high level of her potential rival, and further evidence of his vulnerability, not having the confidence to imagine Gloria could want him. By this time, of course, nearly everything he said touched Chris to the quick, as if her entire being were a fingernail filed down too far. She sat near him on a white sofa, trying to look dispassionate and polite, even as she hung on his scent. Every once in a while he would breathe in her direction, and the hair on her arms moved.

Almost everyone had left the party. Across the room, in front of the fireplace, Nina seemed deeply, greedily involved with one of the camera crew. That interest came as both a surprise and a relief to Chris. Surprise, because she had always imagined that stars had each other offscreen as well as on, and because she had not thought Nina secure enough to couple with an inferior, as a man would. Relief, because loyalty to a hostess had been stressed at Bryn Mawr, along with language skills, so Chris would have been prepared to step away from Tony had Nina wanted him. Just as she would have surrendered him to Gloria Steinem, whose views she did not particularly share, but whose articulation and hair she admired.

Tony got up from the sofa and passed potato chips, like a monarch donning ordinary clothes to move undetected among his people. "I had these flown in from Safeway," he said to Nina, holding out the bowl.

From where she sat, Chris could see the curve of Tony's buttocks, through his tightly fitted jeans. They were athletically rounded, glorious, moving her as Josh's did. She put him out of her mind more speedily than she had his father, trying to redevote her concentration to that which was centerstage in her life, commanding, Bovarian, rife with tragic implication, the drama of a woman unappreciated, rather than unappreciating. Tony whispered beneath his breath that he would get rid of everybody, have his driver take her to her hotel and then double-back, so no one would know she was spending the night with him. How thoughtful he was, how sweet his sensibilities and firm his bottom cheeks.

She was shaking in the darkness when she returned to him. The air had turned cold; she warmed herself with her own arms. Above the white stucco house a wafer of moon lit the night. Stars clustered, incandescent, constellations she had not seen outside of planetariums moving through unpolluted skies, whole galaxies spinning, glittering through indigo heavens. She rang the bell.

He opened the door, smiled at her, took her hand, moved to usher her inside. "Look at the sky," she said, wanting him to kiss her once, at least, beneath the planets and meteors that sailed in spangled array above them, brilliantly arranged for their tryst, too radiant to be there just for everyone.

"More stars than there are at MGM," he said, and laughed. "You get it? Louis B. Mayer used to say that Metro had more stars than there are in heaven. But with the way things are in the movie business, even on the smoggiest night in L.A., there are more stars than there are at MGM."

"I got it," she said, and wondered why he didn't kiss her.

"I guess I'm probably one of the few genuine stars left."

"Can we go inside?"

"Don't you want to look at the stars?" he asked her.

"If you want to," she said.

He stood for a few seconds, craning his neck backwards. "Nice," he said, and led her into the house.

She stood in front of him, reached up to touch his hair. He stopped the motion of her hands, stepped to the fireplace. She felt confused, thwarted. First, he'd dismissed the stars, then brushed aside her tender gesture. Didn't he want her? Didn't he need what was soft, loving?

Blue white coals glowed on the grate. He took a shovel. "I'll just warm up our bedroom."

Heat flooded back through her. It was not that he didn't respond. It was simply that he was as eager as she, hungry to consummate the attraction raging since that long-ago night in the restaurant, with only Evelyn sharp enough to perceive, Pandarus disguised in Dior.

He transported a few coals at a time into the bedroom, then waited, smiling, at the threshold, his hands extended as though ready to whirl her into a waltz. "Well, come on," he urged.

126

She stepped forward. His fingers threaded hers, led her inside. She took a moment to appraise it all, to note the coals glowing in the corner hearth, the white tufted drapes walling the room, sealing the window behind the oversized bed, giving it an aura of mausoleum. Fitting, she supposed, auguring a love so complete you could die having had it.

"You like my place?"

"Yes."

"My place likes you." He kissed her, first on the outside of her lips, then deeply, his tongue thrusting all the way inside her mouth. It was minty on top, but sour on the bottom. Harry's mouth was clean throughout, like the rest of him, as though he managed to shower even there, running torrents through his teeth. She felt disloyal thinking about him, and brought her attention fully to the hands siding her breasts, measuring, appreciative, if a little too hard-pressing.

Releasing her, he reached into the closet and handed her a nightgown, red chiffon, laced at the bosom. She noticed his hands for the first time. To her surprise, the nails were bitten down to the pinks, dirty underneath what was left of them. She tried to concentrate on the lingerie. Did he have it on hand against someone's coming to fondle him back into cheerfulness, like Cinderella's slipper kept on tap by the prince? Was she the right size?

She hurried into the bluebird-tiled bathroom. On the plane coming down, she'd drunk tea; the little packet of sugar the attendant had given her had a bluebird on it. As with all the desperate voyages Chris had made in her life, it appeared rife with symbolism, almost as heavy as the eyes with which she'd searched the symbols out. A bluebird had seemed too obvious, simplistic. That she stood, now, in his bathroom, bluebirds flying the walls, struck her as neat, not in the California sense of the word, but the cosmic. How well designed it all was.

That which was offered on the plane as the point of the journey, manifested in his bathroom. She slipped the nightgown over her head.

Her breasts were a little too full for the tightness of lace across them, so they bulged from the top, transforming her into the heroine of an eighteenth-century novel, featuring procrastinated rape. Well, she would not procrastinate too long. She opened his medicine cabinet, rinsed her mouth with the minty solution she found there ("Gargle me," it called out to her Alice), crushed some sweet-smelling violet granules between her fingers, patting the crystals onto her breasts and her thighs.

She looked at herself once, critically, in the mirror. The sun, in the worshipful, oiled consecration she had made of herself, had toasted her skin to the color of hazel nuts, making her teeth and the whites of her eyes seem to glow, picking up the deep brown of her irises, turning them chocolate. Her hair had an ashen tint to it, softening the brown. Her body, except for the heaviness of breasts, was slender, graceful. That still surprised her. She looked to herself like a woman used to being desirable. In her mind she always expected to see the chubby little girl who had lived for so long a time, more than two thirds of her life, really, enough to turn her brain fat, give her fat eyes, clouded with her picture of herself, and her immaturity. She was amazed to see who she really was, not quite convinced of that pretty woman's reality.

He was in bed waiting for her, underneath the covers, backlit by the glow from the grate and the rectangular dial of the radio. Music, gently middle-of-the-road, beamed from a station in Texas, pervaded the room, carried her to him on a gentle tide.

His arms went around her. She moved to return his embrace. But her hands were locked at her sides, fixed by the iron pressure of his wrists, a wrestler's grip, souvenir of his earlier career. His lips were harsh on her mouth, moving down to her breasts. "Jesus, they're gigantic," he said, burying his face between them.

Her fingers pried loose, moved towards the unruly tousle of his hair. "Don't do that," he instructed, annoyed, and, lifting her nightgown, swooped down like a carrion bird to bite her mons.

She almost protested. But insecurity and good manners bound her into silence. She was not rude enough to make him feel he was less than a wonderful lover, not experienced enough to know if, in fact, that was what he was. Perhaps those who danced more frequently in the courts of Eros, having tired of the ordinary, thrilled to being bitten in such places. Like those who marched to a different drummer, perhaps they fucked to different pipes. It was doubtless her own limitations that made him seem marauder, transformed him into Hun, pillager, herself a village. It was inconceivable that this man for whom so many women hungered could know nothing about a woman's body.

She thrust herself forward, trying to get him to move onto his back, as though by taking the initiative, she could gentle the motion, slow his attack. "Okay, okay," he muttered, tolerant, rolling over.

He was not even hard. It saddened her as much as it surprised her. Harry had only to touch her, to grow massive. She considered it his weakness, to find her so exciting, rather than Tony's not to. She moaned, and pressed her breasts against his penis, felt the stirrings of life, ministered to his oddly abrasive balls with her nipples. He was erect now, reaching for himself, pulling her rudely towards him, penetrating her with no preparation, jamming into her, crying "Yeah, yeah, yeah, yeah, yeah," like a Classic Comics version of Molly Bloom.

Sorrow washed over her, little tides of compassion. How

129

terrible to be the symbol of it all, and not understand, not know. His inadequacy touched her more deeply than technique might have, almost as deeply as gentleness would. She groaned, as adept at pretending as he was offscreen more generous. And while, all over the world, women fantasized that the husbands that rode them were Tony Candella, Chris imagined that Tony Candella was her husband.

Just before she dropped off to sleep, the radio played "The Impossible Dream," followed by the theme from *Love Story*. Chris was nearly seized by a fit of giggling, conjecturing that God, in a bawdy mood, was so in tune he had even programmed a station in Texas to illustrate what an ass she was. In the morning, she awoke enraged. What had she done? Why? She tried clearing out of herself, with a bath, the anger, the remorse, nearly scalding her skin with the temperature of the water. Tears brimmed in her eyes, so the bluebirds seemed to float around the walls. (*"Ecch mir a bluebird,"* her grandpa would have said: *some* bluebird of happiness she had flown into.) She dropped the violet granules into the tub around her, letting them dissolve with her disappointment.

But what kind of a woman was she, judging her love by how he was as a lover? Wasn't that shallow of her? More shallow than anything Tony had done? Perhaps it wasn't lack of consideration that sent him plundering so clumsily around her body, but simple passion, hunger that could not be controlled by anything so contrived as technique. She would not be swayed by her great passion turning out more travesty than Traviata. By the time she came out of the bathroom, she had persuaded herself the infatuation continued. Still asleep, he seemed to share her conviction: his hand was defensively clutching the back of what she now realized was his toupee, as if he had to keep her from ruffling it, driven by affection.

The more flawed he was, the greater became her sympathetic passion; when she saw the lifts inside of his shoes, she nearly swooned. The poor soul. No wonder he considered himself vulnerable. A crueler woman than she would have laughed, might even, God forbid, have said to the *National Enquirer* that the women who thought he was so terrific should know what she knew. Shorter than he seemed, balding, and a bust in bed. He became, in an aggregate of the pitiable, irresistible.

She wanted to indulge him, give comfort. Wasn't that a major portion of loving, to give comfort? Tender sweetness to buffer sadness, excuse the faults that were not really faults at all, except the world set up such false, overwhelming expectations. It was all right, she wanted him to believe, not to be tall, to lose your hair, to fail as a cocksman. Admirable, even, to be other than a blade, when your sword was reputedly so sharp, and God knew there were ample opportunities to have it honed. She felt affection for him, passion basted with rue. He seemed like her long-lost, never-was friend Marilyn, dead because she hadn't been whore enough. Had she had the mentality of a whore, she might have been contented to be used. But always she had searched for magic, teachers, something that would lift her above the body people saw, make clear her sensitivity, her longing for the spiritual, the intellectual. Chris was sure she could sense that same yearning in Tony.

She made breakfast for him, scrambling the eggs with devotion, seasoning them with solace, her adolescent captivation restored. She felt slightly wounded because he made plans to be with his buddies for the day and didn't invite her along. As if she couldn't get enough of him, resented his wanting to buzz motorcycles in the desert.

"All these honcho games," she sulked unprettily, hating to lose him, not being able to stand being without him, she was

131

sure. "You don't even care what beauty is. You don't even watch the sunset."

"I'll watch it tonight," he said, quietly, charitably. "I'll watch it with you if you'll let me."

They watched from his patio. She could hear the irregular, hurried rhythm of his breathing, sense his impatience. She did not delude herself it was restlessness to be with her. He'd invited his cohorts back to a barbecue after their afternoon of motorcycle riding, sparing them the option of giant shrimp.

"That's nice," he said, as the sun sank behind the left nipple of the curious mountain.

"It isn't over yet," she said.

But he was already barbecuing, his attention on the sizzle of beef, rather than the dazzle of sky.

The hamburger meat had been flown in that day from Hughes Market in L.A., on the private plane he'd rented to the movie company for the duration of filming, with the small proviso he could bring in friends, and necessities, like hamburger meat. After they'd eaten, the group, consisting of Tony's driver, wardrobe man, dialogue coach, and chiropractor moved inside the living room. They started playing a game, each one having to tell a tale that was either a lie or a true experience, the others guessing which. The dialogue coach, a tall, lean brunette with a flatter Midwestern accent than Tony's, told in garbled tones of living in an apartment in New York, in a building across from a well-known stage actress who exercised naked in front of her window.

"Did you use it as a visual aid?" Tony asked. His friends fell down laughing, slapping their thighs, rolling around on the floor in a display of mirth that made Sammy Davis, Jr., seem restrained.

Chris tried to become a part of their laughter, joining in, struggling not to seem alienated, apart from it, croaking as the laughter was, overly hilarious. In truth, she had always had a curiosity about the locker room, what went on there. It was too deep a wound in Harry to ask about; her connection with jocks was in other ways limited. So here she was, finally, one of the boys. And what boys. It intoxicated her, acceptance into the fraternity. There had been no sororities at Bryn Mawr to encourage people's feeling set apart; she'd taken that wisdom with her, steering away from joining clubs. But how wonderful it was being let in, to a brotherhood. Her delight deepened because of the obvious ease Tony felt with his friends. Real love, she understood, demanded nothing of the beloved, not even that he be as happy with her as he was with his buddies.

"Who was it?" she asked the dialogue coach. Tony had guessed the story was a lie, as had the other three. Only Chris had labeled it truth, appraising the dialogue coach as not inventive enough to have made it up, which correct estimate entitled her to a free question.

"Lotte Lenya," said the dialogue coach, sending them all to the floor again, rolling around, laughing.

She was not afraid of their telling she was with Tony. They were obvious Musketeers to his D'Artagnan, pledged to silence, loyalty, not only friendship, but their payrolls depending upon it. She was his now, marked, staked out, more respected for being chosen by him, interesting him enough for a second evening. Gamely, she played with his friends, and when they departed, well after midnight, even more gamely slipped into the nightgown, as if there were something really to look forward to.

She went into the bedroom. The bedside lamp was on, so she could see him clearly. He was lying on the bed,

133

naked—totally covered with hair. That part she hadn't absorbed in the darkness, not having time or chance to touch him. All the more she loved him. His having so much fuzz on his body, and so little on his head, deepened her humanity, as if the more cruel ironies were tossed him by nature, the more kindnesses had to come from her. Touching him, though, was another story. Harry's skin was satin, warmed; Tony's was silken Brillo. She reached behind him. Even the curve of his lower back, his buttocks were furred. Appalled at her feeling of repugnance, she ran her tongue the length of him, and came to rest where she found no hair: his toes. Generously, she began to suck them. When she did that to Harry, he would groan with pleasure, the tip of him beseeching her, bobbing up and down slowly with every touch of her tongue, signaling her like a buoy, begging attendance with her mouth, importuning her lips to the core of his longing.

She waited for Tony to call her north, to entreat her to go down on him, or, in this case, up, afraid to look, afraid to check whether that, too, was pelted. But her worry was uncalled for. He had, apparently, no great need of her personally, no wish to cajole her into service. She could hear him beating like the wind above her head, raised her eyes to see him grasping himself with forefinger and thumb, whipping away.

At the last minute, he seemed to remember her. "Watch my face while I'm coming," he said.

It was, she had to admit, an impressive performance, filled with contortion and grimace as real as though he were actually experiencing something besides himself, death perhaps, or feeling. After he was valiumed-out unconscious, his hand protectively on the back of his hairpiece, Chris closed herself in the bathroom and laughed out loud. Not so much at him, as at herself: he hadn't even needed her there. For all her anguish. After she had practically sprinkled herself with fairy dust to deeper enchant him. She had pictured herself as the heroine of a great romance, and had turned out to be a bit player in his porno fantasy. How foolish women were, herself especially. And how perfect for her part of the American dream that she had looked to a movie star for the thread to the cosmos, and found only a needle.

"You're a much better person with Harry around," Nina Warren said in the bar of the Playa de Cortés. "No wonder you ask his permission. You're silly without him."

"I am?"

"You behave like a little girl," said Nina reprovingly.

Chris could not tell if Nina was making reference to Tony. As far as she knew, none of the company, except for his retinue of loyal followers, had any idea there had been something between them. There hadn't been, after the second night. Three hookers had been flown in on his private plane, like hamburger from Hughes. Chris's relief had been monumental, perhaps outdistancing even Tony's.

"It's hard to believe you're the same woman who writes those songs," Nina said. "People see you mooning around so dippy, so childish. They don't realize when it's over you go back and use it all, change it into poems and melodies and lyrics. I wish I could do that, but I sure don't wish I was as silly as you are." She took a long drink of her tequila sunrise, drained it of everything but the bloody splash of grenadine.

Chris studied Nina for levels of approval, searched her animated face for the judgmental, saw nothing that would indicate she was talking about sex. She envied Nina's guilelessness, humping her brains out, not trying to make it into anything, no apparent guilt, no backward glances, just doing it, like setting-up exercises in the morning. Why couldn't Chris emulate that uncomplicated approach, letting sex go for what it was? Obviously it was too late for that now, since attachment was programmed into her in superabundance. Besides, she would not be so foolish again. Not now that she really appreciated her husband.

"He's coming for Easter," she said to Nina.

"Who?"

"My husband."

"Oh, good. For a minute I thought you were talking about the Second Coming, and You Know Who. I couldn't have handled that. It's enough that you're silly."

"I won't be anymore," Chris said, chastised, littler even than the little girl Nina so objected to. "They're all coming for Easter. My children, too."

"Splendid," said Nina. "I like you better when you're intelligent."

All the arrangements were made. Harry was excited to get her phone call, too wise to have instituted the communication himself, too smart even without Harvard. Street smart, they called it in New York. But it was more than street smart, it was Marriage Smart. Giving her enough freedom to keep her tied.

They arrived on Palm Sunday, her husband and her beautiful children, the sun breaking around their heads, haloing them with radiance. At the far end of the airport, Tony stood by his private plane, bidding farewell to one of the hookers. Chris saw with sudden and total clarity who the real movie stars were, fell desperately in love with all of them, her family, scrubbed to meet her, cheeks and eyes glowing, heads full of genuine hair.

She introduced Tony to them, saw him check out Harry, eye to eye, wondered how much shorter he was than Harry, really. Saw him check out her son, look at his impressive head, felt the envy that had to be in him, not at the cap of glory alone, but at the gravelly voice, a challenge to pretense; the tough-little-man stance, already, at six, more valid than his own. Saw him look into the black-eyed openness of her daughter's face, with no deceit in it, knew there was nothing that real anywhere in his life, and pitied not only that truth, but that it probably didn't matter to him.

"He walks funny," Harry said, watching Tony retreating into the distance.

"He's been having problems with his back," she explained.

"He probably fell off his shoes," said Harry.

That night, she and Harry made the best love of their married lives, as if he intuited what had been at stake, whose triumph it was now. He gifted her with infinite erotic tendernesses, turning her slowly, like a lamb on a spit, barbecuing her with his tongue. Piercing her. Scalding her womb.

She avoided the movie company for the rest of their stay, frolicking in the primitive pleasures of Guaymas, the touristy joys that none of the company imagined existed. Tony was headquartered at his desert villa, so they never ran into him again.

Never afterward was there reference made to what might have happened in Guaymas. Never was the question asked what she had done before they arrived.

Only once, several months later, did Harry make even oblique mention. Chris was in their bedroom at home, restlessness gone, the flats of her fingers idly moving over the shine of Harry's back, feeling how smooth he was. They were watching a late-night talk show. The guest was Tony Candella.

"I'm a romantic man," he was saying to the television host.

"Is he?" Harry asked her.

"Is he what?"

"Is he romantic?"

She did not answer him. It didn't really seem a question at all, but a disclosure, the other shoe dropping, ending the suspense of waiting, wondering if he knew. More than acknowledgement. A statement. Over the charred bodies of battle, his own Gettysburg Address, a declaration that they were engaged in a great civil war, testing whether that union or any union so conceived, and so dedicated could long endure.

Four

A FTER CHRIS returned from her trip to Guaymas, the
fiasco with Tony Candella that proved such an un-
solicited boon to Harry, and to Harry and her, she
settled into her marriage with a sense of total joy, a new
awakening. From her kitchen window, she could watch the
morning flutterings of a family of blue jays, fattened by
breadcrumbs she threw them. So the bluebird at the end of
the journey hadn't been the one on Tony's bathroom walls.
Gore Vidal was right without meaning to be: the bluebird *was*
in your own backyard. Even bromides arranged themselves to
her satisfaction.

It made life very simple, being in love with her own husband. She never had to be on edge at parties, like the women
who were still searching, their dissatisfaction only a shade less
obvious than their cleavage. It came as a great relief to know
for sure there was nobody better out there.

Like the wily, aggressive blue jays in her backyard, her
house was not quite what she had conjured in her mind,
nothing eastern shore of Maryland about it, but picturesque
all the same. On a palm-lined street in the flats of Beverly
Hills, it glowed like a greeting card from Mexico, black tile
roof, white stucco, black iron shutters, lacking only bright
bougainvillea over the eaves to make it a miniature Playa de

Cortés. She had great affection for that hotel now, for the locale of Guaymas, a sentiment close to the alumni-ish loyalty she felt for her college, as if Guaymas had been the site of her continuing education, her most important extension course. She considered herself graduated with honors, grown up at last, the spectre of her lingering adolescence banished. She forgave herself her childishness because she had never had a chance to exorcise the girl. Now, the woman was coming to rest.

She adored her children, she loved her husband. He had returned from that same holiday with the tacit understanding that their future depended on its being "their" future, not just hers. A friend of Harry's from the record days had fallen on hard times. As the road to hell was paved with good intentions, the drives of Beverly Hills were lined with promising, gifted people who hadn't connected. To be a man in the world was to run the risk of failing. To be a man in glittering sectors was to run the risk of failing conspicuously. Together, Harry and his friend opened a health food store. Anguish made positive was a wish to restore. So health flourished in California, an entire culture of anguish made positive.

Harry did well in the health food business. It did not return his easy jocularity, strip him of the gray disappointment hanging over him like an old man's shawl. But it pleased him to be making money. His pride was to some degree repaired, as well as a certain dignity of posture. If he could not quite achieve the swagger of those who had made it in snappier tempos, he could at least square his shoulders again.

He took strength from Chris's renewed attachment. In his "Bagel Days," as he called them, the Bronx equivalent of Salad ones, he was used to being doted on, by relatives, coaches, even the men he served under in the Navy. In the beginning of his record career, it had been the same: no one just liked him, they were totally won. So he suffered more than alienation when the partiality of his peers was withdrawn from him: he suffered great confusion. He had not changed, only his circumstances had. That this was business, and business was basically hard at its heart, or, more accurately, had none, was something he could not quite grasp.

In like fashion, he had been stunned by Chris's pulling away from him. Family, in his estimation, equated with sanctuary, the one place you could always be assured of forgiveness. And he had not committed a crime: all he'd done was not succeed. History offered a pageant of bounders, ne'er-do-wells, none of whom could he take comfort from likening himself to, riddled as he was with conscience, genuine ambition, the irreconcilable need to be a hero. His natural role had always been that of a rescuer, bailing out his team, rushing to the defense of smaller men beset by bullies, joining brawls where the odds seemed out of balance for the weaker adversary. His love affair with Chris had also been a save: he had seen very clearly the pressures she was operating under, and knowing there was no way she could stand up to Evelyn and her family, placed himself firmly between Chris and harm, sometimes even stationing himself in the doorway, her personal bouncer, eighty-sixing the cruelty. Even after he'd pulled Chris like a delicate figurine from her wadding, even after she'd had success, and people knew who she was, she'd periodically backslid into insecurity, succumbing to fear, doubts about herself. At such moments he would soothe her, as with melody, stroking her back, touching her hair, whispering words of reassurance, ministering affection like balm, as if he could fix her certainty about herself, as no one had been able to fix his arm.

To have her considered a heroine, then, fame being the local measure of mettle, was, although a source of pride to him, a burr. Not that he himself did not think her plucky, resolute, spirited, all qualities that were clearly heroic. But her unflinchingness, her dauntlessness in the face of the over-whelming, were a part of her nature because of his shielding her. As much as he admired her, he wanted to be himself admired. It was inappropriate as well as inaccurate, heroism in a wife.

He did not mean to be prejudiced, tried to shuck off the conventional view of women, even as Chris struggled to rid herself of the conventional view of men. Glorying in her accomplishments, he hungered for them to be matched by his own, all the while laboring not to let his conflicts surface. The important thing was, he loved her, they loved each other. Nothing could undermine that, he was sure. He had told her he loved her, hard as expressed sentiment was for him. He had told her he loved her on every occasion she'd pressed him, and some she had not. When her esteem was at its lowest, and she would go through her bouts of anxiety, when her publisher disappointed her, when the people she'd looked to for ap-proval and confirmation showed themselves as uncaring, he would fill her up with love, spin it round her like a silken cocoon, nourishing her with his concern. Needed, his capacity for giving was boundless, his love unlimited.

To have her withdraw, then, as she had, becoming distant, had diminished him as no career setback could have. That he was back in her life, that they were once again a passionate part of each other, relieved him as from a high fever. He could sleep at night without the muscles of his face contorting. He could shave without avoiding his own eyes.

Chris, in turn, was fortified by his trying again. It was a testament to her, the testament to himself, as though he understood, finally, that a man did not have to be embattled by a woman's seeming strong. She was not really strong, except where her will was concerned. Her will had been indefatigable. Having fixed very early on the conviction that life had meaning, she had no choice but to be a survivor.

Anxious to see how it all came out. Waiting for the forces of good to triumph. Having the temerity to expect them to.

She absolved herself for her indiscretion in Guaymas, since it had, in fact, deepened her love for her husband, her gratitude for her children, rearranged her priorities and even her appraisal of what glamour was. "Tony Candella Saved My Marriage," she could fantasy on the cover of the *Ladies Home Journal* as she did her supermarket shopping. There was joy now in the choosing of produce, complete attention she could pay the selection of each egg, finding interest where before there had been only chores. She strode through Safeway with the amused realization that she was delighted with what she had. Lives that counted were in her hands, and the fruit she picked to feed them. Peace. It came as a surprise for her. What she had always imagined happiness was action.

She reconsecrated herself to her children, extending the same forgiveness she bestowed on her infidelity to her past neglect of them. In the bad years with Harry, she had handled her disappointment by focusing all her energies on her work, welcoming promotional tours: getting her songs plugged, taking the energy and new friendships on the road like plasma, to restore, revitalize. Harry had always been home, so there had been no need to worry about the children. Less worry than if she had spent too much time with them. Much as she loved them, she had nagging feelings of incompetence in their presence, lacking the selfless gift of being able to deal with vomit, cuts, household accidents, without herself becoming sick, terrified. Harry was at his finest at such moments, like the best fireman at a disaster, soothing, chastising, filled with pity and mercy and warnings against future sharp edges, not watching what you were doing.

Besides her natural inability to cope in a crisis, there were in Chris seeds of her mother. She could feel them bursting inside her at moments of provocation and stress, little buds of

Evelyn, fury at the children, violence. She tried not to give in to anger, but it frightened her that it existed in her. She understood that her mother's rage had come from over-whelming frustration at life's not turning out the way she expected, at men's not being the solution, at having never fulfilled any potential of her own, in her delusion that women's measure was strictly the measure of the men they attached themselves to. The wrath ofthat disappointment had erupted on her children. Having passed her mother in enlightenment, she was sure, it disturbed Chris that she could feel as furious with her daughter as her mother had been with her. The boy played her with cleverness, knowing he had her captive; he was wily as well as winning, so sidled up to her favoritism. But the girl had angry eyes: she could not forgive her parents the second child. She would explode in little tantrums, triggering Chris's buried hostilities towards Evelyn, turning her into her own mother. It was a loathsome chain of reactions, like a horror movie gone psychological, becoming that which you most feared.

So all in all it had seemed simpler, safer to leave the children to Harry, saving herself for the good parts, the fondling, the holding, the outings, the singing of lullabies. It was the love in her, after all, that she wanted to transmit to those around her, the poetry in her spirit that she wanted to trans-late into song, affection she hoped to transfuse to her children, not rancor. It shamed her that there was anything unkind inside her, so rather than reveal herself as flawed, she con-signed them to Harry. Besides sparing her, it had seemed a generosity to him, making him feel useful, which there was no doubt he was, when you saw him with the children.

But now that he was working again, had a business of his own, Chris wanted to reclaim them. Now that she was glad to be in what she had begun to regard as a trap, she struggled for convention, hungered to be their mother. There was a kind of religiosity in her new approach to home. She would not have minded demeaning herself, doing that which was hardest for her, like scrubbing, even though the maid did it better, and Harry did it better even than the maid. Chris cooked with the same kind of creative devotion she gave to her music, inventing, departing from standard recipes, risking the whimsical critiques of her family. ("Do we have to eat gourmet again?" Josh would frown at her. "Can't we have hamburger, like regular people?") And when they weren't at school, or with their friends, she played with her children. Read to her children. Tried to comfort pains she could not perceive but understood.

The only residual effect of the seizure Josh had suffered as a baby was a slight degree of what the doctor called "gross muscular discoordination." So from the time he was old enough to hold a ball, Harry worked out with him, bringing him along through T-ball until he burst full bloom into the nine-year-old ranks of Little League, outsizing all but the twelve-year-olds on the team. Gamely, Caroline joined the minor division, endeavoring to win at least a small piece of the macho pie, to capture Harry's attention. She had the natural heavy-footedness of her mother and, unacknowledged, her mother's contempt for the athletic. But her longing for her father's regard sent her plodding twice weekly to second base until he criticized her fielding and she quit the team.

"I've outgrown Little League," she said to Josh, hoping he would have the sense to take a cue of maturity from her and lose interest, retiring their father from the ball fields, where he went faithfully, daily, it seemed to Caroline, even now that he was back at work.

"That's because you stink," said Josh. He had grown into a burly child, caps of curls arguing the cherub in him. He was as husky as Caroline was long and lean, embarrassed still at being tested out as mentally gifted, when all he wanted was the life of a jock.

Chris felt little waves of love and loss when she looked at them, because the babies were gone and she hadn't studied them enough, condensed them like a fragrance, a sachet she could put in her drawers and smell always as they had been, a memory lingering on her clothes. But aside from darts of wistfulness, because there was no way to squeeze them back down into what they had been, her feelings were those of contentment. There was no question in her mind she was one of the fortunate women. God had proven not only didactic but entertaining, having moved her through a ribald Wife of Bath adventure in Guaymas, to serenity, itself vaguely satiric in Beverly Hills.

The restless women of the neighborhood talked of earthquake weather, when the air was very hot and very still. Chris refused to think of earthquake. Along with consciousness-raising tendencies, living in California also carried with it the risk of metaphysical inclinations. She had come to discover that that which you feared, you often brought on yourself, that those around her who worried most about illness were those who were most often ill. So she would not allow herself to think about earthquakes, because she didn't need disaster in her life. Still, she could not help noticing how silent it was.

Nor did she entertain for long the thought of being other than prosperous. She tried not to focus on money, since it had been so prominent a part of Evelyn's catechism, leading to what Chris regarded as that woman's spiritual ruin. Worry about money made you small, as worry about illness made you ill. In the eyes of the community, ever on the alert for failure as it was for earthquake, Chris was a success. Although it had been a number of years since a song of hers had broken through at the top of the charts, she had been consistently productive, hardworking, adept at earning a living. True, there were moments of doubt, times when she wondered if people wanted her any more, when performers turned down what she considered the best of her songs, recordings were buried, hits failed to materialize. Like the shock of finding out her publisher had been holding out on her, such events always triggered feelings of unworthiness, reaffirmations of Evelyn's long-ago contention that no one would like Chris's songs, because of how unlovable she was. At those times, Harry would nurture her confidence with his compassion, stroking her back, stroking her ego. The abandoned child in her, seeking parental love and guidance where there was only business, the little girl who had looked to her publisher for protection when she couldn't even trust him for royalties, gradually, over the years was put to rest.

So, like earthquake, real financial trouble had never been a part of her thinking, except in a nightmare quarter in the corner of her mind. The quarrel with her publisher she was sure would be resolved. She still found it difficult to believe they had wanted to short her, had, in fact, cheated her of tens of thousands of dollars in royalties, as her accountant speculated, those white-templed, genial fellows in silk suits, guardians of her biggest hit, the song that had become a standard. Her attorney was hopeful of reaching a settlement before the case even came to court, since a number of other writers and creditors had moved against the publisher and collected. There were rumors of personal parties charged against company profits, weddings, vacations in Europe, allegations of drugs bought for record stars and disk jockeys in exchange for air play. More bad publicity was something her attorney was sure the publisher would want to avoid as much as going to trial.

Chris had defrayed the actual knowledge of what the long, drawn-out battle was costing her, asking her lawyer to submit a bill when the case was settled, in the manner of expecting the devil to wait till death to collect a soul. She had a fear of legal fees that amounted to phobia, passed on to her by her mother, who, having finally abandoned her suit against Chris's father for child support, was now suing him for legal fees spent trying to collect child support.

So it was with some apprehension that Chris accepted her lawyer's invitation to lunch, since he had never asked her to lunch before. She was conscious of the ticking of the invisible meter that measured out her life in dollars, how many per hour she did not even dare speculate. She had never asked him his fee, knowing only that he was considered the finest in his field, his firm the best in entertainment law. Always she had been to see him in his office, talking very fast. That he had invited her to lunch, at of all places *Ma Maison*, filled her with genuine alarm.

The restaurant blossomed around her with an insincerity as thick as its sauces, a canopy of bright colors shielding it from sky and any illusion of reality. Bordered with fresh flowers, as well manicured as its clientele, it was distinguished by a snobbism surpassing even its patrons', including the celebrity tic of an unlisted phone number.

"You can't get blood out of a turnip," her attorney said, life juices oozing from his rare *steak au poivre*, as though by way of illustration. "They've gone into bankruptcy."

"But they have all my money," she said.

"Not anymore." He was a pleasant-looking man in his forties, with a Brooks Brothers cut to his collar and his out-look, a demeanor he had transported from Manhattan, and Harvard law. It was a button-down policy of his firm to deliver bad news in person, a tailored courtesy which helped to account for their charge per hour. But it was out of personal esteem for Chris that he had taken her to *Ma Maison*, urging her to order the fresh asparagus even though he intended to pick up the tab, not even charging it to her under *disburse-ments.* "They say they have no assets."

"Can't we take them to court?"

"We could. But it's going to end up very costly, and there's very little chance we could recoup. I don't want to add to your legal bills. There's already a lot on the clock."

Around them, people bustled, even while sitting down. Fallen beauty queens struggled to seem less than middle-aged, former European skating champions inhaled their way through lunch, as though skintight pants were still easy for them. Sons of movie stars ordered white wine in impressive French, their manners as courtly and easy as their fathers', dispelling Rona's allegations that life was not easy for the children of the famous. A table occupied by movie producers and movie producers manqué—all of whom were known to despise each other but could not find anyone else who would eat with them—lied to each other about deals they had and exchanged the latest joke to come out of Hollywood about Hollywood.

"So-and-so dies," related a Mephisto-browed dealmaker, filling in the name of a notorious liar among producers. "And he goes to hell, where he's chained to the most revolting woman ever, for all eternity. So he looks up, and he sees Bo Derek, and she's chained to so-and-so." He gave the name of another notorious local, this one an admitted thief. " 'You don't understand,' says the Devil. 'He's *her* punishment.' "

All the men at the table dissolved into peals of laughter, more raucous than rollicking, the forced cackles of which television tracks were made. All of them had heard the joke before, had called the East coast to be the first ones to in-troduce it there. But apparently it seemed funnier than ever, since the man who was telling the joke was the one the joke was usually told about, and didn't know.

"What am I going to do?" Chris asked.

"I'm afraid it would be wiser to fold. Even if we went to court and got a judgment, there's nothing to go against. The judgment would be unenforceable. And, as I said, I don't want to add to your costs. I wish I could tear up your bill, but I have an obligation to the firm."

"I understand," said Chris, not understanding.

"Have a dessert," the lawyer said. "Lunch is on me."

Perhaps, she thought, as she walked the distance to Harry's store, she had been unwise to give up a policy of God forbid. If she had lived in fear, like the average woman in her civilization, thinking of the worst that could happen, then the worst happening would not have come as such a terrible surprise. She had thought it well-advised to walk, although her lawyer had offered to drive her. Besides good exercise, it was a kind of arrogance, priding herself as she did on being the only one who walked in Beverly Hills, other than the Mexican maids, a habit that not only cleared her head, but pointed up her difference, her individuality, if only to herself and to the police, who had seen her at it often enough in her neighborhood that they no longer stopped her for questioning. But she had worn her silks to lunch, *Ma Maison* in her mind equating with a paddock where everyone had to appear as a champion horse, or risk being made into Jello-O. So she was sweating, the sun plowing through an unhealthy layer of smog to tint the air yellow, to heat her back, to wilt her hair and what was left of her spirit.

Harry would restore her, of course. Harry would say since there was nothing else to do, punt. She had half-waited for the lawyer to tell her to punt when she asked him what she was going to do, because that was Harry's answer in untenable situations, and seemed, in truth, the only solution, getting out of impossible situations with a joke. As panicky as she felt, as drained, as riddled with anxiety, she could almost feel herself being restored a little at the thought of how Harry would handle it, how they would handle it together. The future was before them, after all, the best place for the future to be, she half-smilingly noted to herself. She would write other songs, as he always told her when the one she thought was going to be the biggie didn't make it. They were young—well, fairly young—and strong, they had each other, the children. It was only money.

His store was on the corner of Robertson and Third, in the midst of what was unofficially named "Decorator's Row." With a touch of the personal style he had always shown, he had turned his place, too, into a kind of showroom, for grains and teas and vitamins and fruit, displaying them with the same *éclat* some would exhibit fabrics. There were other stores in town owned by men who had failed in the flashier entertainment enterprises, where those who had torpedoed them in the past were now the most faithful customers, so relieved at no longer being competitors they could not do enough to keep the other in business, executives of note perched among the merchandise like Lana Turner on a stool at Schwab's. No such air of celebrity reigned at Harry's. Those who moved past his cash register had no consciousness of him in past capacities. Not that Harry was embarassed at seeing the people he'd known when his future had glitter on it, before life had proved to be compromise; he'd just never informed anyone he knew about the store. If they happened to frequent it, or come by accident, he almost always made it into the back room before they saw him, so he wouldn't have to hear how pleased they were at how well he was doing.

Chris moved between the cases of kefirs and cheeses, her nostrils pricked by the milkily sharp scent of yogurt, the heat of her cheeks slightly cooled by the proximity of refrigeration, the panic inside her somewhat stilled at the nearness of

Harry, the refuge she knew he would be to her. Through the small glass rectangle in the door into the supply room, she could see the reassuring width of his back, T-shirted, muscular, leaning over bundled cellophane trail packs, raisins and seeds, dates, almonds in ribboned packages, meticulously ordered on top of packing cases. In the midst of the health-ridden order, pencil behind his ear, Harry stood, like a head-liner playing the waterfront, a little too big for the room.

She supposed it was the out-of-placeness of him, the geniality he could no longer display, that loaned to the scene an aura of sorrow. As if he were not consigned to a business that didn't cheer him, or make use of his particular talents, but rather to a curious circle of hell that was Southern California, chained to the unappealing and boring, as the liars were to Bo Derek. Chris had considered relocating, fleeing to the sanctuary of Connecticut, or someplace she had fixed on in her mind as open, honest, Thorton Wilderish, where they could live and flourish as a family, where worth was judged by what you were. It was her greatest hope and, she understood, possibly her fantasy, that such places still existed, where the seasons changed and people didn't. But at any mention of moving, Harry stiffened, blanched, as if he could not bear separation from his wound. In time, she had come to convince herself that she, too, loved living where they were. And it was, as they said, wonderful for the children.

"You look beautiful," Harry said. "Where'd he take you?"

"Ma Maison."

"That'll show up on your bill. How was your lunch?"

"It was a New York phone call," she said, using a private language, a joke of Harry's invention. There was nothing more depressing than a New York phone call, the one where you called your folks and asked how everything was, and they told you.

"What happened?"

"My publisher's bankrupt. I can't get any of my back royalties. There's no point even trying to take them to court, because they're judgment proof." She waited for something wonderful from him, wry, funny, to put it all in perspective, the way only he could, the street savviness that would make it all bearable, comic, human. Instead, he went ashen, his skin a cyanotic testament to what anxiety about money did to people.

"You can't get any of it?"

She shook her head.

"I told you not to go with that lawyer," he said, grim lipped, his mouth a severe thin line.

She struggled to remember. Had he? He prided himself so on not interfering in her career, offering support and reassurance, but seldom saying or doing anything that would lead her in a conflicting direction from the one she'd decided on, or her agent advised. "Harry doesn't know everything," was the anthem her mother had sung all through the marriage, and, as if in acceptance of Evelyn's appraisal, he had gradually seemed to withdraw from putting his opinion on the line. Had he said anything about the law firm? Phrases pulled at her memory, welling up like waves of nausea inside her. She could hear the word *punk*, bugled to her brain, in Harry's voice. Had he said that? Had she failed to pay attention because that seemed to be his appraisal of everyone humorless, in a suit, and a job they couldn't lose?

"You can't blame him," she said. "It would be the same with any lawyer. There's nothing to go after."

"He should have moved in on them years ago. But he was too busy taking his time, piling up goddamned memos, building up your bill . . ."

"Harry, please . . ."

"You should never have gone with that publisher. I told you about them."

155

Had he? It had been early in their marriage when she'd signed with them, and he was still in the record business. They had shared plans and ambition then. Had he told her, or had he been as impressed as she that a company that big and flashy wanted her?

"They offered me the best deal," she said lamely.

"Well, that's you all over, isn't it. Always going after the best deal. No thought of human values." He threw his hands up in despair.

Who was he talking to? All the people who hadn't wanted him? Giving an apologia for his present position, as if *that* had placed him where he was, as if his frailty had been giving too much thought to human values in a society that honored them only at Share shows. Had she been as sensitive as he, would they not be having this discussion now, would she have come away with the small fortune she had lost, was that what he was saying?

"Harry, why are you mad at *me?*"

"I'm not mad at you," he said, furious.

"Hey, Harry. Pussycat, baby, sweetheart." She threaded her voice with irony, using show-biz terms of affection that they both knew meant none. "It's only money."

It was only money. At a time in the country's history when calls to emergency clinics were on the rise, heads of households were pleading for help, alcoholism was on the increase—as was suicide, because of inflation, unemployment, and recession—it was only money.

She understood, without being able to relate to it completely, people's panic about money. She had never really experienced poverty, or even physical inconvenience, except in the beginning of her life, when her parents had moved in with her grandparents and all their grown children, with nine people sharing one bathroom. But that had seemed folksy, homey to her, riddled with the smell of her grandma's cooking, a spate of avuncular arms around her. When Evelyn pointed back to the hardship of those circumstances, Chris remembered them as the happiest days of her life.

Her impoverishment had seemed to be only where affection was concerned. Always there had been enough to eat: too much, from the size of her; always there had been enough for her mother to run away, dragging Chris along, Evelyn's single concession to parental feeling. Most important, there had always been ample funds for education, the center of Chris's life, the one arena in which she could dance, transported to grace by her brain.

That same education, as she grew, had fostered an incipient socialism, an understanding that the world would not be a happy place until everyone was taken care of. That that philosophy was revolting to Evelyn had strengthened Chris's conviction. Not enough, of course, to have her reject the lavish gifts of higher education paid for by her stepfather, but enough to make her contemptuous of him for being a stockbroker. When she finally forgave Sonny that, because of the humane man behind the veneer of limousine, she began to relax about money. There were enough difficulties in the career she had chosen without imposing on herself false pride, unnecessary indigence. She accepted his substance as she would have patronage from the de' Medicis.

So she had never felt what it was to be involved in financial struggle, could not begin to grasp Harry's point of view. In the beginning of their relationship, she had journeyed with him to the Bronx, cast her eyes down at the graffiti on the elevator, as if her being discreet, ladylike, pretending not to notice, would eradicate the simple horrors of a bad neighborhood, a demeanor she carried into everything, averting her glance from the scenes of accidents, as though that would stop the flow of blood. At the same time she was quick to note aloud how noble she thought his rise, how sensitive his person, considering his origins. ("I never even knew I came from a slum," he was to say to their children, "until your mother pointed it out to me.")

He, on the other hand, never fully comprehended her roster of agonies. They had journeyed to the boarding school in Connecticut to which she had been consigned with her parents' divorce, where her adolescence had painfully unfolded. They walked by the lake where Lionel Lindenbaum had betrayed her, never turning up at the boathouse, saw the tennis courts, the glassed-in classrooms bounded by magnolia trees heavy with waxy pink blossoms. "This is where you were so unhappy?" marveled Harry.

Once, in her sixteenth summer, studying music at Tanglewood, Chris had had a debutante roommate who fell in love with a Jewish dental student. "Don't encourage her," her father counseled. "You can think they love each other, and they can think they love each other, but the first time they have a serious quarrel, it'll come out, and she'll say to him, 'You can't possibly understand, because you're a Jew.' " That an equal disparity of thinking could apply to herself and Harry—not because of religion, but money—confounded her.

"Fear does strange things to people," a close friend told her, a man who had stayed their friend throughout the roller coastering of their fortunes. She had begun making the rounds of everyone she knew for counsel, much in the way she had consulted friends in the beginning about whether she should marry Harry.

She had never seen him so joyless, so angry, fury not even slightly contained or disguised. He fumed and stomped around their kitchen with each bill that came in, wondering aloud how they would manage, with her career in the slump that it was, and what they would have to pay the goddamned lawyer. Her gorge would rise at the lumpishness in him, the unprotectingness of her protector, the fear that he should have quieted compounded by his ragings. In fact, she had received the lawyer's bill, been struck nearly insensate by the size of it, called and pleaded for an accommodation, which her attorney said he regretted not being able to give her, because of pressure from the firm. In the end, he agreed to wait a few months for payment. She could not find the courage to tell Harry how much they owed. She wanted to run away, except she was too responsible. Besides, she couldn't afford it.

"But you have to tell him," said her friend Miriam, a delicate-featured, amazonian blonde with gorgeous breasts and an appetite for life matching her size. They were lunching at Phillip Scully's, an unpretentious restaurant on the easternmost boundary of Beverly Hills, adjacent to a motel almost nobody noticed was there, on a street too conspicuous for adultery. "It's a sign of disrespect for Harry that you don't tell him about the bill. My God," she exhorted, fiercely going at her spinach and mushroom salad. "How can you put yourself through that, *alone*? Now's when you need support. That's what a husband is for."

Miriam had some confusion about what her own husband was for. He was a workaholic who was not home very often, in spite of, or perhaps because of, Miriam's having inherited several million from her father. That which should have lessened the pressure on her husband seemed rather to compound it, as though he had to prove he could still be richer than she, even if he worked for a living. "You take him out to dinner tonight and you tell him."

"And if he can't handle it?" Chris asked.

"Then you find someone who can." A giant mushroom was

splayed on her fork, dripping vinaigrette. "For better or for worse. That was the agreement. You're a lovely, intelligent, unusual woman, and if he can't come through at a time like this, then there are plenty of men who would fall all over themselves to be with me." She took a ferocious bite of the mushroom.

Chris wondered if Miriam had heard herself, picked up the slip her tongue had made, a replay of an ultimatum she had given, or failed to give to her husband. "How's Manny?"

"How would I know," Miriam said, chewing. "I never see him."

"You ought to get out more," Chris said. "You ought to use what you are."

"Not me," said Miriam. "I have no wish for a career. A woman's place is in the home."

"You really believe that?"

"Certainly," Miriam said. "Someone has to be there."

Chris invited Harry out to dinner. They ate in silence, pretending interest in the food. Lately they had done almost everything in silence, out of strain and a hostile sanction for peace to continue, as though words might have brought revelations of truth neither was willing to expose. She discerned the real root of his anger, that it was she who played in arenas that were off-limit to him, she who had the creative outlet he had lost. That her accomplishment had brought with it a financial burden was intolerable to him. All of that she fathomed. What she still could not comprehend was how ugly money had turned him, stripping his features of sweetness, making him droop lidded, deadening the color of his skin, the light in his eyes.

They walked home from dinner. She could feel him tolerating her custom of walking, regarding it as one of her cloying idiosyncrasies, like searching for God. Unmarked by him were her experiences of tree-shaded bridle paths, clumped geraniums fronting the sidewalks, jacaranda blossoms like lavender tree fairies fallen to earth, enchanting her footsteps. He agreed to walk with her this evening without protest or comment, intuiting there were revelations coming.

She told him about the lawyer's bill, her tongue thickening on the figure owed. "They're kidding," Harry said. "Thirty-three thousand? What the hell for?"

"Depositions, disbursements. Lawsuits are expensive. I'll show you the bill."

"You show me nothing. Throw it away. Don't pay them."

"We have to pay them."

"And what'll they do if we don't?"

"They'll sue."

"Perfect," Harry said. "If they represent themselves, they won't collect shit."

"But they'll come after us."

"Don't include me in, this. It's your problem. Say you're bankrupt, like your publisher did."

"But we have assets. The house. Your store."

He turned so pale he looked luminous: she could see him against the night. "They can come after my business? I bust my ass to get it going, and they can come after *me?* Because of what *you* did?"

"Harry . . ."

"When they couldn't even get our royalties?"

"*My* royalties! *My* royalties!" Exasperation flared up in her, blotting out vision. "You finally have a chance to carry me! What about all the years I carried you?"

"I see. How long have you waited for that one?"

"As long as I could. I probably would have waited longer, only you didn't let me." Waves of disappointment rose in her, sickening her. "For better or worse," she said lamely.

"When does it get better?" he asked, as though it were the moon that pulled at him, the planets and stars that placed themselves in opposition to his happiness.

He didn't have the money for the lawyer. The store was showing a profit but just enough to keep ahead of the bills, which were monumental with inflation, without the balloon of lawyers' fees. He told her to tell them to shove it up their ass. She didn't have the nerve to tell them anything. She was afraid of lawyers, afraid of their ability to make trouble, and make it legally. She was afraid, too, that her inability to pay them might cause a finger to be pointed at her in the community, might make more glaring the length of time that had passed since her last marked success. Everyone assumed she was rich. To admit she was not, to fall seriously and publicly into debt, might not just cover her with scorn but also cloud her chance for any future success. People only liked to do business with those who didn't need it. She sold her engagement ring to make a payment to the law firm, not telling Harry it was gone because she'd learned better than to tell Harry.

As once, long ago, romance and marriage had been the center of her dreaming, she now began to fantasize about divorce. She did not have the courage herself to move in that direction, did not dare allow the strain it would be on the children, or risk their choosing to be with Harry. Instead she took her consolation from the marital rifts of her friends, drinking in terrible news, pumping women for details of divorces as she had once been greedy for the particulars of weddings. As previously she'd believed in the myth of romantic marriage, she now began to believe the myth of romantic divorce.

"Well, I thought of using Marvin Mitchelson," said Miriam, "but I'm afraid he's a little too show biz. I want this to be an ending with dignity, nothing Lee Marvin about it. And Roy Cohn would kill Manny. I don't want to hurt him. I just want out."

She and Chris were lunching at Scully's again, and, to show the extent of her rebellion, Miriam had ordered chicken Wellington at lunchtime, having abandoned the charade of keeping herself in shape, she'd announced to the restaurant. No more salads. Breast of chicken sautéed in butter, with pâté, in a homemade pastry crust. The hell with all of them. "I had the locks changed while he was out of town. Of course the impact was somewhat lessened by the fact that he didn't come home for three weeks." Miriam cut through the tender gold pastry, took a forkful of delicate white meat, propelled it eagerly into her mouth, chewed it as though it were Manny.

"What did he say when he found out?"

"He begged. He pleaded. Told me how much he loved me. But I did what my lawyer said. I visualized Manny in a motel in Cleveland, lying on top of a blonde, and just hung up."

"Was there another woman?"

"I doubt it. He didn't have enough for me." She impaled a broiled mushroom, dripping butter.

"Who's your lawyer?"

"Elmer Chadsey. Not as merciless as Roy Cohn, but enough. I almost used Adam Wilkerson, the one from San Francisco, he's so attractive and calm. But it seemed better to have a local, don't you think? He knows *so* much." Her green eyes sparkled as they had a few years before when she'd talked of the landscape architect laying out the grounds of her home, the one she was going to live in, forever, with Manny.

"What are you going to do?"

"Who knows? Go to the Riviera, Paris. I haven't really made any plans. I'm just luxuriating in my privacy."

"I thought you didn't like being alone."

"That was only when I thought I needed him. Now that I made the decision to get him out of my life, I dance around the bedroom."

"Alone?"

"Certainly, alone. I thought I was hungry for affection, because I wasn't getting any from Manny. What I really wanted was seclusion, the chance to be by myself without the hurt of waiting for him to come home. I'm orgying in solitude. It's better than fucking."

"I can imagine," said Chris, although she couldn't. All her early life she had lived in dread of loneliness. Now it seemed a privilege, one that would probably elude her because there was no way to have a life separate from Harry, not without selling the house and paying the lawyers, whose fee would doubtless be even more terrifying than the one she was already having to deal with on the quiet. And maybe she would lose the children. The children.

She contacted women she hadn't seen for years, the moment she heard they'd split with their husbands, lived in a wine-littered revelry of vicarious divorce. She took them to lunch at Scully's, like a welcome wagon for the separated.

"You better quit going out to lunch so much," Harry said one evening. "I saw you coming out of Scully's today. That's three times this week. Who's going to pay for that?"

"It's cheaper than getting a *divorce!*"

They were about to eat in the breakfast alcove, even though it was dinner. The dining room was something they never used except for company. They seldom invited friends anymore. There was nothing to celebrate, certainly not life. The breakfast alcove was a little too cheerful for her present mood, even at night, painted bright yellow as it was, hung with shiny copper pots and pans, thickly green with hanging plants, as though there were air there, a jungle of gladness.

Outside, the winter rains had started, sending hillsides sliding into canyons, gouging out chunks of the countryside, like caterwauling harpies seizing with clawed hands pieces of earth as tithe, in exchange for the usually clement weather, the privilege of living in California. Chris did not feel protected by the flatness of their neighborhood, the thickness of the walls, her house. There was no such thing as a fortress; she understood that fully, now. Money pulled at people the way the rain was tearing at the roof. The plaster on the wall at the top of the stairway was turning to the consistency of wet Saltines.

"Dinner," she called to the children. Josh was finishing his homework in his room. She could feel him making an ostensible show of the effort he was putting in, against the pounding of notes from the living room, where Caroline practiced the piano.

"You know, it's very hard to concentrate," Josh said, once they were all seated at the table. "With Rachmaninoff in the living room."

"Who?" asked Caroline. Her shoulders were curved slightly forward in a posture she'd adopted since the realization that her breasts were going to be bigger than Brooke Shields's.

"She doesn't even know who Rachmaninoff is," Josh sneered. "And she wants to be a pianist."

"Oh, *that* Rachmaninoff," Caroline said.

Josh cut his meat. "Half of that," instructed Chris. He cut it in half, looked to make sure she had seen, and, fork in his left hand, raised it to his mouth. "Use your right hand," she said.

"Don't you ever get tired of watching me."

"No."

"I can't really blame you," he said. "I *am* great looking."

"And *so* humble," said Caroline.

"You're just jealous because you don't have anything to

brag about." He looked at his mother to see if she noted his wit, then turned to his father. There was an expression on Harry's face that made Josh eat faster. "Tommy Ehrlin's parents are getting a divorce," he said, swallowing before he said the word.

"I'm sorry to hear that," said Harry.

"His father's taking him to Hawaii for Easter. Where are you taking me?"

"The Santa Monica pier."

"How come we don't go on real vacations anymore," asked Caroline. "A whole bunch of my friends are going to Palm Springs."

"We can't afford it," said Chris.

Harry looked at her with hostile eyes, darts of yellow in the green, like flashes of criticism. That she told the truth about money, when it was the custom of their particular society to do anything but, added to his anger at their circumstances. It was a constant prickle in his spine that his car was not a status luxury automobile like those of most of the people in Beverly Hills, who, though they might have been hurting, at least had the courage of their pretensions.

"Why can't we go someplace cheap, where we could fish?" Josh asked.

"Fish, yucch," said Caroline. "Why don't we go to Palm Springs and play tennis?"

"You weren't invited," Josh said.

"Of course she was," said Harry.

"Then we're going? I can use my new rod?" Josh had been gifted for Christmas with an expensive fishing rod, a boy's sportive equivalent of the Mercedes Harry had been unable to buy himself. The costliness of it riled Chris as much as the diamond earrings Harry had given her, with the falsehood implicit in them. A fishing rod was a fishing rod. Her ears should have stayed intact, without diamonds they couldn't afford.

"Maybe," Harry said. "How about where they made the movie with that big stiff?"

"What big stiff?" Chris asked, knowing perfectly well who he meant. In happier days, she might have made jokes to herself. Harry was too generous: the most she would have described Tony as was "a little stiff."

"What's his name?" he said. "Where we went to visit you."

"Guaymas?" said Josh. "Could we go back to Guaymas?"

"Guaymas is the pits," said Caroline. "Mango pits." She shrieked at her cleverness.

"Aren't you embarrassed that you have her for a daughter?" Josh asked Chris.

"If we hadn't had her, we wouldn't have had you," Chris said. "She was so wonderful, we thought we'd try for another one."

"You should have quit while you were ahead," said Caroline.

The tension between Chris and Harry transmitted itself to Josh, erupted. He was disruptive in school, as though acting out what was going on in his home, little cracks revealing themselves in him. The easy charm he'd carried cookie-cutter style from his father was transmuted into bluster, braggadocio. Teachers called to complain. Chris tried telling Josh how wonderful he was, to calm him down, holding him, assuring him there was nothing to be worried about. He broke from her grasp, whirled angrily onto the playing fields, as though only with bat against ball could he express himself.

In like manner, Harry made Little League the center of his life. Every afternoon after school he was at the park, pitching to Josh and the other members of the team, fulfilling beyond any obligation his role as coach. In between scheduled games and workouts, he held informal batting practices. It amused him in an ironic way that he pitched the boys nothing but strikes, afternoon upon afternoon, without his arm hurting. He was like a machine, now that it didn't matter, so caught up in his team, he escaped from under his own shadow.

Chris, on the other hand, felt a growing sense of dejection which she tried to counter by taking long walks. But coming home she would feel despair at the sight of her house, as though her spirit were going to be corked up inside it, airless, inspirationless. The house depressed her, black and white as it was, like her life seemed to be now, empty of color.

She decided to paint the front door red. In the absence of bougainvillea—would they ever plant it now, or was it too late for anything to begin?—she thought it would be cheering to have a bright door. She painted it herself, while Harry and Josh were at Little League practice, so she could surprise them. Heartened by her small but glaring achievement, she walked to the game. Red-paint-spotted fingers stretched into the twisted gray metal opening, she clung like a climbing animal to the chain-link fence by Josh's dugout, studying his every motion, giving herself over to full admiration of her son.

"Rally time!" he cried singsong to his teammates, a junior version of Harry, spurring them on to courage, victory in the face of terrible odds, as they came in from the field, four runs behind. His white, green-striped, green-numbered uniform loaned him both swagger and pathos, catapulting him closer as it did to a boy's concept of manhood. To the left of the dugout crouched Harry, in white shorts and a green T-shirt with "Coach" inscribed in white on the back, a gift from the mothers of the team, who sat in the stands regarding with envy Chris's marriage, as she envied nearly all of them their divorces.

"All right," Harry shouted to the first batter, a ten-year-old with yellow ringlets dancing from beneath the visor of his cap. "Make him throw strikes, Andy. Don't help him."

"Be aggressive! Be aggressive!" shouted Andy's father from the stands, having lost his wife to the head of a production company.

The boy fanned his bat, struck at air. "*Strike*," Harry cried, annoyed. "That was at your ankles. Don't help him."

A few feet in front of the dugout, Josh warmed up, swinging two bats. His moves were those of a practiced sportsman, veteran of several seasons in the majors. "Come on," he prodded Andy. "You can do it."

Andy popped up to the infield. A sigh of disappointment emanated from the stands. "It's okay, pal," Josh sauntered past him on his way to the plate. "There's next time."

Chris could see his firm, round bottom pulling at the muddied seat of his pants, wondered why the sight of it stirred her so. Was it memory of baby cheeks, and the tender feelings once offered those, or was it loss, an interdiction on pinching, caressing? Possibly it was just the round little-boy beauty. All the boys had sweet derrieres, as varied in shape as their haircuts, Italian cherubs on display, with Josh the Michelangelo.

He stepped to the plate, half-crouched, bat poised, menacing the pitcher. There was the crack of bat against ball.

"Out of here! Out of here!" cried Harry exuberantly as the ball flew long and high and Josh started a grinning tour of the bases. The center fielder ran back to the fence, jumped high in the air, and caught it. A groan rose from the stands, echoed in Chris's throat. Slump shouldered, Josh circled second and headed back towards the dugout.

"Don't come off the field a loser!" Harry instructed. "Get tough!"

Josh made an attempt to square his shoulders. Bravura failed him. His sweet petulance of lower lip, the pink bud bursting incongruously in the feisty little face, betrayed him, quivering. He stepped down into the dugout, leaned his arms against the wooden siding, rested his green-capped head on the backs of his hands.

She suppressed the impulse to run to him. Why did it have to hurt so much, losing? What was there in human nature that so diminished its own glory by seeking glory?

She studied the field: good healthy boys who didn't sleep at night waiting for the next day's game. Well, when they were men, they would sleep. Why could men sleep, and women couldn't? She and Harry had not said happy words to each other for months now, and yet he slept.

She supposed, to be fair, that sleep in itself was a kind of healing, an escape, a way for him not to have to deal with his discomfort, his unhappiness. But just now she had no particular wish to be fair: she wanted him to be as uneasy as she was. She wished she had the nerve to shake him from his slumber so the two of them could suffer equally.

"What's that?" Harry asked gravely, as they pulled into the driveway. There had been silence all the way home, Josh brooding about the first loss of the season, and Harry contributing to the gloom, taking it all as seriously as his son, his victories now being reserved for the diamond. "What have you done to the door?"

"I painted it red," she said.

"I can see that. Tomorrow you'll paint it black."

"No, I won't."

"It looks like *The Amityville Horror*." said Josh. "I'll be embarrassed to invite my friends. Paint it black. I vote for black."

"Childhood is not a democracy," Chris said. "You don't get a vote."

Harry was out the other side of the station wagon, jaw set, muscles in his cheeks visibly clenched. He spoke over the top of the car, as though it were the Berlin wall. "I want it black! *Black!*"

The argument raged till they went to bed. Listless, wakeful, she heard his snoring as long as she could stand it, and went into the bathroom. Scrawled on the mirror in lipstick was: I WANT IT BLACK! NO DISCUSSIONS!

What rose in her gorge with the greatest ferocity was the fact that he had used her lipstick. Even that. No ownership even with that. "He'll drag you down" Sonny had warned her. Never had he dared imply that Harry would even appropriate her lipstick to badger her. Well, what had she expected? That he would use his own lipstick? That was the real root of her rage, wasn't it? That fear had womanized him—making him petulant, dirisive, weak—all the clichés of character with which men labeled and associated their harridan sisters. Words, concepts as vilifying to men as "aggressive" was to women. She had expected Captain Marvel and gotten someone as frightened and vulnerable as herself.

She slammed into the bedroom, turned on the lamp by his bed. "Get a lawyer!" she shouted.

He opened his eyes, warily, and half-mumbled, half-accused. "How dare you do that! How could you make such a change and not even ask me?"

"You would have said *no*," she yelled. "You know nothing about decorating."

"I know that a red door looks like shit!"

"You don't know everything, as my mother would say."

"Like shit!" he shouted, sitting up, his back against the wall.

"It lifts my heart! If I'm going to come back to this house where I don't want to be with you, there's got to be something that makes me happy!"

"I want it black!"

"Get a lawyer," she said, exhausted. "I'm ready. I'm finally ready."

"I don't have to get a divorce because you're afraid to admit you made a mistake painting the door."

"I made a lot bigger mistake than the door!" She slammed out of the room, noting with pleasure the crash of wood against frame, hearing a picture fall on the other side of the wall. It was only after a moment that she remembered Josh slept with his door open.

Guiltily, she made her way down the stairs, turned on the hall light, peered into his room. His arms were propped up on the pillow behind his head. His eyes were wide open, riveting hers.

"Oh, honey," she said, and moved towards his bed. "I'm sorry if we woke you."

"What were you fighting about?"

"Nothing. It was silly. Go back to sleep."

"Mom?"

"Josh."

"If you and dad get a . . ." he swallowed. ". . . divorce, you know I'll have to go with dad, because you haven't got a steady job."

A laugh escaped her, a gasp of pain made merry, because the world was such a joke. All the years she'd labored to keep her success inconspicuous, so Harry wouldn't be made to feel worse than he felt, so the children wouldn't be confused by her prestige, and their father's lack of it. All the later years when she'd realized there was no need to veil her accomplishment, because the children did it for her, seemingly turned off by what she had done, as though to laud her would be to denigrate their father. Both of them patent male chauvinists, even her daaghter. And now Josh had said what he'd said.

"You understand, it doesn't mean I don't love you."

"I understand," she said, and kissed him, pressed her face close to the pillow, picking up the slightly gamey, sweet, little-boy smell of him. Well, the truth of it was, she supposed, she was a male chauvinist too, hoping he would be the one to grow up a hero, trying to soothe his fears, as unbecoming as they would be to a man. She felt ashamed of herself, even as she was suffused with love for him.

Spectres of her childhood danced in the room. She could hear screams and shouts, the breaking of milk bottles, the hurling of lamps, feel the pulling of her limbs as father and mother fought over her so literally her grandfather had to separate them, screaming they were tearing her apart. Always she had sworn she would never allow that to happen to her own children, never do that, fill them with terrors of loss and separation like she had suffered. Most of her young life she had doubted she would even have children, that anyone would love her enough to want her, to give her children. And now her son was next to her, riddled with a child's worst anxiety. Making terms for his future, arbitrating for her release of him.

"You want to sleep here, as long as you're fighting with dad?"

"No thank you," she pulled herself away, started for the door. "But it's the best offer I've had for a long time."

"See you in the morning," he said.

"See you in the morning," she echoed.

"Love you."

"Love you."

173

"*Bonne nuit.*"

"*Bonne nuit.*" Litany concluded, she moved across the hall into Caroline's room.

"What was all the yelling about?" Caroline asked.

"Nothing. Don't worry about it." She smoothed the covers near Caroline's face, felt the warmth of her cheeks. Why didn't she have the dream for her daughter, project her into the future as fearless paladin? Caroline was the fashion plate, flirtatious, consecrating herself to the superficial, nothing Chris encouraged or demonstrated by example but nothing she wished to interfere with. It was a strain of incipient femininity of the most cliché kind that Caroline rebelliously evinced as though to counter her mother's struggle. Her very nature hearkened back to Evelyn, as though frivolity and acquisitiveness had been passed to her unimpeded through the genes. Why did it come as such a relief to Chris that, if someone had to have these characteristics, it wasn't her son?

"I think you better go on that vacation," Caroline said. "You and dad need to blow off a little steam."

"Is that your advice?"

"Definitely. Even," she sighed, "if it isn't Palm Springs."

Chris made her way up the stairs, her fingers crumbling the portion of wall made soggy souvenir of storms passed. No roofer was available for fixing it, sought after as they were, like movie stars, in the aftermath of floods. So it sat like a sore on ter marriage, a boil that spoke of internal infection. Collected tears.

She went back into her room, switching off the light in the hallway. Harry was sleeping. She couldn't believe it. Sleeping. With all that had happened, with the end of their marriage a distinct possibility, he'd been able to fall back to sleep. She simply could not understand men.

Where had she gone, Diana of the Woods, what had become of her myth? Had there ever been a man who would stand ready to protect a woman, to be always wakeful, to defend her, and, at the same time guard against his own murder at the hands of a would-be successor? Was there ever such a trait in man, even mythically, to be filled with such fealty, preparedness, simply in exchange for a woman's love, and being called king?

Surely, she thought, that myth, like so many things laudatory of man, had been promulgated by men. Women knew better. Women knew their husbands were sleeping.

Five

"JESUS CHRIST," Evelyn said. "Guaymas. How did you find this place?"

"How did you find *me?*" Chris asked, trying to rise above the sudden sensation of drowning. Not enough she had found dead lovers on the beach, been questioned by the police, was in turmoil about her marriage. As if the gods meant to see how many thunderbolts she could field at once, there stood her mother, in the middle of the Playa de Cortés.

The lobby yawned about Evelyn like the mouth of hell, the only locale gaping enough to contain her luggage. It was piled in several red-sueded mounds, while near her, two taxi drivers argued in Spanish over the way they would divide the fifty-cent tip she had given them to bring her and her suitcases, in caravan, to the hotel. "First answer my question. How did you find this . . ." Evelyn indicated the umber-stoned floors, the high, dark-beamed ceilings, bolstered with ancient rail-road ties. "This so-called place?"

"It's where I visited the movie company five years ago," Chris said weakly.

"Well, I can understand its having a certain charm if you're hanging around Tony Candella. But Harry?" Disdain hung in the air, like the scent of mimosa.

"How did you find us?"

"How do I find anyone? How did I find your father to serve him with a subpoena for child support? Tenacity. Genius. Get me a room. Or do people here live in caves in the sides of mountains?"

"Lower your voice, please, mother."

"They can't possibly understand English. Education can have reached this part of the world no more easily than I did. Six hundred Mexicans and their chickens, on a 'luxury' train." She brushed the ghosts of them from her beige linen suit. "I haven't been on a train since my honeymoon with Sonny, who was too much of a coward to fly, not that it did him that much good staying alive."

She ran manicured, black-pearl-ringed fingers through her auburn hair, checking it for feathers. "Why did you pick someplace so hard to get to?"

"We thought it might keep you away."

"Hell hath no fury like a serpent's tooth," Evelyn admonished. "Now get mummy a room at this . . ." She looked around skeptically, at white-painted stucco walls hung with oils of the Virgin, wrought-iron sconces. ". . . hotel."

Behind the large mahogany desk fronting the lobby, with its small wooden mailboxes like beehives, ornate brass room keys dangling from hooks set into the wood, the desk clerk stood looking more pained than apologetic, as if people should know better than to ask him for rooms at Easter time. He was silver haired, with brown skin, slightly shiny, like his hair, as though both had been pomaded. "I'm sorry. We're completely booked."

"What about the bodies they were carrying out when I arrived? Weren't they guests here?" Evelyn smiled, charming herself with her deductive capabilities.

The desk clerk looked extremely unhappy. "Yes, they were."

"I'm not superstitious. I'll take their room."

"The police must examine it."

"Police? Then it wasn't the food?"

"Mother . . ."

"Of course I was jesting." Evelyn smiled, radiating the amount of irresistibility she considered fair portion for an underling in an inaccessible village.

"When they're done, can't I have the room?"

"I will ask the police captain."

"I'll be glad to make it worth your while." She opened her beige lizard purse, pulled out a ten-peso piece. The desk clerk looked unimpressed. "Isn't that enough? How much is that in real money?"

"Forty-four cents," Chris said.

"Oh, in that case," Evelyn took out another one, pressed it into his palm.

"I will do what I can," he said, unenthusiastic.

"You seem like a clever man." Evelyn conjured a lifetime of admiring glances, shot them through the hazel of her eyes. "I'm sure you'll manage."

Once Evelyn entered her room, Chris knew there would be no more sanctuary. What little sense of privacy and preservation she had left, had flown like a winged bird at the sight of her mother. But there was no way she could refuse to let Evelyn have a bath, to cleanse herself of "the nightmare journey," as she put it to Chris, adding that she herself could have easily been a writer what with her sense of imagery, probably more successful than Chris had she only applied herself and not wasted so much time catering to the needs of her husbands.

She was splashing happily in the bathtub, emitting little groans of pleasure at coming to rest in warm water, asking questions that Chris could use as openings to reassure, to flatter. It was her custom, since childhood, to act more or less as a Greek chorus to her mother, sighing when she sighed, lamenting the injustices Evelyn saw heaped on herself. On the occasions when Chris asserted her own arguments and concerns into the soliloquies, she had to deal with accusations of self-centeredness and vanity, none of which she could handle at the moment, so thought wisely to contain. She had not even been able to plead inconvenience to herself in her mother's wanting a bath, even though she knew what Evelyn really wanted was a chance to go through everyone's drawers.

Through the door which Evelyn had left ajar to enhance their camaraderie, Chris could hear the splattering of waters, a merriment, a purge. Bathing was the only activity her mother really enjoyed that did not have hors d'oeuvres or a potential husband in it. "Dead lovers on the beach," Evelyn mused, splashing. "How grisly. What happened?"

"Nobody knows yet."

"Were they young?"

"Yes."

"Then they were stupid to die." Evelyn sighed, deeply, enough air and bathos in it to affect even Chris, heartless as she was, as Evelyn was always telling her. "Maybe they did it to liven things up. Nothing livens things up more than *death*." She paid tribute to the word, investing it with the respect she might have for the extra man at a dinner party.

"What made you come here, mother?"

"Why, I wanted to see my successful daughter, of course. And my adorable grandchildren. Where are they?"

"Caroline's sunbathing by the pool, and Josh went fishing with his father."

"Such devotion. It's absolutely sickening. He must have gotten it from you. It certainly didn't come to him through my genes. How you can still be that much in love eludes me."

"I'm not," Chris said. She sat down on the bed, the nub of

182

the maroon and yellow bedspread scratching against the back of her legs.

"After all, you're my daughter, and blood will tell. You'll grow weary of him one day."

"You're right."

"Granted, you have a longer attention span than most women, but you aren't blind. You'll wake up one morning, the scales will fall from your eyes, and you'll see him for what he is."

"I already have."

"You can't go on forever deluding yourself." There was a sudden silence from the bathroom, palpable, thick with the busy hush of Evelyn reviewing, the wheels of her mind spinning, in reverse. "What did you say?"

"I said I already have."

There was a crash of waters from the tub. In a moment, Evelyn was standing in the bedroom, beach towel wrapped around her, water dripping down her still-remarkable legs. "Are you kidding me?"

"I'm afraid not."

"Afraid? What have you got to be afraid of? That you're finally wising up? Nobody can love anybody forever, especially Harry." She leaned over and kissed her. "Now we can start looking for someone worthy of us."

"Mother, please. Don't make it into a celebration. I'm trying to work it out."

"You've worked it out. The miracle is that you stayed with him as long as you did. That flop."

"He isn't a flop. He's just had a hard time."

"My God, how you go on defending him. Why?"

"Nobody ever loved me before Harry."

"What nonsense," Evelyn said. "That isn't true. Your father was crazy about you when you were little. Of course, he might have acted like that just to aggravate me."

183

"Don't say anything to the children."

"How are they? The little princess, and that adorable boy who hates me?"

"They're all right. Just don't say anything. I don't want to spoil their vacation. I'll talk to them when I've made up my mind, and we're home."

"Very wise. Very wise. I always waited till my children were snug and secure in their own little beds before I told them about my divorces."

"I haven't said that was what I was going to do."

"You don't have to say it. I understand you better than you do yourself." Evelyn patted herself dry, checking her motions in the mirror. "All these years of pretended selflessness. It had to be a strain."

"I wouldn't have been anything without him."

"You would have been exactly what you are."

"He pulled me together."

"*He* pulled you together. He's not strong enough to pull himself together, much less a fierce-willed creature like you. If I couldn't rip you completely apart, how could he possibly have pulled you together. With *that* mother." Evelyn went back into the bathroom, carrying her bathing suit.

"I thought what people were wasn't the fault of their mothers. That's what you always said."

"Well, in his mother's case, I'll make an exception. But I do get weary of being blamed for everything. You blamed me. Your sister blamed me. Sonny even blamed me for Norman. I was only his stepmother. *I* didn't drive him crazy. It was in his genes." She was back out of the bathroom now, in her designer bathing suit, her trim little body slightly rounded through stomach and hips.

"People make their own destinies. You can't just go on blaming your mother. Do I get your royalties? No. Have I ever asked for them? No. If we don't get the benefits, we shouldn't get the blame. Not that I want anything from you. But what you are is what you are, and has nothing to do with me." She started looking through the dresser drawers.

"Will you please stay out of those?"

"You've certainly gotten neater, I'll tell you that much."

"Those are Harry's."

"Fastidious, isn't he? His mother must have potty trained him too early. Not that I blame her. The things mothers have to do. Diapers!" Evelyn shuddered as though the task were still before her, loaded.

"I'm sorry I inconvenienced you," Chris said.

"You needn't be ironic with me, dear. The truth is, I had no idea what to do with you. I'm sorry I wasn't a good mother, but why did you have to be so dependent and *clinging?*"

"I was a *child.*"

"Well, when I was a child, I did things for myself. My mother didn't have time for me. She had too many children, she had to help pop out at the store, she had to clean, she had to cook. She had no time. Nobody took care of *me.* I had to do everything. *Everything.* And do I resent it?" The question hung in the air, trilling with her fury.

"I'm sorry."

"For what?"

"That you didn't have a happy childhood."

"Happy childhoods are overrated," said Evelyn. "I had no time for a happy childhood."

"Well, I want to make sure that my children do."

"You can't live your life for your children," Evelyn said. "If you're going to live your life for anyone, it ought to be your mother." A smile flashed across her face, brightening it, brightening the room. Evelyn's trump card: knowing how outrageous she was, tempering it with charm and the suggestion that she didn't mean the things she said, even though she did. "I read an article that children of divorce overcompensate with their own children, trying to be better parents than comes naturally to them. You really can't love them that much, dear. I mean they're cute, but they *are* children."

"How did you find me?"

"I called your accountant. Don't get mad at him. I told him I wanted to give you some money, because I understood you were having a hard time, and I needed to give it to you right away. It was only a little untrue. I would give you money in a second, if it wasn't all tied up in stocks from those awful people on the elevator who keep giving me bad tips."

"You don't have to listen to them."

"How can I take a chance? I didn't listen to Morton, after years of sitting through his boring stories, eating all those nights at Quo Vadis and never ordering the rack of lamb—he was so stingy. And all I got out of him was his goddamned stock tip. If I had listened, I would have made half a million dollars. How can I ignore the people on the elevator?"

"You never listen to anyone else. Why do you listen to them?"

"Don't get smart with me. If you were as smart as you think you are, you'd be rich, and then you could take care of me, and I wouldn't have to be preyed on by people in elevators. Why is that? Why aren't you rich?"

"My publisher cheated me. I had to sue to try and collect my royalties. I ended up having to pay a fortune to a lawyer."

"You should get a cheaper lawyer," said Evelyn. "You should get a lawyer who would work for you for less and at the same time handle your divorce. Maybe we can find one who'll do it all out of love for you. I'll write to the spa. It's loaded with eligible overweight men, and we'll get a discount for sharing a room."

"I don't want to go anywhere," Chris said. "I'm not looking for another man."

186

"You're too loyal to think about it so soon. That's what mothers are for. Divorced!" she canted, the "Bell Song" from *Lakmé*. "I thought you'd stay married forever, just to spite me."

"I have to work it out by myself, mother. You've got to go away."

"Go away? But I came here to help. Not that I don't have a million places to go, a thousand invitations. Is there anyone attractive here?"

"The most attractive ones are dead."

"It's usually like that at resorts," Evelyn said, and slipped into a chemise cut of the same cloth as her bathing suit. "Oh, you mean the young couple."

"They were such a terrible color." Chris shivered. "I've never seen a corpse before."

"That's because you never went to dinner with Morton," Evelyn said. "Are there any older men here?"

"How can you only think about one thing, and think about it all the time?"

"Well, where do you suppose you got your gift of concentration?" Evelyn asked, waltzing to the French doors, peering down from the balcony at the beach. "I could have probably been a writer myself—you know how many good ideas I have—if only I hadn't wasted myself on my damned husbands. And Morton, he was the worst. Imagine his not leaving me anything." She turned her back on the sea, as if that, too, had yielded up nothing but promises. "But now we can begin again, the two of us. We'll be wiser this time. No more losers."

"Harry isn't a loser."

"You must be realistic. Don't defend him now, when you finally have the sense to despise him."

"I don't despise him."

"Don't deny it. There's nothing so terrible. Most women can't stand their husbands, they just haven't the courage to admit it."

"You're no one to make judgments. You hate marriage."

"I love marriage," Evelyn insisted. "I just hated the men I was married to." She moved to the sink and started mascaring her eyes. "I'm so happy I found you. We'll have such a good time at the spa. Especially now that you're beautiful. You were *not* a beautiful child."

"So you always told me. I remember the day I was going for my first appointment at the Brill Building, I was fifteen, and you said to me, 'Nobody will buy your songs because you're fat. You could write the score of *Oklahoma!* the way you look and nobody would buy it.'"

Evelyn stopped the fluttering of her hand. "How long are you going to go on remembering the things I said to you?"

"Probably all my life."

"That's because I speak truth." The mascaraing recommenced. "Who would have known it was the score of *Oklahoma!*, the way you looked? But look at you now. My God, you're beautiful. You could probably write *My Fair Lady* now."

Chris laughed in spite of herself.

"What's so funny," Evelyn said.

"You are."

"Well, it's nice you've started appreciating me. We'll have a wonderful time at the spa."

"I'm not going to the spa."

"You just keep saying that." Evelyn smiled. "I remember when you said you'd stay married forever."

A wind whipped up from the Sea of Cortés, brisk, unexpected. As it was the middle of the day, the Mexican sun was so intense, that for Chris, lying by the pool, the breeze seemed a forgiving caress, cool fingers whisking the heat from her skin. On the chaise next to her, Evelyn was relating tales of the last three men she had met, who had all been crazy about her, she said, but had turned out unacceptable. The first had used bad grammar, the second wore loud ties, the third Evelyn had introduced to her girlfriend, Mae, just to point out to him how lucky he was to have a woman of Evelyn's caliber. To her astonishment, they had gone away on a cruise together.

"Five weeks to the Greek islands," said Evelyn. "My God, how could he take *her?* She's never even been to the same party as Jackie Onassis." Evelyn suspired her grief at the shortsightedness of millionaires and rubbed some more lotion on her breasts.

The desk clerk had advised her that as soon as the maids had cleaned up the victims' room, she would be able to take occupancy. By now the identity of the dead lovers had been established. The woman, Alana O'Connor, was an heiress from San Francisco, which fact emerged when the police examined her passport case, with the *aviso* that the person to be notified in event of emergency was the Hibernia Bank on Sutter Street. Once that call was initiated, bankers and attorneys in abundance were on the phone from San Francisco to the hotel, men of such substance they managed to get through, in spite of the erratic nature of Mexican long-distance.

Evelyn had heard, to her sorrow, that the male of the ill-fated pair had been nearly as rich as the woman. She had already lamented the friendship that would have sprung up between them, as she enchanted him with stories of her past and witty observations by the pool. When the holiday was over, he would doubtless have invited her to San Francisco, introducing her to everyone substantial in that community, having his mistress give a luncheon for her, because if there was one thing Evelyn had always been smart about, it was making friends with women, especially when the target was their man. How they would have taken her to their collective, terribly social bosom. It was a tragedy past imagining, the loss of such valuable contacts, and so young. She mourned them in a way that was almost personal, and would have regretted the loss even more had it not meant her getting a room.

"The key," the room clerk said, handing it to her. "You understand, of course, it's only temporary."

"Life is only temporary," Evelyn said, "as we know from this morning. How long can I stay?"

Chris found herself experiencing a certain shortness of breath as she waited for an answer. Perhaps destiny or the room clerk had the strength that she lacked to hasten Evelyn on her travels.

"Until the attorney arrives for the lady O'Connor. He comes after tomorrow. As soon as he can make arrangements."

"Well, perhaps by the time he gets here, you can find another room for me." She smiled her most ravishing smile and underscored it with a quarter.

"We are completely booked."

"Maybe someone else will die," she said pleasantly. "We have to be optimistic."

No cutting edge serrated Evelyn's observation. There was about her such insouciance, the fact that she viewed the world as a personal convenience was forgivable. Many were those who, having spent enough time in her company, wondered why the universe had the illusion it was laboring for itself.

She asked the room clerk to have her luggage taken upstairs, and gave him another quarter. Then she turned to Caroline, who was basking on a chaise a few feet away, soaking up rays with a fierceness of concentration that augured serenity. "You want to go with . . ." Evelyn lowered her voice to a whisper, "Grandma. . ." She raised it to normal level. ". . .and help her unpack."

"I have to get tan," said Caroline.

"Musn't overdo it, darling. Be sure to use a lot of lotion. It's never too soon to start protecting your youth." Evelyn turned to Chris. "You shouldn't spend too much time in the sun, either. Although there's a Jap in Santa Monica who can fix you no matter how withered you are. Do you want to have your face done before we go to the spa? I'll treat you."

"I'm not going to the spa. And I'm not having my face done."

"I'm not saying that you need it," Evelyn demurred. "You look ten years younger than you are. I just thought maybe you needed a little lift to your morale."

"No, thank you."

Two black-uniformed soldiers, armed with carbines, slung leather-strapped over their shoulders, walked through the patio towards the beach. Evelyn raised herself on one elbow, touched her harlequin-framed sunglasses and peered at them. "Apparently they've called out the militia. What a shame. Such a rich, young woman." She sighed and lay back down. "Imagine his taking Mae on a cruise. To be trapped on the high seas, where there's no escape! At least if they're dreary at the spa, you can leave. But a ship! How could she stand five weeks with him. He's the most boring man I ever met."

"Then you're well rid of him," Chris said.

"He wouldn't have lasted that long. He's had three coronaries."

There was a familiar-sounding whoop of excitement; Josh came running towards the pool, a fish dangling from his fingers. "Mom! Come down to the dock!" He was naked to the waist, tugging at her hand, his hard little shoulders browned from the sun, slightly too red at the bony extrusions.

"You should put a shirt on," Evelyn said, "You're going to burn."

"Where did she come from?" Josh said distrustingly.

"Don't say *she*," corrected Evelyn. "Have some respect. I'm your . . ." she lowered her voice. ". . . grandmother."

"Show a little kindness," said Chris.

"Here," Josh said, going over to Evelyn's chaise, holding out the fish. "This is for you."

"Isn't he gross?" Caroline said. "Isn't he rude? No wonder I'm your favorite. Yucch."

"Who taught you about gifts?" Evelyn looked at the fish disdainfully. "Your father?"

"Now, now," said Chris.

"Can't we go down to the dock?"

"Don't you want to help me unpack?" asked Evelyn.

"You're staying?" Josh asked with undisguised alarm.

"He's the worst," said Caroline. "You're right to leave me everything."

"I'm not going so fast," Evelyn advised her. "Give me a kiss, you wicked little boy."

His dark eyes moved to Chris, an entreaty in them, as though she might grant dispensation not to be a grandchild. She nodded. Reluctantly he moved towards Evelyn, kissed her on the cheek more charily than he held the fish.

"How was your outing?" Chris asked him as they walked towards the dock.

"It was great! Dad only threw up a couple of times."

From a boat moored at the end of the dock, a white-haired, wizened fisherman unloaded Josh and Harry's catch, handing up pails of grouper and sea bass to a sailor. Harry stood on the pier slightly lime faced, his back toward the proceedings as he took deep breaths of air.

"We even caught a shark," Josh enthused to Chris.

"Santiago! Santiago!" he shouted, running towards the old fisherman. "Show my mom the shark!"

The old Mexican smiled a smile like a rotting picket fence, every other tooth still holding fast to his gums, and handed up a three-foot shark. The sailor laid it on the dock, where it thrashed weakly, oozing red slime from its belly. "Look," Santiago said, "babies." He reached up and cut a neat slash along the underside. Six tiny sharks, like tadpoles, slithered from the gash.

"That's gross," said Josh.

"I sort of liked it," mused Evelyn.

Josh picked up the biggest of the baby sharks and threw it into the water, peered over the edge. "It's alive, it's alive!" he noted triumphantly. "It's trying to swim." He ran back and got the other tiny sharks and threw them, one at a time, with expressed gentleness, into the ocean.

A pelican swooped down, then a second, outsized gray wings flapping. Their giant, jowly, dewlapped bills scooped beneath the water, breakfasted.

"Oh," Josh lamented.

"It's all right, darling," Evelyn consoled him. "They're better off. What's life without a mother?"

Harry turned, his face waxing more bilious, pallor intensifying as though there were, in fact, ghosts, the most threatening of them alive, and related. "What are you doing here?"

"It's wonderful to be greeted so warmly by your favorite son-in-law."

"I didn't know I had any competition," Harry said.

"Well, you never can tell," said Evelyn. "Any day now Angela may leave the reservation and settle down." She offered her cheek.

"You don't want me to kiss you," Harry said. "I've been puking."

"What a gift for poetry," Evelyn said. "It reminds me of my first honeymoon. No wonder your marriage lasted as long as it did," she said to Chris. Chris shook her head in warning. Harry caught the look between mother anddaughter and started away from the dock.

"Why are those soldiers on the beach?" Josh asked. There were eight of them now, darkly garbed, sinister carbines strapped in place to their shoulders, black boots planted in the sand, more firm of step than the police, more steady in conviction of their own importance.

"They must be performing some drill," Chris said.

"Don't be silly," contested Evelyn, ignoring Chris's face making. "They're there because of the killing."

"What killing?" Josh said unbelievingly.

"A man and a woman," Evelyn gossiped merrily. "Your mother found them dead on the beach." She caught the pained expression on Chris's face, finally, too late. "Well you can't shield your children from *all* the realities. Enough you try to fool them about your marriage."

"What does she mean?" asked Josh.

"Don't say *she*," said Evelyn. "Say . . ." she lowered her voice. ". . . grandma."

The color of the sea on Harry's face had blended softly with his gloom, shadowing his cheeks, dulling his eyes to gray. "Your mother," he said, coming out of the shower, towels wrapped around him. "That's all that was missing."

"You talk like I invited her."

"How the hell did she find us?"

"She called Leonard and told him she had money for us."

"How did she know his name?"

"I gave it to her once when she said she needed an accountant."

"You set all your own traps," Harry said. "You landscape with quicksand. Then you walk outside to admire what you've done and you wonder why you sink."

"You don't have to make me feel worse than I feel."

"My mother doesn't even know we have an accountant, much less his name."

"Your mother is not likely to leave us several hundred thousand," Chris said, fuming, hating herself for falling into the trap, which, in this instance, at least, he, not she, had set with his righteousness.

"Well, neither will Evelyn. She'll blow it all."

"That's her privilege. At least she has it to blow."

"I see," he said darkly. "My folks are contemptible, because they have no money."

"I never said that."

"You don't have to say it. I know what you think."

"Do you?" she asked, and filled her brain with all the venom she felt for him at the moment, aimed it at him, mentally daring him to pick up on it, sticking her tongue out in the subtler manner of those who were getting on, and fancied themselves mature.

"I don't know why we came on this trip," he said, disgusted. "You're doing everything you can to make it unpleasant."

"You mean like getting you seasick?"

"You put a man down for being ill."

"Seasickness is a form of anxiety when people are afraid they're not in control."

"Really? Okay, I admit it. I'm not in control. God is in control, the ocean is in control, and you and your mother are in control. I surrender. I give up!" He picked up the hair-blower from the sink and turned it on, whipping his fingers through his silky, dark hair, as though victory lay in good grooming, and well-coiffed, he could once more into the breech, resuming conquest.

"Is that it?" Chris moved closer, trying to make herself heard over the noise of the hairblower.

"Huh?"

"Is that how you win all your arguments? Making sure nobody else can be heard?"

"I have nothing more to say," Harry said.

"That's been true for a long time." Chris slammed out of the room, abetted by the wind, which hurled the giant oak door against the frame with hurricane force. She was rather surprised by the impetus, the accompanying impressive sound. It was a demonstration of fury on the level of her childhood memories of her parents. As much as she had promised herself independent footsteps, and nothing of violence in her life, she found it wonderful, orgasmic, fulfillment of potential she didn't know she had. Having discovered it in herself, she guiltily rejoiced in expressing it, noisily applauded by the wind.

In the flower-decked patio by the pool, heavy branches of twisted coral trees made wide circles of shadow. The trees were like no other trees Chris had seen, limbs blown back on themselves by the constant force of the wind, becoming self-protecting, gnarled arms embracing gnarled arms. Like people defending themselves, Chris mused. Unwound, they might have reached to touch a portion of sky.

Beneath a vine-covered latticework trellis, Evelyn sat plying Josh with Coca-Colas. "I'm going to have the fish Josh caught for lunch," she announced, as Chris approached their table. "Isn't that colorful? They're preparing it in the kitchen. I ordered some for you, too, Chrissie. Ceviche for an appetizer, and bass for an entree. Doesn't that sound healthy?"

"Yucch," said Caroline from her chaise, outside the boundary of the shade.

"Don't make those awful noises, dear," Evelyn advised. "They're liable to catch in your throat and choke you."

"So are the fish he caught," Caroline said.

"You're just jealous because we wouldn't let you come fishing."

"I was *invited*. I just have better things to do with my time."

"Like grow giant jugs," Josh said.

"Fat ass!"

"You know, children," Evelyn said. "When I was a little girl, it would have been very easy to hurt my brothers' and sisters' feelings . . ."

"Then why didn't you?" asked Josh.

"She didn't have time," Chris said. "She had to help her mother."

"We all struggled. We all helped each other. We cried with each other and made jokes. No one can be counted on more than family, family is very important. And now my brothers and sisters are the best friends I have in the world, except for Enid, that bitch."

"Ceviche?" the waiter said, offering tomato-sauced fish piled high in sundae glasses.

"For the two ladies and the large little boy," Evelyn instructed.

"Not me," said Josh. "I'll wait for my hamburger."

"Why are you eating hamburger?" asked Chris. "That's all you ever eat at home."

"I don't like fish. I like to catch them and study them, but not eat them."

"Study them?" Evelyn queried, proferring interest to Josh like a present she had found for him on her travels.

"I'm going to be a marine biologist," Josh said.

"Is there any money in that?" asked Evelyn.

"I don't have to worry about it, because I'll have my eight-hundred-thousand-dollar bonus for signing with the Dodgers."

"Really?" Evelyn said, losing interest as her eye noted an

elderly man diving into the swimming pool. "You ought to taste this ceviche, Caroline. It's really delicious."

"I'm not hungry."

"Then why don't you take a dip in the pool, and ask that nice man if he's married?" She looked back at Josh. "Are you that good an athlete?"

"I'm excellent," he said.

"Fair," said Caroline.

"How do you know? You don't even come to the games."

"I see you enough without watching you show off on the field."

"I don't show off. When you're excellent, you don't have to show off." The waiter set his hamburger in front of him. "*Gracias*," Josh said.

"You have a slight lisp, dear. Why don't you give him diction lessons?" Evelyn asked Chris.

"His speech will adjust when the braces come off, the orthodontist said."

"Good. If he's wrong, let *him* pay for the diction lessons. A lisp would be unbecoming in a baseball star. Baseball." Evelyn shuddered. "You should never have moved to California."

"I'm going to be a movie star," Caroline said.

"Not if your skin is wrinkled. You've had enough sun. Go in the pool and talk to that nice man." Evelyn returned her attention to Josh. "Why do you have such low ambition, a boy with your brains?"

"There are plenty of smart athletes," Josh said. "Tom Hayden was a Rhodes scholar."

"Why don't you want to be president?"

"Mom says I don't have to."

"That's right," Chris said. "I excused him. It's not a rewarding job."

"Great to have the pressure off," Josh said, grinning.

"Then maybe it'll be Caroline," Evelyn said. "She can be a movie star, and then president. It seems to be a natural progression."

"Presidents elected in a year ending with zero never live out their terms," Josh advised.

"Don't run in a zero year," Evelyn advised Caroline.

"She couldn't get elected," said Josh.

On the beach, hotel maids were raking the sand, while black-uniformed soldiers supervised. Josh half-raised himself out of his chair, craned his neck to see. "What are they doing?"

"Probably looking for valuables'" Evelyn said, smiling at the waiter as he removed her appetizer and placed her fish in front of her. The smile was of the intensity that she usually reserved for the nonworking classes, but there was a possibility that the old Mexican in the pool was observing her, and, rich though he was, would be pleased to note that she had no prejudices. "A watch, or something they might have dropped. God, I hope her bank had an inventory of her jewelry. I hear she had the most fabulous emerald collection. A shame I couldn't get to it before the maids." Evelyn cut into her fish, raised it to her mouth. "Umm. This is delicious, Josh. You're a great fisherman."

"Thank you."

"Don't talk with food in your mouth."

"It helps cover up my lisp."

"Don't be rude. I was only trying to be constructive. It wasn't said to hurt your feelings. Where does he get his manners?"

"The same place I got mine," Chris said.

"I always taught you to be respectful to your elders, although maybe Josh doesn't realize that's what I am, because I look so young. I should never have wished on you a child that would give you as much trouble as you gave me."

"He doesn't give me any trouble."

"Uh-huh. Just like you used to tell me how happy you were."

Chris looked at Evelyn beseechingly. "And of course, you were telling me the truth," Evelyn amended, realizing her error, which had not been deliberately cruel, but unthinking, like much of her life.

"What can they figure out from finding a watch in the sand?" Josh asked.

"Maybe what time the people actually died," Evelyn said. "Maybe the murderer stepped on it the moment of the killing. That always happens in mystery stories."

"Maybe they just need a watch," said Josh.

"Is he always this salty?" Evelyn asked.

"Don't say he." Josh wiped his mouth with a napkin. "I'm going to go down to the beach and watch them."

"May I please be excused?" Evelyn coached.

"I didn't know you did anything wrong," Josh said, smiling. "May I please be excused?"

"My God, you're fresh. But your fish *is* delicious. You have a brilliant future as a sportsman."

"I'm already a sportsman, like my dad." He was gone, running towards the sand.

"Come sweetheart," said Evelyn to Caroline. "Taste this."

"I'm too hot." Caroline sat up.

"Then take a dip in the pool. Near that nice white-haired gentleman."

Caroline splashed into the water. "She's so good," Evelyn said. "What an angel. She reminds me of myself."

"Me, too," said Chris. "I guess that's part of the problem."

"It's lucky you have one nice child, at least." Evelyn sailed on, unheeding. "I don't know why you're so crazy about the boy." She looked off towards Josh, his muscular little back rippling as he moved towards the sand. "He obviously adores Harry. What are you going to do?"

"I don't know."

"Of course, they have that joint-custody ruling now in California."

"That's too confusing for the children. They have problems getting their bearings. You can't split them in half. It makes them schizophrenic."

"You are no expert on what makes people schizophrenic," Evelyn said heatedly. "Schizophrenia is chemical. It has nothing to do with what you do to them. It's in the genes. And they weren't my genes. They were Sonny's genes. Norman wasn't even mine. I was his stepmother. Angela was schizophrenic from Sonny. Is it my fault she wants to be an Indian?"

"Nobody accused you of anything," said Chris.

"Why would you want custody, all they do is turn against you. Bring you grief. When you can find them." Evelyn sighed, ate a piece of fish. "Still, I guess you have to go through the charade of trying to keep them. It's a pity you didn't get friendly with those Mafia people in the restaurant days. You could have hired a hit man."

"I don't want Harry dead."

"Really? You're much more generous than I am. I would have welcomed the murder of any of mine."

She narrowed her eyes and watched Josh's progress. "Maybe it's just as well that he prefers Harry. If he goes with him, at least you won't be saddled with an angry adolescent, the way I was. He's cute now but in another six months the testosterone will start to flow, and he'll get difficult, the way they all do. He's already testy. I never saw a more adorable little boy than he was. You should have stuffed him when he was four."

"I couldn't stand to lose him," Chris said, her eyes filling. "I love him more than myself."

"Well what's so hard about that? You're not so lovable." Evelyn laughed, a slightly cackling sound. "The truth is, you'd adjust. Maybe it would pain you for a little while, but you'd see you were better off. Most men don't want to be saddled with other men's children. When you met Harry, you hadn't grown into yourself. You could probably get anyone now. I never knew what you saw in him, that Adonis from the Bronx."

"I loved him."

"Well, your sense of values was always a little peculiar," Evelyn said, and signaled for the check. "Searching for *meaning*. Searching for *truth*." The waiter set the check on the table.

"The truth is, I think it's over," Chris said, starting to cry.

"Nothing to feel sad about. The truth shall set you free, with the help of a good lawyer." Evelyn totaled the numbers, checked them. "Did you notice the group of Arabs in the lobby? Some sort of oil sheik, I imagine, they always are. I don't think I could give myself to an Arab. But I wish I knew their room number. I could sign it on the check."

Chris wiped her eyes, gave a little choke of laughter. "You see, you feel better already," marked Evelyn. "We're going to have such a good time at the spa!"

Once in her room, Evelyn unpacked, placing an assortment of creams and lotions in the bathroom, emptying out an entire suitcase of makeup and blenders onto the sink. Sadly, to her way of thinking, the police had done a lretty thorough job of clearing the place out, so there was very little she could deduce about the couple, not having been given even a few minutes to go through their drawers. The maids had changed the sheets on the beds, so Evelyn could not see if they had slept in one bed or two. She wondered if he had been impotent, if the heiress, perhaps, had been pregnant, which in Evelyn's estimation would have been reason enough for suicide, there being no therapeutic abortions in the melodrama of her imagination. Evelyn was no particular fan of the ERA. She could not conceive of becoming her own benefactor. But certain deeply feminist principles were a part of her character, without her realizing they were feminist principles, among them a conviction that it was not the destiny of all women to be mothers, certainly not to enjoy that role.

Possibly, she hypothesized, the man had killed Alana. She was richer than he, perhaps too much for his ego, in conjunction with her being brighter, which women usually were, another feminist conviction Evelyn had never proclaimed publicly, since the secret of her success, such as it was, had always been pretending to be stupider than the men she spun webs for. No healthy respect for women led her to such a surmise, but disdain for males based on intimate knowledge. Such was the clemency of her nature, nonetheless, that she was willing to begin again, forgiving, merciful, exculpating, in direct ratio to his Dunn and Bradstreet rating, which—she had learned from being married to Sonny—it was wise to run before becoming involved, though in her case not in the business sense.

Not the prospect of financial harbor alone sent her skiffing around erotic seas. She was thinner skinned than she'd been in her youth, and the world seemed colder. So she would have welcomed a warm fat body next to hers at night, to buffer the loneliness, the winds that blew around the years. But a man had to plight a definite troth, or, being too old to take her home to mother, invite her several times to dinner, before she'd consider, as she still called it, "putting out."

It was this wish not to appear easy, even at an age, in a time, when sex was no longer a favor granted, or more, an index to personal morality, that gave Evelyn her veneer of Republicanism, which, along with a subscription to *W*, was all she had in common with Nancy Reagan. To have been told that she seemed like a woman of that stripe would have horrified Evelyn in equal measure with an accusation of feminism. In truth, she was neither traditionalist nor rebel, joining in the ranks of absolutely no one, very much her own woman, at least until she could find a suitable man, at which point she would be quite willing to pretend she could subvert herself. As long as he lasted.

The lawyer for Alana O'Connor arrived at noon the following day, already a day too late as far as three out of four family members were concerned. Josh and Harry's discomfort at Evelyn's presence had been palpable, Chris's nervousness at her situation intensified, since her mother's being there necessitated moving Josh back into his own room, so Evelyn would not take note of an empty bed and want to move into their quarters.

Harry drank too much at dinner, anesthetizing himself against the cloaked stilettos of his mother-in-law, while Josh chugalugged Coca-Colas in a frenzy of swallowing. Only Caroline seemed charmed with the visitor, appraising the rings Evelyn promised to leave her, diemissing some of them as too large, old fashioned, not pretty, but wondering aloud why Evelyn had to wait till death to pass them on.

"Where did you get those earrings?" Evelyn asked Chris at dinner.

"Harry gave them to me for Christmas."

"I had no idea you liked such *small* diamonds," Evelyn said. "If I had known you would wear anything so small, I had some I could have given you made from baguettes on one of my rings. But I gave them to Angela. She probably sold them to buy lithium."

"You have a slight lisp," said Josh. "You ought to take diction lessons."

By the next noon, when the manager regretfully informed Evelyn that the *abogado* for the O'Connor woman had arrived, and she would have to move on, Chris welcomed the news as she might have the Second Coming. Evelyn had continued her unwitting assault through breakfast, succeeding in driving Harry and Josh back to bed, as though daylight were too bright for their spirits. Chris had discovered them napping together. Harry's hand extended tenderly towards Josh, whose fingertips touched his father's, like the Sistine Chapel depiction of Adam being given life by God. It was such a beautiful sight, so enraging, that it intensified her fury at her mother's coming, forcing them into an even more obvious alliance.

With the unpremeditatedness of a tornado, Evelyn was oblivious to any damage she had done, concerned only with where she would blow to next. "Maybe I could go from here to Guadalajara," she mused, studying the travel folders laid out on the table in the lobby as two bellmen stood piling her luggage on a trolley.

"They have the most beautiful roses in the world in Guadalajara," said the manager helpfully.

"I hate roses. I'm allergic."

"What a sadness," the manager mourned.

"Not really. It makes men give you things that don't make you sneeze. Like jewelry."

"Very good, very good," he said, smiling, shaking his head with obvious approval at her wit. She looked at him appraisingly, studied the vaulted dome of the lobby, calculated what the manager of such a hotel probably received in the way of salary, and lost interest in him.

By the French windows leading out to the pool, in quiet conference with the police chief, stood the dead woman's attorney, a slight, fair man in his early forties, with a San

Franciscan's comportment and style. He was dressed in a custom three-piece suit, as though he had come directly from the courtroom and was on his way to cocktails at the Fairmont. He gestured slightly as he spoke, to underscore his words. His hands were pale, with long, graceful fingers, a musician's hands, artful in their economy, expressive. Evelyn could almost tell what he was trying to say from their movements, and wished he would get to the part about the emeralds.

He looked up and saw her watching him. He smiled politely, causing a momentary quickening of her heart rate, although he was clearly too young for her, unless she went back to the Jap for another quick tack. Or maybe he liked older women. Maybe his mother hadn't shown him enough affection, the cold cow, although Evelyn understood how hard it had been for her, too, and would be respectful when they were introduced in San Francisco after he'd begged her to go back with him, to meet everyone in his circle, all of whom would adore her.

The entire progression of these thoughts took place in the literal twinkling of an eye. His were, like his hands, unusual, a very pale, luminous lavender, almost transparent, the color she had always expected from lapdog interviews with Elizabeth Taylor, who had the power to cloud men's minds, even Truman Capote's. Evelyn had found herself once in an elevator on the way to a charity party, standing next to Elizabeth Taylor, to discover that mythic woman as short as herself, with jewels that were mostly turquoise and eyes that were actually blue. Oh, maybe a little lavender. But not the vivid violet she had been led to believe would rivet her, as the lawyer's did now.

The aesthetic characteristics of men were not usually paramount in Evelyn's appraisal, since fineness of feature seemed to her an index of how easily they could be manipulated. Much as she enjoyed piloting those who imagined they were in charge, she preferred a bit of a struggle for the helm. So she had picked for herself mainly coarse-featured fellows, whose bellies bruited their bank accounts and a gusto for battle, which Evelyn much preferred to peace.

The attorney was on his way to her. In the time it took for him to cross the lobby, she had already rejected his kind offer to share the room, unless it was clear there would be nothing between them. They could handle it like *It Happened One Night*, with a screen instead of a hanging blanket between the two beds, and he would lie there night after night longing for her. Finally, lust would overwhelm him, in spite of the delicacy of his hands, the exquisiteness of his eyes, the correctness of his tailoring, and he would knock over the screen and have at her, deaf to her protestations. And marveling at her breasts (she would have to drop a thank-you note to the Jap), losing himself in the warm of her, he would beg her forgiveness, entreat her to let him make it up to her in San Francisco. In the meantime, he would insist on her accepting one little brooch embezzled from the estate. No one would know it hadn't been the hotel maids who took it, but she would have to be careful not to wear it to dinner at L'Etoile.

"Mrs. Sterne?" he said.

"Yes?"

"I'm so sorry to have to inconvenience you." He extended his hand and shook hers. "I'm Adam Wilkerson."

"How do you do." She found him, close up, even more attractive, the long, straight line of his nose, a testament to generations of aristocracy, his jaw as rigidly imposing as his eyes were soft. Given the unmistakable purple tint that Elizabeth Taylor didn't have, he lacked the thick double lashes she did, so his eyes, light lashed as they were, lids nearly naked, were staring, innocent. Slightly bald faced, ingenuous was the look they gave him, contradicted by his manner, the sophistication of his smile. Not that Evelyn was impressed by externals.

"I regret your having to leave the hotel."

"Well," she said bravely. "It was only my first holiday since my husband died." She did not mention that at Sonny's death, he had been married to someone else, as he had for a number of years before that. Paltry details, they seemed to Evelyn, undercutting the immediate drama of their exchange, to be saved for another time, possibly when they were ensconced in front of the fireplace in their suite at the Stanford Court.

"I wish there was something I could do."

She waited. Maybe they could have a little too much wine their third or fourth night together, and she could make it less of a battle for him.

"But, unfortunately, I'm here on a very sad mission . . ."

"I understand that."

". . . And my wife and son are with me."

"Oh," said Evelyn, the vision of the Stanford Court crumbling in an earthquake that once again leveled San Francisco.

"I hope you find other accommodations," he concluded, brisk now, businesslike, obviously finished, a master at making his point.

In her heart of hearts, Evelyn was sure she was relieved. Now that she looked at him really carefully, he seemed a trifle epicene. The truth was she like men closer to brutes, which made the guidelines clearer. Nor was she totally comfortable with Wasps, even though she'd read most of the novels of Henry James, and much preferred them to Philip Roth's. She supposed Wilkerson's mother would have made things difficult for them, since, although she and Evelyn were probably around the same age, Evelyn was a generation younger, and a Jew.

So, she felt nearly happy: adventure was bound to wait for

her someplace else. The very inconvenience of the locale she was leaving, the fact that the airport no longer had commercial traffic and was open only to private planes, loaned to her departure an air of mystery, since she had no idea where she was going or how she would get there. Difficulties were opportunities inside out, she assured herself like a fortune cookie.

In the forecourt of the hotel, with its crowns of bougainvillea, the fountain seemed to flow farewell to her as Chris, Josh and Caroline waited to bid her good-bye. Nobody asked where she was going: Chris because that might encourage Evelyn to camp nearby; Caroline because it might lead to an invitation to accompany her grandmother, the declining of which could affect how much jewelry she would get, when; Josh because he didn't care. He knew from how tired his father was, too heavy with sleep to even come down to say good-bye, that it was good she was leaving.

Still, he was generous with his kisses, holding up his mouth, accepting her embrace as though he believed she liked children. Caroline, too, was an example of affectionate charity, clinging to Evelyn's arm as if reluctant to be parted from her, holding her hand up to the light to catch the full glint of the rings on her fingers. Even Chris participated freely in the physical masque of farewell, giving her face to the too-bright imprint of her mother's lipstick.

"Good-bye, you naughty little boy. Good-bye, little princess. Good-bye my favorite daughter." The last was an endowment Evelyn had finally decided to grant, since the most recent detective's report placed Angela with the Peyote Indians in the desert near Taos, New Mexico, the only locale primitive and hostile enough to keep her mother at a distance.

She stepped into the cab, piled inside and back and above with her luggage, heavily roped. "How much would you charge to drive me to Guadalajara?" Evelyn asked the driver.

"I hope she doesn't come back," said Josh, watching the dust rising in the road behind the taxi.

Lunching by the pool that afternoon, Chris noticed an attractive blonde woman and her son. The woman was of a type Chris had always admired: statuesque, not in the body, which was rather flat chested and slender, but facially. She had the carven, pale, marbleized features and high cheekbones of heiresses, with cornsilk hair and enough assurance never to have it done. Her fine blonde hair was drawn back into a simple knot at the back of her neck, a style Chris recognized from the girls with whom she had gone to college, those who had prepped at Brearley and Spence, whose breezy diffidence she had tried to emulate, along with their handwriting, a squat, very neat little print that spoke of notebooks filled with information they would never have to absorb, because of how pretty they were. The sight of the woman caused in Chris a kind of Junior League epiphany as she realized how hungry she was for the bright conversations of her undergraduate days and the friends who had surprised her by turning out to have ideas.

The son was flaxen haired and spindly, the same aristocratic heritage that had gifted his mother with a statue's face having passed to him narrow shoulders and bony knees. He looked to be about Josh's age, perhaps even a little older, although nowhere near his size, robust as Chris's offspring was with the blood of peasants.

"Why don't you go play with that boy?" she asked Josh.

His face was half-buried in a hamburger, as if he would have been swallowed by it, instead of vice versa, and that would give him refuge from the strain of the morning. "He looks like a wimp."

"Musn't judge by appearances," Chris said. "Why don't you go over and talk to him when you're finished eating."

"Okay," said Josh, with an alacrity that surprised her. He did not usually want to play with other children. Sometimes it occurred to Chris that his dependence on Harry was an affectionate camouflage on Josh's part for Harry's dependence on him. Harry had abandoned him. There were youth, the ones that had not abandoned him. There were relationships with other fathers in Little League, but these were community friendships, not the kind you picked up the phone for and said "I need to talk to somebody." So Josh was his only buck feedback, the single important male in his life. Chris realized what a burden it had to be for the boy, having always to be there, to deliver for his father. She felt an uncontrollable affection for him, for his loving kindness, the pretense of not really wanting friendships his own size. She leaned over and kissed him.

He brushed her away. "He's not going to want to be friends with me if I have a mushy mother."

"It's good you're trying to get Josh to make some friends," Caroline observed, watching Josh and the blonde boy splashing in the pool. "He doesn't have a million friends, like I do. He spends too much time with dad," Caroline noted. "Why don't you find a friend for him, too? Somebody with a tennis court."

"His name is Nicky," Josh related animatedly to Chris as he ran back, out of breath, dripping, water plastering his hair, making matted brown triangles of his lashes. "His mother calls him 'Nick-o-loss.' " He became imperious, a socialite, affectionate but arch. Then he was gone again, sprinting, cannonballing into the pool with a shouted "YOW!" sending a giant spray into the air, dousing the sleek composure of the blonde.

"I'm so sorry," Chris moved to the chaise beside her. "My son is very rambunctious."

"That's all right." The woman raised herself on her elbow and, shading her eyes, checked Chris over. "I'm delighted Nicholas has someone to play with. I didn't know there would be any American children. I'm Denise Wilkerson."

Chris introduced herself. "Did you just get here?"

"My husband is the attorney for the O'Connor estate," said Denise. "The woman who died?"

"Oh yes. Very sad."

"Sad when she was alive, too," Denise said. "It's amazing nothing awful happened before. She was a strange girl, spooky. Always trying to donate her money to cultists, anarchists, lunatic causes. When the list of names came in from Guyana we were all pretty relieved Alana wasn't on it."

"Who was the man?"

"Jimmy Moffatt. Charming, shallow. No sense of values at all. You understand I'm not telling any tales out of school. This has all been raked over in the papers. Alana's death is the biggest thing to happen to newspaper circulation in San Francisco since Patty Hearst."

She signaled for the barman, with his portable cart. "Adam came within an inch of handling that one. Fortunately the Hearsts decided they wanted more flash. That would have taken years out of our lives. He cares so much." It was a complaint, in tones too elegant to whine, as a poor woman might have said "He drinks, and beats the children." "A Sauza sunrise," Denise instructed the barman. "Would you like something?"

"Thank you," said Chris, and ordered the same.

"Her affair with Jimmy seemed to mean she was off her noble kick, at last. She even started wearing jewels, her mother's emeralds, as if she finally thought it was all right to be rich."

"Are they missing?"

"Some of them," said Denise. "But you can't go by that. They might not have been stolen. She gave one to a waiter at the Top of the Mark because he brought her an Irish coffee after the bar was closed."

"A madcap heiress."

"Oh, I'm not sure about the cap. Although I don't mean to speak ill of her. I rather liked her. There was something pathetic about the importance she kept trying to give everything, as though she couldn't bear the thought life might be trivial. Besides, I owe her the fact that we're here. It's been years since we've had a holiday together. My husband takes his work so seriously. He never sees our son."

Chris drowned momentarily in envy: a man who never spent time with his child.

"Does it seem too much like dancing on the coffin, to make this into a vacation?"

"It seems like a really good idea," said Chris, sincerely, since it seemed to be her own fortune to be making her vacation into a coffin, but without the dancing.

As the boys decided they wanted to go fishing the next day on one of the big boats that left from San Carlos, it fell to Chris to make the arrangements. Denise opted to stay at the hotel, having had enough boats in San Francisco, where the family yacht was berthed. Harry declined to go, having had enough sea, as did Caroline, having had enough Josh.

Caroline had watched with concern the growing antagonism between her parents. Divorce was a pretty good bet to come out of marriage, she understood living in Beverly Hills, from the split parentage of most of her contemporaries, the predominance of girlfriends with different names from their mothers' husbands. She had not been programmed into fear at the prospect of failing as a wife, however: marriage was a definite part of her plans; it just included the probability of divorce. Divorce did not seem to her as tragic as much as part of the road, sad only in its effect on the children. She was not sure, however, if she intended to have any, since they might turn out to be boys.

As for the immediate problem of her parents' splitting, she had dealt with it in her mind, deciding that if her father moved to Westwood, as divorcing fathers seemed to, she would stay with her mother in their house. If her mother moved to Westwood, since she did so much that fathers usually did, Caroline would stay with her father. She had stronger feelings about allying herself with her room, her closet, and Beverly Hills than with either of her parents, as alienated as she felt from everything except her friends and Judy Blume. Her father spent all his free time with Josh. Her mother spent all her free time with her songs, and even the time that wasn't free, sitting in her music room with the door closed, writing, listening to records. Or else she went out for walks where she didn't particularly want company because she was thinking. Thinking. All the time thinking. It puzzled and saddened Caroline, because she would have been glad to go with her mother on an excursion she understood, as they had gone to Japanese Deer Park and Magic Mountain when she was a little girl. But the lunches and movies and shopping trips that had taken the place of those seemed forced, heavy with duty, the only real joy in her mother's life, her work. Since Caroline felt as apart from that as she felt from baseball, her one true feeling of belonging was to the house, She herself had found it when a classmate of hers had told her her parents were divorcing, so somebody else's bad luck had turned out to be good for Caroline. She had felt as clever as the real estate lady her mother had seemed to admire, as though the house had afforded her a rare chance to help, to contribute, to tell her mother something she didn't already know. So the house in a way was hers, as nothing else was: they would not have been in it without her. In the awful event they sold it, and both moved someplace else, she had made the sad optional plan in her mind of going with whichever parent didn't have Josh.

The free expression of feelings that did not take place between mother and daughter was an unfortunate omission, since both females would have been astonished by the alikeness of their anguish. Chris, too, was suffering from a sense of alienation from her family, as sure she was as unloved as Caroline, filled with regrets that she hadn't squeezed herself into the traditional mold. She was sure her daughter looked at her with disapproval, would have been happier with the customary mother, as Evelyn would have been happier with a prettier, dumber little girl. Chris suspected the real reason for the lopsidedness of her life was her brain, and being an achiever. All around her she sensed antagonism, the difficulties she had fallen into a manifestation of the quiet contempt society had for accomplished women, as though it weren't natural, their becoming something other than partners. In Africa, when there was not enough food, the women went hungry. In America, with not enough success to go around, there was hidden resentment when any of it fell to a female.

This curious, unspoken prejudice was fast becoming a part of Chris's consciousness. Like a Jew in an anti-Semitic society, she did not quite deny what she was, but avoided mentioning it, not waiting anymore for the question 'What do you do?,' feeling a sense of nearly fatal relaxation when people asked the vocation of her husband. She was no longer of the opinion that intellect in women was a particular asset, having noted

215

from reading about the trial of Jean Harris that the women jurors were as offended by her as the men. It was Harris's attitude, her pride, combativeness, and too-quick articulation that had doomed her. That, and her history of privilege. Women did not take heart from educated women, but rather felt threatened by them, as much, or more, than men. Certainly the woman jurors had seemed uncomfortable and angry rather than sympathetic, unable to relate to Mrs. Harris's plight, the angry wit she had displayed. The verdict seemed to Chris to come with a sense of force and relief that the headmistress could be put away, as if it were not just the killing she needed to be punished for.

So there seemed to Chris to be a quaint hypocrisy in the magazines flushing the periodical stands, celebrating career women, scouring industries for leaders with breasts beneath their blazers. It struck her as a hollow revolution, with only those women who had always been exceptional remaining truly exceptional, the rest being flushed out into the job force, pressed into the forefront, when all they wanted was to remain in hiding. Where would it lead? To a civilization of females convinced they had to be special, because their chance had come at last, whether or not they wanted it? Competition had driven men mad in America, ulcerated their stomachs, attacked their hearts. Was that to be the new medical map of women, cracking them under the strain? Or would they mince back into traditional roles, parading complacency and subservience, drum-majoretted by Phyllis Schlafly? Evelyn had said the truth would make Chris free, but intuiting the real opinion the world had of bright women, the truth was making her reactionary.

She longed to become oblivious, thick, thin on sensibility. As her early life had been a struggle to sharpen her mental capacities, she now wished to dull them, struggled for a kind of coma, a blur of perception and awareness that would make her acceptable, maybe even welcome at the hostile hearths of the closet misogynists, among whom she feared were a number of her sisters. As undimmed as might have been her secret hope for enlightenment and inspiration, on a conscious level she aspired to a stultifying of awareness, lest, like Jean Harris, she be tried and found not wanting.

It surprised Chris then, as the fishing boat glided out of the marina of San Carlos, to find herself feeling as bright as the morning, and delighting in it. There was an unaccustomed paleness to the day, silver streaks in the sky, dawn not yet completely surrendered, still attaching itself to night. Across from Chris, Adam Wilkerson lounged on the stern bench, thick, nearly lashless lids half-closed, dozing. He had spoken almost not at all since the cab left the hotel, as if reticence were part of his attire. But his voice had struck her as exceptionally gentle, soft with a hook in it, pulling people along. In two white deck chairs bolted to the deck, the boys, her own, sturdy and dark, the other, pale and spindly, rehearsed their catch of yellowtail and giant tuna. Manuel, a white-haired fisherman, deep creases on his face intensifying the darkness burned in by the sun, set their lines for trawling, while a Mexican sailor steered the boat from the flying bridge.

Pelicans sailed their own regatta on currents of air, coming to rest, clustering on giant brown rocks rising from the sea. Shrieking, staring, the heavy-billed, homely creatures marked the small boat's passing. Seagulls whipped by with gentler grace, as though challenging the obtuse expressions of the pelicans, their right to the name of bird.

Chris studied the profile of her son, joyously trawling his line on the top of the water. Into the grin was insinuated the half-frown of the man of serious purpose, aware of the magnitude of the task he had set for himself. His hair, so weighty it was not even stirred in the wind created by the boat's swift maneuvers, sat like an undisciplined monk's atop the sweet, belligerent features. From the other chair Nicky watched Josh's every movement, as though all the memberships in the San Francisco yachting club could not grant the assurance of a boy who had actually caught a shark. Aware of admiring eyes, his mother's, and his friend's, Josh struggled to look jaded, slightly world weary, sea weary.

On the stern bench across from her, Adam Wilkerson, in white duck pants and a red and white striped T-shirt, struggled to relax. Somnolence, like his ensemble, seemed not his habit. His long, slender fingers twitched, as though they could not adjust to repose.

The boat moved farther out into the water, leaving behind giant brown rocks crested with white, carrying their doltish burden of pelicans. To the right of the boat, a great grotto loomed, a mammoth arch of yellow gold rock, the water beneath it viridescent, a prairie turned liquid. Caught in the break of current, the waves began to tower in size. Pulled by the rips and swells from the luminous hollows of the grotto, the boat began to pitch.

As though he were only pretending fright, Josh made an apprehensive comic grimace at Nicky. But the attempt at humorous ease was wasted, as Nicky moved in full stagger to the side of the boat. Adam signaled to Manuel. He took a pail, filled it with sea water, and doused Nicky as he threw up over the side.

"Why'd you make me buy you such a big breakfast?" Adam called to his son. "Wasting all that money on the fishes."

Chris studied him. To be so callous, he should have been taller, more muscular, his body a keener index to his lack of feelings. It didn't matter how fine their fingers were if their sensibilities were hammers.

Manuel signaled to the sailor to guide the boat into peaceful waters. The gesture came too late for Josh. His head was over the side, his square sturdy hands gripping the taffrail, while Manuel drenched him. Chris was on her feet. "Don't add to his humiliation by babying him," Adam cautioned her.

She was tempted to ask him what he knew about sons, having spent so little time with his own. Her first opportunity to comfort Josh without Harry's being there first, and she had to brook the meddling of a stranger. But she did not move to embrace her son. The least of them, the slightest, even one who seemed dressed by Barbie as Ken goes to sea, could still intimidate her. Instead, she said very softly, "Are you all right?"

"Don't tell Dad," Josh said feebly.

Manuel directed the four of them through the cabin to the bow of the ship, where their faces would catch the wind. Settling their backs against the windshield, the boys sat, wet hair dripping onto their faces, which for all the dissimilarity of features and size seemed connected now, made kin by shared misadventure. Their fingers, white knuckled, gripped the stanchions as the boat moved into quieter waters.

Chris took off her jacket, folded it into a pillow for her head. Leaning back, she missed the cushion, and hit her head on the bowsprit. Adam laughed.

"So you see, Nicky," she said. "It's nothing personal with you. Your father just takes delight in anybody's discomfort."

"What does that mean, what she said?" Nicky asked his father.

"It means she's a very bright lady," Adam said, smiling.

When the boat returned to calm waters, the boys moved to the back of the boat to resume their fishing. Chris was still resonating with Adam's compliment, all the more baffling, considering how convinced shewas that she wanted to be stupid. She looked at him without seeming to look. He was still smiling. She tried to find smugness in it, sarcasm, something that would make him dislikeable. But in fairness, he seemed pleasant enough, if a trifle too manicured.

"Do they know what happened to Alana O'Connor?" she asked him.

"Cocaine laced with sodium cyanide," he said.

Chris shuddered.

"They haven't determined yet if it was double suicide, or murder."

"Was she suicidal?"

"Only in her causes. Everyone was so glad when she took up with Jimmy Moffatt. He promised to convert her to a life empty of meaning. Constant parties. Long lunches at Trader Vic's."

"They made me sad, they were so beautiful together." Chris clasped her hands around her bent knees, rested her cheek against the inside of her arm. "They seemed always to be touching each other. As though they couldn't stand to be separated. They reminded me of someone, and I couldn't figure out who. Then I realized it was me and Harry."

"Your husband?"

She nodded.

"That's nice," he said.

"It was a long time ago."

"Josh is a fine boy," Adam noted. He and Chris walked on the pier several feet behind their sons, who proudly trailed two burlap sacks loaded with their catch. Josh's arm was around Nicky's shoulder, as though to console with cama- raderie the unintentional wound of catching more snapper.

"So is Nicky," she said. Around them, fishermen hauled in harvests, in boats named for women, and Jesus, while sailors stripped barnacles from yachts christened with variants of repose. Adam's fingers lightly threaded the inside of her arm. She was aware, in the heat, how cool his fingers were.

"It's nice they found each other," said Adam.

"Well, when people are supposed to meet, they do."

He looked at her very carefully. She noticed for the first time the color of his eyes.

"Adam Wilkerson," she said, connecting, "the attorney."

"I thought that had already been established."

"A friend of mine was going to use you for her divorce."

"Really," he said. "Isn't it a small world."

"Apparently."

Moving up the tile-inlaid steps to the second-floor landing and their hotel room, Josh twice reminded Chris of her promise not to tell Harry he'd been sick. "Why are you so worried?" she asked him. "It only means you're human."

"I don't think he should know that about me," he said, his step slowed by the enormity of the burden he carried.

"Come see what your son did," she called to Harry, while Josh loosened the neck of the burlap bag to better display his catch.

"An octopus." Harry gave an appreciative whistle.

"You should have come," Josh said. "They were jumping into the boat."

"Was it rough?"

"Not really." He shot his mother an apprehensive look.

"Come," Harry said. "We'll take them down to the kitchen. They can make us ceviche for dinner."

"We have a date for dinner," Chris said, in a constructedly casual tone. She did not want to alert him to how much she was looking forward to the evening, how pleased she was that one of the mythic lawyers had turned out to be such an appealing man. She sensed Harry would resent an attorney, because of the burden that fraternity had imposed on them, would resent any man who might become her rescuer. She felt a momentary flash of shame: she hadn't even been aware of that in her thinking, but there it was, there was Adam Wilkerson, suddenly, the one who could get her out of it. "With Nicky's parents."

"Nicky?"

"My new friend. My fishing buddy." Josh looked up at his father, checked him for signs of hurt. "I didn't have as much fun with him as I would have had with you."

Harry smiled and started to pick up the sack. As sensitive to his son's feelings as Josh was to his, he left it for Josh to carry. But, as the boy lifted it and started down the hallway, Harry held it from behind.

The children decided to stay at the hotel and eat dinner together, Caroline generously agreeing to supervise the boys, almost English in her accord, as if she were about to be mother, pouring tea. The Wilkersons, Harry, and Chris chose to assay the country club at San Carlos, built specifically to cater to the tastes of Americans, according to the taxi driver.

There was already a certain elegant cast to the evening. Harry was in his best jacket. Chris had forgotten how suited to sartorial splendor he was, seeming half again as tall, an imposing figure of a man. She felt touched and slightly saddened, to see how much better he seemed to feel about himself when slightly resplendent, as if he had set that aside, along with the rest of his dreams, being handsome.

His sense of warm jocularity seemed also somewhat restored, as he twitted Denise without letting her know he was being wry, obviously amused by her imperious diction, according it the same tolerance he showed the marbleized speech of Chris's Bryn Mawr friends. He had come to the conclusion that the overly educated were, in their way, as laughable as the thugs, there being no real difference between the privileged and the criminals when it came to making assholes of themselves.

"I understand your boy is quite a ball player," Adam said to Harry as the cab made its way across the single-stripped highway passing mountains into desert.

"The best," Harry said. "He's a superathlete."

"Takes after his father," Chris said. It was important to her to have Adam like him. She wasn't sure why.

"Were you a ball player?" Adam asked.

"I pitched for the Dodgers."

Chris was more than surprised. That was a piece of information he had stopped imparting so long ago, even to intimates, she was baffled by his telling it to a stranger.

"The Los Angeles Dodgers?" Denise asked, sounding at once impressed and appalled.

"In those days it was Brooklyn."

"And you're from New York," Adam noted. "That must have been the American Dream come true."

"Yeah," Harry said. "Well, that's the thing about the American Dream. It's always over."

The country club, attesting to sleek aspirations in its design—one glassed-in wall running alongside the night-lit golf course, tailored to what was imagined as American taste—was, nonetheless, crowded with only local celebrants, parading what they thought was American style. A tinny orchestra played next to the dance floor, in imitation of country-club bands, its music like elevator Muzak, running too slowly.

The maître d', obviously struck by the authenticity of the

223

garb and attitude of the Wilkerson party, gave them the first available table. Harry and Denise were seated, their backs to the wall; Adam sat on Chris's left.

On the wall behind Denise and Harry, between them, was a wide mirror, silver framed. Chris looked into it and found Adam staring at her. It was a look at once so frank, so openly appraising, and interested, that there would have been about it nothing even vaguely suspect were it not taking place in full view of their partners, and yet, literally, and exquisitely behind their backs. Adding to that intensity was the fact that, once meeting, their eyes did not let go. His held her riveted, as if he knew full well the power he was setting loose there and had no intention of pulling back, no thought of stopping, no confusion of purpose, or letting her mistake what the look was, how deep it went, how far he meant it to go. The deep lavender color of his eyes buoyed her, tuning her up like a cello, with strings a little too tight, so her whole torso vibrated. His look did not go, as the look she had thought she was searching for all her life would go, to the center of her soul, to the core of her being. It went, quite simply, all the way inside her eyes.

She felt devoured by him, thrilled, the woman she thought she had become reawakened as girl, giddy, faint. All the air was suddenly sucked out of her.

Both their heads were vaguely inclined in the direction of the two opposite, so it seemed as though they were listening to the conversation. But she heard nothing. It was as if she was lifted, closeted in space with him, timeless, in a vacuum, the two of them locked in each other's eyes. She could feel heat rising in her, feel her blood rushing through parts of her body she hadn't remembered existed. Explosions in her toes. And still, he kept on looking at her, telling her more clearly than with words how much he wanted her.

It was still a surprise to her that a man could find her so

224

desirable, a kind of biblical charge, as if she were set in a cinematic pageant, miscast as someone that men wanted. That a man looked at her with covetous eyes, set fires loose in her.

It was she, finally, who had to look away. She did not speak very much during dinner, only half-attempted to eat her food, because her hands were shaking, and she was afraid Harry would notice her fork if she tried to raise it too often to her mouth. Mostly, she rearranged the contents of her plate. She did not dare to look again in the mirror.

They did not touch, except for the brushing of hands as Adam helped her from her chair, and into the cab. They avoided shaking hands while saying good-night in the lobby of the hotel, as if neither wanted contact that was swift, impersonal. They did not really touch, as touching went. They didn't have to.

She could not sleep all night. Harry's snoring no longer bothered her: he seemed part of a story unrelated to hers. Even the love she felt for Josh, asleep in her bed when they'd gotten back, a poignant tribute, seemed separate, consumed as she was with what had happened with Adam, what was still happening. What was the matter with her? Never in her life had she been easy, a pushover. Oh, maybe in that foolish whatever it was—she could not call it an affair—with Tony Candella. But that had been the girl in her dying. She owed a little honor to the girl, no matter how silly she was. What was this, then? Who was acting like this? Surely not a mature woman. One who had never been a roundheel, turning out to be a roundeye. Knocked over by lavender eyes, and the wanting behind them.

She went outside on the balcony and sat, with her arms wrapped around her knees, studying the moonlit expanse of water. How funny was the originator of those heavens that stretched above her, sending her seeming salvation again, in the guise of a *lawyer*. Was it another test, the way the movie star had been, a test she had failed and passed at the same time? Was it to see how much she had grown since that first time in Guaymas five years ago? To see if she was over being foolish, flighty, had become sensible at last, mature, an inspiration to herself, wise enough to pass him by? Then why was she so excited, exultant, enraptured?

And why was he someone so clever at divorce: The answer to an unhappily married maiden's prayers. Wasn't it still after all, after everyone, the mind of a maiden? Whispering rescue, rescue, rescue, rescue.

Six

I N THE morning, she went for a walk on the beach, and gave him up, a step at a time. Adultery was the reason for most marriages ending, she supposed, because women didn't have the courage simply to admit it was over; they had to make it be over, with someone else. If her marriage was to come to a close, Chris wanted it orderly, not a hysterical, passionate flight into another man's arms. Oh God. She could practically feel him. Remembering his fingers on the inside of her arm, the gentleness of his touch, she wondered if she hadn't chosen a stupid time to be wise.

Her rope-soled sandals offered only slight protection against the hazards of the beach near the hotel, bumpy with large round rocks and pebbles, littered with beer cans and mango pits. It angered her that this most singular, visually dramatic portion of earth should be peopled by those with no appreciation of its beauty, scarring the waters where their own children swam. On the first day of their visit, Chris, Harry, Josh and Caroline had made a pilgrimage to the beach at Algodones, site of the area's most fabled sunsets. "Catch-22" beach it was called, after that portion of airstrip built by the film company, leaving behind its display of bombed-out buildings, mock ruins where people now lived, Hollywood's ravages being less impoverished than some of Mexico's splendors. The beach had become a lure to locals because of the spectre of movies and glamor. When Chris and her family arrived, it was so thick with garbage, they could not maneuver to the shore.

"Why don't they throw it in the garbage cans?" Josh had asked miserably, looking at the cans set up along the beach, all of them empty, watching emaciated cows nosing through the rubble for corn husks.

"You have to say to them, please don't put anything in the garbage cans," their taxi driver had said. "You have to tell them, if you throw it in the garbage cans, you go to jail. Then, they put it in the garbage cans."

Chris supposed it was all men's ignorance, intensified, desecrating the earth, abusing what was privilege, beauty, flaunting the brutality of a nature insensitive to the wonders of the planet, even as it made a show of observing them. Well, there was no way to clean up the beaches, but she could keep her own life polished, and not add to the dark scar of a marriage failed the blemish of adultery. She and the universe had both forgiven her Tony Candella: what would be unforgivable was if she hadn't learned anything. The purpose of life was to grow, to evolve, to move into the next adventure equipped with lessons from the last. One thing she knew for sure: it was all downhill from eye contact. The lusty act itself could never touch the hot, subtle promise it had held in the mirror.

Besides, Adam was perfectly happy in his marriage, Chris was sure of it. Denise was the right wife for him, sleek pillar of the community, slightly bored, slightly boring. Men like Adam would never be comfortable with wives who were trouble, complicated women who might take some of the energies they laser-beamed onto their careers. Denise was the right partner for him, enough for him.

230

He would have argued with Chris, she knew that much about him already. Being a craftsman in the courts of law, he probably would have argued effectively, persuaded her, tilted her into bed. It would be better not to be with him, not to see him alone. She wondered how they would manage to sneak off, planned the opportunities. She brought her attention back to the beach, and gave him up, leaving him a footstep at a time in the sands and rocks behind her.

When she got back to the hotel, he was sitting by the pool. He smiled at her, past Denise's sombreroed profile. It was all there, straight ahead, what she had seen in reflection. Desire. Lush. Delicious. She could taste him.

Harry was splashing in the pool with Josh and Nicky, raising them, one at a time, to his shoulders, becoming their diving platform. Nicky had a look of total happiness on his face, a freer joy than Chris had observed there. Harry had captured him. The Pied Piper of Beverly Hills, loosed in Sonora, stealing the hearts of other men's children, even the other man who could steal his wife.

She lay down on a chaise next to Caroline and tried to imitate her absorption in the sun. Caroline was chocolate now, her skin darkened to the color of her eyes, cheeks burned berry bright, slashes like paint along the bone. Something like peace sat on her countenance. Chris struggled for the same expression, as though she weren't waiting for him, smelling him, feeling him walking toward her. She could actually feel him through her face, blazing into heat from more than sun.

"Good morning," Adam said. His voice stroked her spine.

"Oh, good morning," Chris feigned surprise, as though she hadn't seen him through closed eyelids, been struck by his shadow.

"Did you sleep well?"

"Yes," she lied. "And you?"

"Not very well." He sat down next to her.

What was he telling her? And telling her honestly, as directly as he could with her daughter sitting there beside them, her great dark eyes suddenly wide open, not even squinting against the sun. Chris had the distinct impression Caroline saw it all clearly, where it might lead, and with whom. Like a teenage heroine on a science fiction planet, she seemed already to have sent telepathic alarms to her father, who was lifting himself out of the pool, clambering towards them with athletic grace but not too much speed, as if he felt no panic about what was going on. Not that anything was.

"You have a remarkable way with children," Adam said to Harry, "I've been watching you with my son. I think I've lost him to you."

"He's a nice guy," Harry said, adjusting his big frame into a chair.

"I envy that in you, being able to guide Josh through Little League."

"Thank you," said Harry. "There are some things I envy you."

How much did he intuit, Chris wondered. He had always known what was happening to her before she knew it. Did he have eyes in the back of his head? Had he seen what was happening in the mirror? Even in his sleep, had he perceived her wakefulness, known what rendered her so restless?

"They found a note from Alana O'Connor," Adam told Chris. "The police arrested an old *mariguano*. A bum who must have been the first one to the bodies. He tried to sell her watch. He also had a pair of her earrings, and the note."

"What did it say?" Chris asked him.

"I'll show it to you," Adam said, getting up. "It's in my briefcase. Come."

Caroline was on her feet with a swiftness totally out of character, alert, like a soldier who had just received orders,

232

stationed beside her mother. "Nobody invited you," Harry said.

"Oh." She slithered back down on the chaise.

"We'll be right back," Chris said.

"Uh-huh," Harry said, and closed his eyes.

When they had turned the corner, and were safe in a cluster of trees, out of sight of those by the pool, Adam reached for her hand. "Not even that," Chris said.

"Why?"

"Because if we touch, we won't be able to end it."

"What makes you think we can end it now?"

His eyes were nearly purple, deepened against the backdrop of fuchsia bougainvillea. His very slightness moved her. She had had enough of manifest strength, looking up to men she couldn't look up to.

"We have to."

"Why?"

"Because you're happy with Denise."

"Are you happy with Harry?"

She felt a flash flood of laughter cascading through her. My God, she could get him wholesale. Evelyn would be ecstatic. Lustrous at last in her mother's eyes. One of the top attorneys in the country, and he'd do her divorce for nothing. Well, almost nothing. Chris was suddenly reminded of a number of friends who'd gotten involved with their gynecologists. Well, was it that different, looking into her divorce?

"We'll be leaving tomorrow," he said, urgently. "We have to take the bodies back."

"What did the note say?"

"I can't show it to you. I only used it as an excuse to get you away. But wouldn't it be interesting if it said something like they did it to stay in love."

"Sad."

"If I promise not to hold your hand, may I kiss you?"

233

"If it's good-bye," she said. "Only if you understand it's good-bye."

"I understand," he said, and kissed her then. As his look had gone no deeper than her eyes, but all the way inside her eyes, his kiss went no deeper than her lips. And as the kiss was all there would be, it felt like everything.

Harry rubbed a spot of dust from his Gucci loafers, the one status symbol he still clung to. Feet of clay, he thought, could at least be well shod. He had been silent most of the afternoon, politely but unenthusiastically inviting the Wilkersons to dinner, his relief ill concealed when Adam declined. As the two of them dressed for dinner, Harry listened to Chris prattling a little too merrily, the Trapp Family Singers covering their escape with music. Not all the words in the world could conceal what he heard bleating inside her.

"Did you have a nice talk with Adam?" he finally asked.

"We didn't talk very much," she said. "We weren't gone long."

"I noticed."

"You look wonderful in that color. Very handsome. You should wear brown more often."

"Did he tell you to say that? Did he tell you to mix me up by being nice to me, and then you can change the locks on the doors like they do to those other poor schmucks, and everything will go the way you want it?"

"What set you off?"

"How long am I supposed to play the patsy? How long am I supposed to act like I don't know what's going on? With your mother the cheerleader spurring you on, the Dallas Cowgirl of Divorce. Did Adam tell you to be nice to me as a tactic?"

"We didn't discuss divorce."

234

"Shame on you. He's supposed to be one of the best. He really could have helped you work me over."

"I don't want to do that," she said.

"What do you want to do?"

"I don't know." She reached all the way inside herself for courage. "I think I want out."

He was quiet for a moment, a terrible quiet that came from the same realization she had, that her words had not been spoken in anger. "You can't have the kids," he said, at last. "They're mine."

"I think they should have a chance to decide . . ."

"It's already decided. You were never there."

"That isn't true."

"Oh, maybe in the beginning, when they were a new field for you. But when they needed you, when it wasn't convenient . . . You perfect example of a working mother . . . You were never there."

So it was finally out in the open, the accusation. Bad mother. There were worse things a woman could be than ball-breaker.

"You were never there."

"Don't say it again," she pleaded.

"I just want you to know I'll fight you."

"You don't have to fight. They can go where they want." And where would she go? To the spa? What would she do without them? What would they do without her? As elusive as she might have seemed, she had always been their mother, a presence. True, they could survive without her, although according to the studies she'd read they would be more likely to experiment with drugs, to have their grades suffer, to be disoriented and confused because of divorce, and single parenting. What a cold euphemism.

She knew that the children of "shared parenting"—cute expression—fared no better, experiencing even greater disorder, not knowing where they were when they woke up, the tangle of their lives reflected in their sleeping as well as their homework. She would not do that to her children, petition for some days with one parent, some with the other, cloud those bright, clear minds with even more turmoil. Of course she would insist on sharing the important decisions affecting the lives of her children. But she knew what custody battles really were: a twist on the game of "Keepaway."

Josh had already made his preference pretty clear. She could review in her mind the mistakes she'd made; she could go back in time and hold him so close that Harry couldn't get him; she could make herself the one who had pressed her mouth to his, her spirit to his, her mind to his. But there were no spells to be cast in custody cases, no clocks to be magically rewound. He was probably lost to her. Caroline, Chris assumed, would also choose her father. Chris could not imagine that her daughter loved her. Caroline stared at her with what seemed to Chris the same reproof in her eyes as Evelyn.

So she was ready to surrender them, to acknowledge her womanly role of coward, and give them up without a battle. But what would she do, in between melodies? Who would fill the spaces? What was this myth of independence? She had thought she loved Harry best for setting her free, it being an endowment of men to emancipate women, contributed to by the women themselves, to make it enduring, like a perpetual trust at a college. Generous men granted a tenuous freedom, giving women a chance to make mistakes while silently entreating them not to. This act of liberating while tacitly beseeching a woman to stay captive was a clever tyranny, a variant of which he seemed to be using now. Letting her go without malice, without entreating her to stay. Not using any leverage, except the children. The children. Nothing to keep her in her place, but gravity.

"If they want to be with you, you can have them," she said.

236

"Okay." He averted his eyes as though vanquishing her shamed him. He resumed his grooming, inspecting himself in the mirror, touching the collar of his soft brown shirt, to put it exactly in line. His eyes lost their paleness, the milky yellow that invaded their green when he was angry or challenged. "God, what a prune she is, that Denise. Adam must be a very constipated man to be married to her."

It was an ancient manner of attack, one he usually reserved for men he viewed as menacing their relationship, a technique she had not picked up on in the early days of their marriage, when it hadn't occurred to her she might ever be interested in anyone else. She had come to recognize his style only with Tony Candella, the witty onslaught, the subtle lampooning. That he was doing it now with Adam, prodding her with the implication of his coldness, tightness, the suggestion Adam would not be giving enough for her, open enough, loving enough, the way Harry had been once, was both touching and infuriating. It meant he understood what a threat Adam was, but not that she intended to do nothing about it. He had no idea the transformation that had taken place in her. Understandable, really, since she hardly grasped it herself.

As she saw the reason for his carom shots at Adam, she now understood Harry's behavior the previous evening. How wily he was. Like variation on Evelyn's theme that the way to a man's heart was through friendship with his wife, he'd been parrying Adam by wooing him into camaraderie. Chris realized now he'd done that through the years—she could conjure in her mind a line of men who'd seemed interested in her, but who after lunches or tennis with Harry had mysteriously disappeared. She suddenly saw with dazzling clarity the clever way he had guarded his nest, tried to disarm Adam with his honesty, his openness, so that Adam would have had to say, when Harry cut them loose, sent them off alone: "I couldn't do it to Harry."

Well, it hadn't worked. But he'd certainly given it his best shot, she had to say that for him. She felt mildly amazed at the number of shots she hadn't noted, and happily surprised by her own restraint. Maybe everybody was turning out more interesting than she'd anticipated.

Dinner was a strangely quiet meal. Caroline kept looking at her mother, eating more greedily than usual, her dark eyes moving anxiously around the somber, high-ceilinged hotel dining room, preparing for troubled news.

"I ate too much, I need to take a walk. Want to come?" Harry asked Chris.

"Sure," said Josh, wiping his mouth with a napkin.

"He wasn't speaking to you," said Caroline.

"Wrong," sang Josh, a tuneless melody. "It was you he wasn't speaking to."

"Anyone can come who wants to," Harry said.

"I'm going to have dessert," said Caroline.

"Be careful it doesn't go to your jugs," sneered Josh.

"Doesn't it embarrass you," Caroline asked Chris, "to have a son who's a swine? It's just like Alice in Wonderland. You think you've had a baby, but what it is is a pig. Oink, oink," she tried to nasal after him, but he was already out of earshot.

"You should try not to let him bother you," Chris said.

"He doesn't bother me. It probably bothers you because you love him. Don't you?"

"Yes. I love both my children."

"It should be easier to love someone who *isn't* a swine." Caroline pointed to the strawberry tart on the cake tray the waiter held out to her, smiled with pleasure as he set it on the table. "*Gracias.*"

"*Esto,*" Chris said, indicating a chocolate layer cake, like Caroline, dulling her uneasiness with food.

"*Este*," Caroline corrected. "*Este*."

"Sorry."

"That's all right," Caroline said, a sudden relaxed maturity on her face, as if the combination of dessert and being able to correct her mother had catapulted her into self-possession.

"You're a wonderful color," Chris said. "Are you having a nice vacation, even if it isn't Palm Springs?"

"It's all right," said Caroline, a slightly dour expression pulling at the corners of her mouth, tugging her back into sullen insecurity. "I just wish we could go someplace normal."

"Why are you so sour with me, sweetheart? All your friends have so much fun with you, all their mothers tell me what a darling girl you are. Why do you change when you're with me?"

Caroline shrugged. "Maybe because I don't know what to talk to you about."

"You can talk to me about anything you want to."

"All you care about is your work. All you talk about is your work. You should hear yourself on the phone. You could make a recording." She sighed, and stuffed a strawberry between her ripe red lips, sugary pectin deepening the color.

"I didn't realize that about myself," Chris said. Nor had she realized how often Caroline overheard her conversations, or how interestedly.

"Well, listen sometimes. Everything is your work. *I'm* your work."

Chris was stunned by the hurt in her daughter's eyes. Just before they had left on vacation, Chris had received the Bryn Mawr Alumnae Bulletin, which, with the curious synchronicity her life seemed to be taking on, was entirely devoted to the problem of children and work. "The most difficult aspect of holding a professional job and having a family is the continual pressure that forces you to compromise, and do less than your very best at work and at mothering," it said on the back cover. The contents had been a catalogue of anguish: women who had had children right after college, whose lives were now empty; women who had never been able to have children, and desperately tried; women who had never wanted children, and had chosen a career; and, most agonizing of all, a divorcee whose husband had been given custody because she was a "Career woman," and so, by definition, wasn't considered interested in her children by the courts.

The bulletin had unloosed in Chris a kind of free-floating distress because what it really meant was there wasn't any answer. No matter what choice a woman made, it seemed to be wrong.

"I don't feel like that," Chris told her daughter. "Really I don't. I love you, Caroline. Why do you always pull away?"

"Maybe I'm not smart enough for you," Caroline said. The great dark eyes welled with tears, half-filling, so their radiance was intensified, floating in sparkle.

"Oh, honey," Chris said, and put her arms around her. "That isn't true."

"Yes it is," Caroline said, her eyes overflowing.

Chris held her close, her own tears coming to greet her child's. What a bitch it was to be set loose in a changing world—even worse than being unintentionally one of the changes. If Caroline was in so much pain, how must the rest of them feel? What was Harry going through? Not enough that he was bright, and once had been funny; what could he really contribute to Chris? What could he give on a creative level? How from his world of disappointed reality could he ask to join her in the dance?

The only one who could really keep up with the nimbleness of her thought was Josh. And he was so terrified by that link between them—the unnaturalness of being smart, like his *mother*—he sped to the ball fields to be like his father, struggling to become obtuse. Uncomfortable for all of them was having her as mother. So it wasn't just the bright woman who suffered in a society where women were not supposed to be bright: it was her whole family.

That night, she did not sleep again. Adam was still a factor in her wakefulness, but slightly diluted now, a part of the entire puzzle. She went to the balcony and observed the blossoming moon, wondered if she would ever sleep again. She had read recent data that revealed falling in love released a chemical in the brain, phenylethylamine, which was why lovers couldn't sleep, were short of breath, lost their appetites, moped around, sighing. Depression whipped into speeding, an amazing high, fed by the thought, the sight of the loved one. Was that what was loose in her? Was it Adam who had triggered it? Or was it other kinds of love, the curious anguished affection she felt welling up in her, like Caroline's tears, for that daughter she had always imagined didn't love her. Who loved her better than anyone, Chris saw that clearly now; loved her with the same fierceness Chris had loved Evelyn, only to be rejected. So those weren't Evelyn's eyes that had been looking at her out of her daughter: they were her own eyes, looking at Evelyn. God, what a trip, not in the California but the human sense.

How thick everybody was, coming at whatever ailed them from the angle of their own pain, never imagining that everyone else was in comparable agony. Why was love, in all its aspects, so complicated? Why couldn't it be simplified, maybe even packaged. Maybe they could isolate that drug, market it, and everybody could take it all the time. Women could take it when they were with their husbands and feel the way they did when with their lovers. Society with its Judeo-Christian ethic could continue peacefully, if pharmaceutically. Families would be preserved, marriages saved.

And what of her own marriage? Having acknowledged that she wanted to be released, speaking the words, so the truth was floating around her, had cast her curiously adrift, as if the subterranean wish for divorce had been her ballast. Harry seemed sadly subdued. It felt like a war was over, and everybody was dead, no one left even to recount what the issue had been that caused the battle. No standard on the field still waving. Only broken bodies, vanquished spirits.

She could hear him snoring. Quietly, she moved to his bed and eased him on his side. The snoring stopped. If only all the sandpaper agonies of marriage could have been so easily handled.

She studied his face. Handsome it was, clearly that which the world considered appropriate for masculine beauty darkly present, high, wide forehead, thick eyebrows, imposing nose, a jaw with a stubborn set. But what of the part that was not appropriate, a too-tender spirit inside, a genie in a bottle. A man who could rescue a baby, but whom money set to trembling. Well, didn't everybody have their personal dragons? Why was she as unforgiving as he had been craven?

She moved her glance around his face as though it were her fingers and could tingle them both back into infatuation. That was the best part, wasn't it? Wasn't that really what she felt for Adam? Wasn't infatuation the most you could feel, when something was new, and you didn't know it well enough to feel anything deeper, or be bored? Keeping it exciting, giving it its freshness, making it too alive with unknowables to compartmentalize, too surprising to be tedious?

What turned it into love? What made it become more caring than wanting? When did you desire more for him, than from him?

Love was a key to transcending or it wouldn't be love. But transcending what? Transcending self to get to true joining? Transcending the joining to get to God?

God. She could practically hear the voice of Bette Davis, saying "How very amusing." A struggle you didn't dare have in public, didn't speak of, even in private, unless you were very sure of the people you were with. The love that dared not speak its name was out of the closet, dancing in the streets, becoming part of the platform of political parties. But people still spoke in whispers of God.

In the East the erotic was a stepping stone to God, the fusion of man and woman, a way to higher incandescence. Sex was a creative act, sacred, raising man from the ordinary world to the unknown. But in the West the erotic was secondary; in America, it had been refined to an unavoidable embarrassment, the poor relative at table with too hearty an appetite, making lusty noises.

The East, she supposed, was an irrational reference point, since besides sanctifying the erotic, it also prayed to a God that was Father and Mother. Any woman worth her pillar of salt understood that God was a masculine principle, or why would He have made it that much harder to be a woman? Unless it was that the whole struggle was spiritual, and women were that much more capable of enduring—maybe even long enough to find out what the lesson was.

She moved back over to her bed, where her son had chosen to sleep again, as if he could balance favoring his father by giving her his nights. He did not cry out in his sleep now. No incubus riddled his dreaming. No horrors of losing at Little League, or being abandoned, or falling, or any one of the myraid nightmares of childhood seemed to disturb his rest. She lay down beside him. He felt almost peaceful next to her, as if the holiday had cleansed him, the waters, even polluted, providing a cure.

She turned and studied his face by moonlight. How beautiful he was, how much more voluptuous of feature than either of his parents, with his full, pouting lips, and strange, wide-set eyes, Oriental in their mounting, mysterious. What was it she felt for him so different than anything she had felt for his father? Not maternal love simply: it was not what she felt for Caroline. Why? Because he was a boy, and boys were better? Even the psychologist Chris had taken them to for testing, in their double-bright babyhoods, when Caroline was six, and Josh was four, even she had said, when she checked the results, "Well, isn't it lucky that the more gifted one is the boy." A *woman* psychologist who had risen not only above the pigeonholing of her sex but had literally lifted herself above crippling disease, a deforming arthritis. Even as she sat, twisted in her chair, a triumph over impossible obstacles, the woman had rejoiced that the greater capabilities were the *boy's.* The living argument against chauvinism, arguing for it.

When would it end? Where would it go? How would women ever be free? And if she packed very quietly, could she run away with Adam?

She saw him in the lobby, just before he left the hotel. In his three-piece suit, armored for his forays against the windmills of civilization, he looked bigger, more solid, as if the appropriate garments for his field added weight to his convictions, made his footstep surer. What gave businessmen greater comfort in clothes that made them uncomfortable, Chris wondered, and what was it in women that responded? Maybe it wasn't just little girls that liked to play dress-up. Maybe boys, too, hungered for their turn to look impressive. She marveled at being so stirred by the sight of him in those clothes, when what she had been sure she wanted was to see him naked.

Denise came into the lobby, instructing the bellman about the luggage while Adam settled the bill. From the hard wooden bench on which she sat, Chris observed them, noted how suited they really were to each other, Adam and his prune. Wasn't that odd, how Harry could still do that to her, turn her off someone with a word.

"Well, good-bye," Denise said, coming over to her, kissing both her cheeks, San Francisco society French.

"Good-bye," Chris said.

"And say good-bye to Josh, and Caroline and . . ." she hesitated.

"Harry," Chris said.

". . . Harry . . . I've got to go get Nicholas," Denise said, and left the lobby.

What was there about Harry that made it so hard to remember his name? Was it that same, sweet inconspicuousness that had mitigated against him in business, his reticence to impose himself, as imposing as he had once been, as imposing as his physical presence still was. A powerful figure of a man, who seemed nonetheless to make not enough of an impression, as if he preferred remaining in shadow. No longer Superman failed, or Captain Marvel, but Lamont Cranston, not with the power to cloud other men's minds, but to cloud his own. To try and make himself invisible, because there was not much to parade. "What do you do?" was almost everyone's first question. Having no answer that satisfied his spirit, the image he'd once had of himself, he preferred to remain anonymous, and so did. No noteworthy achievements except his beautiful unit, and that about to be dismantled. Chris felt a spasm of indignant rage for him and wondered if, in a better world, people would be judged by their quality and not their accomplishments.

How peculiar passion was, especially adulterous passion. In the presence of Tony Candella she had come to hunger for her husband. Now with Adam moving toward her she was filled with righteous indignation for Harry.

"Will you call me?" Adam said, in a voice just above a whisper, filled with urgency, intimacy.

"I don't think so."

"Don't be afraid to change your mind. It's a woman's prerogative."

"A man said that," Chris noted.

He looked amused. "What would a woman say?"

"I don't know yet. I'm working it out."

"Well, when you do, don't hesitate to call me. Good luck." He held out his hand.

She shook it, trying for the brusque manner of business, struggling not to feel his palm. "I hope your life will be joyful all the time."

He smiled at her, a little ruefully. "It's not supposed to be joyful all the time."

Sometimes, she realized with a quickening of her heart, the best love affairs were the ones that didn't happen.

The plane that carried the coffins of Alana O'Connor and James Moffatt, escorted by the Wilkerson family, was owned by a member of the board of the Hibernia Bank, an adoptive uncle of Alana's, and was slightly smaller in size than *Air Force One*. Evelyn, alighting from the private jet that had transported her from Guadalajara, was moved by the sleekness of the funeral plane to cast about her eyes for its owner. Seeing the slender, slightly sunburned San Francisco lawyer climbing the ramp, his path once again crossing hers, she was moved to cry out, "Ships that pass in the night!" waving merrily to him, in case he just couldn't bear it and had to ask her to come with him, wife, son, coffins and all. He looked at her with a slightly puzzled frown, waved unsurely, and went inside the plane.

"Probably his wife is a very jealous woman," Evelyn explained to the porter carrying her bag.

He did not understand English or Americans. But he smiled at her as though he cared what she was saying, a look of total blankness in his eyes. It was a reaction Evelyn had long been accustomed to seeing in her husbands, so she felt almost at home, in spite of the fact that the airport unsettled her, as had the trip. It was the first she had ever taken in a private jet, placed entirely at her disposal, or as her pilot had said, "*a sus ordenes.*" It had struck her as all very daring and Hemingway, a fantasy she had never particularly entertained, her only imagined privately airborne adventures being courtesy of Brut, at the side of Cary Grant. Like most callous hearts in handsome disguises, he had foiled her, first by never meeting her, then by marrying someone he met. There seemed to her to be very little balance in the universe, awarding the few attractive men in their seventies to women in their thirties, whereas women like herself, (even looking not a *day* over forty-five—well, maybe a few days) were forced to forage for crumbs. Not that her new conquest was a crumb, exactly, but he was no Cary Grant, and for that she would never forgive either of them.

Nor had she enjoyed the physical aspect of her journey, bumpy as it was, through threatening skies. As grateful as she was to be on land, she seemed to be faring no better. By the time her taxi reached the Playa de Cortés the roads were awash in a downpour. In the single suitcase she'd brought with her was a bathing suit for the afternoon, a hairbrush and makeup, and a change of dress in case she spilled on herself at lunch. That she had not thought to bring another pair of shoes was less evidence of bad planning, in her mind, than of the general hostility evinced by the entire locale, which she considered was trying to reject her personally, like her daughters, the one disappeared in the desert, the other finding the most obscure corner of the world, offering neither easy access, nor quick escape. Unless, of course, one had met a Mexican millionaire in Guadalajara, and he'd placed at one's *ordenes* his private jet.

In spite of the deluge, Evelyn felt practically merry. It had been a long time since anyone paid tribute to her in terms she could understand. She had been driven to the plane in his private limousine, found the cabin bedecked with roses, which she'd quickly thrown onto the runway, spraying the cabin and the air around her nostrils with *Norell*. So she supposed if her shoes were ruined by the same skies that could rain a mustachioed surprise, it was small sacrifice.

But hearing the squish of her soles as she made her way along the sheltered arcades of the hotel's first floor, a blustery wind rendering her protection of small suitcase nearly useless, she resolved that Chris's future holidays would be spent someplace easier to get to. Either that, or Evelyn would make Jorge buy a helicopter.

She climbed the stairs to Chris's room and pounded heavily on the door. "Who is it?" Josh cried from inside.

"Let me in," she said, pounding. "Let me in."

There was silence from inside. "Not by the hair of my chinny-chin-chin," said Josh after a moment.

"You're going to have to do something about his mouth," said Evelyn as Chris opened the door.

"I thought it was pretty funny," said Chris, laughing.

"How come you're back?" asked Caroline. She was sitting on the floor, wedged against the French doors of the balcony in a slightly collapsed posture, looking upward, checking the clouds for the sun that had to be behind them. Josh settled himself on the edge of Harry's bed, placing himself between Evelyn and his dather, who lay sleeping, one hand flung over his eyes.

"I've met a Mexican millionaire!" announced Evelyn joyously, slipping out of her shoes, setting them in front of the fireplace, where twigs and twisted branches crackled orange flames. "He's crazy about me. He sent me here on his private jet. Imagine. He said if I wanted I could bring you all back to

Guadalajara, as his guests. He has the most fabulous home. Like a castle. Start packing."

"No, thank you, mother."

"*Madre,*" Evelyn said. "Call me *madre*. My God, these floors aren't even carpeted." She sat down on a chair, put her feet up, and made a face. "I can understand your wanting to stay here. It isn't beautiful, but it certainly is uncomfortable."

"I like it," said Josh.

"Is it sunny in Guadalajara?" asked Caroline.

"Brilliant sunshine," Evelyn said. "Brilliant everything. Roses, for those who like flowers. For those of us who don't, planes at our disposal, to fly anywhere."

"What about Palm Springs?" Caroline said.

"Is that where you want to go, my little darling? I think first you should see Guadalajara."

"Can I?" Caroline asked her mother.

"I want you to stay with us," said Chris.

"I don't understand you, Chrissie. All your life complaining that I never showed you enough affection, and here I am, trying to give you a wonderfal holiday, andyou're not even excited. Why don't you get excited about things, like your husband. Look how animated he is." She indicated the sleeping Harry. "Hmm. The rest of the virtuous. He's probably worn out from all his success and hard work."

"All right, mother. Is that why you came back?"

"I told you why I came back. Jorge loves me. And I love you. You and your beautiful children, even though one of them, I won't say which one, is wicked. Imagine, Jorge will send me anywhere I want to go."

"How about the moon?" asked Josh.

"You know, you're really a very naughty little boy. I don't know why your mother worries so much about giving you up."

"What's she talking about?" asked Josh.

249

"Good-bye, mother."

"I'm not leaving so fast. My shoes have to dry."

"You can have a pair of mine."

"Don't bother. You buy them at Chandler's. I've checked the insoles."

"What did she mean about giving me up?" asked Josh.

"Why don't the two of you go downstairs and play," Chris said. Caroline's eyes were on her, ebony now, with the darkness of the day, the sudden shadow on the room. "It's raining."

"Go play in the lobby."

"There's no one to play with," Josh said. "Nicky's gone."

"There are other children."

"They're Mexicans," said Josh.

"Don't be a bigot," said Evelyn. "You yourself may become Mexican by marriage very soon." She smiled at Chris. "You're going to love Jorge. He's so vigorous, so volatile! You should see him lose his temper! It's like Sonny in the old days."

"I would have thought you had enough of those," said Chris.

"Well I haven't. I'm not ready for serenity. I still want sex and violence."

"Go downstairs and play," Chris instructed her children, opening the door for them.

"They can get it on television." Evelyn shrugged. "Why try to hide it from them in their family?"

"Do old people have sex?" Josh asked, just before Chris closed the door behind him and Caroline.

"He is, he's absolutely wicked," Evelyn said. "No loss to you at all. You're lucky he doesn't love you."

"He does love me." Tears stung Chris's eyes. "Why'd you come back? To hurt me? To hurt Josh? To hurt us all?"

"I would never hurt Caroline. She has impeccable taste.

Nor would I hurt you. I came back to show you I love you. Your trouble is, you don't know how to deal with people on your own level. Always sinking to those unworthy of you, for what you consider *love*." Evelyn mocked the word.

"Well, that's what you did for my self-esteem."

"Oh come on. It's a little late in the day for you to blame your *mother*. You're thirty-three years old, that's what I told Jorge. Time you started blaming yourself. Whatever you are now is your own doing. At least it will be, as soon as you unload that loser."

"Stop calling him that."

"Why must you defend him even when it's over? The fact that he's a failure isn't your fault."

"Well, it isn't his—"

"Whose is it, then, *his* mother's?"

"Maybe. Maybe she did for his self-esteem what you did for mine."

"Don't blame her. She's a very good-natured woman, no matter how she dresses. All this crap about self-esteem. What people do is based on their brains, and their guts, and he doesn't have enough of either."

"That isn't true."

"Why do you cling to him? Why do you protect him?"

"He protected me."

"From what? Your trouble is, you can't face reality. Just like you don't want your children to face it. It's a terrible world, filled with murder and mayhem and hatred, with people assassinating nuns and presidents and popes. And none of the killers are mothers. You just don't know where to put the blame. Put it on your husband, where blame belongs. Stop being so strong about some things and a weakling where you should be strong. Get a divorce! It isn't a failure, it's a sign of growth. Nothing about you is a failure, except your husband."

On the bed, Harry stirred. "You see," Evelyn said. "He recognizes his description. Harry. I never even liked the name. Aristotle Onassis. *That* was a name."

"If I had married Aristotle Onassis, my son would be dead."

"If you had married Aristotle Onassis, you could have bought all the sons you wanted."

A snort escaped Harry. "That, too," marked Evelyn. "You really got a package."

"I'm having a terrible dream," said Harry, from underneath his arm. "I'm dreaming that the storm brought back your mother."

"Go back to sleep, honey," Chris said.

"Honey? You still call him honey? What hypocrisy! Or is that just California?"

Harry's hand moved off his eyes. Warily he opened them. "Oh, my God, it's true. I was hoping I'd wake up and be home in Kansas." He pulled the pillow from behind his head and put it over his face.

"Very funny," said Evelyn. "I can see where your son gets hie non-sense of humor. Why would you even care about custody? Why would you want him when he's so much like his father?"

"Get her out of here!" Harry said, muffled, from underneath the pillow.

"Come with me to Guadalajara. Get Caroline and come with me. Leave them both."

"Put your shoes on, mother. I'll take you to a taxi."

"I'll take her to a taxi," Harry said, and sat up.

"Don't make a show of gallantry for me," Evelyn said. "I know what you come from. And I am here under the aegis of Jorge Rodriguez, a *gentleman*."

"Mother's found a Mexican millionaire," Chris explained.

"You better knock him off before he learns English well enough to understand you," said Harry.

"Don't get nasty. Just because my daughter finally has the sense to see you for the failure you are, and divorce you."

"I'm not so sure who the failure is," Chris said. "I think I'm the failure."

"Women cannot be failures. They can only marry them."

"Not anymore. It's a new world, mother. Women have their own chance to fail."

"Not me!" said Evelyn, blithely, and went to the fireplace, checking her shoes.

"Well, I don't want to be like you."

Evelyn stiffened. "That's good, because you can't. In order to be like me, you would have had to be dazzling in your youth, dazzling. And you weren't. The only reason he married you was because he thought your family was rich, and they'd make it easy for him."

"Well, we fooled him, didn't we?"

"Not that he deserves any better. With all your faults, you're still miles above him. Him and his little brute. I look at him, I see this . . . sinking ship."

"You better watch your mouth, Evelyn," Harry said, "or I'll let you have one straight in the chops."

Evelyn turned to Chris. "Are you going to permit him to talk this way to me?"

"She's going to *permit* me to do nothing." Harry was on his feet now, moving toward Evelyn. "I'm the man." He pointed to his chest. "Do you understand that, *I'm* the man."

"I understand it, Harry. I'm thrilled to death that you finally understand it."

He started for her, hand upraised. Chris rushed between them. His hand cracked across her cheek.

"I saw that!" Evelyn shouted. "I saw that! Unprovoked violence! I'll be a witness to it in court."

"I bet you will. What will you wear?"

"Don't you see, you can get them both now! No judge would award children to a man who beats his wife. Caroline

253

will pick you anyway, she knows what side her bread is buttered on. She'll pick you just like you picked me, because you wanted my old clothes."

"I wanted *you*," Chris said. "I wanted you. When are you going to understand that?"

"*Now*. I understand it *now*. You can have me, and Caroline, and that little delinquent too, though why you'd want him is beyond me."

"You'd better go," Chris said.

"And leave you alone with him, as violent as he is? He's crazy. I always knew he was crazy, even if he doesn't come from a good family. I saw him hit you. I'll testify to it. Should I wear my Chanel, or borrow a housedress from his mother?"

"Shut up," Harry said darkly.

"Please get out," Chris said.

"You'd side with him, after what he did to you? You'd drive your mother out in the rain? What's the matter with you? Are you deranged?" Evelyn put her shoes on. "It must be Sonny's genes."

"Sonny was my stepfather," Chris said.

"You were always more like him than me."

"Thank you," said Chris.

"So smart. Always such a little smart aleck. You're as wicked as your son. And to think I was going to have Jorge give you money to help you out of your troubles." She walked toward the door, squeaking from her insteps. "I certainly don't intend to ask you to the wedding." Her hand was on the knob. "But I still expect to be invited to the divorce."

The wind slammed the door behind her. "Are you all right?" Harry asked Chris.

"I'm all right."

"I didn't mean to hit you." He was leaning against the marble mantel of the fireplace, his head bent, as though he were looking at the fire. "She makes me crazy."

254

"I understand the feeling."

He sighed, a great release of air. His wide, muscular back, its breadth emphasized by the T-shirt he wore, seemed rounded, as if to the defeat the world had imposed on him had been added a drubbing by his mother-in-law. In his own way Harry had always seemed to carry rank, distinction—not the high nobility that came from birth but what was well meaning, exemplary. With all that had happened to him, or failed to happen, he had never displayed the boorishness Evelyn attributed to him.

But now he had. With Evelyn's curious ability to bring out in those around her their darkest fears about themselves, she had in that moment transformed Harry into the villain she thought him.

Chris moved to the fireplace, touched his back, rested her cheek against the expanse of it. "What's that for?" he asked. "You like getting hit?"

"I'm sorry she did that to you."

"I shouldn't have reacted."

"You'd have to be made of steel not to react."

"I am made of steel," he said, and smiled, a little mournfully. "But your mother carries kryptonite."

She smiled. Her arms went around him.

"She's right about my being a failure."

Her arms fell away. No matter how sorry you felt for a man, it seemed he could always feel sorrier for himself. "That's not true, Harry. You've kept us going with the store."

"The store." He walked to the French doors, watching the rain beating on the glass. "I'm so sick of yogurt. I wanted to be with people, greet them, give them things that made them happy. Like music, and fattening food. Yogurt. Wheat germ."

"Not everybody gets their dream," she said softly. She'd assumed love would provide all the answers, that marriage

255

would be her refuge. Faced with her own disillusion, her grief, her guilt, because it wasn't the way she'd expected it to be, she felt little darts of pain when she looked at him, little waves of loss. Well, the Lord must have loved bad marriages, she thought, or He wouldn't have made so many of them.

"Maybe I ought to get out of this business," Harry was saying. "Chapter Eleven. If at first you don't succeed, bankrupt."

"Why don't you stop feeling sorry for yourself?"

"It isn't just me I feel sorry for. It's you. I feel so helpless to support you. I mean, really support you. To pull for you when things are good and back you up when they're not. The way Adam could. You should have married a lawyer."

"If I'd known what a good client I'd turn out to be, I might have." She smiled.

"But we did have a lot of fun in the beginning," he said.

"Not just the beginning."

There was a knock on the door. "Open up, it's me, Josh." He was soaking wet, the inverted bowl of chestnut hair matted down, weighted so it hung below his lashes, half-obscuring his eyes, as though he'd failed to listen to Chicken Little, and the sky had fallen on him. Raindrops, like tears, nestled in the hollows above his high cheekbones, glistened against his freckles. "Is she gone?"

"She's gone." Chris reached for the bottom of his shirt, started pulling it over his head. He stood docile, letting her undress him.

"I saw her go," Josh said, inside his sodden T-shirt. "I hid behind a pillar." His face pulled free. He looked at Chris with dark, uncertain eyes. "Is it okay that I didn't say good-bye? I was afraid if I said good-bye she'd kiss me and tell me how bad I am."

"You aren't bad," she said. "You're wonderful."

"You're right," he said, but he was shivering. She put her

256

arms around him and felt how cold his skin was, how fragile his spirit was, for all the stockiness, how woundable, for all the braggadocio. She held him tight against her and felt pity for how assailable he was, how assailable they all were, living in a world waiting to chip holes in them, with battlefields waiting to claim them. She had closed her eyes, and he was eleven. She would close them again, and he'd be eighteen.

Harry came out of the bathroom, carrying a towel, and started rubbing Josh's head. "If you saw her go, how come you asked if she was gone?"

"She always comes back," Josh said.

"Where's Caroline?" Chris asked.

"She's on the phone in the lobby, trying to get through to the Mexican weather bureau." His hair rose in thick clumps from the friction of the towel, making little horns of light. "What did grandma mean about giving me up?"

In divorce, as in nudity, caught with your pants down in front of your children, you were not supposed to cover up with gestures and actions that spoke of embarrassment. That would only deepen the child's anxiety, his sense that there was something to be ashamed of, the conviction that his life would be shattered, and that, somehow, it was his fault. Knowing how essential it was that she be straightforward, Chris still answered: "Nothing."

"Dad?"

"Josh?"

"Would you mind if I talked to mom alone?"

"Not at all." He picked up his sweatshirt from the chair. "I'll be in the bar if you need me."

Josh waited till the door was closed behind his father. "Mom?"

"Josh?"

"Are you and dad going to get a . . ." He swallowed. ". . . divorce?"

"I don't know."

"That was what grandma meant, wasn't it? You're afraid if you do I'll go with dad. That's it, isn't it?"

"Would you go with him?"

"Yes. But that doesn't mean I don't love you. It's just that he needs me more than you do."

She ducked her face into the full wet thatch of his hair, smelled the rain in it, the little-boy eagerness, the heat. "That isn't true," she said.

"Sure it is. You know it is. What would he do without me?"

She turned away then, quickly, and put the faucets on full in the sink behind her so her tears could splash freely and he wouldn't see. Ducking her face down close to the recessed bowl, she splattered water in it, flushing her eyes.

"Crying in the sink," he said. "That's pretty organized."

She laughed, into her hands, into the water, into the tears. He put his arm around her, pressed his cheek against her jeans. She reached behind her and touched his head while he patted her bottom, in solemn imitation of the comfort she had given him when he was a baby.

"Is it true?" Caroline asked Chris. Josh had gone to join Harry in the bar, dropping his bomb on Caroline in the lobby as he raced through. "Are you really getting a divorce?"

"I haven't made up my mind yet," Chris said.

"Well, he says he's going with dad. So can I stay with you?"

"Of course you can. You can stay with me even if I don't get a divorce." She put her arms around her daughter. Caroline backed off slightly.

"Grandma Evelyn said I could come live with her. I saw her in the lobby. She said you really don't deserve me." Caroline walked to the window, looking out at the rain. "It's a hundred and two in Palm Springs."

"How do you know?"

"She let me call the weather bureau in Los Angeles and charge it to her boyfriend. Do you really think she'll marry him?"

"I don't know."

"If she does, she'll get stationery with her name that says 'New York and Guadalajara.' She says if I come live with her, she'll order me the same stationery. And she'll give me all her rings."

"That must be pretty tempting."

Caroline shrugged. "I think I'll get them anyway."

Chris put her arms around her daughter, a kind of hospital-visiting compassion in the embrace: materialism was no less a disease than many let loose in the world. She saw the source of it, coming from the same place as Evelyn's: envy and neglect. Her own neglect of her child. When it seemed there was not enough love, you had to find someone who loved you, so you ended up loving yourself. No better way to prove deserving than to decorate yourself with pretty things. What love there might have showered from Chris had been deflected into tiny arrows of criticism, so sure she was that Caroline didn't love her. "All that glitters is not gold," she softly counseled her daughter.

"I know that," Caroline said. "Grandma told me. There's also diamonds."

That night, both children elected to sleep in with their parents. Caroline waited in Chris's bed. Josh attended his father. The room was unusually warm, the maids having reset the fire in the hearth with unaccustomed efficiency. No gustiness of wind moved chill currents past the windows, the calm in that part of the earth coming after the storm rather than before.

"You coming to bed, dad?" Josh asked.

Harry sat in a chair by the window, a book open on his lap. "I think I'll read for a while."

"Okay." Josh settled into the pillow. "*Bonne Nuit.* See you in the morning."

"See you in the morning," Harry said.

"This is a comfortable bed," said Caroline.

"Good," Chris said.

"Much more comfortable than mine. It's a nice hotel, but the beds are too hard. This one isn't though. This one is just right."

"Good-night, Goldilocks," Josh said.

"Good-night, baby bear," said Caroline.

"I'm having a really good time," said Josh.

"That's good," marked Harry. "Go to sleep."

"I'm having a very happy childhood."

"I'm glad."

"Did you have a happy childhood?" Caroline asked her father.

"Ecstatic."

"Really?" asked Chris, slightly surprised.

"I wasn't just loved. I was adored. My family thought the sun rose and set on me."

Josh put his hands behind his head on the pillow and contemplated his past. "I can remember practially everything about my childhood. I remember when we lived in the house on the hill . . ."

"The house on the hill," Caroline chorused. "You remember the raccoons that came and looked in the window?"

"I remember when dad taught me to swim . . ."

"Me, too," Caroline joined in. "And remember when we went to the pony rides on Sundays?"

"I remember when I got my Big Wheel, and dad taught me to ride it . . . And I remember one time I had something yucky in my hair, some kind of gook . . ."

Chris looked at him sharply. They had never discussed his illness, his seizure. He hadn't even been two, and yet he remembered.

". . . and dad was there," he said.

"Don't you remember me?" Chris asked, struck.

"I do," Caroline said.

"Not me," said Josh. "I only remember dad."

"Well, then, your memory's not that good," Harry said quietly. "Your mother was *always* there. She had important things to do, but when you needed her, she was there."

Tears blurred Chris's vision. She turned off the lamp between the beds and kissed her children good-night, her mind spinning. She could suddenly picture Harry at all his jobs, when the right moment came to promote himself, unable to knife a competitor.

She looked down at the face of her daughter, the darkness curling around her, turned to look at her son. He had put her on notice to constrain herself, advertising to the evening the happiness of his childhood, sending out like a riptide warning: don't mess around here. Marveling, as at a sunset, at the beauty of his circumstances, trying to keep them from changing, to stave off the coming eclipse. How crafty he was. Not nearly as artless as his sister. Molding circumstances, in stead of being molded by them.

Well, she would not be manipulated: people survived unhappy childhoods. She had, sort of. And if Harry was an example, maybe happy childhoods weren't all they were cracked up to be. Maybe they were illusory, deceptive, because the world didn't think the sun rose and set on you. The world kicked sand in your face, even if you weren't a ninety-eight-pound weakling, even if you were a big hand-some man with a barrel chest who stood very tall before circumstances started beating you down.

But had he really been beaten down? Or wasn't he simply what he was . . . a kind, loving man who didn't know how to hurt, even when it meant his own victory. And wasn't it not just their marriage that was fucked, but all of society? It would not be society, though, that provided the solution, if solutions there were going to be: it would be the individual marriages, the couples struggling for salvation, allowing themselves to change. And if it was going to get better, wasn't it really up to the woman to make it better? Because she was smarter than he, more flexible. Not that she meant to let him know.

She moved to the chair where he sat, reading, and said to him very softly: "You sure don't know how to kick a guy when he's down."

"Or even when he's up," he said.

They laughed. She reached for his hand. Maybe the real truth of white man's burden was having to be a man. Maybe all genitals were, really, were metaphorical dross, something you had to get through, so you could move on to the good part, the spirit of it. Maybe the higher you got, the less confused you were by sex and gender. Maybe it was all a struggle to get to the understanding that transcended wisdom.

Perhaps the real quest was finding the solution in yourself. Attaining wholeness all alone.

Harry looked at Chris, puzzled by her touch. She opened the French doors, taking care to be quiet so the children would not awaken, and signaled Harry outside.

The moon was full now, radiant. She could see the glint of a single silver strand among the hairs on his chest. Even boys got older. She opened his robe, pressed her lips to his flesh.

"What are you doing?" he asked her.

"Has it been that long, that you don't know?"

"That's how long it's been," he said, and bent to kiss her, to receive her mouth, to reach for the flow of her. Her hands explored the velvet casing of his testicles, sprang him to life.

He moved against the wall. She climbed him. Held aloft by his arms beneath her thighs, she rode him, beating the space between them, whipping the air into an erotic wind. She wept with joy that she could still feel something for him, sorrow that it could not be more, relief that it no longer had to be everything.

When it was over, they held each other. She kissed the wrists that were powerful enough to lift her, forgave the character that was not. Love, she supposed, was a process, like everything else. Going through changes, not always at the pitch of glory. Where was it written they had to be heroes, she told herself. Maybe, sometimes, what heroes were, were men with the courage to be kind. And women with the courage not to look for heroes.

"You sweet, lovely man," she whispered. "You tender soul."

"And not a bad dancer," he said.

They stayed for a final sunset. She sat on the balcony, her son at her right hand, her daughter close behind him. Caroline had her eyes closed, face angled slightly forward, as though she would catch the last of it on her cheeks for those returning from Palm Springs. Josh seemed visibly pleased that he had developed at least an outward show of patience for something that smacked of so little action. He looked serene except for the fingers checking his braces, as though he could not fully buy what he and Caroline had been told: that they were working it out. That everything was going to be all right. Chris understood his not being able to accept it fully. She wondered if she, herself, believed that everything would be all right.

She watched the sky changing, muting through brilliant swirls of orange, red-crusted clouds, to pink, mauve, gray, like the vanishing of youth. Well, there were still some beauties coming up: twilight, evening, stars. It would not be so painful now, home. Not such a terrible place for a woman in a revolution, watching the firm asses of the boys in Little League. Here it was, then, finally, surrender. Allowing life to unfold.

She felt strangely restored by this mystical place, with its curious power. As though God had struck up through the earth to fling mountain against desert and sea in a testament of inconsistency, unexpectedness, contradiction. Perhaps in the quiet tides and shifting sands the test was to find what was steadfast, the mountains inside you. Perhaps in a place where the sun sank so fast, you were speeded to sharper perceptions. As foolishness had saved her marriage there the first time, perhaps discrimination had saved it the second. Maybe there would be invisible rewards. Maybe she would fulfill herself as a woman, as a human, as a spirit. Maybe she could do it all.

She understood marriage now. Men had fallow times, and so did women. You filled in for each other. It was a partnership, an exchange. To keep a marriage nourished, to keep it going was as hard an endeavor as any she had striven for. Noble. She had always wanted to do something noble.

Tears started flowing slowly from her eyes. She wondered if it was the beauty of the sunset, or having to start all over again, like the constant application of alcohol to newly pierced ears. After a while you were moved to keep it together because of all the time you'd put into it, like an investment, admiring that it had lasted. At least her ears had healed.

Harry stood to the left of her chair, making a visible effort to show he was taking in the glory. Poor soul, he was only a man. Giving men's kinds of gifts, that women had to go through pain to carry. Diamonds in her ears. The Beverly Hills version of crucifixion.

But that's what marriage was: a kind of crucifixion. An agony that became an ecstasy when you found out you had the strength to endure.